THE BLOOD BROTHERS

The son of a missionary, David Beaty flew every Coastal Command aircraft type from Beaufighters to flying boats, operating throughout the war against ships and U-boats over the Arctic, Atlantic, Baltic, Skagerrak and Mediterranean. The author of *The Complete Skytraveller*, he has written many best-selling novels including *Excellency*, *The Proving Flight* and *Cone of Silence*. He now lives in Sussex with his novelist wife Betty.

DAVID BEATY

THE
BLOOD BROTHERS

A Methuen Paperback

A Methuen Paperback

First published in Great Britain 1987
This paperback edition first published 1988
by Methuen London, Michelin House,
81 Fulham Road, London SW3 6RB

© 1987 David Beaty

Printed in Great Britain by
Richard Clay Ltd, Bungay, Suffolk

British Library Cataloguing in Publication Data

Beaty, David, *1919–*
   The blood brothers.
   I. Title
   823′.914[F]
   ISBN 0-413-19330-6

For B, as always

CONTENTS

Author's Note

I am most grateful to Nanette Butler, a native of Hamburg, for reading this novel and for making valuable contributions.

While the book is based on certain episodes in my life and the Battle of the Atlantic, the characters, with the exception of historic figures such as Hitler, Dönitz and Prien, are all imaginary, and I would emphasise that this is a work of fiction, not a history of the U-boat war.

BOOK ONE
9–10 June 1944

The bearded man in the battered white hat heard the sound of engines and looked up. As he did so, the turned-up collar of his Navy raincoat fell away to reveal the Iron Cross with Swords and Diamonds round the neck of his uniform jacket. Standing stock still, head right back, he watched twenty enormous bombs emerge from the bomb-bays of twenty American Army Air Force Liberators.

The date was 9 June 1944. The biggest invasion the world has ever known was three days old. Allied airfields had been established round Bayeux, and tanks were racing to encircle the U-boat bases on Brittany's Atlantic coast.

The bombs were still falling, but now the man in the white hat was actually running *towards* them, till a mountain of smoke erupted in front of him and a hurricane of blast knocked him down.

But next moment he was up again, running through the blinding dust, through the gates of Lorient harbour, past the sentries prone in their slit trenches, past overturned trucks, past a flaming oil tank, down the steps into the vast concrete cathedral of the U-boat shelters.

'Exec!' His voice echoed back at him through the half-darkness. 'Are the men all right? Is the boat all right?'

A light flashed on. It glittered on empty water, illuminating only Kessel's battered U95 where three years before had berthed the victorious boats of the aces Prien, Schepke and Kretschmer.

The man in the white hat caught his breath. 'U2452,' he shouted. 'Where is she?'

'Here, sir!' Busch's voice came reassuringly from the far end of the bunkers.

'You all right, Otto?'

'No damage.'

The light lifted to the ceiling. It illuminated a thin crack from which fragments of cement were falling like snowflakes onto the sleek grey shape below.

'Ten direct hits and that's all the Tommies could do, sir!'

Someone shouted, 'Three cheers for the Todt Organisation!'

It was well known that the Kapitan had a *poule* in the Organisation which had built the shelters, and the man in the white hat joined in the laughter as he inspected the seventy-one men lined up on the aft deck before dismissing them to their stations.

'When do we sail, sir?'

'Midnight, Exec.' He looked at his watch. 'Two hours yet.'

The man in the white hat returned Busch's salute and made his way down the open hatch of the conning tower into the glittering belly of the U-boat, his eyes lovingly taking in every new mechanical detail. This was the first of the wonderboats, the Type XXIs, twice the size of the old workhorse VIICs, and with every possible device for destruction and self-preservation.

Already the crew were at their supper. As he pushed open the door of his cabin, he could smell the scent of hot goulash mixed with the reek of fresh paint and diesel oil.

From two photographs on his desk, the eyes of a fair-haired girl and a white-haired woman followed his every movement. He came inside, sat down in the only chair, and took off his hat.

For more than a minute he stayed quite still listening to the hum as the Base Maintenance Engineer checked the six huge electric motors powered by a posse of vast batteries; and to the roar as he changed over to testing the two diesels that gave almost as much power; and to the click of tube doors opening as the torpedomen inspected their twenty charges.

Then he put his right hand into the inside pocket of his jacket and carefully drew out a blue sealed envelope. Opening it, he picked up a red flimsy covered with teletype.

As he read, he began to smile.

At last!

He had been given what he had always wanted, what he had repeatedly asked for. Now here it was in his orders, with a personal message from Dönitz: *I know that you will never fail me.*

Nor would he. He was filled with an unshakeable confidence. He knew now what he had to do. And he would do it. All the disasters and disappointments of the past year would be wiped out by this one fantastic feat. The honour of the U-boat Service would once more be glorious, bright, unconquered. The orders ended with the words: *Go in and sink the target.*

And what a target!

The Admiral had simply signed off *Papa*. The smile on the face of the man in the white hat broadened.

'You look pleased, sir!'

Looking up, he saw his Executive Officer standing behind him.

'Very, Otto.'

'Dangerous?'

'No picnic.' The smile was still on his face. 'Can't tell you yet, but I can say we've been given the ultimate privilege of topping even Prien's feat of sinking the *Royal Oak* at Scapa Flow.' A fanatical glint came into the grey eyes. 'We shall win, Otto. We shall –'

Filtering into the cabin, dance music interrupted him.

'The radio,' Busch said apologetically. 'After supper, the boys like to listen. Just for a little. You understand . . .'

'Let them! Let them enjoy themselves.'

A girl sang of waiting for her sweetheart underneath the lamp-post outside the barracks gate, the guttural German softened by the husky sweetness of her voice.

'Lili Marlene,' Busch supplied unnecessarily.

The man in the white hat nodded. 'Brings back memories, eh, Otto?'

'Yes, sir.'

The man in the white hat began drumming his fingers in time to the music as the two of them listened.

The girl's voice sank in a slow syrup of saxophones. Instead a man's voice suddenly announced in colloquial German, 'This broadcast is for our friends in U2452, about to leave Lorient. We know all about you. We know what you are going to try to do. If you sail out of port with a white flag on your periscope, we shall respect you as brave men and treat you honourably. But if you choose to fight, you will be destroyed.'

The man in the white hat was already out of his cabin. The smile had left his face. He was racing along the companionway shouting, 'Turn that *verdammte* thing off!'

By the time he reached the radio room, there was total silence.

'That station!' he demanded. 'What was that station?'

The radioman said sheepishly, '*Atlantiksender*, Sir.'

'*Atlantiksender*!' From that station was the last time he had heard her voice. 'Poison kitchen Atlantic . . . that's what Papa Dönitz calls it, *Giftkuche Atlantik*. I'm ashamed of you!'

'Sir,' said a torpedoman,' *Atlantiksender*'s all we can get in the bunker.'

'So you listen to lies? Enemy propaganda! White flag, eh? We will go out of port with all my victory pennants flying! Once more we will make history! No eyes will see us! We will be invisible! Inviolate! We will never surface! No depth charge can touch us at 400 metres. We will fire our torpedoes without ever seeing or being seen. And we will achieve the greatest feat of naval warfare ever. It will show the enemy that with our wonderboats pouring off the prefabricated assembly lines, they can never win! It will the turning point of the war! And all the time, you will be as safe as houses, I promise you! You have my word . . .'

The smile had returned to his face. He made a joke. The men laughed.

The watch changed. Busch sent the electricians and engineers to recheck motors and batteries now that the Base Maintenance party had completed their work and left. The steel shell reverberated with the familiar sounds of shouted orders and men's footsteps.

Routine returned. Two hours later, U2452 slipped out of the shelter into bright moonlight on her electric motors, turned in a flurry of white waves and followed a minesweeper across the harbour. At midnight exactly she nosed between the gap in the stone arms of the breakwater and proceeded on the surface to the north of the Ile de Croix.

There the minesweeper turned and hooted, the crew cheering from the deck as pennant after victory pennant was hauled inside the U-boat's conning tower.

'Diving stations!'

The man on the bridge took off his white hat. As he did so, his eye was caught by the tiny white scar on his right thumb. A momentary memory of times past flashed through his mind and then was gone as he acknowledged the cheers.

Lingering on the deck, the crew of the minesweeper watched him disappear down the hatch, watched the nose dip, watched a white flash of water envelop the conning tower. U2452 slipped lower and lower under the sea till all they could see was the tiny schnorkel, like the head of a sea-serpent moving rapidly north-west.

An hour later, an echo from that metallic breathing apparatus was showing up as a minute green spike on a radar tucked away in what appeared to be just one of a group of French trawlers that was fishing off the coast.

A man's voice said in English to a radio operator sitting beside him, 'U2452 . . . course 315 degrees. Speed sixteen knots.'

That message went straight to the Submarine Tracking Room in Whitehall and to Western Approaches Command in Liverpool. Top Secret Orders were flashed to all naval bases and Coastal Command stations.

Three hours later, a man in a battered blue hat wearing the purple and white striped ribbon of the DFC under his wings was standing beside a white Liberator with his eight-man crew, watching a tractor emerging from the early morning mist, towing a trailer loaded with a big cylindrical object covered in a white sheet. It was guarded by a posse of RAF Regiment and all the Station armament officers.

The little procession lurched up to the open bomb-bay. The aircraft crew were ordered to get on board and keep right away.

The man in the blue hat grimaced as he climbed onto the flight deck. Always bloody bullshit with Top Secret stuff! The Mark XXIV Mine, that's what They called it, but he and his crew knew it was nothing of the sort.

Ten minutes later, a squeal from the hydraulic pump in the bomb-bay announced the bomb-bay doors closed. The empty trolley was towed off by the tractor. One by one, all four engines burst into life.

Ghost-like in grey air, the Liberator crawled round the perimeter track and lined up at the end of the muzzy flarepath.

The man was still wearing the blue hat as he opened up the engines to full take-off power.

Wallowing like a whale, the Liberator groaned down the full length of the runway to the red boundary lights and tottered up into the fog.

'Course 330 degrees, Skipper. Speed 160 knots.'

'Roger, Navigator.'

The man in the blue hat turned the control column spectacles starboard. As he did so, he caught sight of the small white scar on his right thumb.

Still there, he thought. Still there after . . . how many years?

BOOK TWO
20 April 1928–10 June 1944

I JOHN

'Ouch!'

The smaller boy tried to withdraw his right thumb, but the bigger boy held it in a vice-like grip and pressed it hard against his own bleeding thumb.

'Now we are blood brothers, John!'

The moment John Blake had arrived with his parents at the Swains' bungalow for Henry's birthday party, the bigger boy had whisked him off to his bedroom to show off his principal present – a real Scout knife with a wicked blade which he had promptly dug into both their thumbs.

'That hurt, Henry!'

'Cry-baby!'

The bigger boy put away the knife and laughed. 'Come on! Tea! Race you before Papa says grace!'

He pelted out of the room followed by the smaller boy still sucking the blood off his thumb.

At the far end of the veranda, watched by the parents of both boys and a small fair-haired girl and her mother already sitting at the table, Sinhalese servants were putting silver trays of sandwiches round the big white birthday cake.

Henry Swain and John Blake scrambled onto the two empty seats as the Reverend Swain began grace.

'Lord, hear us on this happy birthday anniversary that we –'

Through half-closed lids, John Blake could just see the white Customs buildings and the grey warships within the Colombo harbour breakwater. He could hear the shouts of the coolies and the grunts of the elephants working on the extension to the Mission School of which the Reverend Swain was headmaster.

'. . . and hasten the time, oh Lord, when the whole world is a family as united as our family in Christ here today.'

'Amen to that!' said the Reverend Blake, and everyone opened their eyes.

'A cucumber sandwich, Mrs Monteith?' The Reverend Swain lifted up the plate and offered it across the table to the little girl's mother. 'Or perhaps you, Alexandra,' he smiled at the little girl, 'would prefer tomato?'

The grown-ups chatted. The three children simply munched their way through the sandwiches, saying nothing.

Then the candles on the cake were lit. Henry was bidden by his father to blow all nine out in one breath.

He succeeded, of course. Henry never failed. Everyone applauded, but none so ecstatically as his mother.

'Gut, Heinrich!' she exclaimed. 'Gut!'

'Well done, Henry!' said the headmaster, as if his son had done something very splendid. 'Bravo!'

Henry's mother was statuesque with raven-black hair. Henry's father was a little man with pince-nez and a ginger beard, not at all like Henry, who was big and burly with thick hair like his mother's, only a light golden brown.

But then there was no reason why Henry should be like his father since, as the Blakes were never tired of discussing, he was not poor Septimus' natural son, being German through and through. How that could be, John didn't know, just as he didn't know what was natural and what was unnatural.

But they were very nice to Mrs Swain, talking about the new German cruiser that was coming in July on a goodwill visit, the first of its kind since when – well since when . . .

John didn't hear *since when* for the Reverend Swain remarked with diplomatic speed that everyone was so pleased Germany had now joined the League of Nations. Alexandra's mother, Mrs Monteith, the wife of the Naval Commander, looked scornful.

A little embarrassed by it all, Mrs Swain turned to John and asked in her strange guttural voice, 'And when will your ninth birthday be?'

He gave her a little shy smile. He felt sorry for Mrs Swain, though he didn't know why. 'Not for another seven months, I'm afraid, Mrs Swain.'

'Alexandra has to wait longer than that, haven't you, Alexandra?' said Mrs Monteith.

Alexandra went on eating birthday cake.

'Alexandra!' Mrs Monteith had eyes of battleship grey. 'How long have you to wait?'

'One month and four days.'

'*One year*, one month and four days!' corrected Mrs Monteith. 'Alexandra isn't half as good at arithmetic as she thinks she is.'

The passing round of the sandwiches and cake done, the five grown-ups switched their attention away from the children. Henry began to kick John Blake under the table, and John continued to look at Alexandra, as he had done for most of that tea-time.

'Alexandra has never really had any schooling,' Mrs Monteith was saying.

'John will be taking the entrance examination to Kirkstone on my furlough,' said the Reverend Blake. 'Our passages are already booked on the *Warwickshire*. As are those of Brother Swain and his family.'

John Blake scowled at the news and aimed a retaliatory kick at Henry which connected only with the table leg.

'Septimus wants Heinrich to go to Kirkstone too, you see,' said Mrs Swain. 'That's his old school. The school for the sons of our Ministers.'

Mrs Monteith nodded her head. 'I know. In Barminster. Not far from our Imperial School for Officers' daughters. Alexandra will be going there when we're posted home.'

Home meant England. John had never been to England. Alexandra had never been to England either. Only Henry had seen Europe, and all he remembered about Germany before he came out to Ceylon five years ago were the schnitzel and sausages and a grandpapa with a beard.

Nobody else on the Protestant mission field knew much more about either Henry or Germany. Everybody had expected the Reverend Septimus Swain to remain a bachelor to the end of his days. But then, during his first furlough after the Great War, he had gone to a teaching course at a Lutheran college in Hamburg and had come back with Helga and Henry.

John Blake liked Mrs Swain. She wasn't concerned, as were his parents and the others, about who she was and where she had come from. She made gingerbread men with currants for eyes and gave them to him and Henry and Alexandra.

He liked the Reverend Swain, too, for he was gentle – 'other worldly' his father called it. He seemed perpetually to look for the best, not the worst, in other people. He taught other religions like Buddhism and Hinduism at his school, which worried the Reverend Blake as the Mission was financed from the Kirkstone Protestants' funds.

How Helga had 'got' Brother Swain remained an endless speculative exercise on the Mission. That she was a German was considered unfortunate. As a race they were not to be trusted.

She dressed Henry either in sailor suits or the khaki shirt and long knickerbockers tucked into knee-length stockings that he had on that day. John was wearing his best tussore suit, which at least was cool. Alexandra was in white lace with a big straw hat tied down over her golden hair by a blue ribbon under her chin.

The grown-ups became suddenly aware of the silent children. 'Now run along!' said Mrs Swain.

They were being dismissed, bidden to disappear into the Swain garden of burnt-brown lawn, tall palms, shrubs and paw-paw trees.

'You lead the way, Heinrich!'

He didn't have to be told. He was way ahead of Alexandra and John, panting down the verandah steps, pretending to be a steam engine.

'Not so fast, Heinrich! Remember your little guests!'

He paid not the slightest notice. He leaped up the bank crowned by oleander bushes and vanished, still chuffing.

Mindful of his still bleeding right thumb, John Blake put out his left hand to help Alexandra down the steps. From up on the verandah, he heard his mother say, 'I think my son is quite taken with your daughter!'

'At that age,' said Mrs Monteith, 'they have their little love affairs. Then they grow out of them.'

'Heinrich has grown out of them already!' Mrs Swain sighed. 'If indeed he ever had them!'

Behind him, John Blake could hear the bubbles of laughter and the tinkle of tea-cups. Still hand-in-hand, he and Alexandra began crossing the lawn towards the gap in the oleanders through which Henry had disappeared.

'I wonder where he is, Alexandra?' he said, just to say her name, because he didn't care if Henry had disappeared for ever.

'Henry is a silly boy,' pronounced Alexandra.

'Yes, isn't he, Alexandra?' he said eagerly. 'I'm not a silly boy, Alexandra. I'm a –'

'Henry is a silly-billy!'

'He is, Alexandra!' And then he whispered, because he ached to hear her say it, 'I have a name too, Alexandra.'

'Yes, I know,' she said. And then she stopped and dropped his hand and called imperiously, 'Henry!'

He came then, popping up from behind the oleanders on the top of the bank. He began to make faces, his open hands pressed to the sides of his head, wiggling his fingers.

'I'm the king of the castle! Get off, you dirty rascal!'

Then suddenly he turned calling over his shoulder, 'Betcha can't catch me!' and disappeared back into the oleanders.

'Alexandra,' John Blake said, 'don't take any notice of him, Alexandra!'

But it was too late. She had started to run away from him, pushing the bushes back and laughing and shouting, 'I'll catch you, Henry! I'll catch you!', now disappearing herself, leaving only the shaking branches behind her.

He took his time to follow them. He wasn't going to show his eagerness. He thought perhaps Alexandra would call out, 'John, where are you, John?'

But she didn't. So eventually he made his way through the oleanders too, and found himself in a clearing at the bottom of which was a gully through which a stream ran, glinting in the sun.

Across it a kind of rough dam had been made of planks a couple of inches thick, so that there were two levels, the top part being about eight feet above the lower level.

Green ooze leaked out of the joins in the planks onto the weedy water below.

It was beside this dam that Henry and Alexandra were standing.

'Here he is!' Henry shouted.

'I caught you, Henry,' said Alexandra, taking no notice of John. 'Henry, I caught you, didn't I, Henry?'

Henry simply fixed his stare on John. 'Aren't you going to, then?'

'Aren't I going to *what*?'

'Walk the plank.'

'*What* plank?'

He pointed to the upended plank that divided the stream and stretched out across to the other bank. '*That* plank!'

It was a very narrow plank. And it was a long way to the opposite bank.

'It's the only way to get across to the other side,' said Henry.

'I don't want to get to the other side.'

'Betcha can't!'

'I don't bet,' said John Blake.

He wasn't sure what betting was, but he did know it was wicked because he'd heard his father say so in one of his sermons. Drinking was wicked too, and he knew exactly what that meant because the old appu sometimes swayed like a tree in the wind when he served dinner and reeked of bad coconut which his father said was arrack. His mother ran a Missionary Milk Bar in the Port, the place in Colombo where the shops were, and his father used to bring the sailors in to the Mission bungalow after Sunday service and give them warm lemonade. Then his mother would sit at the piano and lead the hymns.

'Are you going to walk the plank?'

'No,' John said. 'No.'

'You can't!'

'I can!'

'Do it then!'

'I don't want to show off.'

'You're scared!'

'I'm not.'

'Alexandra, he's scared! He's scared, Alexandra!'

John looked at her. He was so sure she was going to say 'John *isn't* scared! I *know* John isn't scared!'

But she was still looking at Henry and said nothing at all.

'It's you who's scared,' John said. 'He's the one who's scared, Alexandra.'

'Scared? *Me?*' He gave that frog's-croak laugh of his. 'Just watch me, Alexandra!'

He jumped up then – not cautiously but carelessly – onto the plank, right foot in front of the left.

Then he began walking – not slowly, not with his arms outstretched to balance himself, not hesitating, not swaying, but gracefully as a dancer.

He put one foot neatly in front of the other, his body quite upright, his limbs moving rhythmically, rolling along the knife-edge of the plank in one smooth movement till he reached the other side. And then he didn't jump down on the grass, but simply pivoted on his toes, twisting round and running back along the plank, those two dozen steps synchronised and harmonised into one movement till he was back where he started, and only then did he jump down.

Alexandra clapped and clapped. Only then did she look at John Blake. 'Now it's your turn,' she said.

John Blake fell over things. He knocked things over. He dropped things. 'The boy's clumsy,' his father used to say. 'He can't even catch a cricket ball!'

He took his time getting onto the plank. He started off, one cautious foot in front of the other, feeling for the edge like a blind man.

Then he began to go faster. It was really quite easy. It was just like swimming, which he could nearly do. All you needed was confidence.

And then half-way across, his right foot caught his left. He swayed. He looked to the right – down beyond the plank, down, down, *down* to the mesmerising green water below.

He began wobbling. He flung out his arms to steady himself. Everything went hazy. The world had started spinning around him. Then he was toppling, *toppling*.–

It seemed a long way down. Suddenly a warm squelchy mass enveloped him. He couldn't see anything for the weed over his eyes, and he started kicking his legs and shouting.

Then he heard running footsteps, and when at last he managed to clear his eyes and dog-paddle to the bank, standing there were his parents and the Reverend and Mrs Swain and Mrs Monteith.

He struggled up onto the grass beside them.

'John!' said his mother. 'What *have* you done?'

'I've fallen into the water, Mother.'

'But how, John? *How*? she demanded, but without waiting for an answer she bundled him dripping wet across the grass, up the verandah steps into the Swains' back bedroom. Out of the almirah, Mrs Swain took a sailor suit of Henry's.

'Slip him into this, Beatrice,' she said, leaving his mother to effect the change.

John viewed the clothes with misgivings. The blue trousers were much too big and the square collar was more like a cloak, while the hat almost covered his eyes.

When he and his mother returned to the verandah, both Henry and Alexandra started giggling.

Fortunately, leave-taking was brief. Commander Monteith had arrived from an important conference with the Admiral, Far Eastern Fleet, at Naval Headquarters, to take them all home in his Ford.

John squeezed in front between the Commander and his mother. His father, Mrs Monteith and Alexandra sat in the back.

Nobody said much as the car weaved between rickshaws and

bullock carts. The Commander was always silent, anyway. He used to bring the sailors to Church Parade – that was how the Blakes knew the Monteiths – and he called John's father 'Padre', which the Reverend Blake liked. But he never used to stay for the sing-song and the warm lemonade.

When he dropped the Blakes in the portico of their bungalow, as John climbed out of the car the Commander caught sight of the name on the ribbon round Henry's *Kriegsmarine* hat.

'*Kronstadt*, eh?' He shook his head disapprovingly. 'Led us a hell of a dance in '18 before we caught her. Never thought I'd see an English boy with *Kronstadt* round his hat. It's a strange world, is it not, Padre?'

Three months later, when they embarked for England, it was Henry who wore the offending hat, Commander Monteith – in fact none of the Monteiths – were there to comment. Newly laundered and starched as it was, Henry wore the hat with exuberant pride, a pride made more vociferous and voluble by the sight of the visiting German cruiser lying almost alongside the *Warwickshire*.

The Reverend Swain paid off the rickshaw coolie, and Henry, goggling at the cruiser, swept off his cap and waved it round and round his short-cropped head.

'The sea,' said Mrs Swain, putting an arm round Henry and shading her eyes with the other, 'is in Heinrich's blood. The sea and ships.'

She looked momentarily very sad, John thought, as if having the sea in your blood was not necessarily a good thing. As the Swains and the Blakes trooped up the *Warwickshire*'s gangway, she kept darting little fascinated glances towards the cruiser, which were not missed by his parents.

'Once a German always a German,' his father remarked cryptically as they inspected their cabin.

Mrs Blake nodded. 'And I presume she meant Henry's father was a sailor?'

'It is not unlikely.'

'In the German Navy? Fighting against us?'

'I wouldn't be surprised if he was.'

'Was Helga married to him?'

'I would be very surprised if she was.'

'Then he is –'

'Quite!'

'I often wonder how poor Septimus became involved.'

'God moves in a mysterious way.'

'And now Septimus is not to come with us?'

John pricked up his ears. It was the first he had heard of this change of plan.

'He felt he should wait till the school extension was completed.'

'But surely,' his mother began, 'others could –'

'Quite,' his father said. Then he lowered his voice and added, 'God may realise that Septimus is better on his own.'

'Won't he be lonely?' John could not restrain himself from interjecting.

Neither of his parents replied. His father said severely to his mother, 'Little pitchers have big ears,' and sent him up on deck with strict instructions not to lean over the rail.

Henry was already up there and leaning over the rail, and still waving his hat towards the German cruiser. John wondered if God might realise that he too would be better on his own at Kirkstone without Henry. In fact, in his opinion most people, except his own mother, would be better off without Henry.

Then shortly after his parents came on deck, the ship gave a loud blast that echoed round the harbour. A disembodied voice announced, 'All ashore that's going ashore', and John saw the sad and grieving expression of the Reverend Swain's face.

He wondered if his father noticed it as he shook their hands. '*Bon voyage*, Brother Blake.'

'Till our next meeting, Brother Swain.'

John averted his eyes as the headmaster kissed his wife goodbye, 'Write often, Helga.'

'Of course I will, my dear.'

But John couldn't avert his fascinated eyes as the Reverend Swain put his arms around Henry, and held him tight.

'Take care of your Mother, son.'

'Yes, Papa.'

John felt himself momentarily overcome with a terrible sympathy for poor Septimus Swain. He found it difficult to understand how anyone could feel sad at being parted from Henry. Perhaps it was something to do with Henry not being his natural son.

He watched the headmaster descend the gangway to the tender, then turn to wave as the boat chugged past the German cruiser. He looked very small sitting there, a tiny ant dwarfed by the warship's high steel sides.

John forgot the Reverend Swain's sadness in the excitement of departure. Everyone crowded the rails and the German cruiser played 'A Life on the Ocean Wave' in salute, which seemed to delight the passengers.

Mrs Swain exclaimed hopefully, 'We Germans and you British, we all love the sea, do we not?' She looked from Henry to John. 'You are both sons of the waves.'

Few of the passengers loved the sea so much as the voyage progressed. The cabins were small and the decks narrow and the weather windy. The dining room was cramped and they were all at the same table for meals. Mrs Swain insisted on always talking German to Henry.

'His German is so rusty,' she explained. 'I must see he brushes it up before we arrive in Hamburg.'

The meaning of that enigmatic remark was debated by the Blakes in the privacy of their cabin. As the voyage progressed, further remarks that Mrs Swain let slip indicated that she and Henry were not after all going to stay with Septimus' cousin in England, as had been supposed, but would be going on to Hamburg in the *Warwickshire* to her parents' home.

There were a lot of other children on board, and Henry soon established himself as their leader. He was always playing deck quoits and deck tennis and ping-pong. It went without saying that he always won.

Then there was the Children's Fancy Dress. Mrs Swain spent days stitching Henry's costume. Mrs Blake didn't bother, simply bundling John into his mackintosh and sou'wester and putting a placard round his neck labelled SKIPPER'S SARDINES. Henry, in the blue and gold uniform of a *Kriegsmarine* Admiral, naturally won first prize.

The climax was the apple-bobbing. It was a blustery day, with a north-westerly wind chopping the Mediterranean into pale pieces. Hanging from an overhead beam, three dozen apples swayed on their strings like pendulums.

The boat was pitching and rolling. Apples were connecting with the competitors' faces like cannonballs. A number retired from the field, crying it wasn't possible.

'Not possible?' said the Sports Officer. ''Course it's possible. Here we are! The winner! What's your name, sonny?'

'John Blake, sir.'

At prize-giving, he was presented with a toy fire engine by the Captain. Shortly afterwards, two elderly women told the Reverend Blake that they had seen his son put the apple to his mouth with a lightning stroke of his left hand.

His father made him give the fire engine to the boy who was second – Henry Swain – in spite of Mrs Swain's pleas that he should be allowed to keep it.

Altogether, John wasn't sorry when the *Warwickshire* docked at Tilbury.

Henry and his mother waited by the gangway to see the Blakes off. The ship was going on to Hamburg that afternoon.

His mother embraced Mrs Swain and his father said, 'We shall be seeing you when you bring Henry to Kirkstone, Helga.'

Mrs Swain cupped John's face in her hands and kissed his forehead. She looked into his face. 'I shall think of you often, John.'

He felt that same inexplicable sadness swoop over him.

And then Henry was shaking his hand and making a great business of their two thumbs touching, '*Auf Wiedersehen*, Brother John,' he called after them. '*Auf Wiedersehen!*'

For all his *Auf Wiedersehens*, Henry Swain did not appear at Kirkstone.

That was the only good thing about John's first day – listening in the great echoing Assembly Hall to a prefect calling the roll of new boys from Ames through all the As and then the Bs to Blake, right through to Yablon at the end of the alphabet – and not hearing the name of Swain.

Everything else about the school filled him with gloom. From his first glimpse of it through the taxi window, crouching like a stone lion on the hilltop above Barminster, he had known he would hate it. In all his life he had never seen so much heavy stone, such narrow slit windows, walked down so many flagged corridors, felt so cold, or seen so many rows of boys uniformed in grey flannels and blue blazers.

Now the headmaster was coming onto the dais and with a 'Thank you, Roxburgh', taking the roll-book from the prefect.

A tall, gaunt, black-gowned man, he did not move as other men did on two feet, but came across the dais with a loud thump and a scrape and another loud thump, walking on two wooden legs.

'Mr Colville has a very gallant war record,' his father had told him in the train from Nottingham where his parents were spending their furlough before going back to Ceylon for another seven years. 'Unfortunately, he lost both his legs on the Somme.'

The information had not adequately prepared him for Mr Colville. Blake hardly heard what the headmaster told the new boys, except that it was about pulling one's weight and not being a slacker and team spirit and living up to the school motto *None for himself but all for the school.*

'Now,' the headmaster finished up, 'you are each assigned an older boy to show you the ropes.'

Blake's older boy was a pale sandy-haired eleven-year-old with a missing front tooth and freckles, who introduced himself as Nash.

Together they claimed Blake's attaché case from the entrance hall and began the long walk down corridors smelling of disinfectant and boiled cabbage, past classrooms, across playgrounds, up a stone staircase to a dormitory lined with twenty-five white coverleted beds each side, divided by a brown linoleumed aisle.

Nash pointed to the bed nearest the door. 'That's yours. Over there is Roxburgh's, the prefect who called the roll. The others are awful, but he's quite decent. And this,' he indicated the bed next to Blake's, 'is mine.'

All the beds had a wooden screen behind which was a locker, a lead basin and a cold water tap.

'Baths are at the far end,' Nash told him. 'You get one a week. Lavatories are called "pets". A friend is a "case". A maid is a "dumb". All non-Kirkstone boys are "purds". The food is foul. But you'll get a "prog" – that's a feast – if your House wins at games. The chaps are all right, but beware of Foxy Fanshawe.'

Nash began to walk away. 'I'll be back later to take you to supper.'

Left on his own, John Blake unpacked his case and filled his locker with socks and shirts. The dormitory was very cold and still. It smelled of that same disinfectant, mixed with carbolic soap and linoleum polish. He felt a sudden desperate longing for the rattle of tea-cups on a verandah and the warm spice-laden scents of his distant home. He was relieved when Nash returned and took him downstairs for supper. He was more relieved still when it was time to go to bed.

'Silence!'

An immediate hush. Out went the lights. Now there was only the sound of the prefect's feet as he walked up and down, and the rustle and creaks as boys settled themselves down in their beds.

Blake lay perfectly still. He longed to escape into sleep. Most of all, he tried not to think about his problem, a problem which was worse than not being able to play rugger and as painful as parting from his parents. He couldn't tie his own tie.

In the golden-scented faraway days of Ceylon, on the rare occasions he had worn a tie, his ayah had tied it for him. His mother had tied it for him that morning. When he finally drifted off to sleep, it was to dream of the war hero headmaster thump-scrape-thumping after him to strangle him with his tie.

He woke next morning to the ringing of a bell and sounds very like thump-scrape-thump. He saw a man with waxed whiskers wearing a blue-striped butcher's apron ringing a big brass bell, and a boy holding a copper kettle who was asking him for fourpence.

'Hot washing water,' Nash explained. 'Fourpence is Jenkins' charge.'

Blake produced the coins, washed gratefully in the hot water and began to dress. He put on his shirt, short trousers, socks and shoes. Then he took his tie and went over to the cracked mirror in his cubicle.

Now came the moment of truth.

He hoped that the knack might come to him. He did in fact pray it would. The prayers produced nothing but a tangled mess. Then in the cracked mirror, he saw a terrible sight.

There was a face behind him. A face with its wide mouth curled into a wry grin – Roxburgh.

'Turn round, Blake.' Roxburgh put his hands on his shoulders and spun him round. 'What's the trouble? Can't tie your tie?' Without waiting for Blake to answer, he began to untangle the ends. He held them up under Blake's nose. 'It's very simple, Blake. Once over, twice over, up through the middle and slot through the knot. Then pull tight! How's that?'

He turned Blake round to look at himself in the mirror.

'Oh, that's fine, Roxburgh. Thank you, thank you very much.'

He made to move off, but Roxburgh held his shoulder.

'Not so fast.' Deftly, he unfastened Blake's tie. 'Now do it yourself, Blake! You're a big boy now!'

Red-faced and sweating, Blake faced the mirror again. 'Once over, twice over, up through and down.'

Triumphantly he spun round.

'Not bad,' Roxburgh said, pulling it tighter, seemingly oblivious of Blake's relief. That small relief joined the relief of not having Swain at Kirkstone as being just about the only decent things that happened to him that first week.

Everything else seemed very strange and he felt very isolated. He found it impossible to get a 'case'. All the other new boys paired off and he was the one that was always left to walk on his own. On the Thursday half-holiday a ramble was organised. Everyone else was delighted. Having no one to pair up with, Blake trailed along behind the two most unpopular boys in the class, Samuels and Jacobson, dark boys with large brown eyes and big noses, who reminded him of Mrs Swain. He knew it wasn't wise to be too close to them because of their unpopularity which was catching, so he kept his distance.

The mystery of why Henry Swain had not turned up at Kirkstone was unfolded in a letter from his father. 'Mrs Swain has decided after all to send Henry to a German school.'

Another one up to God, Blake thought, adding it to the tie-tying. If only He would also provide a 'case', His score would be three. If he had a friend, Blake felt he would belong. And painfully finding his way in this strange world with its strange language and strange code of behaviour, he recognised that the most important priority was to belong. It was even more important than being good at games or despising girls. Everything he could do to make himself more acceptable, he did.

In the second week of November, it was announced that Chapel would begin later on Remembrance Day, that poppies would be on sale outside the Masters' Common room and all boys were urged to give generously. Blake had intended to spend his Saturday sixpence on three Milk Flakes, but joining the queue of boys at his housemaster, Mr Marshall's poppy table, he spent the lot on a silk poppy with black stamens and pinned it onto his lapel on the way to Chapel.

It was a solemn and moving and funereal occasion. It began with the singing of 'Oh God Our Help In Ages Past'. Then the Lord's Prayer, then the Chaplain reading very slowly 'They shall not grow old as we who are left grow old'.

Standing at the lectern, towering above the silent seated congregation, the headmaster kept looking at his watch.

Suddenly he lifted his head, 'The School will rise.'

They obeyed as one man. Still as stone, heads bent, they stood there listening. Not quite sure what he was supposed to be listening for, Blake suddenly heard the sound of guns.

Now there was absolute silence. Nobody seemed to breathe. Cars had stopped along the road outside. There was no scrunching of tyres on the gravel, no distant whistle of a railway engine. Only the clock went on ticking.

Blake kept his eyes straight in front fixed unblinkingly on the School War Memorial just opposite the front First Form pews.

Heavy embossing edged the glittering plaque. Three columns of names were carved in front of English county regiments, the Royal Navy and the Royal Air Force. Below in Gothic letters was engraved TO THE GLORIOUS MEMORY OF THOSE OLD BOYS OF KIRKSTONE WHO DIED THAT WE MIGHT LIVE.

Blake stared reverently at all those names. For a school that was a charitable religious foundation and had no OTC, there did seem to be a lot of them. There was also a large brass space at the bottom, as if it were waiting for more names.

Beside him, Nash stood rigidly and proudly to attention. His father had served in submarines during the war. All Blake could produce was the friendship of Commander Monteith, and he remembered to his shame that afternoon in Colombo, standing in front of his war hero in an enemy hat. Then the guns went off again, and the knowledgeable Nash whispered, 'The maroons!'

With all stops out, the organ shattered the silence. The school began singing fervently 'I Vow To Thee My Country'.

And majestic in his long black gown, the clicking of his wooden legs echoing round the Chapel, the headmaster began leading the school out, singing

> *The love that asks no questions,*
> *The love that pays the price,*
> *The love that makes undaunted*
> *The final sacrifice.*

At the War Memorial, the headmaster stopped, took the poppy out of his button-hole, and stooping painfully, laid it reverently on the stone below the plaque.

Behind him, the whole school did likewise.

Not quite the whole school. To Blake's disgust and dismay, he saw a boy in his class called Wagstaff just ahead of him walk past the Memorial as if it didn't exist.

'There is no point in glorifying war, Blake.'

Wagstaff was a gangly boy, all arms and legs with protuberant melancholy eyes. He reminded John Blake of an octopus, except that he was harmless.

The time he picked to deliver himself of those sorrowful pacific words was the second Monday in February as they were trudging downhill from the Upper Field through the half-darkness of a winter afternoon.

'War is *not* glorious.'

Wagstaff flicked snow off his sweater. As usual, Blake had not distinguished himself on the rugger field. The harassed games master had been too busy to teach him anything.

'Isn't it, Wacky?'

'No, Blake. War is *la rage*. Madness!' he translated obligingly. Wagstaff was good at languages, which earned him no respect amongst Kirkstone boys, for languages were considered sissy. 'As Christians, we should turn the other cheek. In the Great War, my father was a CO.'

'CO of what, Wacky?'

'Which just shows how militaristic you are, Blake! CO of nothing! A Conscientious Objector. What all Christians should be.'

Blake wondered what Mr Colville would say to that – but not aloud. They had reached the changing rooms. Inside was a long trough of hot dirty water into which all the boys scrambled. Wacky and Blake were the last in, and Blake the last out by a long way.

He was just drying himself hastily in the now empty changing room, when he heard a peremptory whistle. Turning his head, he saw approaching him a big ginger-haired boy with glittering green eyes and a long foxy face. It was Fanshawe, fully dressed and carrying a wet towel. The boy Nash had warned him to avoid. And so he had.

Till now.

Blake looked around desperately for Nash, Jenkins, Samuels, Jacobson, or even Wacky. But they had all rushed off to Early Tea. It was as if he had been swimming around with a lot of minnows who had suddenly smelled a shark.

He was naked and alone.

Foxy advanced, fingering the towel lovingly.

'What's your name, boy? Answer me!' He raised the towel. 'Quickly!'

'Blake.'

Foxy looked outraged. 'I don't like the name! Give me three good reasons why I shouldn't thrash you for having it!'

Blake couldn't think of one. In silence, he stood and shivered as the wet towel descended on his back and his legs.

Wacky would have been proud of him.

He was too scared to hear the approaching footsteps, but Foxy heard them. He retreated through the outside door as neatly as his namesake. When Roxburgh put his head into the changing rooms, Blake was alone again.

'Hurry up!' the prefect snapped. 'No wonder your teeth are chattering if you take so long to dress!'

He looked too cross to suspect what had been happening. It was shortly after that, however, that he volunteered to give Blake a few rugger lessons, and a month later told him he had quite an aptitude. 'You're fast on your feet,' he said, 'and you've got pluck.'

Amazingly that was true. He who was scared stiff of Fanshawe and of not belonging had no fear at all on the field. It was as if there was this well of courage inside himself, waiting for someone to discover or some eventuality to bring out.

Next year he made the Junior XV and with that came the passport to belonging. He was one of the set. He could look down on Samuels and Jacobson and pour scorn on Wacky's pacifism. He realised he owed it all to Roxburgh. When his parents' furlough was up that autumn, and they had returned to the mission field, Roxburgh became the only person in the world to whom he could turn. Though his parents wrote regularly, they had become as shadowy as those vanished days with Henry and Alexandra in Ceylon.

So he began to build a Kirkstone world around himself with Roxburgh as its main supporting beam. He worked hard and climbed up steadily in class. Out of the windows of his new world he looked towards becoming a prefect, to an Oxford scholarship and a good job in the Colonial Service. His father's letters told him of Henry's continuing achievements. In his own way he tried to match them. When his father wrote that Henry had joined the Hitler Youth, he sought enlightenment from Wacky one Saturday lunchtime as to what that might be, guessing that it was something like the Scouts.

'No,' Wacky shook his head. 'More like an OTC. If Hitler becomes Chancellor, they'll bring in conscription. The Germans are preparing for war.'

Everyone laughed that idea to scorn.

Wacky stuck to his gloomy guns and there being nothing much else to do, Blake and Nash, Jenkins, Samuels and Jacobson took him off to scrag him.

Naturally he didn't hit back, but rocked on his feet like a pop-eyed Aunt Sally and though they did nothing more than give him a bloody nose, Roxburgh got to hear about it and virtually read the riot act to them.

That night as Blake was getting into bed, Roxburgh asked him if he knew what Fascism meant. Dipping into his meagre knowledge of Latin derivatives, he answered, 'Is it something to do with sticks bound together, Roxburgh?'

'Something, yes. Sticks to beat people who don't agree with you. It's mob rule. It's violence. It's the opposite of democracy. It's what you lot did to Wagstaff.'

'I won't do it again, Roxburgh. I promise I won't.'

From then on, he treated Wacky's outrageous statements with tolerant laughter.

At the end of his third year, his mother wrote that not only Henry Swain but also Alexandra were doing very well. Alexandra had passed the entrance exam to the Imperial School and would be starting there in September. The idea of her proximity filled Blake with a strange dismay. He had learned over the last three years to regard girls with dislike and mistrust, and those feelings uncomfortably overlaid his remembered admiration and enchantment with Alexandra. His classmates, he noticed, seemed to dislike girls less as they got older. The voices of some of them were breaking. They had spots and boils, and one or two had begun to shave sporadically.

The fact that his own voice had not yet broken landed him in his deepest humiliation. The school put on a big play each year in the Spring. In 1934 it was 'Androcles and the Lion', and he was dragooned by Mr Marshall, the geography master, into the hated role of Lavinia. He couldn't think of anything more degrading.

'Why me, sir?'

'Because you're the best actor we've got,' said Mr Marshall, but in fact, it was because Nash was the Centurion, Lavinia's lover,

Fanshawe was the Lion, Jacobson and Samuels were Christians, and Jenkins had grown too tall and shaved every other day.

Privately, Blake feared it was because he looked sissyish and his voice hadn't broken. But he enjoyed the acting, except the embraces with Nash.

Fanshawe enjoyed the acting too. 'A natural for the part,' Mr Marshall said, as Fanshawe horsed around in the lion skin.

These days Blake found him less intimidating. He even essayed a joke. 'You should wear that skin all the time, Fanshawe! You look quite human in it!'

His own costume was a long blue dress belonging to Mrs Marshall. With it, he wore a fair flowing wig that came down to his waist. Mrs Marshall daubed red grease paint on his lips and black round his eyes and exclaimed on the length of his lashes.

'My, my, who is this young beauty?' Mr Marshall pretended to be bowled over. 'Why, it's Blake, God bless my soul!'

Strangely enough, that first night the audience seemed bowled over, too. Blake lost himself in the play. For two hours he became Lavinia, and Nash was a Roman Centurion.

But the second night was disastrous.

Just as they were all being made up by Mrs Marshall, her husband came backstage to announce that the Imperial School girls had arrived.

'I didn't know they were coming, sir.' Blake was moved to pipe up indignantly.

'Oh, yes.' Mr Marshall rubbed his hands. 'Hadn't you heard?'

None of his fellow actors seemed dismayed by the Imperial School's invasion of the boys' school, but then none of them knew Alexandra. Blake tried to comfort himself with the thought that she would be too young to attend. It would be Sixth Formers only.

'You're not cold, are you Blake?' Mrs Marshall asked. 'You're shivering so much I can't do up this button.'

When she'd gone and he had a moment on his own, he peeped through a crack in the curtains. His eyes travelled over lines of girls in gym tunics. And then he saw her. In the second row. Dead centre. A girl, but not as other girls. That fair hair had been cut short, but was still as beautiful. She was chatting to the girl on her left, smiling and tossing her head.

Blake stood there with his heart hammering, every word of his lines flying out of his head like escaping pigeons.

'Your cue,' Mr Marshall hissed through Blake's wig, and gave him a forward push.

Blake wobbled on stage like Charlie Chaplin. He still couldn't remember his lines, but he could see the fair head in the second row suddenly jerk up. He was aware of blue eyes regarding him with the intensity of instant recognition.

He was cringingly aware that there was no question now of being Lavinia. He was Blake dressed up in an old dress with a hot wig and melting greasepaint. It was worse than having a sailor cap on with *Kronstadt* round it. He lost count of how many times he had to be prompted. But he could count the number of times he met the vivid blue eyes.

And as hard as he tried not to make a fool of himself, she tried not to laugh. He saw her cover her face with both her hands, rocking herself backwards and forwards in a paroxysm of silent mirth.

Others were not so restrained. He tripped over his dress. Laughter broke out all over the house.

Afterwards people were very kind. But Mr Marshall did say crossly. 'I thought you'd got over your clumsiness, Blake.' Roxburgh took the sting out of it, saying lightly, 'All in all, I enjoyed your second performance rather better.'

Blake felt he had lost some of his new-found status, and that some aura of girlishness clung to him like remnants of greaspaint. Then to give this fear the lie, his voice broke. When he telephoned his aunt with whom he was to spend Christmas, she didn't recognise his voice.

And along with the breaking of his voice came other tumultuous physical phenomena. What with the boils, the pimples, the brown whiskers on his upper lip and chin, and the strange disturbed feelings within himself, he seemed to be changing into a Dr Jekyll and Mr Hyde. The face that looked out at him from the little mirror above his cubicle washbasin had a distinctive Hyde-like quality. He did not take Biology, being well on the Arts side now. But he picked up scraps from those that did and books that were banned.

One night, finding him hastily trying to conceal a book, Roxburgh confiscated it, adding, 'I'll lend you one that sets it out rather better.'

Privately, Blake found what he read simultaneously reassuring and depressing. At least he wasn't a monster, but the Lord, he felt, could earn no marks for that side of Creation.

He returned the book to Roxburgh a week before the end of the summer term. Roxburgh was leaving. He had won an Oxford scholarship.

'Like you will one day,' he told Blake. 'Meantime you're on your own.'

And though he missed Roxburgh more than his parents, his world was strong enough to do without the main beam.

He matriculated with four distinctions. He was made a prefect. Just after he took Higher School Certificate, his parents returned for furlough before again returning to Ceylon. Before going up to Oxford at Christmas 1937 to take the scholarship examination, he wrote to Roxburgh, telling him he was coming up. But the letter was returned, marked *Gone Away*. He had probably taken his degree early, Blake told himself, but the letter gave him a strange chill.

He fell in love with Oxford at first sight. Its grace and beauty enchanted him. In its own way, it was like his distant childish love for Alexandra. News of her achievements, like those of Henry Swain, went winging to Ceylon to his parents and then boomeranged back to him. Both sets of news had certain bullet-like qualities. Alexandra was doing brilliantly. A form above her age group, and top of that. Henry was similarly achieving. He was at a special school, distinguishing himself in athletics and archery.

He read other things too on that journey back to Kirkstone. When they stopped at Swindon, the paper boys were rushing up and down the platform yelling about the Nazis putting pressure on Austria. He bought a paper and studied it. Wacky's pet obsession, Hitler, was at it again!

Next morning a notice had appeared on the board saying that as part of cementing happier international relationships, a party of twelve German boys from a school called Trefeld founded by Benedictine monks would be arriving on 9 February 1938 for a six-week visit.

'Hitler's fooling us, Blake! This friendship ploy is all eyewash!'

Blake laughed, 'But friendship is what you preach, Wacky!'

'You'll laugh on the other side of your face, one of these days, Blake! Hitler isn't going to go away. Nor is Fascism. And it'll be our generation that cops it!'

'*You* won't, Wacky.'

'We all will,' Wagstaff said sombrely.

Poor gloomy Wacky, Blake thought, through the hymns and the prayers.

He went to stay with his aunt in Yorkshire for that Christmas. There was snow on the ground when he returned to Kirkstone. The pipes froze in the dormitories. Ink became black ice in the classroom inkwells.

On the first Sunday evening, as usual, Mr Colville preached the sermon. It was usually about the School's misdoings the previous term. From his stance at the lectern this time, everyone knew that something more unpleasant than usual was coming. Perhaps some boy had been found talking to a 'dumb', or imbibing cider.

The headmaster cleared his throat. 'Many of you will remember William Roxburgh,' he began, 'a brilliant scholar and sportsman, a fine Senior Prefect, a credit to the school. With profound sorrow, I have to tell you now that he was killed in action during the defence of Teruel, fighting in the International Brigade.'

Blake was too stunned to hear the rest of Mr Colville's eulogy. Childish tears pricked behind his eyes. A lump came into his throat. Then his sorrow turned to bitter cynicism. The Germans and the Italians were fighting on the side of the Spanish Fascists. It had probably been a German bullet fired by a German gun from a German hand that had killed Roxburgh. Wacky was right. They were spoiling for a fight. He hated the bastards. Hated the only German he knew – Henry Swain.

As they filed out of Chapel, he averted his eyes from the War Memorial. The name of Roxburgh would soon be carved in that empty space. It was as if the Memorial had reached out to gather him in.

But sorrow for Roxburgh gradually subsided. More immediate things were filling his mind. He won a scholarship to Minton College. The news came to him as he, Nash, Wagstaff and Fanshawe were making tea and toast in the privileged confines of the School Prefects' Room. A telegram dated 9 February was delivered by a pale shrimp of a First Form boy. On it Mr Colville had written, 'Well done, Blake!'

As Nash had already won a scholarship to Oriel and Wagstaff to Jesus, the mood in the School Prefects' Room was very comfortable. The significance of the date had entirely slipped Blake's mind.

He was just holding another piece of bread up to the fire, when he heard the sound of marching feet. Fanshawe, who was standing by the window drinking his tea, called out, 'Here come the monks now!'

Blake put down the toast and rushed to the window.

'God Almighty!' Fanshawe said, choking on his tea, 'Did you ever see such an ugly bunch of bastards?'

Looking over his shoulder down to the playground below, Blake saw a dozen strapping young men in black jack-boots and brown uniforms.

And there in the centre was Henry Swain.

II HEINRICH
9 February 1938–3 September 1939

'John! John Blake! By God, but our *Wiedersehen* has been a long time coming!'

The moment Blake came through the archway into the asphalt playground with the three other boys, Heinrich Swain had recognised him, taller, more muscular, but in his step the same hesitation, the same oddly innocent expression in his eyes, a familiar welcoming face in Papa Swain's unfamiliar, unwelcoming country.

And by God, had it been unwelcoming! The rough cold Channel, the winter fields of the so-called Garden of England, the rain-soaked cliffs of Dover, the dilapidated buildings, the mean grey streets, the sooty railway station, the dirty train that left Paddington half an hour late, the shabby frowning people that crowded it.

'I told you, Herr Ritter,' he said to the Master as they boarded the bus at Barminster station. 'I told you the English would not like us coming in uniform.'

'You know everything, Swain!' Herr Ritter had smiled at him indulgently. Heinrich was popular with the Masters. He was clever, he was ear-marked for great things.

But he was less popular with his peers. 'He *thinks* he knows everything,' Varenfordt, their Jugendschaftsführer, corrected. He was haughty and thin-lipped, with a duelling scar under his left eye. 'That is somewhat different!'

Heinrich let that pass. Varenfordt was jealous of him. Varenfordt was no cleverer and no braver and considerably less strong than he, but he came from a powerful Prussian family, though no more powerful, he was sure, than the Hartenburgs, his own family, used to be.

As the bus climbed the hill, Heinrich had told his eleven Trefeld comrades about his friendship with Blake and how he himself had very nearly gone to Kirkstone.

'Then as usual you had the luck of the devil!' was Varenfordt's comment.

Heinrich would not deny it. Compared to Trefeld with its three hundred acres, the place looked more like a prison than a school, all high walls and sombre grey buildings. Where was the green and pleasant land that Papa Swain had sung about in the Mission Chapel?

But it was not their place to criticise, as he had reminded Varenfordt. The visit must be a success. The High Master had drummed that into them before they left. The Führer himself had written in *Mein Kampf* that friendship with Britain was imperative! Together they would resist Communism. For though Britain was declining, its Navy was the envy of the world, admired and imitated by the *Kriegsmarine*, into which all twelve Trefeld boys hoped to be going. Their behaviour must be beyond reproach. They must show their hosts the qualities of men of the Third Reich.

With a warm friendly smile curving his lips, his eyes bright with unaffected pleasure, Swain put out his hand. 'Last time I saw this man,' he told Varenfordt, 'he was walking off the ship that brought us from Ceylon. Almost ten years ago!'

They had had fun, John and he, on board that ship. He had won all the competitions. Except one. John had cheated in the apple-bobbing and been given the prize. Mother had been furious, had wanted to go to the Captain. 'No, Mother,' he had said, 'Let John keep his fire engine! He's only a baby!' But the Reverend Blake had insisted.

Grandfather Mendelssohn had met them at Hamburg docks. He had bright black eyes like Heinrich's mother, but his hair and beard were white and he walked with a stoop. He looked as old as Methuselah, and that had been the first shock.

The second was the house they lived in – an old house overlooking the sea, his mother had said. But the hired car took them to a very small terrace house, and only from the attic window could be seen the river Elbe, over the Blohm and Voss shipyard.

'Come and greet your grandmother!' His mother had said. Lying on the pillows of a bed that had been set up in the downstairs sitting room that was afterwards *verboten* to him, was a brown wizened little woman who held out her arms and held him so close he thought he would be suffocated.

Heinrich had lived in the attic room with the sea view. His mother's bedroom was just below. On her table beside her bed, she had two photographs. Of course one was of Papa Swain who had adopted him. But the other was of a handsome bearded naval officer – Kapitänleutnant Hartenburg, his real father, Captain of the sea-raider *Kronstadt*, sunk in the Malacca Straits with all hands and all guns still firing at five British cruisers.

Not that Heinrich ever knew his father. He was killed before he was born. But his mother used to tell Heinrich about him – how he was a *Junker* from a family in East Prussia – which must, he realised later, have been as noble as Varenfordt's – how brilliant he was at school, what a fine sailor he was, how kind he was to her. She was full of stories about the Hartenburgs – of their estates, of their wealth, of their fine mansion. But when he asked to go and see those grandparents, she would shake her head and say they were dead.

And his mother's parents never once mentioned his father or any of the Hartenburgs.

Heinrich was put to school at a *Gymnasium*, a high school where the curriculum had remained unchanged since his mother's day.

His mother obtained a position as a saleslady at a Hamburg department store. Papa Swain used to send her money. Grandfather Mendelssohn had a small pension from the government administrative job he had done all his life. So Heinrich did not really notice during those first years in Hamburg that they were short of money.

His mother had never laughed much in Ceylon. Now she laughed less. Grandfather Mendelssohn was the one who laughed most. He used to walk with Heinrich in the parks, skate with him when the Alster Lake was frozen, take him to the zoo.

Without Grandfather Mendelssohn, he didn't know what he'd have done. He was very musical, a descendant of the great Mendelssohn family. There was a piano in the house, but he rarely played it because of disturbing Grandmother. Instead he used to take Heinrich to concerts, and was delighted when his old friend Otto Lerner, a tall shambling widower, taught Heinrich to play the violin.

Papa Swain wrote to him every week. He wrote back, though not very often. He would ask his mother when they would return to Ceylon.

'Sometime,' she would reply.

But the months passed, and then came the World Depression. His mother lost her job in the same winter of 1931 that his grandmother died. Unemployed men gathered in the *Hopfenmarkt* and along the

Fleeten – narrow canals full of barges and bordered by warehouses. The Communists were massing, his grandfather had said, just as they had done nine years before, when the city was torn by riots and fighting which was only stopped when a cruiser and three torpedo boats entered the harbour.

Then came the summer of 1932. Five hundred firms closed in Hamburg. Government salaries and pensions were cut. Now there was only a trickle of money coming into the house, and they lived on black bread and potato soup.

But at least he was fourteen that next year and he could sit the examination to enter the *Kriegsmarine*.

'You'll never get in,' his grandfather said. 'Nineteen places. Three thousand entries.'

'I'll get in,' Heinrich said. 'My father was the Commander of the *Kronstadt*.'

His grandfather simply shook his head and said nothing.

He didn't get in.

'The Admirals and the Captains choose only their own sons,' his mother said. 'It is a wicked system.'

'It is a wicked world, my dear,' said his grandfather.

When they were alone, Heinrich suggested they should write to the Hartenburgs. 'A powerful family will have influence,' he said. 'Surely they would help?'

But his mother simply repeated that all the Hartenburgs were dead.

'Never mind,' he told her. 'I'll get in next time!'

But for the time being he had to work to bring more money into the house. He hung round the docks till the men on the barges came to know him. He used to walk down to the Blohm and Voss yards, where they built boats and seaplanes. He used to look through the iron gates so often, one cold January day the foreman had him in and gave him a hot cup of coffee and showed him round the assembly sheds. For the next month, he had a job there as a sweeper. But then he got his real chance – deckhand on a steamer that plied between Hamburg and Rotterdam.

He took the *Kriegsmarine* examination again that year. Again he didn't get in.

His grandfather shook his head. 'You can't beat the system.'

'It is a new system now!' his mother shouted at the old man. 'There is a new spirit in our Germany now. Germany is awakening into strength and prosperity!'

Heinrich knew what she meant. The Nazis were now in power, and this was what Adolf Hitler had promised.

'He must join in,' she said. 'He must *belong*!'

But his grandfather simply started laughing. Not his usual laugh, more like a growl.

There was a row when he wanted to join the Hitler Youth. His grandfather objected. It was his mother who supported him. It was good fun. They learned map-reading and navigation, sailing and gliding. He got free transportation to summer camps in the Black Forest, and sang songs round the pinewood fires. There were girls of the *Bund Deutscher Mädchen*. That time in Schloss Fassen was the first time in Germany he really noticed them.

At Schloss Fassen, there were a lot of fair-haired, blue-eyed girls with their hair neatly plaited and hanging down their backs. But there was one dark-haired one called Anneliese who knew more than a thing or two. She had a tent on her own, being a Leader, and in the small hours he used to pull out the peg on the entrance flap and slither inside to find her arms waiting for him. She gave him her photograph which his mother found in his desk drawer and which at first made her angry. But when she heard she was the daughter of General Frankel, a military advisor to the Führer, she remarked how pretty she was and encouraged him to write to her.

Then came that Red Letter Day – 20 January 1935. Ignoring her ally France, and in spite of the Versailles Treaty, Great Britain signed a Naval Treaty with Germany, allowing her to build battleships and U-boats. There was going to be a big expansion to the *Kriegsmarine* and many more jobs. Unemployment had come down from six million to almost nothing. He got a job as a machinist at the Blohm and Voss yards. Every morning he went into the yards under a banner inscribed in huge red letters WE HAVE OUR FUHRER TO THANK THAT WE ARE WORKING HERE TODAY. HEIL HITLER!

This 'Heil' was the new greeting. *Heil Hitler*. Everyone said it instead of good morning. Everyone, that is, except grandfather.

'Heil only means salutation, Father,' his mother told the old man.

'Salutation?' He gave that laugh again. 'Damnation! Pure pagan! Pagan as that filthy swastika!'

'Father, Hitler has given us back hope. Just you see! Germany is entering a new era.'

He shook his head. 'Not for the likes of you and me.'

That year he took the Naval examination again. And this time he was selected. Better than that, he was to go, after Compulsory Labour Service, to a new sort of establishment, where the best boys in the country would be trained to be Leaders. His new school would concentrate on future officers of the armed services.

His mother was delighted. 'What did I tell you, Father?' she said.

His grandfather said nothing. Heinrich thought he was pleased, but those days it was hard to tell what he felt. He had taken to the bed in the sitting room where Heinrich's grandmother had lain when they first arrived. He had developed a cough. It was winter of course, and very cold. Best place was bed for him, his mother said. But two storeys above him at night, Heinrich could still hear him coughing.

He did not, after all, go to Labour Camp. Because his grandfather was ill, he was allowed to do his service for the Community assembling prefabricated U-boats that had secretly been built in Spain. That way he could stay at home and help his mother.

The way ahead now was clear. The economy was booming. No longer was there unemployment. There were only two blots in those two years. His grandfather became worse in the winter of 1936. One evening just before Christmas, while Heinrich was sitting with him, he suddenly reached out for his hand and held it tightly.

'Look after your mother, Heinrich. She will need you.'

'I will. I promise.'

'You're a good boy.' He lay back on the pillows. 'And a strong boy. You always keep your promises. Now I can rest.'

He closed his eyes. That was the last time Heinrich saw him alive.

The second blot happened just before he went to Trefeld. He and his mother had had dinner at a good restaurant in Hamburg as a celebration and farewell. As they were walking home through the Friedrichsstrasse, suddenly there was the clatter of shattering glass, footsteps running, people shouting. In the lamplight down one of the side streets, Heinrich saw a shop window had been smashed in. Boxes and shoes were scattered on the pavement. A man with blood on his face and a weeping woman were surrounded by three jostling youths.

His mother clutched his arm, but he pushed her off and rushed down the street. He collared the nearest of the youths round the neck, twisted his arm behind him and threw him to the ground. He sent his fist crashing into the jaw of the next one; the crack of bone on bone excited him.

His blood-lust was up. When the third youth ran off, he made to pursue him. Then he saw the word *Jude* scrawled all over the shop door and the brickwork. He stood rooted momentarily to the spot, chilled by something more than disgust – an inexplicable, premonitory fear, as if the huge jagged hole in the shop window was a tear in the veil of the future.

He stopped to help the man pick up the scattered shoe boxes. Nervously, his mother crept up to join him.

'Come, Heinrich, please! Don't spoil our last evening!' She put her hand through his arm, drawing him away, back to the bright lights of the Friedrichstrasse, murmuring, 'The city is so lawless . . . the Communists are everywhere!'

'Louts,' he had said angrily, 'drunken louts! You must not go out on your own at night!'

She promised that she wouldn't.

That night after he kissed her goodnight at her bedroom door, she had said abruptly, 'We are not Jews, you know, Heinrich!'

'Of course, I do, Mother! Whatever made you say that?'

'Your grandfather . . . his name . . . you might have thought . . . his father was of Jewish birth, but he was baptised by his parents into the Lutheran church. He never went inside a synagogue. Never! Your grandmother was pure German through and through. As you are, Heinrich.' She kissed him again with what seemed to him to be relief.

But the conversation left him feeling uneasy, and in some way vaguely besmirched.

He left for Trefeld next day. And suddenly he was in a young man's paradise – and forgot about everything else.

For here was everything.

Five hundred years before, the Benedictines had built their monastery by the side of a vast lake, which soon became a celebrated centre for learning throughout Germany. The Nazis had built on it substantially and turned it into a dream of youth. Motorboats and yachts sailed the lake. Gliders rose from the fields, fast cars and motorcycles raced round a cinder track. There were sports fields, swimming baths, two gymnasiums.

There was also a parade ground and a rifle range. Instead of monkish habits, staff and pupils wore peaked khaki caps, tunics, breeches and field boots.

Lessons were in the morning. Mathematics were in military

terms: if the bomber flew at 212 kilometres an hour and the fighter at 314 kilometres, where and when would they intercept?

The afternoons were given over to sports and games, driving instruction and flying lessons, sailing and car racing. In the evening there were lectures from high-ranking officers – Field Marshal Göring, Head of the *Luftwaffe* came, so did General Frankel, and so did Captain Dönitz, of the new U-boat arm. Occasionally there was a musical evening, listening to Wagner – but not Mendelssohn – and singing the *Horst Wessel Lied*. Sometimes the more right-wing pupils added an extra verse – *avenge Horst Wessel*. Though he neither knew nor cared who Horst Wessel was, the song and the shouting aroused something hot and challenging inside him.

In the spring, they lived off the land for six weeks, engaging the 'enemy'. They had *Wehrsport*, or war games, where 'lives' were rubber bands round their wrist. Break the rubber band and you 'killed' your man – a kid's game of tag, Heinrich thought, much preferring manoeuvres where real ammunition was used.

His mother was pleased that he was happy, proud that he was nearly always top in everything, though that made other pupils envious. Knowing his background, they called him '*der Engländer*'.

Of the twelve who were selected to go to the English school, it was natural that Heinrich should be one. The other senior pupils were Varenfordt, Fische, who came from a rich industrialist's family friendly with Goebbels, and Kassel, whose father was in the *Kriegsmarine*. Eight juniors, or *Pimpfe*, made up the party.

Now all twelve were drawn up in two columns of six on this English school yard, and Heinrich had John's right hand in his.

Varenfordt echoed his last words. 'Ten years! It's a wonder you recognised him!'

John's handshake was cool. A boy behind him with a large head came forward. 'I'm Nash, Senior Prefect.'

Heinrich introduced the others. 'This is our Leader . . . Varenfordt.'

Varenfordt clicked his heels – doing it to annoy, as always.

'I'm Wagstaff,' said a tall beanpole with horn-rimmed glasses.

'Fanshawe,' said a big man with orange hair.

'And this is Fische,' Heinrich said.

Fische clicked his heels too. But Kassel didn't. He hurried over the *Pimpfe*'s names. Nobody gave the Nazi salute. At least they'd taken to heart what he'd said about that.

These four were apparently the Heads of Kirkstone's Houses. Each of them was to take three Germans to look after.

'Naturally I shall be with you, John,' Heinrich said. 'And you two *Pimpfe*' – he chose the two best-mannered – 'with John and me, too!'

Fische went with Wagstaff. Varenfordt with Nash. Kassel with Fanshawe – each with two *Pimpfe*.

Off they all trooped with their hosts to the four dormitories – cold barrack blocks with twenty-five beds. Flannels, blazer, ties and school cap lay on each of the beds that had been provided. They put their uniforms carefully away in the cubicle lockers, and emerged looking like overgrown Kirkstone boys.

Nash then gave them a guided tour of the school. Trailing behind the others with Blake, Heinrich kept up a continuous description of what he'd been doing.

'What will you do when you leave here, John?'

'I'm going to Oxford in October.'

'And afterwards?'

'The Colonial Service, I hope.'

'You're lucky, you British, to have colonies and a Colonial Service. We Germans only have the armed services.'

Blake gave him a sharp, almost hostile look, and Swain went on quickly, 'And such beautiful colonies! Ceylon! I often think of those times. Remember my ninth birthday?'

'Vaguely.'

'I remember it *vividly*. The day we became blood brothers.'

We are having a good time here, Heinrich wrote to his mother next day. *When next you write to Papa Swain, be sure to tell him how much I am enjoying his old school* . . .

He was fond of both his mother and his stepfather, and he had never understood their separation, particularly as they corresponded regularly and Papa Swain's letters that were passed on to him were always very loving and concerned both for his mother and himself.

But troubles started almost immediately. Coming out of the dining hall on their third day, Kassel asked in German, 'Enjoy your breakfast?'

German speaking was *verboten* while they were here. As a double reproof, Swain replied in English, 'Very much.'

'As an Englishman, you will of course like bread and porridge,' Kassel said, but this time in English.

Coming back from Chapel on the next Sunday, Fische declared in his execrable English, 'Such church-going the Party would not like.'

'Nonsense, Fische!' Swain enjoyed the English hymns. Just for that time in Chapel, he was back beside his mother in Papa Swain's church in Colombo.

In class, Shakespeare and English literature were meekly accepted. Latin and Greek meant nothing to them anyway.

But at Trefeld, German physics, not in accord with Professor Einstein, German history and German geography had been taught. Fische objected to the British versions. But the worst was Varenfordt, who turned a geography lesson into an impassioned denunciation of the Versailles *Diktat*.

By the second week, the lessons for the Germans were confined to English literature, Greek and Latin. After all, it was argued in the Staff Common Room, they were here to improve their English, and Classics would certainly help their etymology.

There were not many opportunities to let off steam.

Freezing weather made the Upper Field too hard to play rugger on. It was not till the end of the fourth week that the weather became warmer, and for the first time Heinrich and John walked up the steep hill together.

John was in shorts and a football jersey carrying his boots, Heinrich was in flannels and blazer only, because he hated wearing the long black mackintosh that made him look like an SS man.

The First XV were playing against a Catholic Public School. Blake stood well behind the others at full back.

Heinrich watched while they rolled in the mud. Beside him on the whitewashed line, boys were calling out encouragement or execrations. But after fifteen minutes, Heinrich's attention wandered to what was happening on the other side of the stone wall.

A number of girls in white blouses and navy blue gym tunics and black stockings were playing lacrosse.

He had heard that there was a girls' school just down the road from Kirkstone. He had seen neat crocodiles of girls out walking in the lanes. But nobody had told him that their playing fields were next door to the Upper Field.

Now his attention became riveted on a girl with short blonde hair who appeared to be dominating the others.

He watched her leap into the air, intercept a pass between two of her opponents, streak through half a dozen other Boadiceas and slam the ball into the net.

'Well played, sir!' he shouted in the English fashion, remembering what they used to call out during the tennis matches in Colombo.

She looked up, saw him, but pretended not to.

He watched her, spellbound. Ten minutes later, she scored again. It was like that, leaning against the wall with his chin resting on a flat stone, that Blake found him.

'That's not allowed,' he said.

He was sucking a quarter lemon. Apparently it was half-time, when they changed ends and had a rest,

Swain looked at Blake in amazement. The Kirkstone boys' attitude to girls was a source of amusement to the Trefeld contingent. What with calling the maids 'dumbs' and not looking over stone walls at the girls playing games, Varenfordt was speaking for them all when he said that 'These boys don't know one end of a girl from the other!'

'Why?'

'They don't like it!'

'Who are they, anyway?'

'The School. Daughters of serving officers.'

'Do you know any of them?'

'Only one,' he paused. 'To be more correct, I *used* to know her.' He paused again. 'You used to know her, too.'

'*I* did?'

Blake nodded. 'In Colombo. But you'll have forgotten.'

'What was her name?'

A whistle blew. Blake immediately left him and shot back onto the pitch for the second half of the game. Heinrich resumed his appraisal over the wall of the performance of the blonde-haired girl.

She was running up the white line now, the ball in her lacrosse stick, not thirty yards away from him.

A small spark of recognition had been energised when he'd first set eyes on her.

Of course!

He watched her feinting past two hefty girls towards the goal. Just as she was about to make her throw, one of the defences tackled and brought her to the ground.

'Foul!' Heinrich called out, just as he'd heard the boys call out on the rugger touchline.

Curious eyes were turned in his direction. Then a whistle shrilled. He thought a penalty was being awarded. But no, it was the end of the game.

The fair-haired girl got up and called, 'Thanks for your support!'

He took off his ridiculous little Kirkstone cap. 'My pleasure!'

She began walking towards him. A dark-haired girl, following behind her said, 'Go on, Alexandra! Introduce us!'

'I would if I knew his name.'

'He doesn't look like a Kirkstone boy,' said a small girl with pigtails.

'My name's Diana,' said the dark-haired girl.

Heinrich reached across the wall for her hand and raised it to his lips. 'Mine's Heinrich.'

'Sounds German.'

'It is German.'

'Alexandra,' said the dark-haired girl over her shoulder, 'that should give you a clue!'

'I remember,' Alexandra said. Then she added in fluent German, 'Why don't you give us your famous balancing act on the top of the wall?'

'You remembered all along,' he said back to her in German.

She laughed. 'What on earth are you doing here?'

'We have been sent to learn English.'

'You mean there's more of you?' asked Diana hopefully.

'Eleven.'

'Where?' There was a concerted rush to the wall, followed by cries of, 'I can only see Kirkstone grizzlies!'

Alexandra leaned on the other side of the wall beside him. 'You seem to have made quite a hit.'

'Always do.'

'Still the same boastful little boy.'

'Still the same beautiful girl.'

She gave him a sideways smile.

'Why are you laughing at me like that?'

'Just remembering.'

'Remembering what?'

'Remembering you and John Blake.'

'He's here at Kirkstone.'

'I know.' She began to laugh. 'I've seen him.'

'Why are you laughing?'

'Oh, nothing!'

'He came to see you?'

'A Kirkstone boy coming to see an Imperial School girl?' She laughed again. 'You must be joking!'

'*I* would have done.'

There was a scurry of girls away from the wall. Suddenly Alexandra and Heinrich were alone.

'Here's Miss Hawkhurst,' she said. 'I'll have to go.'

'Who's Miss Hawkhurst?'

'The headmistress.'

Coming up over the horizon was a woman in a tweed skirt and sweater.

'You'll get into trouble.'

'Nonsense! I'd simply kiss her hand and ask leave to call on you.'

'She wouldn't fall for that. No permission without parents' approval. That's the rule.'

'Then get their approval.'

'They're in Hong Kong with the Far East Fleet.'

'Then I'll just walk in.'

'You'd never get past the Lodge. Do go! Quickly . . . *quickly*! She's coming!'

The woman was walking purposefully towards them. Alexandra moved away.

'Herr Ritter,' Heinrich Swain said in the archaic English that the Master preferred, 'I have had the good fortune to discover that an old family friend is a pupil at the august Imperial School. Naturally I would like permission to –'

'How old is she, Swain?'

'I never ask a lady's age, Herr Ritter.'

'Old enough.' He shook his head vigorously. 'As I suspected.'

'Herr Ritter, you do not even know what it is I am requesting!'

'I can guess, Swain.'

'It is simply a little gesture of politeness.'

'Now if you had been Kassel, or Fische or Varenfordt even, my answer might have been different. It's your reputation, Swain. By saying "no" now, I am simply protecting you from yourself. You have a weakness for women, Swain.' Herr Ritter smiled indulgently. 'One day, a woman will seal your fate.'

Having attempted to achieve his goal legally, he would simply have to achieve it illegally by taking the first opportunity to slip away. But there was no opportunity that weekend, nor the next. It was as though every minute of the boys' time had to be occupied. Heinrich remembered a favourite saying of the Reverend Blake: 'The devil finds work for idle hands to do.' That might have been the Kirkstone motto. When they weren't in the classroom, or joining in rugger games, or running, or jumping, they were being taken with their English hosts to look at the sights.

Sitting together half-way down the bus and arguing, Fische and Wagstaff made such sightseeing trips uncomfortable for everyone. Fische had convinced himself that the Aurora Borealis was an anti-aircraft searchlight, and developed a phobia about British war pre-paredness. He got really excited at the sight of a black aeroplane taking off, which he identified as a 'powerful Whitley bomber'. Wagstaff countered with continuous sermons on 'Hitler's Napoleonic aggressiveness'.

To part the pair of them and to bring peace to that expedition to Fry's chocolate factory, Swain marched quickly up to the seat beside Wagstaff and, smiling in his most winning way, asked if he might sit beside him.

That meant Fische had to sit somewhere in the middle. The bus was full because everyone at Kirkstone was perennially hungry and the prospect of free chocolate samples had ensured that every seat was taken. Blake, arriving at one minute to two, was the last aboard and got the last seat.

Before he sat down, he counted heads. 'That's everyone,' he shouted up to the driver.

Then as the driver turned on the ignition, up jumped Fische, waving his hands excitedly. 'I must my seat change,' he called in his clumsy English. 'Now! At once! Wait! Here I cannot sit!'

'What *is* on his seat, d'you suppose?' Wagstaff asked Swain owlishly.

Ribald suggestions were made. Then an appalled silence fell as Fische pointed accusingly at Samuels sitting next to him. 'This is a Jew! I cannot next to him sit.'

Swain closed his eyes. He felt his stomach turn inside him. He was back, not just with his mother in the little street off the Friedrichstrasse, but at home when he had kissed her goodnight. 'You are not a Jew, Heinrich' echoed through his mind.

He was glad he wasn't a Jew, but appalled that she had had to tell him so, appalled at that tiny fragment of Jewishness that might lurk in him. He had been taught that Jews caused problems, and he did not want to know about them. Of all the lessons at Trefeld, Racial Studies was the only one he disliked. Fische, the upstart, the *Dummkopf*, loved them.

'No, I will not sit down,' Fische was shouting to the boys around him, brushing the sleeves of his jacket as if Samuels had contaminated him.

Swain rose slowly to his feet. Now he would have to act the smiling diplomat. He would say, 'I was keeping your seat for you next to Wagstaff, Fische.' And he himself would sit next to Samuels.

But before he could get to Fische, Blake had come forward and grabbed Fische by the shoulder. As if an anger too long held in check was bursting from him, he shook Fische, then shoved him forcefully down in the seat. 'You'll sit there, Fische, if Samuels will still have you! Or you'll get off the bus and report to your Master!'

Fische went pale with anger. Stunned by surprise, he remained seated. Relieved, Swain returned to his place beside Wagstaff, and engaged him in a discussion of Thomas Mann.

'Is that to show that all Germans are not anti-Jewish?' Wagstaff asked.

The bus accelerated away. But it was an uneasy, subdued journey. Swain kept thinking he'd seen a different John Blake, one he almost admired. As together they walked round the huge vats of churning chocolate in the factory, Heinrich said, 'I thought you handled Fische very well. I apologise humbly for his bad manners.'

But he was careful to say it out of earshot of the other Germans, and because he knew he'd done that, he liked himself a little bit less, as he liked John a little bit more.

'The Führer has liberated Austria!'

As the four senior German boys were walking up the stairs to the School Prefects' Room on the morning of 14 March. Fische began excitedly gabbling in German about something he'd heard on the radio.

They came through the door into an icy atmosphere. Headlines in the newspapers lying on the table announced HITLER MARCHES IN AGAIN.

Swain tried to explain to Blake that Austria traditionally belonged to Germany.

'You British,' Varenfordt told them, 'know nothing of German history.'

'But we do!' Wagstaff retorted. 'Murder of Dollfuss. Persecution of the Jews. Confiscation of property. Imprisonment of–'

'Many of your aristocracy support Herr Hitler,' Varendfordt interrupted. 'They see him as a bulwark against Europe's real enemy, Communism.'

'The Führer has thrown off the chains of Versailles,' Fische said. 'He has released the Rhine, Sudetanland, and now Austria from imprisonment.'

The bell rang out then, and the eight of them went down to Chapel in ominous silence.

The hymn for the day was 'Praise The Lord For He Is Glorious'. Varenfordt led all the Trefeld contingent except Swain in singing 'Deutschland Über Alles', which had the same tune.

The atmosphere became icier. The British were now hardly speaking to them. In retaliation, Varenfordt and Fische began to make pointed remarks.

'This is a school for *Unteroffiziere*,' Varenfordt declared, after he had counted the number of Sergeants and Second Lieutenants on the Chapel War Memorial.

'And Jews,' put in Fische.

'And Communists,' Varenfordt added. 'Did you see in the space below Second Lieutenant Zangwill the name of W. K. Roxburgh, International Brigade?'

When Herr Ritter announced that the Germans and the British would celebrate the last day of the visit with a game of *Wehrsport*, Varendfordt said, 'We just can't wait!'

Everyone cheered except Swain. Next Saturday was his last chance to see Alexandra, and he had planned an altogether different schedule.

During the Friday morning break, he slipped outside the Kirkstone gates and telephoned the Imperial School from the kiosk.

'Who is that?' demanded a female voice suspiciously, when he asked to speak to Miss Alexandra Monteith.

'The name is also Monteith,' he replied with dignity. 'I am Alexandra's Uncle Henry. I happen to be down here on business and would like to arrange a meeting on Saturday afternoon.'

It worked. In a cool self-possessed way Alexandra said, 'Of course I'd love to see you, Uncle Henry. On Saturday at three, Diana and I are going to Charlstone Wood to sketch the church.'

'I'll be there,' he told her.

Alexandra had grown to be a girl after his own heart!

After lunch the next day, the Trefeld boys assembled in the playground wearing yellow armbands. The Kirkstone boys wore red. Wagstaff had refused to attend.

The gym master and Herr Ritter were the umpires. The rules were explained. The rubber bands, their 'lives', were distributed.

The headmaster blew the whistle. Everyone shot out of the playground. Varenfordt shouted to the Trefeld boys in German, 'Keep together! Don't get isolated!'

The British force under Nash disappeared into the trees to the north of the school. Varenfordt led the Germans towards an old quarry, where Heinrich told him that he would take up position 'as a sniper'.

Hiding himself behind an outcrop, he watched the Trefeld boys disappear westwards. Then he ran across the fields in the opposite direction and down the steep unmade lane into the valley. Climbing over a stile, he made his way upwards across the meadow to the fir trees at the top of the knoll known as Charlstone Wood.

He saw her as soon as he rounded the hill. She was still a long way away, but he would recognise the way she held herself anywhere. The short dark-haired girl was with her. They were shading their eyes and looking down at the church immediately below them.

Alexandra didn't turn until he was on them. When she did, she spread her hands in mock surprise and said, 'Why, Uncle Henry!' in that soft breathless voice of hers.

He was not usually shy, nor was he an English boy, virginal in his pursuit of the cricket ball and the university scholarship. He had a healthy knowledge of women. But Alexandra affected him differently. Her hair, as she tossed it carelessly back, rippled gold in the sunlight. Her skin glowed and her eyes shone bright and blue and teasing.

'You know Diana?'

He bowed stiffly. 'Of course!'

'You almost clicked your heels,' Alexandra said severely.

The dark-haired girl gave him a distinctly admiring smile. 'It's just his continental good manners.'

Alexandra raised her brows. 'Really?'

'It's a pity they don't teach such manners to our weedy youths,' Diana said.

The three of them stood in the half-shadow, not knowing what to say next.

'You're very tall,' Diana remarked, endearing herself to him, shading her eyes, looking up from her short height as if he were some splendid tree. 'You remind me of that film star . . . whatshisname, Alexandra?'

'Charlie Chaplin?'

'No, silly! Plays opposite Marlene Dietrich. Otto von Something.'

Heinrich was not displeased. He was becoming reconciled to having Diana with them as a flattering chaperone, when Alexandra said firmly, 'Now Diana has to go down to the church to draw the font for her prep.'

The dark-haired girl nodded, but seemed reluctant to leave.

'Do you also have to go, Alexandra?'

She shook her head. 'I can copy Diana's.'

Diana shifted her weight from foot to foot. 'Are you sure you'll be all right, Alexandra?'

Heinrich smiled, feeling splendidly in control of the situation. 'I promise I won't eat her up.'

Diana flushed crimson. 'I didn't mean that. I mean, suppose Miss Hawkhurst sees you?'

'This is an excellent hide up here,' Heinrich said. 'You can see without being seen.'

'Alexandra has an eye for good places,' Diana murmured, thrusting out her lower lip.

He could see she was disappointed, and when she finally gave a grudging farewell wave, he took her hand and carried it to his lips. 'I hope we shall meet again, Diana,' he called in a vibrant Otto von Something voice as she set off down the hill.

Alexandra called after her, 'The church closes in an hour!'

Diana didn't turn round.

'An hour,' Heinrich said very slowly, 'is not long enough to be with you.'

She opened her eyes wide. 'That,' she replied, equally slowly, 'is a very gallant remark, Uncle Henry.'

He nodded, and subsided onto the mossy bank. 'At least let's make ourselves comfortable.'

He held out his hand for her to do the same. She stood for a moment, looking down quizzically at him, her arms folded over her chest, her long black-stockinged legs slightly apart.

When she sat down, it was at a little distance away from him. She clasped her hands round her well-shaped knees and asked demurely, 'Have you enjoyed yourself at Kirkstone?'

'Not much.'

'It looks like a prison to us.'

'There are resemblances,' he smiled, and moved a little closer to her.

'*We're* not allowed any contact with Kirkstone.' She ran her fingers down the pleats of her gym tunic.

He reached over and touched her hand. 'And do you know why?'

She slid him a sideways smile, her head down, so that a lock of fair hair fell over her forehead.

'I have no idea. Perhaps they are afraid they would corrupt us.'

'They are afraid, my dear niece, that *you* would corrupt *them*.'

She tossed her head. 'They'd be lucky!'

'I agree. They would indeed be lucky.' He shuffled closer to her. 'In fact, Varenfordt says . . . no, on second thoughts I can't repeat to a lady what Varenfordt says.'

'Who's Varenfordt?'

'Our Section Leader.' He folded his arms and sat up straight and wide-shouldered. 'A real Nazi.'

'Aren't you?'

'No.'

'But you're at a military school.'

'It's no tougher than Kirkstone.'

She laughed as if he'd made a joke. After a moment, she persisted, 'But you're going into the Services?'

He nodded. 'Into the *Kriegsmarine*, I hope.'

'You'll look very dashing,' she smiled, her blue eyes crinkled up and dreamy. Then she frowned. 'But won't you have to join the Party then?'

'The *Kriegsmarine* is a very professional and independent body.'

'Like the British Navy?'

'Exactly.' They both smiled, finding the similarity reassuring. 'In fact,' he went on, 'the *Kriegsmarine* is modelled on the British Navy. D'you know, I've had to study Nelson's tactics at the Battle of Trafalgar?'

'I must tell Daddy that.' She laughed, and let him take her hand. He experienced a potent mixture of content and discontent. English girls, especially schoolgirls, could have no idea of the potency of their freshness and innocence.

'And where will you go after Trefeld?'

'Naval College.'

'And then a commission?'

'If I'm lucky.'

'Then,' she broke off a piece of feathery grass and tickled his nose with it, '*then* surely you'll have to swear allegiance to Hitler.'

'As Head of State. If he's *still* Head of State. In the same way as your Navy swears allegiance to the King.'

'But you'd have to join the Nazi Party then?'

'There are a lot of high-ranking *Kriegsmarine* officers who are not in the Party.'

She smiled enigmatically.

'Hitler has his good points, you know. He's taught a defeated Germany to hold its head high. He's brought full employment. He's built the best roads in the world. Hospitals, schools, sports stadiums. He has given me a first-class education. And the prospect of an excellent job. He has given a joyousness to German youth.'

Alexandra threw away the piece of grass and resting her elbows on her knees and cupping her chin in her hands, stared ahead at the blue and white distance. Then she asked softly, 'And what's he given to Austria?'

He felt a rush of anger shot with a sensual delight. He liked the way she suddenly brought out her feline claws. He even liked the way she presumed to be his equal in argument.

Sternly he replied, 'Liberation. Hitler has brought liberation to Austria.'

She raised her brows at the tone. 'I wonder if the Austrians would say they'd been liberated?'

'If they're honest.'

'And cooperative?'

'I've answered enough questions. Tell me about *you*.'

She shrugged.

'You're clever, aren't you, Alexandra? You'll go to university.'

'I'm hoping for Oxford.'

'I'm hoping,' he mimicked her tone, emphasising its preciousness, 'for Oxford.'

She tried to put a hand over his mouth. 'Shut up, Henry!'

He caught hold of it, and now he had imprisoned both her hands. He could have pulled her close and kissed her. But he didn't, because he dare not.

So he released her and they both sat decorously again. He plied her with polite questions. She told him she was going to read Modern Languages, but before she actually went up to university, she would spend some months in Germany.

'Where?'

She didn't know yet.

'But promise you will let me know?'

She said, 'I promise,' in German.

Her German was excellent. She spoke it with the most beautiful and beguiling accent. He thought he could have fallen in love with her just for the way she spoke his language. She knew a great deal about German history too. Far more than any boy at Kirkstone. She did not like Hitler. But then she did not like Chamberlain either.

As for her family, she had a younger brother now who would be coming home from Hong Kong with her parents to go to prep school. Captain Monteith was leaving his shore job – at last getting his wish to go back to sea.

'The sea is in his blood, isn't it?' Heinrich said, squeezing her fingers. Like it was in *his* father's. How alike he and Alexandra were!

Time went with unbelievable speed. Far down below, he heard the church clock chime four, and almost immediately a figure appeared at the bottom of the hill. He thought it was Diana and was mentally cursing her for her punctuality, when he saw it was a boy and a Kirkstone boy at that, crouching low as he moved stealthily along the fence.

'What's that boy doing?' Alexandra asked.

'Playing soldiers.'

'But Kirkstone hasn't got an OTC! Look, there's another one!'

Heinrich crouched forward and pulled her down with him. They parted the bushes with their hands, their faces close.

'Who's that big chap with the red hair?'

'Fanshawe. A School Prefect.'

'He can run! He's caught up with that fair one!'

'That's Varenfordt!'

'What sort of game is it?'

'*Wehrsport.*'

He threw himself flat on the ground and pulled her with him. 'We mustn't let them see us!'

'Why?'

'I'm a deserter. I'd be killed.'

'Why did you desert?'

'To see you.' He stroked her hair. He slid an arm under her shoulders and held her protectively close. The presence of the foolish Kirkstone boys, stamping and shouting at no great distance away, guaranteed her virtue, but he felt painfully and exquisitely aware of her nearness.

When the pain outweighed the pleasure, he sat up and listened. Hearing only bird song, he peered through the bushes.

'I think the coast is clear.'

Alexandra lifted her head to look, and flopped back again.

'It's *not!*'

A boy, a slight dark-haired boy, was coming up the hill. He kept straightening and shading his eyes, looking up at the copse.

'It's John Blake,' Heinrich said. 'I think he's seen us!'

'What'll we do?'

'John can't do us much harm.'

'He may miss us. Look, he's going off to the left!'

They watched Blake skirting the copse. Just for a second Heinrich thought he might be going away, but he was only looking for a way to break through the thorn bushes. Suddenly he found one, and came rushing noisily towards them.

Heinrich got to his feet. Alexandra scrambled up behind him.

'I'm out of the game,' Heinrich called. 'Retired hurt.'

'You can't get out of it that way!'

'I am out of it, boy! Go away!'

But Blake came on. He had come right up to them before Alexandra peered out from behind Heinrich.

Then Blake stopped in his tracks. His face flushed crimson as he saw her, but whether with anger or embarrassment, Heinrich didn't know.

Panting, Blake snatched at Heinrich's wrist, tearing at the rubber band.

'Take it, boy!' Heinrich held out his hand smiling and condescending, feeling the sting as the snapped ends flicked his wrist.

'You're dead, you bastard!'

It was then that Heinrich's mood somersaulted. Blake had used the one word Heinrich found deeply offensive. And in front of Alexandra. He clenched his fist. Frustration fuelled his outrage and anger. Without consciously intending to, he shot out his arm and smashed his fist into Blake's red indignant face. Blake rocked backwards, mouth agape in astonishment.

Heinrich was immediately appalled. He heard Alexandra's furious indrawn breath. He began to say 'I'm sorry' when Blake staggered forward and landed a hefty punch on the side of his mouth.

'Stop it!' Alexandra shrieked, grabbing Heinrich's arm. 'Stop it, you fools!'

She pushed herself between the two of them.

Heinrich was not sure that he would have stopped it. He could taste blood in his mouth and he felt an acute urge to have Blake at Alexandra's feet. But from behind came Diana's urgent *hallooo* and the sound of her running feet. 'Alexandra! Quickly! We're late! And I've seen the Hawk!'

Blake had dropped his fists. Heinrich turned away.

'Off you go, Alexandra. Thank you for coming.' Heinrich wiped his mouth with his handkerchief. 'Sorry for the *contretemps*. I'm sure John is sorry too.' He whispered in her ear, '*Auf Wiedersehen*. Till next time. Perhaps in Germany.'

Heinrich did not feel sorry to leave England. The contrast between the undersized unemployed outside the British Labour Exchanges and the big bronzed smiling German youth immediately struck him as soon as he returned. Hitler was right – the British were a decadent race, as gloomy as their weather. In spite of all his hopes and expectations, the only fun he had had was with Alexandra.

A week after he was back at Trefeld, he wrote asking for a photograph, 'preferably not in school uniform'. She replied a month later, enclosing an indifferent snapshot which he found enchanting. He answered at once, enclosing a photograph of himself. *Not that you asked for it*, he added, *but anyway here I am*.

Before he could really expect a reply, the cadets ear-marked for the Navy were sent to Kiel for 'special tests'. Psychological tests, social graces tests, conversation tests, attitude tests, personality tests. All were different, but the most painful was the *Mutprobe*, the courage test, where they had to grasp electrified iron bars while all the time cine cameras photographed their faces.

A third of them were failed, including Fische. The survivors were pitchforked into continuous intense training – at the double.

'*Reise, reise!* went the call at six in the morning, followed seconds later by a naked plunge into an ice-cold pool. And all the time, petty officers shouting. 'Kassel, tidy that disgusting shelf! Swain, what's that woman's photograph doing on your locker? You should have

Admiral Raeder's there to set you an example! Mercke, you wouldn't last a moment in that filthy gas mask! Knees-bend, eighty times!'

Climbing the mainsail on a three-master, manning schooners in Force six gales, chipping ice off the decks, firing twenty-millimetre guns and endless physical training, finished at last with an interview by a man with a high forehead and short brushed-back hair, who asked, *'Willst du zum U-Bootwaffe*, Swain?'

That *du* – in spite of the unsmiling mouth and the piercing eyes, it was as though his own father was speaking to him.

He had expected to go on one of the new pocket battleships. He hesitated.

But only for a second. He had heard of the new Z Plan where priority was to be given to build 300 U-boats. Promotion would be quick and the pay was better. Better still, training would be at Kiel, where the School for Naval Officers' daughters was also located. Alexandra had said in her last letter that she hoped to be attending here. Now she was definitely going to Oxford in October.

'Jawohl, Herr Kapitän! he said with such gusto that his hat fell off and even the Head of the U-boat Fleet smiled.

'The sea is in your blood,' his mother was always telling him, and for the next six months he realised how true that was. He loved the salty sting of the wind as he stood on the conning tower of the little 250-ton U-boats where much of their training was done. Unlike some of the others, he was never seasick. He never minded being drenched through by the waves. The inside of a U-boat with its myriad pipes, its hot reek of diesel oil, rope, paint, sweat and boiling potatoes, all mixed up with a whiff of chlorine, fascinated him. He was never happier than when the U-boat was lying on the sea bed, as he listened to the throbbing of destroyer propellers on the hydrophones or the boom of practice depth charges, or when he was up on the surface, firing the 88-millimetre or aiming dummy torpedoes at target ships.

He wrote to Alexandra, imploring her to arrange to come to Kiel as soon as possible. It was several months before he got a letter back saying she hoped to come to Kiel, 'But there are difficulties!'

He presumed these would be the political events that were causing some tension.

But München and the annexing of Czechoslovakia and the other bloodless victories Heinrich regarded as evidence that Germany was climbing away from a position of abject defeat and poverty, that she was once more climbing back into power and prosperity and peace.

And it followed that as a result, he would bring his mother and himself up out of that little house in the back street behind the Blohm and Voss yards into the power and prosperity and greatness of his ancestors. Certainly the sea was in his blood – but that blood was Hartenburg blood.

He was determined that he would be top of his course and collect the Sword of Honour. But when four weeks later, the examination results came out, though he was top of his course, he shared that honour with Varenfordt. First equals. In the event of such a tie, it was for the *Korvetten-Kapitän* to decide who received the Sword. Varenfordt, for his especial devotion to the aims of the Third Reich, was chosen. To his fury, Heinrich had to watch the smiling Nazi mount the podium to collect the Sword from Admiral Raeder.

His anger and disappointment were assuaged by a letter from Alexandra, saying that her parents had rented a house in Oxford and at last it had been agreed that she could do her three months at the Kiel School for Naval Officers' daughters before going up for the Michaelmas Term.

Swain was away on a fortnight's cruise in the Baltic when she arrived at the beginning of July. As soon as the little 250-ton U-boat returned to Kiel, he rang an ex-girlfriend, Klara the Art Mistress, and told her there would be a party at the U-boat School that night to which she was to bring a busload of girls.

The party was quickly laid on. Prompt at eight o'clock the bus swept into the drive between the two old naval guns, and there was Alexandra, sitting at the front, looking more beautiful than ever in a blue dress with a silk shawl over her shoulders.

He claimed her immediately, pushing away the other cadets round the steps. He put his hands on her shoulders and kissed her forehead – a discreet friend-of-the-family kiss. Then he slipped her hand through his arm and led her along to the Mess Hall where already the band was playing a Strauss waltz.

'At last,' he sighed. 'At last.'

'At last what, Henry?' She looked up at him, her blue eyes questioning, her mouth preparing to be amused.

'At last I've got you all to myself . . . without –'

'The Hawk?'

'No. Without John.' He took her shawl from her and draped it over a chair.

'As a matter of fact, I saw John the day before I left England. On my way to the Minton Ball.'

Swain put his arm around her and led her onto the floor. He felt a little twinge of jealousy. 'Who did you go with?'

'Oh, no one important. He was a friend of John's.'

'And how was John?'

'He doesn't change much.'

Heinrich laughed. 'More's the pity.'

Alexandra didn't smile. 'That's not very kind.'

He twirled her round expertly, his head thrown back, his eyes half-closed, smiling, saying nothing.

'Besides,' she went on, 'I like John.'

'So do I. But he's one of those lads who do everything the hard way.'

'But gets there in the end?'

Heinrich shook his head. 'Not if the end is the other side of the stream.'

They both laughed at that. Then the waltz ended. He escorted her back to the gilt chairs and the little glass-topped tables. He snapped his fingers for the steward to bring them champagne. They toasted their meeting and exchanged what had happened since that afternoon at Charlstone Wood.

'Your father is still in the Navy, of course?'

'Of course! He's a Captain now.'

Heinrich grimaced. 'And here am I on the bottom rung.'

'You won't be for long.'

He took her hand and kissed it, 'Ah, that's what *I* say. But how did you know?'

'Because you are one of those lads who do everything the easy way.' She smiled, gently mimicking him.

'Don't judge my performance on one crossing of the Rubicon.'

'Oh, I don't.' She twirled her glass thoughtfully, 'But I think you're very good at making up your mind what you want, and very good at getting it.'

'Does that frighten you?' he asked.

She opened her eyes in astonishment. 'No, Why should it?'

He wondered if he should tell her that he had suddenly realised he wanted *her*. Wanted her almost as much as climbing the ladder. He decided that such bold tactics were all right with Klara but not with Alexandra, so he simply gave an enigmatic smile and murmured that he was teasing. Then Mercke came up, bowed stiffly, and asked if he could '*die Ehre haben*' to ask her to dance. Then Kassel claimed a dance, and Varenfordt, damn him. But in the end it was Varenfordt who provided the excuse for leaving.

As usual, the cadets were drinking too much, liquor had been spilled on the floor, the party was disintegrating. And Varenfordt whose cure for such ills was a rabble-rousing song, leapt onto one of the tables, threw back his head and began to yell the Horst Wessel song.

He waved his arms for everyone to join in. Kassel began playing the accordian. The room echoed to the roar of male voices, to the ringing primitive chords. Faces were transformed in the passion of the song. Suddenly the party had been pulled together. But into a strange and menacing unity. '*Kameraden, die Rotfront und Reaktion erschossen . . .*'

Heinrich saw Alexandra's lips moving as she translated the words to herself, saw the look of consternation in her blue eyes.

He touched her shoulder, 'Let's get a taxi. Have a quiet drink at a café.' He slipped her shawl round her shoulders.

Purposely he took her home early. On the way, they went to a quiet bar by the quay and drank *schnapps*. He would only allow her one glass because of the champagne they had drunk and because she was still very young. For that evening he cast himself in the role of friend of the family entertaining the Captain's daughter. They discussed Navy matters and school impressions.

But after that night, they met as often as he could persuade her to come out with him, and it was rare that he took her home before the early hours. They went for bicycle rides along the ship canal's banks. They picnicked in the woods. If it was wet, they went to the Schönberg cinema and held hands in the back row. They saw Tyrone Power and Loretta Young in *Café Metropole* and Deanna Durbin in *A Hundred Men And A Girl*.

The fact that there were American films in most of the cinemas and English books in all the bookshops made her feel at home. Alexandra told him that her mother had written in some anxiety about the international situation, especially Poland. But in Germany everything seemed so normal and carefree.

The city was getting ready for *Die Kieler Woche*, the annual

International Regatta, and the harbour basin was filling up with flag-bedecked yachts of all nations.

'Your mother has no cause to worry,' Swain told Alexandra. 'Now the Versailles *Diktat* has been put right, Germany and Britain will never go to war. We will compete, but not fight.'

The U-boat School had a fleet of two-man sailing dinghies to teach elementary seamanship. Swain took Alexandra in one of them right into the basin. Then they moored on the beach at the other side of the estuary and watched the seabirds through *Kriegsmarine* binoculars.

'That's an oyster-catcher,' Alexandra identified a high-pitched mourning whistle. They watched it dive in a flash of black and white and pointed purposeful beak. Like a *Junker*, Swain thought, attacking a submarine. Alexandra suddenly threw her arms around him. It was a moment of great sweetness. He could have stayed there for ever.

'Submarines are dangerous. Wouldn't you rather be on a surface ship?' Alexandra asked him on the way back.

'Certainly not. It's much less pay and much slower promotion.'

'Slower up the ladder?' she smiled.

He was letting her sail the return trip. Alexandra was good in a boat, very quick and nimble, knew what to do at the helm and could reef and luff a sail with the best of them. When her father was stationed at Malta, she and her brother had spent their summer holidays there, and she had done a lot of sailing on Robin Class boats.

That was what gave him the idea in the first place.

At the International Regatta, there was a Midshipman's Cup, open to all nationalities, and it was a tradition of the U-boat School that their cadets competed in the two-man dinghies.

Swain carefully studied the rules of the race. The Captain had to be a midshipman, but there was nothing laid down about his crew.

'You're going to be my mate,' he told Alexandra.

She was doubtful at first, mainly because she thought she wouldn't be good enough. When Swain pooh-poohed that idea, she became as enthusiastic as he was.

Swain went through the School's dinghies carefully. Varenfordt had chosen the newest. He chose the oldest, but with a sharper prow than any of the others. He had 66 out of the water on the slipway, and with Alexandra worked on it till they could barely see in front of their eyes, cleaning up the dents, smoothing the hull, painting and oiling, renewing all the ropes and making sure the mast was firm but still flexible.

Then they took her out on the Baltic.

Those were the days they gulped in the salt-filled air, and spent every spare moment out on the sea. They practised starts, rounding buoys, but not the way the keen types did. Instead of tight against the buoy for the shortest path, they practised a wider sweep round, then cutting in on the windward side when the others skidded too fast to hold their course.

He had told his mother that Alexandra was in Kiel. Now she pestered him on the telephone to bring her to Hamburg.

He was not happy about any visit. Alexandra's Englishness, he thought, would turn his mother against her. She had always spoken of feeling distrust from the British for being a German in Ceylon.

That attitude, Swain realised now, had added a strain to a difficult marriage between a romantic Lutheran widow and a gentle man wedded to the universality of all men and all religions. She had softened now, of course, become totally obsessed in her son and his career. But when at last he diffidently suggested that they go down 'for a night only', Alexandra agreed.

The visit went well. The sun was warm, and they enjoyed watching the boats on the Alster from the grassy banks under the trees. His mother had been delighted to hear about their entry for the Midshipman's Cup.

'You'll win, Heinrich!' His mother turned to Alexandra. 'He always does!'

'If we do,' he told her, 'it will be because of Alexandra. She is a far better sailor than me.'

'How come this sudden modesty?' his mother asked. 'It must be *your* influence, Alexandra!'

Next day before Alexandra was up, when he and his mother were in the kitchen preparing breakfast, she suddenly said, 'When are you going to get married?'

'Mother, what do you mean?'

'You know exactly what I mean,' she said with such asperity, that he thought she was going to go into a tirade against Alexandra, all about the fatality of early marriages and ruining his career.

'Mother, I'm not thinking of getting married. She wouldn't have me anyway.'

His mother gave him a look of such sweetness that for a moment he was back in Ceylon again, to those carefree times of childhood when she seemed so young and used to play with him on the verandah in the evening.

'Never have I heard you say that about any girl!'

He shrugged his shoulders. 'Happens to be true about Alexandra.'

She smiled. 'Now I know she is the right one!'

On their return to Kiel, the Regatta had started with the race of the three-masters to Bornholm Island and back.

The town was gay with flags and loud with bands. There was dancing in the streets, and the cafés on the pavements were full of Swedes, Italians, French, Dutch, Spanish, Americans and a few British. The weather was good, too, bright sunshine and a stiffish wind from the Baltic, just perfect for fast dinghy racing.

The race for the Midshipman's Cup was two days later. The wind was stronger and coming from almost abeam as Swain and Alexandra luffed 66 into position on the starting line.

Thirty-six other boats were bouncing up and down all round them, with the air full of the sounds of the waves slapping their sides, and shouts and the thudding of sails and the sleigh-like jingle of wire riggings. There were four entries from the U-boat School, twice that number from the German battleship squadron, one each from the German cruiser and destroyer flotillas, and entries from several European countries and America. All had different coloured sails – every shade of red, blue, green, yellow, grey, white, even black.

66 was an all-white boat, with white hull and white sails. 'The Virgin,' Varenfordt called it as he edged up in his Number 1 with its crimson sails. As he came alongside, he saw they were both wearing gloves, which Swain had insisted on because they would be doing a lot of trapezing. He was pointing out this effeminacy to Kassel on their other side, when the pistol went and they were off.

Varenfordt immediately took the lead, followed by an American, then one of the battleship entries. Everyone had to tack, and a dozen dinghies were shielding the wind from 66. At the first buoy, they were trailing well behind the leaders, with Varenfordt still ahead.

The Midshipman's Cup had a reputation for being a real rough-and-tumble. The wind had freshened further, and now the smooth veneer of the start began to wear thin. Tempers flared. Boats were running within inches of each other, trying to cut out their wind.

Two dinghies collided and left a debris of broken wood on the surface, the crews clinging to their floating sails and masts.

Rounding the next buoy, 66 slipped up two places. But Varenfordt and the American were still a long way ahead.

There was no time to speak to each other. Both had to know what was in each other's minds, doing what was best for the boat in that sea and that wind. Swain didn't have to tell Alexandra to get out on the trapeze. They both did it automatically, working as one as though they were in some preordained dance ritual, their feet side by side on the gunwale, tiller hard over, their taut bodies horizontal to the sea, soaked by continuous salt waves of water, in an endless tug-of-war against the pull of the sails to keep the bow straight and speeding.

At the next buoy, 66 slipped up another place. Two more laps to go!

Fizzy as sodawater, the sea streamed up their nostrils, stung their eyes, filled their mouths and half-choked them. But the exhilaration lifted them up, tingled them all over. They were dancing a ballet, playing a symphony, flying together through the spray-stained air.

Two buoys later, 66 had edged up to third place. Swain caught Alexandra's eye behind a film of water, sparkling blue like the inside of a diamond. She was as determined as he was to win.

Thirty yards ahead were only the gold sails of the American and Varenfordt's huge crimson expanse of spinnaker.

Then the American began to have trouble with the choppy waves. He slowed, fell back.

But Varenfordt still hung onto his lead. Rounding the buoy for the final dash to the finish, he was still those vital ten yards in front.

Now Varenfordt put on every inch of sail he had, his spinnaker up again and fat with wind, determined to come in between the yellow victory flags in style. Swain saw a smile spread over his face as he pulled away from 66, the race practically in his pocket.

Sick with disappointment, in one last effort to catch him, Swain was about to let out the spinnaker when he looked up and saw that the burgee flag at the top of the mast was shifting anti-clockwise.

The wind had veered.

He felt 66 tremble, called out to Alexandra to lessen sail, when they both heard a crack ahead of them and saw the crimson sail flounder.

The next moment, all that was left of Varenfordt's boat were splinters. As 66 shot past, they could see both crew in the water – Varendfordt's head bobbing up in the sea, his pale cheeks whiter than ever from the water, his eyes glaring malevolently as 66 crossed the finishing line.

The Midshipman's Cup was always given away by a Kapitänleutnant of the *Kriegsmarine*. That year was the submariner's turn, and it was Günther Prien of u47 who called out, 'The winner is Midshipman Heinrich Swain!'

He grabbed Alexandra's hand. 'You too!'

At just thirty, Prien was one of the most experienced U-boat commanders in the flotilla. He stood there on the dais, holding up the cup in both his hands, a wide smile on his good-looking face.

The crowd had started clapping. But no one came forward, because Alexandra was resisting Swain's efforts to accompany him. Prien turned to speak to the Race Administrator. Then he caught sight of the two of them below him and his smile widened.

He shouted down to Alexandra, 'Don't be shy! I am particularly partial to girls!'

The crowd roared.

'You see, I have just had a daughter myself!'

The crowd clapped and cheered.

Alexandra held Swain's hand tightly as they went up to the dais. Prien asked Swain questions about how he got into the *Kriegsmarine*, told him that he too had been in the Merchant Service and asked if he had been assigned to a U-boat yet.

He gave the cup to Alexandra with a kiss. Then they were both swallowed up in the crowd again, and the loudspeakers were announcing the next race.

The rest of that afternoon was like a kind of dream. They floated together, hugging their happiness, out of the harbour, down the cobbled streets, through the market place. They drank champagne at every café in the area. They dined by candlelight in the best restaurant in the Pfalzer Platz. They walked all the way to her school because they wanted their day to last for ever.

They didn't want to be parted – not at the school gate, not in the deserted hall, not in the corridors. They went into her bed-sitting room, and she made a pot of coffee.

Swain heard the clock in the school tower chime midnight, then one o'clock, two, three – and he was still there. Alexandra was very soft and sweet to kiss

He said, 'It was you who did it. It was you who won really.'

'It was both of us,' she said.

The school clock struck four, five, six. Only when he heard steps outside did he leave her and tiptoe down the corridor and then out into the early morning air.

He ran all the way back to the U-boat School, he was so happy. He was planning where he'd take her that night, and wondering whether she would like the dance at the Waltheim Hotel or the Opera, when he saw Mercke looking at the noticeboard.

He called out, '*Engländer*, you lucky sod!'

Swain said, 'It was certainly a near thing.'

'I don't mean the race!' He pointed to a notice in the middle of the board. 'I mean the posting!'

Swain read the list of names against U-boat numbers. At the bottom was *Midshipman Heinrich Swain* to report to U47 at 10 a.m. on 19 August 1939.

'But that's today!' he said.

He had barely time to get into his uniform and pack. Three times he tried to get hold of Alexandra on the telephone, but first they couldn't find her, secondly they thought she was in the classroom when she wasn't, and finally he learned she had gone off in the bus with the senior girls to the Museum at Miesleratz, sixty kilometres away.

All he could do was to get a taxi to the Tirpitzmole. U47 was lying with three other 500-ton U-boats beside the Submarine Depot Ship *Weschel*.

Prien was already on board, wearing a brilliant white cap cover, the U-boat commanders' symbol.

Swain saluted. Prien smiled, welcomed him briefly and handed him over to Endrass, his First Lieutenant. Everything inside the U-boat was spotlessly clean. He was to learn that everything had to be kept that way. Added to interminable practices of everything from firing the four-pounder to abandoning ship, that left the crew little time to think.

There was no room in the tiny officers' mess. As the most junior officer, Swain dossed down on top of the spare torpedoes.

Fifteen minutes later, the klaxon sounded. Both diesels were started. 'Prepare to leave port!' was called and everyone went to their stations for the salute.

Prien stood at the conning tower with the coxswain and the

Officer of the Watch. Swain and the rest of the crew lined the deck at attention as they slipped mooring and edged away from the Tirpitzmole towards the Kiel canal.

Only a handful of dockyard workers saw them go. Watching the waves lick the needle-shaped bow, hearing the bands and the shouting of the Regatta getting fainter and fainter, ordinarily Swain would have felt keyed up with excitement, setting out like this on his first Operational patrol.

But all he could think of was leaving Alexandra.

That afternoon they learned the reason for the haste. The position in Poland had worsened. Not only U47 but thirteen other ocean-going U-boats, twenty destroyers and the battleships *Graf Spee* and *Deutschland* had been despatched to patrol the North Sea – the Murder Sea, the Great War U-boat men called it, because of their casualties.

For the next ten days everyone on board was too busy under Prien's constant practices and inspections to discuss the politics of the situation. But three days later, lying on his makeshift bunk, Swain heard three engine-room artificers saying that the wireless operator had picked up radio messages to the effect that Polish troops had attacked Germany's eastern boundaries.

Next day, Prien announced that German troops, in an effort to put an end to this border fighting, had invaded Poland.

The news was disturbing – but all the activity was in the east. Hitler had said he would never go to war with Great Britain. And Great Britain, Swain reasoned, would be too wise to intervene in such sporadic frontier fighting.

Next day was Sunday 3 September. Swain was on watch on the conning tower, binoculars up to his eyes, looking ahead at an empty grey horizon when the wireless operator called up, 'Captain . . . a special announcement!'

Prien jumped down the ladder beckoning Swain to follow him. The control room below was filled with the sound of military music.

Then a voice announced, 'This is *der Grossdeutsche Rundfunk*. We report a special message . . .'

III JOHN
3 September 1939–
28 October 1940

Listening in his Oxford room to the tired voice of his Prime Minister telling the nation that they and the Germans were now at war, John Blake was struck with the chilling thought that Alexandra might still be in Germany.

He had no doubt she would have taken the opportunity to meet Swain. She had almost admitted as much on the night of the Minton Ball three months ago, when she and his new friend Dacres had sailed into this very room. A rather different and yet not different Alexandra. For Alexandra had the power to change and yet not to change, to merge new and enchanting visions of herself into that potent childish image he carried of her. Perhaps he did all that creating and editing and merging of those visions himself. Perhaps she didn't exist except in his fantasy, like the heroines of Dacres' chivalrous poems.

'I've brought an old friend to see you,' Dacres splendid in white tie and tails had said, brandishing a champagne bottle. 'She insists on greetings.'

And there was Alexandra, framed in the doorway, wearing a long blue off-the-shoulder dress that shimmered and rustled as she came into his cramped little room.

'Hello, John.' She had taken his extended hand and, leaning forward, brushed her powdered cheek against his. He had felt almost shocked at the low cut of her gown, at her black lashes and red nails, and more than shocked that she was with Dacres, the dilettante poet of all people, who had established himself a terrific reputation with women.

'Has the Imperial School broken up early then, Alexandra?' he asked, foolishly trying to merge this new version, while Dacres busied himself with opening the bottle.

'Of course not. She's left school. She's coming to Lady Margaret Hall. With my sister. That was how she swam into my net, wasn't it, Alexandra?'

Now, as he was crossing the quad to have a word with Dacres, he realised that this war would probably be the end of him. Coming up to twenty, the first age group for the threatened conscription, that would be it.

Dacres assumed he'd come to commiserate with one another. As soon as Blake put his head round his door, the poet threw down his pen and sighed, 'God! I can't concentrate on anything *now*. That's *it* for us, isn't it?'

His attitude on the war appeared to be ambivalent. He had already fished out his OTC uniform from the wardrobe. It was hanging over a peg, his new life waiting to be assumed.

'Girls love men in uniform,' he said. 'You'll have no difficulty on that score once you're in, John.'

'The trouble is, which Service?'

'Army, of course. Get into a good regiment.'

He was vague on Alexandra. 'Only saw her once after the Ball. For a very virginal coffee. Wasn't really my type. But I can give you her phone number. Her Mama has rented a house in Park Road. Father's back at sea.'

Dacres got up and flipped through a red leather address book. 'Mayhew, Mirfield . . . Monteith . . . here! Oxford 776. Fond of her, are you, or just a friend of the family?'

'Friend of the family,' Blake said, and rushed off to telephone. While he waited for the operator to put him through, he stared out at the High Street. It ought to have been very different somehow, after such momentous news, but it wasn't. Sandbags had been placed in front of most of the buildings. People went around carrying their little square gas-mask boxes – that was all.

The phone seemed to ring for an inordinate time. He wondered what he would say to Mrs Monteith when she answered, *if* she answered.

Then he heard the click of the line opening and Alexandra's voice. 'It's John, John Blake. I wondered how your family is,' he said lamely. 'With war being declared and all that.'

'We're fine, thank you, John.' She sounded surprised, amused and yet sad. 'Are you?'

'Yes, thank you.'

He couldn't think of anything else to say. Then the war came to his aid. The weird howl of the air-raid siren started up, the first of the war. An air-raid warden in a steel helmet banged on the glass of the box.

'Better go,' he said. 'Bye, Alexandra.'

He had hardly taken a dozen paces down the street when the steady note of the All Clear sounded.

He searched the sky. Far away in a bank of white clouds, he saw a small aircraft. He'd no idea what it was or whether it was connected with the swift ending of the alert. But it looked free up there, somehow. Romantic, even. Something out of Dacres' poetry. That was it, he decided. He knew he'd hate the Army and the sea made him sick.

He would do like Nash and Fanshawe had done. He would opt for the Air Force, and the sooner the better.

He was called to the Sheldonian theatre for his interview on 24 October and already he had begun to feel that he was only half alive. Half of him had already left Oxford. The enchanted Oxford he had fallen in love with was fading before his eyes, as familiar faces disappeared, older men came in, the lights were blacked out, more sandbags muffled the walls and a blustery autumn took over from that hot and splendid summer.

The war was beginning uneasily. The Phoney War. The RAF went out on raids, but dropped leaflets instead of bombs. The rumour was that they had neither the aircraft nor the armament to do better. The Local Defence Volunteers of the very old and the very young were formed, and were promised they would soon get rifles instead of staves. Yet in that first week Cracow was razed and the Polish Air Force and Army were destroyed as the German mechanised juggernaut hurtled across Poland. On the Western Front, the French and British Armies stayed defensive and unmoving, while close at home German submarines sank the *Athenia* and the aircraft carrier *Courageous*.

An English voice on the German radio, soon nicknamed Lord Haw-Haw, called it the *Sitzkrieg*. He accused the French of 'lacking courage' and the British of 'sobering reflection'. The mood at Oxford was not of sobering reflection. It was a strange mixture of anger, frustration and foreboding, as men and women waited to join up. There was a terrible build-up of suppressed anger and violence, as if the young were preparing themselves to fall in love with war.

A man who lived on the same floor as Blake cut both his wrists in the bath. A first-year student shot dead a senior who had been bullying him as he came down the steps of his college Hall.

There was an eeriness like being one of the walking dead, Blake thought, as he walked past the bulbous bulge of the Radcliffe

Camera Reading Room through the Bodleian library courtyard and into the ancient entrance hall of the Sheldonian theatre.

There he sat, mustering in his mind some good reasons for the Air Force to accept him, while he waited for his name to be called.

'Mr Blake.'

All along one side of the seventeenth-century theatre was a dais on which rows of dons sat in their gowns with Lindsay, the Master of Balliol, presiding in the centre. Tucked in at the far end were representatives of the three Services.

They had all his papers in front of them.

'So,' said Lindsay, 'you've chosen the RAF?' He smiled invitingly at a fresh-faced man in Air Force blue with two rings round his sleeve. 'Flight Lieutenant?'

The Flight Lieutenant looked only a couple of years older than Blake. He came straight to the point with, 'Why the RAF, Mr Blake?'

Blake couldn't think of anything more original than, 'I'm interested in flying.'

'How much have you done?'

As he had had only one seven-and-sixpenny joyride in Alan Cobham's circus while staying with his uncle and aunt, he replied evasively, 'Just pleasure flying.'

In fact, evasive was the tone of all his replies. He knew nothing of the theory of flying, not much more about engines, had never worked a lathe as a hobby, nor done anything mechanical, had never joined an Observer Unit, had not been in the OTC and was not informed on aircraft recognition.

The Flight Lieutenant turned first to the Army Officer next to him, as if only too eager to hand Blake on to him, and then to Lindsay.

'Sir,' he said apologetically, 'Mr Blake is an Arts man. He has no engineering experience. No evidence of flying aptitude. No –'

The Master of Balliol interrupted his full flood of no's. 'But Mr Blake is an Oxford man, Flight Lieutenant! And an Oxford man can do anything!'

Two minutes later, Blake came out with a piece of paper on which was written *Highly Recommended for a Commission in the RAF as a pilot.*

He felt enormously elated. He felt as if he'd won some sort of victory, though over what he wasn't sure. In Minton College Porter's

Lodge, he met Nash who'd already been accepted, and told him the good news. Poor old Wagstaff had gone to a Labour Camp. He'd been far too outspoken at his Conscientious Objectors' Board and he hadn't got into the Ambulance Unit as he'd wanted.

Nash and Blake strolled across the Quad to the Junior Common Room for a cup of tea. The day's newspapers were laid out on the table. Blake picked up *The Times*.

Headlines caught his eye. U-BOAT SINKS BATTLESHIP IN SCAPA FLOW. NEWS JUST RELEASED.

He drank his tea as he read the details.

Kapitänleutnant Prien had taken U47 at high tide on the surface through the unguarded and unnetted passage of Kirk Sound, between Kirk Island and the Orkney mainland. At midnight on 14 October, he was inside Scapa Flow and, helped by a calm clear night and the Northern Lights flickering in the cloudless sky, he selected the battleship *Royal Oak* as his target. At 12.58, he closed to 4,000 yards and fired three torpedoes, one of which hit her bow. No notice or action was taken. At 1.16, Prien fired three more torpedoes, two of which hit. At 1.29, the *Royal Oak* rolled over on her side and capsized. Twenty-four officers and 809 crewmen were missing, believed killed. The news had been held up before publication for security reasons.

Churchill had praised the U-boat commander for a courageous feat of arms. Nash, who had been reading over his shoulder, exclaimed, 'How damned stupid of the Navy to leave that Channel unnetted and unguarded.'

But Blake said nothing. He had lowered his eyes to the casualty list given below. A name leapt out at him from amongst the missing officers.

Captain R.M. Monteith CBE, DSC.

He didn't know what to do. He had a sudden sad memory of the last time he had seen the Monteith family together, all those years ago in Ceylon. They had seemed then so assured and invulnerable. A bright and happy picture-book family. Now the war had moved in on them. He wondered if he should call round and offer his sympathy. Did it help people, or did it make things worse?

In the end, he wrote. In fact he wrote the letter several times over before he posted it. The final version remained stilted. It said merely how sorry he was, and please don't bother to reply.

Alexandra replied. Only briefly, thanking him for his letter and inviting him to tea at four that Sunday.

He did not have a good suit, but he got his flannels and his sports coat cleaned. At four o'clock exactly, he lifted the brass dolphin knocker on the door of Number 7, Park Road and let it drop with too much of a thud.

He was trying to think of a few suitable phrases when the door opened and there was Alexandra in a neat blue dress.

'You're punctual!' She smiled at him. 'Come in! Mummy's in the lounge. Straight ahead of you. I'll pop into the kitchen and put the kettle on.'

The lounge door was open. He was expecting a woman with grey hair in widow's weeds and eyes red from weeping. But the woman who rose from the chintz-covered chair beside the log fire had brown hair cut in a fringe above clear grey steady eyes and was wearing a smart flowered print and high-heeled shoes.

'Hello, John!'

Should he kiss her? Should he put his arms round her?

She put an end to his embarrassment by putting her arms round him and kissing him.

'I'm sorry,' he managed to say.

'I know, John. And I had a nice cable from your father.'

'I'm glad.' He realised as he spoke that it was the wrong thing to say. 'We are all so sorry.'

'We did appreciate your letter too.' She indicated the twin of her own chair on the other side of the fire. 'You sit there. Alexandra won't be a moment with the tea. I thought we'd just have it on our laps.'

He sat down. 'That will be lovely.'

'And what are *you* doing, John?'

'Oh, still at Minton.'

'I mean for the *war*.'

He stirred uncomfortably. 'Waiting to be called up for training.'

'Training for what?'

'As a pilot.'

'In the Fleet Air Arm?'

He shook his head. 'The RAF.'

'The next best thing.' The answer had pleased her. 'Peter wants to be a pilot. He's at St Edwards. And Alexandra's at Lady Margaret Hall.'

'Does she like it?'

'Very much. She lives in. Maurice thought it best, living in. Day girls never really fit in.'

'It was the same at Kirkstone.'

'Alexandra told me she'd seen you there.' She smiled. 'And you were fighting that German boy . . . Henry, wasn't that his name?'

He nodded. 'He was in a party from a military school.'

'The Reverend Swain's adopted son. I remember his birthday party. His eighth.'

'His ninth.'

'Of course, you were there, too, weren't you?'

He smiled sheepishly. 'I fell into the water.'

'That's right. Some kind of dare. I can see you now, all dripping wet.' She lay back in her chair. 'That must have been the last time I saw you.'

'It was.'

'Strange how that marriage broke up. The Reverend Swain was such a saint.'

'Yes he was.'

'But that German wife was very strange.'

'She was kind to me.'

'And that awful boy!'

'Henry always thought he could do everything.'

'Well, I suppose he's fighting for Hitler now.'

Blake was on the point of asking whether Alexandra had seen him while she was in Germany, but thought better of it.'

'What did you think of him, John?'

'Well –'

'A typical Hun!' He was suddenly aware of how ice-cold her eyes had gone, piercing grey and sharp as knives. 'But you beat him!'

'Oh yes,' he said. 'I beat him at *Wehrsport*. But I lost the dare.'

'So now it's one-all?'

'I suppose so.'

Go out and get him, John, her whole body seemed to plead. Be my knight in shining armour! Revenge my darling husband and the *Royal Oak*!

The blood-red mouth matched the bayonet-grey eyes. But her voice when she spoke was as quiet as though she was talking of a tennis match.

'Now who's going to win the final set?'

'My mother's quite fallen for you.'

John Blake and Alexandra were sitting in the café of the Regent cinema. Just before he had left the Monteith's house a week ago, he had told her that he had two free cinema tickets to do a review for the *Cherwell* undergraduate magazine and had diffidently asked her to accompany him.

'You're the film critic?'

'This month I am. Let's see what we think of *The Barretts of Wimpole Street*.'

Not much, as it had turned out. But they'd had a talk over coffee and biscuits. One piece of information had emerged. She *had* seen Swain in Kiel. He was a midshipman in the *Kriegsmarine*. Alexandra had then asked him questions about himself, finishing up with his effect on her mother at his visit last Sunday.

Mrs Monteith was at home when they arrived at 7 Park Road for a late tea. She greeted Blake with a kiss and made a great fuss of him. Sitting between the two women, Blake had monopolised the conversation, a habit he had when he was nervous. He talked about the RAF, where he was likely to go and what he was likely to do, not having the faintest idea of either. The *Royal Oak* was never mentioned.

Neither was Captain Monteith. Only his photographed face in a silver frame, his uniform hat very straight, his eyes very serious, regarded Blake steadfastly from the mantelpiece over the fire.

Yet his presence was palpable. He could actually have been there, his aura so enveloped them. Every time Blake stopped talking, in the fragmentary silence when he accepted another sandwich from the proffered plate, the scent of the sea came rushing in through the half-open window, salty as tears. Instead of chrysanthemums, lavender and glazed chintz, the room smelled of steel and rope and guns. He could actually hear that reproof for wearing a German sailor suit echoing back over the years, as he rushed in with another inanity to drown the memory of that clipped naval voice.

All the time he was talking, Mrs Monteith hardly took her eyes off him. They seemed to be holding down that unsaid pact between them so that the glue would dry.

But he had the very definite idea that Alexandra had told her very little of what had happened during her German visit. Twice Mrs Monteith had asked her daughter questions, but had received very evasive answers.

A fortnight later, another piece of information about Kiel was revealed to him. The two of them had begun to meet in the Radcliffe Camera Reading Room, occupying desks E32 and E33 just below a marble bust of Plato. As they came down the curved stone stairs to go to the Cadena Café for tea, over her shoulder as though of no consequence Alexandra had let slip the fact that Swain was in the U-boat arm.

He waited for a tirade against U-boats. But there was none. He waited for a tirade against Swain, in which he would have whole-heartedly joined – but again there was no more mention of him.

Alexandra simply preserved a glazed, unhappy brightness that kept him at a distance – and everyone else for that matter, since that piece of information about Swain had certainly not been passed to her mother.

And yet as the days passed he was convinced that not only the *Royal Oak* hung over seats E32 and E33, but that Heinrich Swain was for ever sitting between them.

And then, on the last Saturday of November, Alexandra was different.

She had not shown up all morning, and Blake was still waiting for her, her place in E33 reserved by a pyramid of books, when she arrived at two-thirty, her eyes red and her nose swollen.

He said nothing, just went on with his work pretending not to notice, till at four o'clock, the usual time for their break, he passed her a note on which was written brightly *Tea-time*!

They got up together. Her face was set and unhappy. Blake led the way down the stairs, and then they walked side by side to a tiny tea shop in Carfax.

They were the only people in the place. Blake ordered tea and toast. Then he leaned over and took her hand.

He said nothing. Neither did she.

The tea came. Then the buttered toast. Both remained un-touched.

The minutes ticked by. A couple came in and took a table in the far corner. From Carfax came the screech of tyres and the sound of bicycle bells.

Alexandra said suddenly, 'John, I'm so sorry . . . but you're the only person I can talk to.'

Then she began.

The Language Department had mutual arrangements with

universities of Scandinavian countries which were not at war to send and receive whatever national newspapers came their way. As a result, German newspapers eventually arrived in Oxford which Alexandra and other Modern Languages students studied as a matter of course.

That morning she had read in the *Berliner Tagblatt* a full account of U47's torpedoing of the *Royal Oak* and the triumphant reception of the crew in Berlin. The front page was a mass of photographs: Hitler and Prien driving down the Unter den Linden in an open car, Hitler decorating Prien with the Knight's Cross with Oakleaves and shaking hands with his officers.

And at the end of the line was the most junior officer – the caption below emphasising that this had been only his second operational patrol – Midshipman Heinrich Swain.

She stopped. Blake was still holding her hand.

'He was under orders,' he said, trying desperately to be fair. 'It wasn't *him*.'

'He was a member of the crew. They were all responsible.'

'The *Royal Oak* was a legitimate target. The people to blame are the Admiralty for leaving the Kirk passage unprotected.'

'It was worse than that. It was *personally* worse than that.' Tears started dropping from her eyes. '*I* was responsible.'

He said sharply, 'Don't be stupid, Alexandra!'

'You don't understand.' She shook free of his hand. 'Henry and I raced together in the Midshipman's Cup. We won it. It was Prien . . . the Captain of U47 . . . who presented it to us . . . to *both* of us!' She started banging the table with her fists. 'Don't you see? How awful! Mummy would kill me . . . and I wouldn't blame her . . .'

The waitress looked curiously over the till at them. From their corner, the couple watched them wide-eyed.

'Oh come off it, Alexandra!' This was sheer hysteria. 'You weren't to know. It was nothing to do with you! It was a recreation . . . sailing. Just a social thing.'

He paused for a very long time. Then he said in a whisper, 'Wasn't it?'

It was her silence that told him. He knew then. She didn't have to say anything.

He stared down at the congealed toast, the cold tea, the little painted rosebuds round the edge of his plate.

After a while he said as steadily as he could, 'Shall we go for a walk?'

Watched by the interested couple in the corner, they got up from the table. Blake paid the bill for the uneaten meal and together they went out into Carfax.

Already it was dusk. People were leaving their offices. Cars with slits for headlights were wheeling around Carfax. A newspaper seller was crying out under the tower of St John's church.

Blake took her hand. They walked past the prison, past the station, turned off to the right to Binsey and then along beside the river to the other side of Port Meadow.

They sat on the stone of Godstone Bridge and watched a flock of starlings rise up from the fields and fly into the darkening sky.

All the time Alexandra had said nothing.

He watched the water flowing through the reeds under the bridge. Now he understood.

He hated Swain for many things. For that day in Colombo. For his ability. For his arrogance. For his boasting. For being a member of the crew which had sunk the *Royal Oak*. For killing Captain Monteith. For loving Alexandra.

But for one thing he hated him more than all those put together.

It was so dark now he could no longer see the reeds vibrating in the current.

He said, 'You love him?'

It was her last chance. She might deny it. She *would* deny it. How could she *not* deny she loved him, an enemy who had killed her father?

He waited and waited, but she said nothing. From far away, a train whistled mournfully into the night.

But she didn't deny it. She just said, 'I'm pregnant, John. I'm going to have a baby.' She said the words slowly with awful clarity as if talking to an idiot boy. 'Henry's baby.'

They walked.

Alexandra had insisted they walk and go on walking. They walked up to the Woodstock roundabout. They walked along the comfortable middle-class roads of North Oxford. They went down to Folly Bridge, walked by the Thames, walked round Merton Fields. They walked on the towpath to Iffley, turning left to the Morris works at Cowley, walked up to Headington and walked across to the Parks and the banks of the Cherwell.

Alexandra talked. It was as though the walking loosened the

floodgates, broke the dam wall of her silence. She talked about her family, about herself, about her visit to Germany, about the war. What she did not talk about – and that was what distressed him because the omission was so significant – was Swain.

He listened uneasily, saying little. Half a moon, dodging in and out of cloud, threw a soft white glow over houses, trees, shadowy human shapes, bicycles and cars, turning the blackout into a ghostly under-exposed photograph.

She talked of her father and how proud she was of him. She talked of her two uncles, also in the Navy. She talked of her mother, of her unswerving loyalty, of her passionate belief in the Navy and the Empire. She talked of her brother, the image of his father, already as dedicated as a Jesuit acolyte to the religion of the Navy and all its works.

'And I love *them*,' she said. 'But I'm different. I've got my own life to lead. Mummy still thinks in terms of the last war. She hates the Germans. Daddy always said that Germany would have another crack at us. He almost resigned when Baldwin signed the Anglo-German Navy Treaty. When I took up languages after Matric, there was a family row. It was only my headmistress who saved the day. She insisted that French and German were my natural bent, and I could get into Oxford if I went on with them.'

They were passing the Ruskin Museum, just before turning into Park Road. It was then three o'clock in the morning. She stopped talking. They went on in silence. Then she exclaimed bitterly, 'Saved the day!'

He tried to think of something helpful to say. But he was too shattered to think, let alone speak. He struggled to crush down his own anger and outrage. Not against Alexandra, for in some strange way he had never felt more tender towards her, but against Swain. He wanted to rail against his heartlessness, to shout out that he hated him for so many things.

But he knew he mustn't. He knew he must keep calm and cool. Take this in his stride. Be mature. Banal words of comfort floated to the turbulent surface of his mind. 'Don't worry, Alexandra. There's nothing to worry about.'

But those were the sort of words you said when you wanted to dash off and leave a person to get on with it themselves. If he could take her in his arms when he said them, they might not sound so bad. But he couldn't. Though she still held his hand, her body seemed steeled against any other contact. And she would dismiss those words as a lie. There was everything to worry about. She couldn't tell her mother the full truth. Blake winced at the very thought himself. There would be the most shattering row of all time.

What then? Go away and have the baby on her own? How would she support it? And anyway, Mrs Monteith would certainly find out, by hook or by crook. That left having an abortion. Whatever that might involve.

They walked up Park Road in silence. At the gate of Number 7, they stopped. The house was totally dark. But behind the perfect blackout, somebody was up and awake.

Faintly over the moonlit darkness, came the sound of *Fingal's Cave.*

'Daddy was fond of music. Seascape sort of music. Mendelssohn particularly.'

A German, he was about to say, but stopped in time.

'She sits up half the night. Reading the books he liked. Looking at old photographs. Putting the gramophone on. That's why I didn't want to go back. Not till she's gone to bed. You see, before I went back to the Radder, I rang and told her I'd be very late home and please don't stay up because I was going to a dance with you. I knew I had to talk. I knew I had to talk to *you*. That's why I've kept you endlessly walking.' She paused, 'I'm very sorry.'

'That's all right. I'm . . . glad you did.'

She gave a little hollow laugh. 'Dear John.' She brought his hand to her lips and kissed it.

The music reached its crescendo. He could hear the crashing of the waves. A Navy wife's mourning, he was thinking, when suddenly the front door was opened and Mrs Monteith was silhouetted against the hall light.

'Alexandra? John, too? Come on in and have a gin and tell me what the dance was like!'

The first thing John did when he sat down beside her in the Radder next morning was to pass Alexandra a note: *I can't work. Let's go.*

She was reading. She shifted her eyes from the book to the note, picked up her pen and wrote *I've got to finish this.*

Then she propped her elbows on the table, put her head in her hands and continued reading.

It had been twelve o'clock by the time they had gone for coffee.

The Carfax café was again deserted. It was there, after the same waitress had brought them their coffee and biscuits and then departed that he said, 'Alexandra, I've been thinking . . . will you marry me?'

She looked at him as if he'd turned into some sort of monster. 'No,' she said. '*No.*'

He kept quiet for several minutes. Then he said, 'I've thought about it and thought about it and it really is the only possible solution.'

'That,' she said, 'must be the most unromantic proposal of all time.'

'I'm sorry. I didn't think you'd want me to be romantic. If you did, I'd . . .'

'I don't.'

'Well, then?'

'I just want you to listen . . . to be a friend . . . I don't see you as, well, someone special.'

'I know that. I'm not special.'

In an altered, but still decided tone she said, 'It's very, very sweet of you, John. I appreciate it. But no.'

'Why?'

'For one thing, I can't tie you down like that.'

'Tie me down? But that's what I want!'

'You'd only be doing it because you felt sorry for me.'

'No, no. That's quite wrong. I'd be doing it because that's what I want more than anything else in the world. What else could you do, Alexandra?' he prompted.

She patted his head.

'I could just have the baby.'

'Your mother would go up the wall.'

'Or I could have an abortion.'

'No.' He raised his voice. 'No.' He had only the haziest knowledge of how one went about getting an abortion, but he knew it was illegal, dangerous and painful and he couldn't contemplate it for her. 'Have the baby and *I'll* look after you.'

'John, you don't know what you're trying to take on. You'd have to love someone a great deal . . .'

'But I do love you. I've always loved you.'

'Ssh! Keep your voice down! The waitress is listening.'

'I don't care if the whole damned world is listening.' He felt suddenly drunk with the excitement of life. 'I love you.'

She got up, grabbed his hand like an elder sister and pulled him to his feet. He had just time to slip half a crown on the table for the untouched coffee and biscuits. The curious waitress watched them go.

'It's very sweet of you,' Alexandra said when they were back in Carfax. 'But I don't want someone to marry me to give the baby a name and make me respectable.'

'I'm asking you because I'm a very ordinary person who'd never have dared to even *think* of marrying you. And now I've got that chance I'm taking it and I'm a very lucky chap.'

Her grip on his hand tightened as they threaded their way across the road. 'You're a kind boy, John, but –'

'No buts about it.'

'But you're very young. And . . . one day you'll meet someone you really love.'

'I *have* done. I really love you. And I'm going to marry you.'

He surprised himself at his own determination. He wouldn't have dreamed, particularly at this time, of proposing to any girl, let alone Alexandra. Had he proposed in the furthest realms of fantasy, he would have done so very diffidently, put off by the faintest frown, the least hint of hesitation. And now he had not only proposed, but he was steamrollering it through, flattening her opposition, forcing his own will on hers.

They passed the jail. They passed the station. He helped her over a stile and they trod again the path through the fields towards Port Meadow, still arguing.

He was totally determined. He had never been so determined in his life. He hated Swain more than ever. The man had fooled Alexandra, hadn't cared about her, treated her like an object, a trophy for his vanity. He hated him so much he could kill him. But the baby was part of Alexandra, and as such was infinitely precious.

'But you can't saddle yourself with a wife and child at your age!'

He said wryly, 'You make me sound like a beardless boy!'

'I don't mean to. But you're just beginning life. You've got the RAF in front of you. And then a career –'

'*If* I'm lucky.'

She said slowly, 'You think you'll be killed, so you might as well marry anyway!'

'If I'm killed, I'll have lived if I marry you,' he said thickly. They were walking along the river bank. He turned his head away to hide his emotion. 'If I don't, I'll have been nothing.'

'That's sentimental nonsense, and you know it! It's very kind of you to ask me to marry you. I'm very honoured. And very touched. But I can't accept your proposal for a very good reason.'

'What reason?' he asked, and immediately wished he hadn't, realising what was coming.

'Because I don't love you.'

They walked along in silence. He had a horrific feeling that now she would talk about Swain, bring out into the open that she loved him, loved him in spite of everything, in spite of being German, in spite of being a U-boat man, in spite of being one of the crew which killed her father.

He said steadily at last, 'I still want to marry you.'

'But *I* don't want to marry *you*! Can't you get that into your head? I . . . don't . . . love . . . you.'

He said nothing for a moment.

'But you might *learn* to love me, mightn't you?'

She didn't answer.

He persisted, though he knew it was best not to. 'People do get to love each other. They . . . well . . . grow into one another. And I'd try . . . I'd try my best.'

'I'm sure you would,' she said then, almost pityingly. 'You're very kind. And good. But you're not –'

'Henry Swain,' he finished for her.

Suddenly it was all too much. She flung herself down on the grass and began crying. Crying in great ugly desperate sobs. Tears coursed down her cheeks. She scrubbed them off with her fists.

'He wasn't any good,' John couldn't resist saying. 'You wouldn't have been happy with him. You may think you would. But you wouldn't.'

That made her cry even harder. 'You don't know anything about it,' she managed to gasp between hiccuping sobs.

Women, John thought, can't be expected to see through men as his own sex could. They admired men for all the wrong reasons. It was all part of Nature's design, he told himself. Though quite what that design was, he didn't know. But it made him feel more in command of the situation to feel he had perceived it.

He sat down on the grass and put his arm round her. She didn't shake it off but her crying didn't stop. 'Come on,' he said. 'Come on, Alexandra!'

'What d'you mean, come on?' she sobbed back angrily. 'I've nowhere to come on to!'

He passed her his handkerchief. 'Wipe your eyes. And your nose. It's no use collapsing in a heap.'

'Now you're giving me the treatment for a hysteric,' she said, her words half-smothered by his handkerchief. 'You'll be slapping my face next.'

'Only if I have to. It's certainly no use maundering over Swain.' He paused. 'I may not be wonderboy, but I'll make you a good husband and I'll be a good father.'

'How very heroic.' She had stopped crying. 'And how very patronising!'

'Come on!' he said again, pulling her to her feet. 'Come on, Alexandra. We're going to have a word with your mother . . .'

He sat on the same chintzy chair in front of the fire that he had sat on the first time he had come to Number 7. Mrs Monteith sat on the other one. Alexandra sat disconsolately on the sofa.

She had resisted all the way home from Binsey fields. Only the threat that he would go and talk to her mother alone had persuaded her to come with him.

Blake told his story as tersely as he could, making no mention of Swain. He was very much in love with Alexandra. He was very sorry in one way that this had happened, but very glad in another because he now hoped to marry Alexandra as soon as possible.

'To make an honest woman of me,' Alexandra put in.

Mrs Monteith turned her head and looked at her daughter. Throughout the unfolding of Blake's story, she had said nothing. To Blake's surprise, she had taken it with no show of surprise, outrage or anger. Navy wives are a good deal more sophisticated than clergymen's wives and clergymen's sons. Though she herself had been fiercely faithful to her husband, she was very much aware of affairs that went on whilst naval husbands were away on the other side of the world. There was a certain directness about John Blake that she liked. Not out of the top drawer perhaps, but he appeared to have the same ideas as she did, and that being so, might be able to knock some sense into that daughter of hers. The circumstances were unfortunate, but the war was an excusing factor. And Blake was made of the right stuff. He was fit and strong. He was going into the RAF. In a matter-of-fact way, she asked, 'When's the baby due, Alexandra?'

'May.'

'Well,' she said, 'the sooner we have the wedding the better.'

'But I'm not going to marry him, Mummy.'

'You're not going to *what*?'

'I'm not going to marry him because I don't love him.'

'You should have thought of that five months ago, my girl,' she said tartly.

'I'm not going to have a shotgun wedding.'

Mrs Monteith studied her daughter carefully. Then she turned her head and looked at Blake. 'John, would you mind leaving us?'

He jumped up very quickly. 'No, of course not, Mrs Monteith.'

'Alexandra and I are going to have a little talk. Perhaps you would come back at four, and we'll all have some tea.'

He came back at four to find all the preparations made. The wedding would take place early in the New Year at the Oxford Registry Office. A quiet one, of course. Just the immediate family. Alexandra and he would go off for a few days' honeymoon. Then they would come back to Number 7 till he was called up. After which Alexandra would have the baby and continue to live at home.

Blake listened. So did Alexandra. She seemed composed and quiet.

'I think that's everything.'

'Thank you, Mrs Monteith. Thank you very much.'

Mrs Monteith rose from her chair. 'And now, come over here and give me a kiss.'

She put both her arms round him and hugged him warmly. 'And now you are part of our family! You are my eldest son!'

Blake asked Alexandra next day what her mother had said.

'The usual things, John. I told you she'd fallen for you.'

He didn't press her. He could guess the sort of things she would say, anyway. They were again sitting in the Carfax café, but now they were actually eating the biscuits and drinking the coffee.

Rather shyly he produced a small box. First thing that morning, he had gone to the bank and had explained some of the circumstances, after which the manager had been kind enough to extend his overdraft. He had then gone to Samuel's in the Turl and come away with that small box.

He opened it and took out the ring and apologised for the smallness of the diamond.

She leaned over and kissed him. 'But John, it's lovely!'

Watched by the curious waitress, he put it on her finger. 'Now you won't be able to get out of it, Alexandra. You'll *have* to marry me.'

He cabled his parents, still in Ceylon and likely to be kept there by the impossibility of getting passages home: GETTING MARRIED TO ALEXANDRA. LETTER FOLLOWS. Though they would certainly be surprised, he was sure they would be pleased.

He told no one else, since none of his friends was left. Wagstaff had departed to his Labour Battalion. Dacres had departed to the Hertfordshire Yeomanry. Nash and Fanshawe had departed to the RAF.

Three days before the wedding on 6 December, a letter from the RAF arrived, telling him to report to Number 1 Receiving Wing at Torquay in a week's time. He told his tutor about his wedding and his call-up at the same time, so that in some strange way they balanced each other out, and Blake collected congratulations on both counts.

Mrs Monteith said at least they'd be able to have four days' honeymoon, and booked the best room in the best Bournemouth hotel that had not already been commandeered.

Alexandra had received permission from Lady Margaret Hall to stay at home and have her baby, continue her studies and take her degree.

So that when the wedding took place at Oxford Registry Office, with Peter as best man, 'all necessary arrangements had been made', as Mrs Monteith put it.

Afterwards they had a quiet family lunch – just the four of them – at 7 Park Road. Then Mrs Monteith and Peter had seen them off at the station.

They had to change at London, where they boarded the *Bournemouth Belle* express.

'It was a lovely wedding day, John.' Alexandra squeezed his hand in the taxi from Bournemouth station to their hotel. 'Thank you for everything.'

But it was not quite over. The wedding night awaited them. There was no hotel porter. John took their bags up to their room. Opening his bag, he unpacked his newly laundered but rather old striped pyjamas and put them under the right hand pillow of the big double bed.

They were the only ones in the restaurant that night. They had a few drinks afterwards in the bar before going back upstairs to their room.

Alexandra undressed in the bathroom. He was already in his pyjamas when she came back in her nightdress and dressing gown.

'I don't want you to see me all big like this.'

He kissed her. 'You look lovely.'

Then there was a moment of embarrassment.

He didn't want to say he'd never been to bed with a girl. He didn't want to say he didn't know whether it was safe or not or what a man was supposed to do on his wedding night when his bride was five months' pregnant.

'You'll be tired,' he said, and kissed her again.

Then he got into bed beside her, and they hugged each other.

Alexandra said, 'You are a dear, John,' and fell asleep in his arms.

Four days later, John Blake went off to war.

The attaché case on the luggage rack of the railway compartment in which he sat was his old school one, now packed by his wife instead of his mother and containing a packet of ham sandwiches, a hard-boiled egg and an apple provided by his mother-in-law. Only Alexandra had seen him off at Oxford station.

'Come back safe,' she had whispered, standing on tip-toe to kiss his lips. She had looked very young and vulnerable. In a sudden rush of protectiveness, he had said, 'You'll look after yourself, won't you, Alexandra?'

'Oh, I'm all right. *You* look after *your*self.'

'I will, don't worry.'

Quite what measures he could take to look after himself he neither knew nor cared. He leaned out of the window, watching Alexandra's diminishing figure until it was finally smothered from his view in a cloud of steam. Then, slumping back in his seat, he stared out at the vanishing suburbs and the advancing grey-green of the Lambourn hills, feeling oddly suspended between his undigested past and his unrevealed future.

He was, of course, delighted to be married to Alexandra. Delighted and deeply confused. It had all happened with such suddenness. He was in the middle of a dream made flesh. He was uncertain how to treat the girl who had so lately and so dramatically changed her role.

For her part, she treated him more as an elder brother than a husband and a not very competent one at that. If anything went wrong in the house, like a fuse blowing or a leaky tap, it was Peter who was good with his hands who put it right. Since Blake had no licence, it was Alexandra who drove the family car when Mrs Monteith could get petrol. The last words Mrs Monteith had said to him were, 'Go out and show them, John!'

But what he was to show them, like the measures to look after himself, remained obscure. All he knew was that she had appointed him as Monteith's Reply.

And one thing was not obscure, he thought wryly, as the Torquay Express rattled rhythmically along at sixty miles an hour. He knew to whom Monteith's Reply had to be made.

Heinrich Swain.

When the train pulled into Torquay station a tannoy started blaring, 'All RAF recruits for Number One Initial Training Wing form up outside the booking office!' Blake jumped down onto the platform and hurried into the motley queue, eager for the transformation into a fighting man to begin.

In the first week, he was transformed into RAF number 969066, was given a hairy grey-blue uniform with a white aircrew cadet flash for its forage cap, a steel helmet, a gas mask, a yellow gas cape, and a pair of red and green identity discs, with his name, number and religion, to hang round his neck, one proof against fire and the other against water, so that his body could be identified satisfactorily. That body was inspected for lice and venereal disease, and accommodated in a commandeered hotel as comfortable as the one in which he had spent his honeymoon.

Drilling in front of similarly commandeered hotels, their windows crammed with admiring evacuated schoolgirls, was elevating to the spirit. They looked very little younger than Alexandra. And their friendliness was a revelation to anyone who had been a neighbour to the Imperial School. Some of the bolder recruits made dates with them. But not Blake. He spent his evenings blacking his boots, polishing buttons and studying. He was slower on morse code than he would have liked and worse on aircraft recognition, and he formed a bitter loathing for the Flight Sergeant who drilled them, with his perennial joke of Blake's two left feet. But he sailed through the maths and navigation exams. Monteith's Reply cleared the first hurdle and was posted north to a grass aerodrome at Prestwick. 'Where I now really begin to fly,' he wrote to Alexandra. 'Tiger Moths to begin with.'

To begin with and almost to end with. They had looked such harmless pretty little things on the winter grass. Easy to fly, everyone said. The instructors were all civilians. Blake's was a large redfaced Glaswegian with a walrus moustache, Duncan McCann, known as Big Mac. Listening to him on the ground was confusing enough, but having clambered into the rear cockpit, Blake found deciphering that glottal accent through the communicating device called the Gosport tube well nigh impossible.

In obedience to it, or what he could decipher of it, Blake looked round the cockpit layout, touched the throttle, put his feet against the rudder bars, and grasped the dual control column.

Then Big Mac hunched his shoulders and put up his thumb. The engine fired, caught, swelled to a steady roar, and they were off, bumping and thundering over the grass. The slip-stream whipped in his face, making his eyes water. He felt Monteith's Reply was about to founder without ever leaving the ground.

Suddenly the control column moved backwards in his hand. He was aware that the engine note had become softer, like a motor-boat on a calm sea. There were no more bumps, no more bangs.

He peered over the side. The green grass had fallen quietly away. He saw the coastline and the grey wrinkled sea far below. A wind sang in the wires. To the right, a shoal of silver barrage balloons hung over Ayr. Then the aircraft banked, turned smoothly towards the gently undulating hills, soared towards a bank of white clouds, and dipped over a miniaturised village.

It was as if the Moth had found its element. And so had he. He was back over the months to the day war broke out, watching the aircraft high over Oxford.

Now more heavily accented information came over the tube. But he didn't care. He simply grunted acknowledgement and they were zooming up and over, on their backs, hanging on by their straps, the universe a breathless blur of blue and white and green and red. Righted once more, they were side-slipping, spiralling, gliding. Then down again to earth, to the bumpy tussocks of the grass runway.

Proudly filling in his new log book, *18 Jan 1940, Tiger Moth 2345, 1st. Pilot Duncan McCann, Pupil Self, dual 15 minutes*, Blake felt a strange mixture of emotions. He was bedazzled by his first real experience of the air. He felt touched by its curious hypnotic pull. It was like being distantly and childishly in love with Alexandra.

Flying was an aesthetic, almost spiritual experience, but he had an awful feeling that he was going to lack the skill.

In that he proved right. 'Yon Oxford education cuts nae ice up here,' Big Mac grunted, as he almost stalled the engine on his second lesson. He told him on the third dual, 'Ye're no in tune wi' her, cuddie!'

Only on the seventh lesson did Big Mac acknowledge that though Blake had a pair of hams for hands, he did have 'pairseverance'. After five hours dual, all the others who survived on Blake's course were going solo. Six had been summarily failed. Only he remained glued to the other end of the Gosport tube, listening to Big Mac's laments.

Then on the second Friday, a cold winter afternoon with the grass still crunchy with frost at midday, Blake managed three circuits and landings without a sound from the tube. They landed and taxied.

The silence was unnerving. He began to fear that despite today's success he was to be given the boot. Instead, Big Mac unstrapped himself, shouted, 'Stay where ye are, cuddie!' and clambered out. 'Off ye go!' He jerked his thumb up at the high blue yonder. 'Ye're on yer own!'

Relieved of Big Mac's weight, the Moth leapt into the air. Blake experienced the physical exhilaration of pulling his world upwards. With awe, he felt the loneliness and exaltation of solitary flight. He played with the power at his finger tips, banking, climbing, gently diving. His hands found a new delicacy. He stared out at the sharply delineated beauty of the winter landscape, at charcoal woods and sombre lochs. He felt admiring but detached – from that earth, from his worries about Alexandra, from his hatred of Swain, from his inadequacy, from his role as Monteith's Reply.

Then reluctantly he came down to land. He sweated, he worried, he over-corrected. Once again his hands turned into pink hams. Afterwards, he thought it was as if Alexandra and Henry Swain and Mrs Monteith and Big Mac were all crowding him. But he managed to get her down all in one piece and actually didn't bounce her. Big Mac came out of the Dispersal Hut and put up his thumb. 'Ye've got guts, cuddie! They're just a long way doon.' He punched Blake in the midriff. For some unknown reason, he reminded Blake of Roxburgh.

Two weeks later, having clocked up six more hours, Blake was on his way with the other survivors to Number Three Service Flying

Training School at Cirencester, his first experience of a pukka RAF Station. They were housed in a large brick-built Officers' Mess. A log fire crackled in the comfortable ante-room, the dinner was excellent, the rooms warm, the white coverletted beds comfortable. Straight away Blake drifted off to sleep, composing in his mind a letter describing it all to Alexandra.

Five hours later he was wakened by the crackle of the tannoy. A matter-of-fact voice announced, 'An aircraft has crashed on the perimeter. All available personnel turn out to search for the pilots' bodies!'

Outside he heard ambulances and firebells, and was aware of a distant red glow rimming the blackout. He had just struggled into his trousers when the tannoy came on again.

'Personnel no longer required! Repeat, personnel no longer required.'

Blake returned to his bed, but this time it took him a long time to go to sleep. He watched the fiery-red edging to the blackout gradually grow dim. He wondered who the poor sods were, and though he tried not to, if that was going to happen to any of his course.

Ironically, it happened to two of the brightest within three weeks. Dickinson, who'd been the first to go solo at Prestwick, and Melhuish, who'd soloed soon after him. But then that had been on Moths, and the Oxford was a monster. Dickinson brought one in so fast they exploded into a boundary wall. Melhuish simply disappeared.

There was a saying that the Oxford gave you either a halo, a bowler hat or your wings. Round the crew room, where the pupils waited in their Sidcot suits for their turn to go up, were photographs of previous courses, bearing witness to this fact. Over the heads of many of those eager young men had been inked in a halo or a bowler hat.

Blake avoided looking at those photographs. They were like looking down when you were walking a tightrope. And a tightrope he surely walked, with a vicious ground-looping stalling monster, bent on throwing him into the ground. It was a monster that he likened in his own mind to Henry Swain. He experienced a feeling of personal triumph when he brought it tamely to the ground single-handed.

But no sooner had he tamed the monster by day than the night-flying schedule went up. As if from another world, Alexandra wrote that all was well at home, the daffodils and tulips were blooming in the garden, but the iron railings had gone for the Spitfire campaign, and Mrs Monteith had begun to Dig for Victory, planting potatoes in the rose bed. Night after night, Monteith's Reply wrestled for mastery of the monster in what seemed like a black cupboard with only the candle-flame brightness of the instruments for company.

Half-way through April, two pupils were thrown off the course, and just before the end of that month, Carter, a quiet studious lad rather like himself, crashed into the Cotswold hills.

It was all a bit too much like the Ten Little Nigger Boys for Blake's liking. But he thought of Henry Swain, the look of scorn there would be in Mrs Monteith's eyes and the sad sisterly commiseration in Alexandra's, and he wrestled on. He had no intention of going back to 7 Park Road in a bowler hat to lift the potatoes.

At the beginning of May, he did his first night solo. Three of them – Renton, Craig and himself – were on that night's schedule. He was second to take off after Renton.

It was a quiet moonless night. Outside, owls were hooting in the woods as they walked out to the aircraft. It was just as eerie inside the cockpit. Like altar candles, the little lights made haloes over the instruments. Blake wished he hadn't thought of haloes as the engines were started.

He watched Renton roar down the runway and take off like a bird. Then he tapped out A in morse on the downward identification light. He received a green from the Aldis lamp.

Cautiously, he taxied forward. Blackness always distorted everything. It seemed that the flarepath, not the Oxford, was moving – coming towards him like a procession of revellers carrying torches. He blinked his eyes, trying to quench his over-active imagination.

He did his Before Take-off Check, already beginning to sweat. Then he opened up the engines. The Oxford lunged forward and surged into the night.

As the wheels left the ground, he felt a moment of exquisite triumph. He climbed to 1,000 feet before turning. A few stars pricked the darkness. Ahead and above he could see Renton's red port navigation light like a ruby spark on the velvet.

The Oxford engines purred sweetly. Blake felt the tension inside himself unknot, leaving him exhilarated and confident.

Half-way round the circuit, he watched Craig's lights leap up into the night. Now they were three little fireflies. They had all made it.

They'd have a noggin in the bar tonight. When it was time to line up with the runway, he saw Renton glide smoothly down.

'Bloody good,' he called generously into the night.

In a moment, the green Aldis lamp gave Blake the clear to land. Descending in a straight approach, he levelled up at the first flare and flew horizontally for six seconds till the wheels gently touched the grass, and then waited till the tail wheel connected before putting on the brake.

He was down! Under the Sidcot, his shirt clung to his back, his mouth felt dry, but he'd done it!

He began taxiing towards Dispersal, drawing into his lungs the smell of crushed grass mixing with the smoke of the paraffin glims. He kept one eye on Craig coming in to land. He was already imagining himself saying to Craig over a jar, 'Saw you come in. Bloody good landing!' It would be a night for mutual congratulation.

Then he blinked at the approaching lights, leaned forward and heard himself shout, 'You're too low, for Chrissake! You're too low! The wall! For Chrissake, the wall!'

After that the world erupted. He caught a glimpse of hell. Craig's wheels touched the wall. The Oxford spun on its back, and with a crack like thunder, exploded. Orange-red flames and black oily smoke billowed into the night.

Blake could feel the heat as he cut his engines, tore off his straps and jumped down. As if in a nightmare, hideously encumbered by his suit, he pounded across the grass, arms going like pistons. Behind him, he could hear voices shouting, the clanging of the fire engine. But they were far away. He would be first. And even as he ran he knew that part of him didn't want to get there. But he forced himself forward.

When he got to the aircraft, the heat drove him back. The whole frame had broken in two. Craig was lying half out of the shattered cockpit on the edge of the flames. Screwing up his eyes, shielding his face as best he could, Blake rushed in, grabbed him and with an almighty effort pulled him clear. Then he saw that the lower part of Craig's body was still in the cockpit.

All he could remember after that was the ambulance coming up while he tottered off into the woods to be sick. He supposed he must have also tottered back to the Mess and consumed a vast number of jars and got very drunk.

The following night he was on the night-flying detail again. The day after that, the Chief Flying Instructor sent for him. Perhaps, Blake thought, he had said something untoward at Craig's crash.

The CFI chattered for a moment about night-flying and then handed Blake a telegram.

Because of potential bad news, telegrams were first sent to the Adjutant who decided how to deal with them. Blake's reaction was sudden apprehension. Awful things seemed to be happening. Now something awful had happened to Alexandra. Then he saw the smile on the CFI's face.

'Congratulations!'

It was from Mrs Monteith – he could never think of her as anything else – EIGHT POUND SON BORN FIVE A.M. TODAY. MOTHER AND BABY DOING WELL. LOVE MUMMY.

'Well, Blake,' the CFI's lean face suddenly assumed a strangely sentimental smile. 'We must try to fix you up with some leave.'

'Thank you, sir. I'd like to see my wife.'

He was suddenly aware that he wanted to see Alexandra more than anything else in the world.

'*And* your son!' the CFI said heartily. 'You'll want to see your *son*!'

Blake said nothing. Had he opened his mouth, out would have tumbled the words, '*I haven't got a son, Sir, you mean Heinrich Swain's son!*'

'Isn't he lovely, John? Just like his grandfather!'

Mrs Monteith was ecstatic – one more boy in the family! Blake stared over the side of the cot at the furrowed face and the dark blue eyes and thought the baby looked exactly like Heinrich Swain.

'Alexandra wants to call him Maurice. What do you think, John?'

Blake was aware of Alexandra anxiously watching him. 'That would be exactly right. It's what I'd have suggested.' What I'd have suggested, he thought, if I hadn't been so busy thinking of Swain.

'Maurice would be very proud,' Mrs Monteith said, 'carrying on his name.'

'He's got your hair, Alexandra,' Blake said, feeling suddenly acutely sorry for Alexandra. Gingerly he touched the fair down with his finger tips. 'And your eyes.'

Alexandra shrugged as if rejecting his efforts.

Mrs Monteith slipped a hand through Blake's arm and looked up at him warmly. 'But your eyebrows.'

Alexandra blushed a deep scarlet. 'All new-born babies look like Winston Churchill,' she said, trying to make a joke. Blake laughed immoderately and Mrs Monteith, who could usually be relied upon to take up the patriotic gauntlet, said fervently, 'May he grow up like him!'

Winston Churchill, now Prime Minister of a National Government, was indeed the man of the moment. That first evening of Blake's leave, spearheads of the German forces had already reached the Channel. Denmark and Norway had fallen. The Low Countries had been overrun, and it seemed that only Winston Churchill stood between invasion and a dishonourable peace. The three of them, Alexandra in her dressing gown, Mrs Monteith and Blake listened to the news in the sitting room.

The French windows were open, and in drifted the smell of cut grass and wallflowers, a mixture that made Blake feel unbearably sad. As a family celebration of young Maurice's birth, and a reiteration of Churchill's fighting words, Mrs Monteith opened a bottle of champagne.

'So what plans have you got now, John?'

Blake laughed. 'It's what plans the RAF have for *me*!'

She inclined her head impatiently, and he went on. 'I've opted for Coastal Command. Working with the Navy. Coastal's the quickest way to get on Ops.'

It sounded all right. Very press-on. But it wasn't like that. He had opted for Coastal Command for a variety of reasons. He doubted he was quick and agile enough to make a fighter pilot. He didn't fancy bombing, especially of cities. In Coastal, you fought uniformed men in murderous ships. But most important of all, Coastal Command's enemy was his enemy. The *Kriegsmarine*. He would be attacking U-boats in general and Heinrich Swain in particular.

'Splendid!' Mrs Monteith topped up his glass. 'So you'll be protecting convoys?'

'Yes.'

'And U-boat killing?'

'I hope so.'

'You can't hope it any more ardently than we do, John.' Mrs Monteith said in a quiet deadly voice. 'Isn't that so, Alexandra?'

But Alexandra had heard the baby crying and had gone upstairs to feed him.

'And how much leave have they given you?'

'A week. I'd finished night flying, so they were generous.'

'Do get Alexandra to go out! It was a difficult birth. She's under the weather. Mopey. Misses you.'

Ah, would that she did, Blake thought as, dutifully obedient to Mrs Monteith's instructions, Alexandra and he wheeled the baby across the park and into the meadows.

May was going out in a blaze of warm still weather. But the news was grim. 'The House should prepare itself for hard and heavy tidings,' Churchill had warned. France was crumbling. It looked as if the whole British Expeditionary Force and two French armies would be cut off in Belgium. For the first time, people talked of the possibility of invasion and thought, though not aloud, of defeat. Blake wheeled the pram and watched a concrete gun emplacement being erected on the river, imagining thousands of Heinrich Swains goose-stepping up the English lanes.

'I'm sorry I brought all this on you,' Alexandra said suddenly, seeing his expression.

'All what?'

'The baby. Me.'

'We've talked about all that. I love you. I told you.'

'And the baby?' She watched him closely.

Blake squinted down at the white wrapped bundle and said firmly, 'I love him too.'

She didn't believe him. But she seemed relieved. Blake toyed with the idea that she too might make the supreme lying effort and tell him, 'And I love you, John!' But being Alexandra, she didn't. She squeezed his arm and said, 'You are a dear, John! You really are!'

After a while, she asked slowly, nervously, 'And Coastal Command . . . why really did you choose that?'

'Oh,' he replied carelessly, his eyes fixed on a group of Local Defence Volunteers ludicrously drilling, 'just my natural aptitude, really. Or lack of it.' He decided to blind her with science. 'They give you aptitude tests, you know. The Coastal Command type of operation suits me best.'

For a moment he feared that she might ask if it were anything to do with the baby and Swain, but she didn't.

Suddenly she smiled. 'Good!'

'And anyway,' he grinned, 'the casualties won't be so high.'

'Touch wood!' She bent down and picked up a twig and made him touch it. He felt absurdly pleased at her concern. He popped the stick in his pocket. It made him feel if not safe, at least wanted.

'You've done wonders for Alexandra!' Mrs Monteith said next day, bringing out the six o'clock gin. 'She's a different girl!' She glanced towards the open sitting room door and the staircase, then walked over to the radio and switched it on. 'She worries about you. She hates listening to the news.'

Blake didn't allow himself to consider why. Small wonder, he thought, that anyone liked listening to it.

The British Expeditionary Force had been driven by Hitler's Panzer divisions to the beaches of Dunkirk. Over the rim of their gin glasses John Blake and his mother-in-law exchanged glances. And then at the end of the news came a surprising item. Owners of small boats were told to report immediately to the harbour masters of Dover, Folkestone and a dozen other places on the south coast.

'Does it mean what I think it means, John?' Mrs Monteith asked in a matter-of-fact voice. 'That they're going to try to take them off with a lot of amateur sailors?'

'Yes.'

'Dear God!'

It all seemed very unreal, Blake thought, sitting on the chintz sofa, nursing his gin, while the warm smell of an English garden drifted through the windows. As Mrs Monteith topped up his glass with a steady hand, he picked up a pamphlet to householders from the Ministry of Information that was lying on the table. With effect from that day, church bells would not be rung except to inform of invasion.

Mentally he echoed Mrs Monteith's exclamation . . . dear God! It had happened in Poland and Belgium and Holland and Denmark and Norway. Later that night in bed he was still thinking about all the Oxford church bells ringing when he drifted off to sleep.

He woke, hearing chimes echoing in his ears, clutching Alexandra protectively to him. But it was only the grandfather clock in the hall, and the baby beginning to grizzle for his two o'clock feed. Blake sat on the edge of the bed beside Alexandra while she fed him. Like that, the baby seemed still a part of her. He could fool himself that they were a little family. He held Maurice while she buttoned up her nightgown. He felt himself soften towards Maurice. His protectiveness began to encompass him.

'I'm very proud of him,' he said, handing the baby back to her. 'He's wonderful.'

She looked up at him, eyes shining. 'I love you for that.'

She put the baby carefully back in the cot and came and threw her arms round him. He felt closer to her than he had ever done before. He thought how nice it would be if she'd left off the last two words. Yet it was something. They had still five more days of leave and he would work on it.

But the next morning, as the three of them finished breakfast, the doorbell rang. A telegraph boy stood on the doorstep and handed him a telegram. He tore it open. RECALLED TO UNIT IMMEDIATELY. REPORT 330 SQUADRON, MIDDLECOMBE MAGNA.

He handed the telegram to Alexandra and went upstairs to pack.

'I'll take you to the station,' she said when he came down with his bag. 'Mother's looking after Maurice.'

'I shall look after both of them while you're away,' Mrs Monteith said, kissing him goodbye in the hall, 'so don't worry!' She didn't actually say, 'Concentrate on being Monteith's Reply', but she did say the naval equivalent. 'I expect things will be busy from now on.'

'What will happen now, d'you suppose?' Alexandra asked him soberly as she turned the car onto the main road. All the signposts had been taken down. Further along, there were jagged concrete teeth on the verge. Tank traps. For German tanks.

'God knows.' Blake shrugged. It all seemed so impossible. He tried to visualise what it would be like, and yet he couldn't. He wondered what it would be like to be on a Dunkirk beach being dive-bombed by Stukas, but his mind boggled.

'But promise me you'll go down the shelter when the sirens go?'

They turned into the station yard. 'Of course I will!' She laughed reassuringly. 'But Oxford won't be a target.'

'And look after young Maurice.'

She looked absurdly grateful for that.

They stood for a moment holding hands outside the RTO's* office, looking at each other, pleased with each other.

And then there was a sudden flurry of activity throughout the station. Ambulances raced up. A long convoy of military lorries and jeeps drew up outside and disgorged orderlies and stretchers.

A whisper ran round the crowded station. A train of wounded was coming in. The remnants of the Expeditionary Force from the beaches of Dunkirk.

Pushed to one side by hurrying khaki-clad men and women

* Railway Transport Office

carrying stretchers, John and Alexandra stood in silence as a long train clanked slowly into the platform.

The doors seemed to open with reluctance. Then it was all there. The nightmare made waking. The dreaded impossible made possible. A Pandora's Box of what war was really like spilling out before his eyes.

Blake wanted to shut his eyes, to not to believe it. He felt Alexandra shaking uncontrollably. Someone near them whispered that these men had been bombed and machine-gunned for two days, hiding in the sand-dunes.

He felt a murderous sickening hatred for all things German. He clenched his fist. He couldn't wait to get stuck in. When a spritely little corporal with a bloodstained bandage round his head began playing 'There'll always be an England' on his mouth organ, the whole crowded station began to sing. They went on singing it, himself included, as the pathetic remnants of England's army was carried and helped away, with a jingoistic fervour he would have scorned a year ago.

Blake glanced sideways at Alexandra. Tears were streaming down her cheeks. But she was joining in.

That sight stayed in Blake's mind throughout the journey, and he arrived in a sombre and determined mood.

At least he was now in the fighting war. At least he wouldn't simply have to watch the vapour trails in the sky as British fighters engaged German bombers and listen to news bulletins of imminent invasion. He would at least be given a first-line aircraft, bullets and bombs and told to get on with it.

'Middlecombe Magna!' the only porter was shouting, at the same time as he was taking down the big nameplate above the platform.

Confuse the Hun was the latest Ministry of Information directive. Outside the station was a pile of uprooted signposts. A woman was doing a house-to-house collection of pots and pans for Spitfires, and twelve Local Defence Volunteers, half of them armed with airguns, half with billhooks, were drilling outside the gates of the RAF aerodrome.

Blake's heart sank. It sank further when he saw there were no runways, just a grass aerodrome. It went right down to his boots when he saw the aircraft standing outside 330 Squadron offices.

'Ansons!'

He was so horrified, he said the word aloud. Older than the Oxfords he had been trained on, these were simply the equivalent of the billhooks the LDV were carrying. As crew, he was given an ancient Flight Lieutenant Navigator on the point of retiring, and a Flight Sergeant Wireless Operator/Air Gunner anxious to remuster to a ground job. Britain must be in an even worse position than he had possibly imagined.

As June turned into July and then into August, that conviction grew, in spite of the heroic efforts of the fighter pilots.

The operations which 330 Squadron were called upon to do made it even less bearable. Loaded with a couple of last war depth-charges, which were far more lethal to the aircraft which dropped them than the U-boat which they were supposed to kill, the Ansons scoured the North Sea for U-boats, accompanied by an assortment of flying club Tiger Moths. 'Don't worry about not seeing any U-boats,' the Intelligence Officer told Blake. 'They see you and dive. And that slows them up and keeps them away from the convoys.'

The convoys he was referring to plied their way round the East Coast, and rewarded the Ansons for their vigilance by taking pot-shots at them. Twice Blake landed with his tail riddled in bullet holes.

The Scarecrow Patrol was how the 330 Squadron pilots referred to themselves. In Blake's opinion, the whole war effort in this area was something straight out of Tommy Handley's ITMA, and was per-sonified by the fête held at the beginning of September on Middlecombe Magna's cricket field, which was held this year, appropriately, in aid of War Weapons Week.

Opened by the Lady of the Manor, the vicar set the proceedings off to a flying start by knocking down three coconuts, painted respectively with the faces of Göring, Goebbels and Lord Haw-Haw, the traitor William Joyce who broadcast German propaganda from Berlin Radio. The band played *We're going to hang out our washing on the Siegfried Line*. A doll dressed up as Hitler sat in a big tin bath, and Blake was urged to 'drown him in sixpences'.

The star attraction was a toy U-boat in a glass tank filled with water which could be sunk realistically by well-aimed marbles at one penny each. Blake became quite adept at it, while to his chagrin and shame the Battle of Britain went on without him.

Two days later, the war touched them a little closer. The bodies of five German soldiers were washed up on the shore eight miles from the station. So when the church bells rang throughout Britain the day after, everyone thought that the invasion had begun and took up their positions. The Ansons were scrambled, the police rolled the barbed wire over the roads, the LDV manned the pillboxes, in thousands of houses housewives sharpened the knives, brought out the old iron frying pans and meat cleavers, totally resolved to put into practice Churchill's words, 'We shall fight on the beaches, we shall fight in the fields and in the streets, we shall fight in the hills, we shall never surrender.'

Blake went to bed that night in an anguish of fear for Alexandra. He was quite sure Mrs Monteith would never allow either of them to surrender. He had nightmares of his mother-in-law and Alexandra in a death-or-glory attack such as Churchill had bidden the civilian population to make on German tanks. He woke up in a sweat, more tired than when he'd gone to bed.

It was a mistake, of course. The invasion hadn't started. Yet. But what *had* started was the bombing of London.

Coming out of the Mess, Blake saw that the night sky to the south had turned a brilliant red. Even as far away as this, he could smell the smoke. London first . . . then where? The next day, he found himself discarding all his previous humanitarian ideas of not bombing cities, and buttonholed his CO, demanding that surely, if they hadn't got anything better, they could at least load up the Ansons and bomb the bastards back.

'We all feel the same,' the CO said. 'But at long last, we're going to do better than that. Coastal have squeezed some Whitleys out of Bomber Command. The Squadron's going up to Leeming to convert.'

Blake and five other pilots were ferried up to Leeming next day. They were all raring to go. Christ, Blake thought, looking down at the golden stubble fields, who'd have thought he would have longed for the fight quite so soon.

The first person he bumped into in the Mess was Jenkins. He was on 102 Squadron, and he'd changed too from the Kirkstone days. He had a hard-eyed old-young look about him. They reminisced over a pint about the visit of the Germans, only now Jenkins called them the Huns.

'First time I ever saw a Whitley was when Fische asked its name and none of us knew.'

'I remember.'

'Well, I know a helluva lot about Whitleys now. And so will you.'

At least Blake found the long cigar-shaped, bat-winged aircraft easy to land. It flew with a characteristic nose-down attitude – though terribly slowly. Not the sort of aircraft to get you out of a tight spot in a hurry.

'All we've done so far,' Jenkins told him, 'is drop bloody leaflets. They bomb London. We drop leaflets. Jesus wept! The crews can't wait to have a crack at them.'

Two days later he got the chance. A maximum effort was suddenly laid on. The target was the German invasion barges, waiting in the French Channel ports to invade Britain – Hitler's Operation Sea-Lion.

Blake was unashamedly envious, and when Jenkins' second pilot was rushed to hospital with acute appendicitis, he persuaded Jenkins to wangle it so that he could take his place. Buttoning himself into his Sidcot flying suit, he found himself pondering what on earth Wagstaff would make of them if he could see them now.

It was a clear moonlit night. Blake could see the shadow of their Whitley as they all trundled round past the dim blue lights of the perimeter track, following the tail of the bomber in front. He felt an almost unbearable mixture of excitement and anticipation and fear, the thrill of being part of a fighting force, the exultation of being about to hit back.

The Whitleys flew at 12,000 feet, the highest Blake had ever been. The Channel lay like a river of gold between the two big black blocks of England and France.

'Enemy coast ahead!'

The Whitley rocked violently. Up came big yellow bursts like chrysanthemum flowers. Blake studied the flak with interest. This is my baptism of fire, this is what it feels like to be fired on, he thought.

But it didn't feel like anything. He felt pleased with himself. Detached. Immune.

Then Jenkins shoved the stick forward. Down they dived, down over the darkened skyline of Calais, over a quick sheen of the harbour, over rows and rows of invasion barges.

'Captain to bomb aimer . . .'

Ahead, he could just glimpse the black bat shapes of the leading Whitleys, the white bursts as they dropped their bombs. Then a different white, the dazzling white of searchlights.

'Steady . . .' the bomber aimer called.

Suddenly the windscreen was filled with a huge orange pulse of light as the Whitley ahead exploded. Now they were caught in a terrifying galaxy of tracer and searchlight. A fly in a fiery web.

'Hold her steady!' Blake gritted his teeth. He wanted to shout out to the bomb aimer to drop the bloody bombs and let them get the hell away. His spurious feeling of detachment had gone.

Momentarily terror burst in on him. He made himself think of the barges down below and hitting back. That's what he'd wanted.

Then the Whitley gave a little bound upwards.

'Bombs away!'

Jenkins pivoted the aircraft on its port wing. Blake caught a glimpse of big white flashes as their bombs exploded. And simultaneously, he heard the rattle of machine-gun fire. The corner of the windscreen starred. A black shape swept over them, its exhausts glowing red.

'ME 109s!' the rear gunner shouted over the intercom.

Jenkins corkscrewed.

Everything became a kaleidoscope of searing colours and black night, a kaleidoscope punctuated by the incessant rattle of machine-gun bullets and the scream of engines. His stomach heaved. His whole body broke out in a sweat.

'Got a burst in his tail, Skipper,' the rear gunner shouted.

They were straightening and climbing. Out of his window Blake saw another aircraft going down in flames. Christ!

But Jenkins was calling to the navigator for a course. They were going home.

Blake saw the shimmer of the Channel now silver in a paler moon, and the black cut-out shape of the Kentish coast. Behind he could see the fires they had started, pink, orange, blood-red. The barges were burning. But he couldn't feel any elation. Not anything, in fact. Except that he had aged by at least twenty years. He had been baptised. He had renounced not the devil and all his pomps, but his youthful self.

The following day, the photographs showed the main basin at Dieppe a mass of steel and wooden rubble. Of the twelve Whitleys which had set out, four had not returned. Jenkins and he drank in the bar the next two nights. He would have liked to ask Jenkins if, over the target, he too had been afraid. But of course he couldn't. Instead they talked about old friends, and then the German boys' visit again. Blake asked Jenkins what he'd thought of Swain.

'A real Hun,' Jenkins said.

Blake agreed.

Then there was another Sea-Lion operation laid on. This time Jenkins did not return.

That night, Blake couldn't face drinking in the Mess. He walked down to the local pub and sat up at the bar drinking beer and whisky chasers and watching the darts.

He tried not to think of Jenkins. But he couldn't help it. He thought of Jenkins and Nash, and Fische and his bloody Whitley. A new Ministry of Information poster was pinned up beside the dartboard along with the perennial ones about *Careless Talk* and *Is Your Journey Really Necessary?* This one, proof of the low ebb of Britain's fortunes, said *You Can Always Take One With You.* Underneath was the picture of a brutal German parachutist being garrotted by a sweet-faced elderly Englishman.

Ironically, the elderly Englishman looked curiously like the Reverend Swain. It was a cock-eyed world. Blake stared at the poster balefully, feeling very drunk and light-headed. He didn't need the Reverend Swain to remind him that he would certainly take a German with him, and that the German he had promised himself would be Heinrich Swain.

Swain's whereabouts was never in any doubt. Gunther Prien was now operating from Lorient, 1,000 miles nearer the British convoys, hotly competing with the blonde giant Joachim Schepke and the quiet Otto Kretschmer to be top of the sinkings table. Since France capitulated, nearly two million tons of ships had been sent to the bottom, many of them by Prien, now revered throughout Germany as the first U-boat ace.

'You British sailors on the Atlantic,' hissed Lord Haw-Haw over Berlin Radio, 'the snorting White Bull of Scapa Flow is coming to get you!'

'I'll get you!' Blake retorted back at the loudspeaker which everyone in the Mess lounge took to be a brave show of optimisitc patriotism.

Next day 330 Squadron was posted to Kilkerry in Northern Ireland to operate against U-boats. At last Blake was on the right collision course with Swain.

'But first,' the CO told them, 'we pick up our hush-hush Whitleys from TRE.'

Those initials stood for Telecommunications Research Establishment – a mundane Civil Service name totally different from the reality Blake found.

The Malvern Hills crawled with hundreds of long-haired bespectacled corduroy-clad academics called Boffins, who appeared to spend their entire lives in makeshift huts playing with tin boxes, valves, transformers, wire and aerials. They all had long strings of scientific degrees after their names, and five of them were Fellows of the Royal Society.

One of the more respectable of them introduced himself in a guttural voice as Dr Schwarz and proceeded to show the Squadron aircrew what he called 'the gubbins'.

'This is it!' Affectionately he tapped a long aluminium box equipped with a round screen, numerous coloured knobs and coils of wiring. 'ASV . . . or to the uninitiated, Anti-Surface Vessel.'

'Looks complicated,' said a pilot.

'On the contrary, *very* easy. Just a miniature of the radars that together with Fighter Command won the Battle of Britain. This little fellow' – again Schwarz tapped the box, but harder this time so the whole contraption shook on its rubber mountings – 'is going, with your help, to win the Battle of the Atlantic.'

Blake studied the instrument intently. 'Will it find U-boats?'

'Provided they're on the surface, yes. If they're underwater the Navy will get them with Asdic.'

'At what range?' Blake persisted.

'Eight miles. Ships at thirty. Land at eighty.'

Schwarz turned a red knob. The round screen was split by a phosphorescent green line, spitting green spines from either side. 'Those are signals or "blips" at various distances up the centre line.'

'What frequency?' asked a pilot.

Schwarz tapped his lips. 'Sorry.'

'You mean if the Germans knew they'd pick up the transmission and get a warning?'

'Fortunately they have no idea the set exists. Indeed, their scientists are certain that miniature airborne radar is impossible. They kicked out their Einsteins because they happened to be Jews. And oh-my-God, is Hitler going to be sorry!'

The doctor's confidence was infectious, especially to Blake. After so many revelations about the RAF's ancient equipment, here was the perfect instrument to find Swain in the vastness of the North Atlantic.

In the lorry that took them from Leeming to Defford, Blake had been rather subdued. The Wingco of 330 Squadron had told him, 'On a big machine like a Whitley, with your limited experience you'll be a Second Dickey for a while', and he didn't look forward to having a Captain over him. Now the Boffins' magic box had heartened him, and he became much more cheerful when, after Schwarz's guided tour, he met his ASV trained crew – a tall, thin, gum-chewing American with Polish forebears called Bronski as navigator, a wiry Yorkshireman, Joe Orton, as chief Wireless Operator, and two dark-blue-uniformed Australian ex-sheep-shearers called Rolf and Harvey as the two other W/Op Air Gunners.

His good humour evaporated a little when he saw that their ASV Whitley had aerials poking out of the wings and running all the way down the fuselage.

'Sticklebacks,' Bronski said.

'Must knock a couple of knots or three off the airspeed.'

'Fifteen.'

The final blow to Blake's good humour came two minutes later when the CO came up with a round-faced moustached Flight Lieutenant in his thirties.

'This is Lionel Pomeroy, chaps. Your new Skipper.'

The whole crew eyed the new arrival warily. They eyed him even more warily after he'd swung on take off and began hand-flying the Whitley so roughly that Rolf in the tail turret complained of sea-sickness.

It was a ninety-minute flight to Kilkerry, and Pomeroy spent the whole time either talking about hunting and fishing or loudly sucking an empty briar pipe.

Cottonflock cloud hung over the mountainsides as they approached their new home. Below them, a listing tanker supported on one side by a corvette and on the other by a large tug was limping out of the Atlantic into Lough Foyle on its way to the naval base at Londonderry, looking like a heavyweight prize-fighter being helped into his corner by two dimininutive seconds.

'Seems to have been in some sort of a scrap,' said Pomeroy.

A sudden spatter of illuminated dots and dashes came up from the gloaming below.

Bronski shouted up, 'They're challenging us!'

'Jittery, aren't they?' said Pomeroy. 'Anybody know the colours of the day?'

Nobody did. Pomeroy dived hurriedly out of range and went into the Kilkerry circuit.

'Like me to do the landing?' Blake asked.

Pomeroy shook his head. 'Captain's job, old boy.'

He carried out a long low approach – wheels down, flaps down, engines screaming – before hitting the runway and bouncing up into the air. There the Whitley suddenly stopped, her bat wings frozen in horror, before coming down to earth with an almighty crump.

The crew could hardly wait to scramble back onto the ground.

A lorry took them to their Sites, for Kilkerry was a Dispersal Camp. Blake's Site was Number Three, half-way up a mountain, a mile from the Mess and two miles from the Squadron Office. The only good thing that could be said about it was that it had a marvellous view.

He stood outside his Nissen hut, staring westwards. Beyond Lough Foyle, beyond Magilligan Point, he could just make out the grey waters of the Atlantic where U47 lurked.

You can always take one with you – the MOI directive came back into his mind. But, he reckoned, it wouldn't be Swain that Pomeroy would be taking with him, but the whole of his own crew.

'Ops in a Whitley, ops in a Whitley.'

In the far corner of the Mess Bar, four drunk pilots were harmonising the RAF ballad to the tune of 'Waltzing Matilda'.

'Who'll come on ops in a Whitley with me?'

Blake watched them dispassionately, quite used to the performance which occurred round closing time almost every night. But Foxy Fanshawe beside him had only arrived at Kilkerry the previous day and was moved to remark, 'Who'd go on ops in a Whitley with anyone?'

Trained at the Cambridge Flying School, he had put himself down for ship-busting Blenheims and was aggrieved to find himself in 330 Squadron. His greeting on seeing Blake was to express surprise that he was still in the land of the living, adding that poor old Nash had had it. 'On a Whitley too. Bloody murder sending Whitleys to Berlin.' He paused. 'But I suppose here you just stooge around seeing nothing?'

'Not quite.'

There was no point in enumerating his adventures of the last three weeks. Pomeroy had lived up to his crew's fears. Letting down through cloud over the mountains on a radar QGH descent, he had allowed the Whitley to get too low and came back with a clump of heather in the hinges of his starboard aileron. Turning onto a new course sent up front by Bronski, he had put 'red on blue' – that is, set up the lubber-lines of the compass 180 degrees out – steering south-east instead of north-west for over an hour. That meant they were over two hours late arriving over the convoy they were supposed to be escorting. Pomeroy also got too close in misty weather to trigger-happy destroyers on the look-out for the four-engined Condors which regularly swept down from Stavanger to Bordeaux to reconnoitre and report.

Sinkings that September reached a record 440,000 tons, five times the amount of ship-tonnage built. Round Inistrahull and through the twelve-mile gap between Scotland and England, the North Channel was now, after the fall of France, the only entry to British ports for the Atlantic convoys.

Pomeroy's crew saw no U-boats. Neither did anyone else in 330 Squadron. It was back to the Scarecrow Patrols, as in the Anson days – except for one thing.

Whitleys began unaccountably disappearing.

McElroy took off in O Orange one fine October morning and never came back. No message. Nothing. A week later, Lawson did exactly the same thing in K King.

Various theories were aired in the Mess. Ice, hit a mountain, jumped by a Condor, shot down by the Navy, the ASV had blown up, they'd bought it attacking a U-boat, the ancient depth-charges had exploded.

It was predictably Fanshawe's idea that it was the 'bloody Whitleys.'

As he explained to Blake, 'These Merlins are high-altitude jobs. At the height we operate, they'll bust! And our bloody Whitleys can't maintain height on one engine!'

Seeing Blake going in to Operations for briefing just before midnight in the middle of October, he called out, 'Look after yourself! Nobody else will!'

Blake had already realised that. Like a hawk, he watched Pomeroy's every movement on the controls. In vain, he tried to extract take-offs and landings, always being fobbed off with, 'Captain's job, old boy!'

He tried again that night as they waited for the briefing to begin, with no luck.

'Another convoy escort,' the Intelligence Officer told them. 'A fast eastbound . . . HX 79. And it's been spotted. According to Roger Winn in the London Submarine Tracking Room, Prien is shadowing in U47.'

Excitement shot through Blake's body like an electric shock. The name lazily lobbed across the quietness of Operations, made all his muscles tense and he could hear his heart hammering. What he had planned for was now being presented to him. Prien was bound to hang on to such a plum prize. He was certain to attack.

'*Rudeltaktik* . . . wolf-pack tactics are being used. Four aces Schepke in u100, Endrass in u46, Bleichrodt in u48 and Liebe in u38 have been ordered to form a "stripe" across the convoy's route. Your presence will at least keep them under and slow them up.'

'We might even sink 'em', Blake said.

The Intelligence Officer smiled. He was a naval officer, and aircraft had not yet sunk a single U-boat with their last war 450lb depth-charges. 'We can all have our dreams and hopes.'

'We might even sink Prien,' Blake persisted.

'Well, of course, that would be perfectly splendid,' said the Intelligence Officer, but he had already lost interest and now he was turning away to prepare his next briefing.

Twenty minutes later, Flight Lieutenant Pomeroy and crew in Whitley S Sugar wobbled off the Kilkerry runway into the blustery night, and turned westwards to do battle with the cream of the U-boat aces.

It was a quiet trip. Though Pomeroy began his usual chat, Blake answered in monosyllables. By the time they reached longitude 13 degrees west, sharing the flying in two-hour stints, silence had descended in the cockpit, punctuated only by the hum of the Merlins and the sucking sounds from Pomeroy's empty briar.

Outside, a misty moon illuminated a calm Atlantic. Shadows of clouds flitted across the water like ghosts. A tracery of eeriness cobwebbed the night like a witch's spell.

Blake sat in the darkness, his eyes never still. They probed each wavetop for the sheen of a steel side, the pole of a periscope. Swain was down there, somewhere on that silvery sea. That spurt of white might be the wash of u47. That curved shadow emerging from a breaking wave might be the bulge of the conning tower.

His whole body was tense, ever moving, his nerve endings alive to the slightest sight or sound.

'Sandwich, John?'

He jumped as though he'd been shot. It was only Bronski holding out the rations tin.

'They're turkey.'

He shook his head. His mouth was far too dry.

'Mustn't miss the convoy.'

'We won't. Got a three-star fix.' Bronski stood still behind him, moonlight playing over his face.

Blake fidgeted uneasily in his seat. 'What's our estimate?'

'Fifty minutes.'

The horizon ahead was battlemented with cloud.

'Any blips, Radar?'

'Nothing.'

On they flew as the moon rose higher over the empty Atlantic. Not a sound came over the intercom. We've missed it, Blake was thinking. Either they're off course or we're off course or . . .

He could stand the suspense no longer. 'Navigator, *how* much longer?'

'Eight minutes. Radar should have the ships now.'

'Well, I haven't!'

Blake had begun counting the seconds. Two hundred . . . two hundred and ten . . .

'Radar?'

'Nothing!'

Another fear struck him. 'Radar's not on the blink?'

'No.'

'Then there *must* be something!'

Eight hundred and twenty-one, eight hundred and twenty-two.

'Radar?'

But this time, Blake answered himself. 'Christ!'

The horizon ahead had caught fire. That or the sun was rising in the west. A bloody crimson etched with black danced and flickered and cascaded in the sky. Showers of red and silver sparks erupted. Searchlights swung crazy beams of shimmering greeny-white, like an upside-down Aurora Borealis.

'Bastards!'

Blake felt a rage such as he had never known. He grabbed the throttles, slammed them hard against the stops. The scream of the boosted Merlins matched his mood as the Whitley dived towards the sea.

'Down! *Down!*' Blake shouted. 'U-boats!'

Starshells went up, covering the red fangs of fire with a white phosphorescence. Black oblongs flickered momentarily into ghost ships before disappearing as the starshells burnt out.

'Blips all over,' Radar reported.

'Radar's no good!' Blake called over the intercom. 'U-boats practically formating on the ships!'

Down below now, a medieval picture of hell had come alive. Devils with tridents, silhouetted shadows, burning cauldrons, even white faces looking piteously upwards as the Whitley shot over blazing ships.

A fan of sea serpents bubbled across the water.

'Torpedoes!' Bronski shouted.

An ammunition ship exploded. Red and green fireworks, followed by flash after flash as the bombs went up.

The Whitley shuddered under the blast, then heeled right over. Thunder echoed down the tube of the fuselage as Pomeroy pulled the port wing up.

Four vessels began scattering at speed, each of them a flaming torch. Fire reached up from the burning oil on the sea, singeing their wingtips, the cockpit so dense with smoke that Blake couldn't see the instruments.

'Can't . . . can't . . .' Pomeroy gasped. 'Can't do more here!'

'We've got to! They're down there! Prien's down there!'

They were right in the middle of the convoy now, running down a struggling line of ships as though taking the salute from a broken army. A merchantman was listing heavily to port, lifeboats strung down her side. A tanker blew up, catapulting men high into the air. The nose of a liner dipped, her propellers frenziedly churning the sea as they took her at full speed down to the bottom of the Atlantic.

The last ship in the line simply broke in two, bow and stern curtseying to each other before simultaneously disappearing.

Dumbly, the Whitley's crew watched the slaughter, their eyes smarting with smoke, their nostrils filled with the smell of diesel oil, as they circled their sinking charges.

Over to port, a large merchantman blew up in a single silver flash. Over to starboard, a cargo of pit props took off like a box of giant matches being flung into the air. Through the windscreen ahead, Blake watched hundreds of tanks and lorries rushing down a crazy sloping deck to drown in the Atlantic like lemmings.

Searchlights flickered over lifeboats, caravans of floating crates, twenty men holding hands in a circle going up and down in the growing swell, a single sailor on a Carley float waving madly, white mushrooms of exploding depth-charges, red sparks spitting from the guns of frantic escorts firing haphazardly at the invisible enemy.

And all the time, the misty moon shone down on the burning sea.

Blake stared down at the water. 'The bastards are there, all right,' he called over his shoulder to Bronski. 'If only we could see 'em!'

But the night went on and all they saw were more sinkings, more fires. Gradually, up on the eastern horizon, came a red dawn to match the bloody holocaust below.

'Getting lighter,' Blake said. 'We'll see 'em now!'

But all they saw were the seabirds pecking out the eyes of the floating corpses, the planks and poles and the upturned lifeboats – the depleted debris of a battlefield.

Bronski shouted up from the navigation table, 'Time to go home!'

He was just passing up a course to steer, when suddenly Blake saw the blue-grey glint of a thin needle shape slithering over the sea.

'U-boat!'

Pomeroy looked up from the instrument panel, 'Where?'

'There . . . *there*!' Blake pointed. 'Bomb doors open!'

'Ah!' Pomeroy pushed his nose down. 'I see him!'

Blake saw something else. The U-boat had turned. On the steel flank of the conning tower at which Rolf was firing with the .300 in the front turret was painted the prancing White Bull of Scapa Flow.

'It's Prien!' he howled, 'Prien in u47! Port! For God's sake, *port*!'

Pomeroy edged to the left.

'Get him! You've *got* to get him!'

Pomeroy centred up, flying just above the water.

'Eight hundred yards . . . six hundred!' Blake shouted. 'Four hundred!'

The U-boat was wallowing in the swell. The White Bull seemed to be dancing.

'Three hundred yards!'

Pomeroy's thumb was still inches away from the bomb-release button on the stick.

'Two hundred!'

Still the thumb did not move.

'The button!' Blake yelled. 'Put your thumb on the button!'

At last the thumb covered the bomb release.

'On target! A hundred yards!'

The White Bull on the conning tower had suddenly become huge.

'Go on! *Press*!'

Blake had a momentary glimpse of men disappearing down the conning tower hatch.

'Too late!' he howled. 'Too bloody late!'

'Oh, no!' Pomeroy put on full port bank. 'I can see bubbles . . . oil. Got him, didn't I, Rear Gunner?'

Up over the intercom came Rolf's voice fraught with the same disappointed fury that Blake felt. 'Overshot, Skipper! And now he's dived!'

Pomeroy dropped flame floats and circled the empty sea while Orton sent the sighting out on the W/T.

Ten minutes later, a destroyer came up and began to drop depth-charges. Five minutes after that Pomeroy turned for home.

'You're not leaving us?' the destroyer flashed.

On Pomeroy's instructions, the Australian Rolf sent 'Sorry' on the Aldis lamp.

Sorry, Blake thought, as Pomeroy left his seat and he took over his stint. That's not the word! Angry, furious, dumb with frustration and disappointment. Death and destruction, murder, torture, burning alive, drowning was spread out in the water below them – and Pomeroy was sorry!

He was still fuming as Bronski came up. 'That bloody man had Prien on a plate! The minute I'm down, I'm telling the Wingco I'm not flying with Pomeroy again!'

'Don't look like any of us'll be flying again.'

'What d'you mean?'

Bronski jerked his thumb to the left. 'Take a look!'

Blake turned his head. A thin white wisp was coming out of the port engine like a fluttering handkerchief.

His eyes went to the engine temperature gauge. The needle was above 100 degrees centigrade and still rising.

Immediately he pushed open both throttles and went into a steep climb.

'Glycol leak!' he shouted. 'Losing coolant on the port engine!'

At full rated power he climbed. 1,500, 2,000, 2,500. Height was money in the bank. Height was their only solution.

'Send SOS,' he shouted back to Orton. 'With our position and course!'

The altimeter needle crawled up to 3,500. Now S Sugar was struggling. Temperatures were off the clock. The oil pressure was falling. Any moment now the engines would seize.

He pulled back the port throttle and pushed the red button. 'Feathering!'

The port propellor slowed, stopped still and stark, its three blades turned like swords to the slipstream.

The needle on the altimeter began to unwind. Just as Fanshawe had said, there wasn't a hope of maintaining height on one engine with all the ASV aerials.

He was quite right. This was what would have happened to McElroy and Lawson, caught 300 miles out with that dreaded white death sentence streaming from an engine and no joy raising anybody on the W/T.

Bronski organised the jettisoning of guns, parachutes, ammunition; everything moveable was thrown out to lighten the aircraft.

Pomeroy came up to take over, but Blake insisted it was *his* stint. There were only 2,700 feet left in the bank. Pomeroy would have simply frittered it away.

Blake flew like a miser, fighting the loss of every penny of height, keeping the Whitley's nose at just the right altitude. But all the time, they were losing. At 200 miles from the coast, the altimeter was registering 1,500 feet and the needle was still falling.

'Prepare for ditching!'

They had fallen below 1,000 feet. The sea looked terrifyingly near and still. Coastal had not acknowledged their SOS.

'Open all the escape hatches!'

Just below them now, the waves seemed to be licking their lips with their white tongues. Nothing was in sight – not a ship, not a seagull, not a piece of wreckage, not even the sun. As the crew huddled up at the front in their Mae Wests, a cold grey overcast hung heavily over them.

'Brace!'

The wings were inches away from the sea. A faint hiss as the fuselage hit. Then a sudden stop, a roaring as the sea smashed the windscreen and came pouring in. The instrument panel crashed into Blake's face.

'Everybody out!'

The nose sank as they scrambled through the top hatch. But the Whitley's wings kept her afloat as the crew ran down the spine of the aircraft to the tail turret.

'Where's the dinghy?' Pomeroy asked.

'Behind the main door.'

The fuselage was settling. Already the main door was covered in water.

'Somebody'll have to go inside to release it,' said Orton.

Blake kicked through the plywood escape cover just forward of the turret, was just clambering down when Pomery inserted his bulk into the hole ahead of him, calling out, 'Captain's job, old chap!' and disappeared down the long thin cave.

The wings were awash. S Sugar was sinking fast.

'He'll be trapped in there!' Blake put his head into the jagged hole and shouted up. 'Come on out! She's sinking!'

Only the wind, whistling over the waves, answered. The five crew clung to the turret, their Mae Wests inflated, as the wings sank and the whole fuselage angled for the nose-down plunge to the bottom.

'He'll never make it back,' Bronski said.

Suddenly the Whitley gave a lurch downwards. Sea water flooded over them, stinging their eyes as the tail began sinking.

'Here you are, chaps!'

From the boiling spume an arm was raised like Excalibur's sword, a hand was holding up the uninflated dinghy.

Blake grabbed it and pulled the wire on the compressed air bottle as the rear turret sank beneath them.

With a *whoosh*, the dinghy inflated. The five of them scrambled inside.

But there was no sign of the Whitley. No sign of Pomeroy. The only sight was the empty circle of the horizon. And the only sound was the slapping of the waves against the dinghy's rubber sides.

IV HEINRICH
28 October 1940–7 March 1941

'Hundred and one . . . hundred and two.'

The Coxswain was counting the depth-charges. Swain was trying to get the spirit level showing steady on the trimming panel. Kapitänleutnant Prien was swearing.

'Goddamned destroyer! *Go away!*'

Another *boom* shook the plates. Momentarily the lights flickered.

'Closer that time,' said the Coxswain.

Prien grunted. 'Won't harm us here!'

U47 was down deep at 300 metres. Let them waste their depth-charges, Prien thought, a U-boat's steel skin was far tougher than the Tommies'. But he was angry about being pinioned down here while the remnants of the fast convoy moved further and further east.

Ping . . . ping . . . ping.

The Asdic beams striking the hull. Joining in was the *whoosh whoosh whoosh* of the propellers – sometimes soft, sometimes loud – as the destroyer circled above. Worst of all, Swain thought, in this continuous underwater symphony were the *bangs*, as Endrass or Bleichrodt or Schepke sent another ship to the bottom.

'That'll be Kretschmer!' Prien called across at Swain as a loud *bang* reverberated against the hull. 'Another big tanker! Damn that bloody aircraft!'

Swain had seen the Whitley first. Standing beside Prien on the conning tower, their faces glowing in the light of burning ships, he had suddenly caught sight of the black bat shape. Next moment there was a rattling of machine-gun fire. Prien gave the alarm. Everyone on the bridge flung themselves down the ladder. The U-boat angled into a 30-degree dive.

It had been a near thing. Not for U47 – the depth-charges dropped miles away. But for Prien. A bullet had gone right through his hat.

He was fingering that hat now, rotating it round and round, as oily condensation dripped down on his head from the Control Room roof. Bearded, dirty, wearing his old reefer jacket with a black silk scarf round his neck, he stared down at the small hole in the white cap-cover – the U-boat captains' insignia – as though he couldn't believe his bloodshot eyes.

'Bloody nerve!' he was saying to Swain, when there was another *bang*.

'Kretschmer! That'll be Kretschmer *again*! He'll be ahead of me now!'

Latest scores in the U-boat sinkings league broadcast by Berlin Radio were Prien 192,000 tons, Kretschmer 179,000. But U47 had had damnable luck on this trip. Their first duty had been the hated weather patrol, sending out half-hourly reports from longitude 30 degrees west. Then they'd been told to shadow HX79. After he'd led Endrass's U46, Bleichrodt's U48, Schepke's U100 and Kretschmer's U99 onto the ships, he'd been allowed to join in the fun, but after sinking three small ships, unaccountably the next eight torpedoes had, according to Prien, been 'duds'.

'The magnetic pistols again,' Prien had shouted to his torpedomen. 'Same bloody trouble we had in Norway!'

Swain had been with him on that Norwegian campaign six months ago. Never had he seen Prien so angry. A British aircraft-carrier, two British cruisers and four large merchantmen had presented themselves as targets at point-blank range. Prien had fired – and nothing happened. He had returned to Dönitz in a white-hot rage, complaining about 'being sent off with dummy rifles'. An Inquiry had revealed serious technical faults in the new torpedoes.

The crews had been told that those had now been righted.

Righted? Seeing his Captain's disappointment, Swain sympathised. Their last five torpedoes had just been loaded into the tubes and they were keeping their fingers crossed that these would be serviceable, when up waddled that black goose of a Whitley. Down they'd had to go. And down they'd had to stay.

It was natural that he should have the most profound admiration for Prien. Prien was the backbone of his U-boat career. With Prien, he had penetrated Scapa Flow where they had sunk the *Royal Oak*. With Prien, he had been fêted throughout Germany, been awarded the Iron Cross Second Class. With Prien, he had suffered the disappointments of the Norwegian campaign. With Prien, he had shared in the phenomenal successes.

Like that fantastic patrol when they had attacked convoy HGF34, sending *Baron Loudun*, *British Monarch* and *Tudor* to the bottom. Two hours later, down went the *Otterpool*. Two days later he torpedoed the tanker *San Fernando*, then the Norwegian *Rondsfjord*. Then it was the turn of *F.B. Goulandris*. On his way home, almost as an afterthought, he sank the *Arandora Star*.

But those successes were with the old torpedoes.

'One day soon, Sir,' his Executive Officer had said on this trip, after the third failure, 'we'll have a torpedo that homes onto the noise of the screws.'

'And that'll go wrong too,' Prien snapped back at him, 'Or some idiot in the *Luftwaffe* will drop one on an English beach like they did with the magnetic mine!'

The English had soon found an answer then – simply degaussed their ships so the mines wouldn't be activated.

Would these vaunted magnetic pistol torpedoes prove to be failures too, Swain wondered, as he watched the hat stop rotating in Prien's hands and the attention of his Captain turn to the second hand of his watch.

'Three minutes,' Prien said at last. 'And no depth-charges. Exec!' he called across to the hydrophone operator, 'Any propeller noise?'

'No, sir.'

'Then we'll have to risk it! Blow tanks! Open vents!'

There was a hissing noise as compressed air forced the water out of the forward ballast tanks. Swain put the hydroplanes to UP. The inclinometer moved from horizontal.

'Two fifty metres . . . two hundred . . .'

'Take her to periscope depth, Chief!'

'Fifty . . . twenty . . .'

Up went the periscope. Seated now, Prien looked into the eyepiece, rotating it round the horizon on the pedals.

'Destroyer's gone!' At least he was pleased about that. 'Surface, Chief!'

'Diving tanks fully blown!' the Engineer Officer reported. 'Conning tower free!'

Prien swung the hatch open and climbed up the ladder. Swain followed.

A fresh north-westerly cooled his hot face. Decorated with white wings of spume, the bows cut through an Atlantic strewn with floating wood and oily debris.

That sight seemed to infuriate Prien even further. 'Not a sign of the convoy! No smoke! Nothing.' He called down the speaking tube. 'Full speed on both diesels! Course zero nine zero!'

An hour later, it began raining. Then mist came down. Visibility sank to less than a mile. Not a sound of screws came over the hydrophones.

Prien's frustration mounted as the weather worsened. When a message from Dönitz he had decoded on the Enigma machine read U47 RETURN TO LORIENT, he was furious.

It was a silent trip home. Off the Ile de Croix they met up in the evening with Schepke, Bleichrodt and Endrass, which didn't improve Prien's mood.

The U-boat crews cleaned up their boats and themselves for the parade into Lorient.

'U47 is going in for an overhaul,' Prien told his crew. 'You'll be getting one week local and three weeks' home leave.'

He had become more cheerful when he had been informed he would lead the flotilla in. On the radio, a great victory was being acclaimed over the convoy with 100,000 tons sunk.

'I'll be going to U-boat HQ at Kerneval to report,' he told Heinrich Swain. 'I'll give them hell on those torpedoes! At the same time I'll remind them how long you've been with me. You deserve your own command. And it's high time you got it!'

The sun was setting in trails of crimson behind Lorient, glowing on the windows of the sea-front cafés and turning the spires into tall black witches' hats, as U47 came home to harbour. Over the calm gilded water, above the soft swish of the wash and the sound of fluttering flags pulsed the majestic beat of *Deutschland Über Alles*.

Head erect, rigidly at attention beside Prien, Swain savoured the sweetness of the homecoming. Closer now, he could see the ranks of uniformed men drawn up below the cranes on the concrete harbour, the dais where Admiral Dönitz waited to greet them, the moving colours of the girls, their arms filled with flowers.

Coming alongside, the girls danced up and down and threw their bouquets. The men cheered so that hundreds of pigeons went winging up over the roof-tops as if part of the triumph display. Glancing up at Prien's face, Swain saw it etched against the skyline like the profile of a god on a Greek coin.

A seductive sense filled Swain of being a super-being himself.

Though not like Prien, a devotee of the new regime, he felt at one with its concept of racial superiority. What other country could have risen like this from the ashes of Versailles, he thought, as following Prien he stepped onto the red carpet and marched up to Dönitz.

Salutes, handshakes, well dones, another medal pinned on Prien's breast. More cheers, more drums, a French girl rushing forward to kiss him on the lips, then another and another.

Then it seemed to dissolve as quickly as it had passed. The sun went down and the streets became shadowy, the glowing windows empty.

He found himself walking the few hundred yards to the *Beau Séjour*, the seaside hotel on the waterfront commandeered for U-boat officers. Though crowds still milled around, he felt a mood of sudden sobriety, almost loneliness. An old woman crouching on a doorstep peeling potatoes muttered something, and a group of men drinking at a pavement café eyed him with that peculiar Breton expression of dumb hatred.

About to walk up the two wide steps to the *Beau Séjour*, Swain glanced to the left.

Suddenly, he had a sudden strange sensation of time spinning backwards. At the far end of the street he saw a straight slender back, and swinging golden hair.

'Alexandra!' He actually said the name aloud. He shoved his attaché case into the commissionaire's hands, and went hurrying down the cobbled street after her.

She had gone, of course. She was no more than a figment of the imagination.

Then, in the quietness, he heard the sound of heels clipping hurriedly away. He saw there was an archway on his right giving onto a passage, which opened out onto another street, and there she was, diminished by distance, her hair unmistakeable in the dusk.

He ran after her, on his toes, quietly, half-ashamed of himself, like a schoolboy. He knew it wasn't Alexandra. He didn't often think of Alexandra. She was part of a different existence. But the figure ahead excited him as she had done.

He was curious to see her face. He knew he would be disappointed. Too often, he had fallen for an attractive pair of legs, or a provocatively held head, or seductive hips, only to find the face cooled all interest. The girl seemed to slow her pace, now quicken it, as if to tantalise him, now down this alley with a glimpse of the sea, now through a narrow passageway stinking of fish at the back of the marketplace. He knew it was risky to walk alone at dusk through this maze, but he had supreme confidence in his own physical strength and the keenness of his senses and he thrived on risk.

At the end of the passageway, she turned left. He followed. She was waiting for him, quite still and quite composed. She looked smaller. Then he saw she had taken off her shoes, and had them clenched in her hands, the high sharp heels, ready to strike him.

She said in rapid French, 'Why are you following me?'

He had no idea what she meant. He had never learned French. He said in German. 'I'm sorry, but I do not understand.'

She frowned. Cool grey eyes stared up at him uncertainly while he stood there, thinking how surprisingly pretty she was, how unlike Alexandra and at the same time how like her. Unlike her because the French girl's face had a certain waif-like thinness, a certain sharpness, and the yellow hair was dyed. Like her because he immediately felt she was special to him.

It seemed quite natural therefore, when the girl obviously didn't understand German, for him to say the same words in English. 'Sorry, but I don't understand.'

She understood that. She looked momentarily wary. Then cautiously, she smiled. His initial judgement that she was special was vindicated. Her smile was charming, slightly crooked, dazzling when it reached the large grey eyes. Yes, she said, she spoke English and in the same breath repeated, 'Why are you following me?'

'Because . . . you reminded me of someone.'

'Of your wife?'

He laughed. 'I haven't got a wife.'

'Your girl?'

He shook his head. 'I have no special girl.'

'You have so many girls?'

'So many that you need not be afraid. You may put on your shoes.'

He proffered his arm for her to balance herself on while she slipped her feet back into the sandals. He found the inadequacy of her protection curiously moving. 'Will you have a drink with me?'

He jerked his head towards the cafés on the waterfront.

'It would not be good for either of us.'

'Then may I walk with you to wherever you were going?'

'If you wish.'

It seemed very strange and yet very desirable to be walking behind her through the narrow streets. She was merely returning home to her little apartment above the *boulangerie*. She lived alone. Yes, he had guessed correctly that she had been to see the U-boats return. She had no love of England. Her eldest brother had been in the French Navy, killed by the British during that treacherous assault at Oran. *Perfide Albion*! Her younger brother was on a cruiser at Toulon.

At the door beside the *boulangerie*, she extended her hand to shake his in farewell, then she seemed to relent.

'Perhaps I may offer you a drink?' she asked with a diffident formality.

The apartment was warm and comfortably furnished. It smelled of freshly baked bread and hot jam. He subsided on the brown over-stuffed sofa and sipped a harsh heady red wine.

Her name, she said, was Suzanne. Under the overhead light with the blackout curtains closed, she looked older than he had first supposed. Late twenties perhaps, but oddly more desirable for that. He pulled her down onto the sofa beside him and kissed her. But that was all. She allowed him to stay for less than an hour. She had to go to bed very early, because she went to work early. She had an important job as an industrial chemist at the Todt Organisation.

'We are building the U-boat shelters,' she said.

'I know.'

Nobody could help but know. The town was crawling with foreigners – Algerians, Africans, Arabs, Poles, Spanish, Italians. Already the thick white concrete walls were showing above the huts of the Base.

'I knew you were clever,' he said, kissing her goodnight, as she pulled him to his feet. 'I like clever women.'

'I am more conscientious than clever,' she corrected.

'And tomorrow after work?' he asked her before she closed the door behind him. 'May I not buy you a drink then?'

She shook her head, hesitated, then said, 'Yes, but here. You may bring some wine. I shall cook you a herb omelette. And you shall stay a little longer.'

He stayed all night. Life had given him many peaks of happiness, and this surely was one of its more splendid ones.

She admired, she told him, the U-boat aces like Prien and Kretschmer and of course himself, more than anyone. It was purely because of her hatred of the British Navy, but he basked in her admiration which was never overdone or cloying. She loved hearing his stories about Prien, how he sank so many ships, and said how honoured most French people were that the aces had made Lorient their Home Base. Lorient had indeed never seemed so much like home as in those warm autumn days.

'The Happy Time' the U-boat men called them.

By the seventh morning of his local leave he had begun to toy with the idea that he was in love with Suzanne. He was thinking of that idea when he returned to the *Beau Séjour* and walked into the almost deserted bar. The solitary occupant at the bar was a middle-aged man sitting quietly and watchfully in the corner. Heinrich was aware of the man's eyes on him as he walked to the counter and ordered a schnapps. So much so that he turned round, whereupon the man raised his glass and said, 'To your good health, Herr Oberleutnant!'

When he had got his schnapps, the middle-aged man stood up and spread his hands. 'Won't you do me the honour of joining me?'

Polite words, politely spoken, so why did they seem an order? Heinrich felt a momentary irritation, but his mood was still benign. The man smiled invitingly and with a shrug, Heinrich took the chair he held out for him.

Close to, the man had light-blue eyes behind metal-rimmed spectacles, cropped pepper-and-salt hair, a heavy jaw and a wide thin mouth. A face to be reckoned with. A policeman's face, perhaps?

Heinrich felt a sudden chill.

'My name is Kauffenstein.' He produced a round metal badge and held it in front of Swain's eyes. 'Fritz Kauffenstein.'

For a moment Swain said nothing. The badge denoted that Kauffenstein was in the *Abwehr*, the German Counter-Espionage Service. At least, thank God, it wasn't the SS, Himmler's men, who, if rumour were correct, were undermining all other organisations, but most of all the *Abwehr*, whose functions they coveted.

'My name's –'

'No need to tell me *your* name, Herr Oberleutnant. You are well known after the *Royal Oak*.'

'Have another drink?'

'Thank you, no. The barman seems to have disappeared anyway.' He smiled. 'But I would like a little talk with you, if that is convenient?'

'Of course.'

Pointedly, Kauffenstein got up, walked to the door of the bar and closed it. Then he returned and sat down opposite Heinrich, his face unsmiling.

'As you will have guessed, it is about this torpedo business.'

Swain nodded.

'The five torpedoes you brought back have now been examined.'

'Were any defective?'

'One was.'

Swain frowned. 'After the Norway fiasco, I thought they had got rid of all that.'

Kauffenstein smiled grimly. 'They had.'

'So why now?'

Kauffenstein stroked his chin. 'There was nothing basically wrong with the torpedo.'

'But you said . . .'

'Defective, I said. This one had been tampered with. Sabotaged.'

Swain felt a twist of mingled anger and apprehension. 'Sabotaged!' he repeated. He cupped his drink in his hand and stared down into it. The one thing every submariner feared. Not the visible enemy, but the treacherous hand. 'How?'

Kauffenstein shrugged apologetically. 'I am no expert. But I understand the explosive in the warhead was neutralised.'

'In what way?'

'I don't know. But I do know it was skilfully done. By the hand of an expert.'

'But how could anyone have access?'

'How indeed! And that, Oberleutnant, is what we intend to find out.' He sighed. 'There are a lot of foreigners in Lorient. Foreign workers . . . but most are of low grade intelligence . . . the men building the U-boat shelters. Arabs. Poles.'

'A Pole?'

'Possibly. The French on the whole are friendly. They don't like the British, especially after Dunkirk and Oran. We have treated the French generously. Our troops have behaved impeccably. Vichy France is pleased with the present arrangements and wish them to continue.' He paused. 'But having said that, sabotage in an occupied country is always possible. Though in this case, we are surprised.'

Swain sipped his drink thoughtfully. 'So the torpedoes that we fired were also defective?'

'Not necessarily. But some, possibly.'

'And what do you want to ask me?'

'Did you notice anything at all before leaving? Anything unusual? However small?'

Swain shook his head. 'It was a normal departure.'

'Think back. *Anything.*'

Swain said slowly, 'The only thing I have noticed is that all the hotel staff can tell you your sailing time before you know it yourself.'

Kauffenstein smiled. 'That's inevitable. So many people are involved in a U-boat departure.' He drew in a deep breath. 'Did you notice anything unusual *after* you'd sailed?'

'*After?* You don't suspect the crew, surely?'

'We have to think of everything.'

'But that's absurd!'

'Yet the spare torpedoes are very available. Men sleep on top of them.'

'They have to, Herr Kauffenstein! There's no bloody room anywhere else!'

'And quite a number of crewmen have torpedo mechanism training?'

'So?'

'Including the officers?'

Swain half rose from his chair. 'Are you suggesting . . ?'

'No, no.' Kauffenstein laid a large hand in restraint on Swain's arm. 'Please. Of course not. My admiration for Kapitänleutnant Prien and his crew is boundless. My enquiries are for your protection. But,' he lowered his voice, 'others are not so clear-sighted. The matter of sabotage is always of great interest to the SS. Their methods are not ours. They find victims, not culprits. One has to walk very carefully, Herr Oberleutnant, very carefully indeed.' He released Swain's arm and pushed back his chair. 'I hear you are getting a command?'

Swain shrugged. 'I have been promised one after my home leave.'

Kauffenstein regarded him carefully. 'Tell me, have you ever considered the disadvantage to a U-boat Commander of having an English name?'

'Mother . . . what would you say if I told you I was thinking of changing my name?'

The following week he had torn himself away from Lorient and caught a train to Hamburg.

He had thought long and carefully about what Kauffenstein had said. When eventually he did get a boat of his own, when eventually he was an ace, would it not sound odd to the German public – an English name?

His mother was overjoyed to see him. She was basking in the reflected glory of his achievements. She had the medal which the Reich gave to all mothers of U-boat men propped against the photograph of his father, and she was keeping a scrap book of newspaper cuttings.

Now they were sitting over the special homecoming supper. The butcher had allowed her a piece of beef. The house was decked with bunting and flowers. The coffee was acorn coffee, but there was brandy to disguise its bitterness. He watched her face over the rim of his glass.

'Your name? Swain, do you mean?'

'Yes.'

'Because it's English? Or because . . .'

'Because it's English.'

She stretched her hand across the table and touched his fingers. 'Have you had trouble, Heinrich?'

'No.' He paused. 'It was suggested to me that I might have trouble. And I think it might hamper me when I get a ship of my own. You know how it is?'

She nodded.

'I know it was like that in Ceylon, wasn't it, Mother? You being a German. Different. So it doesn't just happen here. The British commander who snatched those prisoners from the *Altmark* in Norway, *his* father had to change his name from Battenburg to Mountbatten.'

'So did the British royal family,' his mother said drily. 'From Saxe-Coburg to Windsor. Papa Swain told me.' She smiled across the table fondly.

'And you know, mother, what I will change it to?'

'Yes. To Hartenburg.'

'To my real name. I am Kapitänleutnant Hartenburg's son. A naval man by birth. I wish to be what I am.'

His mother nodded her head several times, her eyes shining. It was a moment of great emotion and gravity. He felt he stood at the crossroads of destiny. Then he remembered his mother.

'And what about *you*, mother? Why not change your name back to Hartenburg, too?'

She shook her head.

'Why not?'

'Because it never was Hartenburg,' she said with a sweet directness.

It was the first time she had confirmed what he really knew. He suddenly remembered four years ago hitting his one-time English friend John Blake because he'd called him a bastard. How angry he had been. How unimportant it seemed now.

'Papa Swain and I were married. Properly and in church. We made our vows. I always try to keep my word. But it is right that you should be called Hartenburg. Just as it is right that I should be called Swain. It is my one link with Papa.'

So the preliminaries to change his name began the next day. He took the train to Berlin and went to see the Central Registrar in person. Things moved fast for U-boat men. He was received with smiling courtesy and told that the necessary paperwork would be completed 'at the speed of lightning'.

Not quite – but almost. Two weeks later, his papers came through. He was no longer Heinrich Swain but Heinrich Hartenburg. He rolled the name round his tongue. He hd been born again. He had gone through a door and emerged a different person in a different, even more successful, landscape.

And as if in confirmation of this, the following morning he received a signal from Headquarters ordering him to report to Neustadt for the short Commander's Course.

Before he left, he wrote to Suzanne. That was the one small cloud on his sunlit horizon. Not seeing her for another six weeks. He told her of his new name and the course and of how much he missed her, how he remembered those sunny days together. He almost told her he loved her. He promised her that he would spend the entire time studying and would get the highest marks.

Like his mother, he had an almost puritanical obsession to keep his word. He received not only the highest marks of the course but the highest for that whole year.

On a cold evening in the middle of February he returned to Lorient – and from the station went straight to the flower market and bought a big bouquet of flowers.

Suzanne had seen him coming from her window, and before he had time to knock, the front door flew open and she flung her arms round his neck.

'Welcome to the Kapitänleutnant,' she cried. 'Welcome to the new Commander of u888!'

He was so excited, he could hardly wait to drink one glass of champagne with her. Saying he'd be back soon, he hurried down the stairs and into the street and tore full pelt to the harbour.

The sky was criss-crossed by searchlights. Every few seconds a bomb went off as the Tommies bombed the new concrete U-boat shelters the Todt Organisation were building.

But he heard nothing and saw nothing. In any case the raid was already petering out. Waving his pass at the sentry on the gate of the Base, he ran down to the wharf.

Schepke's U100 lay under cover beside Endrass's U46. He caught sight of the golden horseshoes painted on Kretschmer's U99, and smiled affectionately at U47, back safely again from patrol.

All the aces were there – and drawn up with them was U888.

His own command! His very own 716-ton U-boat! His new Executive Officer, Oberleutnant Karl Kruger, directing his new crew in stripping down the 4.7 gun!

He shouted across at them. Stopping work, they turned their heads and gazed uncomprehendingly at first at this tall excited figure wearing the brand-new white cap-cover.

Then Kruger summed up the situation. He barked. Men got off their knees, began pouring out of the conning tower. By the time Hartenburg had picked his way over the other boats and reached his command, his whole crew were drawn up on the deck of U888, standing rigidly at attention, and Oberleutnant Kruger stood at the salute.

The new Kapitänleutnant shook hands with each man, memorised their names and their backgrounds. The oldest was Leutnant Fritz Rachman, the Engineer Officer, the youngest were two pink-faced cherubic midshipmen, Sachs and Krancke.

Then, using the conning tower as a pulpit, he addressed them all. They knew, he said, that he came off U47, and now he had his own command, he expected those same standards. Everything would be spotless. Everything would gleam. He expected total loyalty from his crew. In return, he promised them total loyalty and total protection too.

'Only thus can we have success,' he told them. 'And success is what I insist we have!'

The first order he gave was to have a giant jumping shark with ships pouring into its wide open mouth like minnows painted onto the side of the conning tower.

'That insignia has got to be just as famous as Prien's prancing White Bull, understand?'

Everybody did. Everybody worked willingly, Hartenburg had that knack, and he knew how to use it. The crew of U888 spent their time practice-diving, lying doggo on the bottom, firing dummy torpedoes, manoeuvering at high speed, firing the 4.7 at target ships, hosing the drogues towed by Fiesler-Storchs with 20-millimetre anti-aircraft shells, or practising with the escape apparatus.

Nobody got any leave. Nobody even got a night off. And then one Saturday morning, Hartenburg suddenly announced himself 'reasonably satisfied' and everyone – including himself – was given two days' stand-down.

He had worked himself harder than his crew. Not once had he spent the night with Suzanne. On his way to the *boulangerie* he called at a little jewellers in the side street by the market. The proprietor instantly recognised him as a German officer, although he was dressed in flannels and fisherman's sweater. For German officers he brought out little trinkets from under the counter. After that, in the market itself, Hartenburg bought a large bunch of red roses.

Whistling softly to himself, he knocked at the door.

'I hardly recognised you, it is so long,' she frowned, ignoring the roses.

He simply laughed good-humouredly. His crew were proving far better than he had dared hope. He was feeling happy. And he loved Suzanne when she showed her claws a little.

'You know I've been busy.'

'Taking out other girls?'

'No. Licking my new crew into shape.'

She tossed her bright head disbelievingly.

'You know perfectly well that's true.'

'How *could* I know?'

'Everyone in Lorient knows.'

She began to say, 'I am not everyone,' when he pushed forward, grabbed her hand and slipped the gold bracelet he had bought round her narrow wrist. 'I arrest you in the name of the Third Reich.'

She relented then. She stepped back. Up he climbed to the apartment that smelled of warm bread and expensive perfume, and sat down again with his arm around her on the faded brown settee.

'But you have neglected me,' she said, twisting the bracelet round her wrist, her mouth tremulous. 'It is not easy being the friend of a German officer without you also neglecting me.'

'Not willingly, *Liebchen*.'

'Willingly or unwillingly, it is the same.' She drew in her breath. 'But you are not the same.'

'I?' He put both hands on her shoulders and turned her round to face him. 'How am I not the same?'

'Not since you became Kapitänleutnant Hartenburg.' She gazed up at him reproachfully. 'I think Leutnant Swain loved me more.'

'But that's nonsense, *Liebchen*!' He covered her face with kisses, tasted the saltiness of her tears, and for some inexplicable reason felt even happier.

Then Suzanne pulled away from him and went on doggedly, 'With your new name, you have become more . . . more . . .'

For one uncomfortable moment, he thought she was going to say 'German'. But instead, she said, 'Distant. Yes, that is it, distant.'

'I will show you how distant I am,' he said with simulated anger, pulled her to her feet, picked her up and carried her, protesting, through to the bedroom.

He liked it best of all when she was a little angry and sharp and rebellious and he could pretend anger and roughness too. Lying back on the pillows he felt more at peace and happy than he could ever remember.

'Tell me why you are so very happy?' Suzanne asked him, tracing the curved line of his mouth with her fingertip. 'Tell me why?'

He stroked the soft skin of her back. 'I have a good boat. I have a good crew. And I have a good girl.'

She pretended to pout. 'Third. I am third.'

'No.' He cupped her face in his hands and kissed her lips slowly and sensuously. 'You are first to me.'

She caught both his hands, and kissed them. 'And you are first to me. So is U888. It also is first to me. And your crew. For they . . .' her voice trembled with emotion, 'bring you back to me.'

After their simple supper of garlic bread and soup, she recharged their glasses with the harsh heady red wine, raised hers and said softly, 'Let us drink to your crew.'

'Do you want me to name them?' he smiled, with schoolboyish pride.

'Yes, name them.' She touched her breast. 'I will remember them in my heart.'

'And not only can I remember all their names,' he smiled, 'but I know something about each of them. Now Kruger . . .'

She listened to him intently, her beautiful eyes glistening with admiration. He suddenly remembered a favourite biblical quotation of Papa Swain's. 'Better a meal of herbs where love is, than the fatted ox and hatred thereto.'

That simple meal was a truly happy one. The *Coq D'Or* in all its glory could not have provided a better one.

Six days later, Hartenburg was dining at the *Coq D'Or*. But not with Suzanne.

With Varenfordt and Kassel.

It had been Varendfordt's idea. The *Coq D'Or* was where all the aces like Schepke and Endrass went. Having just returned to a tumultuous welcome of flowers and kisses after a five-week patrol off Brazil – during which he had sunk five ships – he was treating Kassel, who was waiting for a boat to be assigned to him, and Hartenburg, who had yet to make his first patrol, with undisguised condescension.

'. . . we came right up to the tanker. Fired at three hundred yards. Couldn't miss . . .'

Hartenburg was on standby and had only consented to come because it was still early in the evening. When Varenfordt wasn't telling them exactly how he sank each of his five ships, he was indulging in some malicious teasing on Heinrich's change of name.

'Hartenburg? I said to the clerk when he told me who was in B41, my favourite room in the *Beau Séjour*, who the hell is Hartenburg? "That's Kapitänleutnant Hartenburg over there, monsieur". And who should he point out but my old friend *der Engländer*! Last time I saw that man, I told him, he had the Olde English name of Swain!'

And then he began talking about what he was going to do on his leave in Paris. 'There is this girl at the *Scheherezade*.' He etched in the air the curves of her body. 'A singer. Beautiful! Black hair, blue eyes.' He paused. 'What about you two? Have you found anything?'

Kassel's fiancée in Munich was well known. Varenfordt showed no surprise when he shook his head. But when Hartenburg did the same, he laughed.

'Engländer, I don't believe it!'

'True.'

'But you're top of the table with the Fräuleins! That little *Engländerin* in Kiel –'

'The one who beat you at sailing, Wolfgang?'

'And so many others too!' Varenfordt pretended to count on his fingers. 'Or are you afraid of consorting with the *mademoiselles*? The Abwehr don't like it, do they? Neither does U-boat Command.' He smiled slyly. 'I'll give you a tip, Heinrich. Reserve such activities for Paris. Everybody does it there. Even the Gestapo!'

From the other side of the restaurant a voice called, 'Wolfgang!' Instantly Varenfordt turned his head.

A handsome fair-haired man was beckoning – the great Schepke, sitting with two lesser aces.

Varenfordt rose. The smile on his face was replaced by a look of admiring obsequiousness. He was being called over, the up-and-coming junior, to join the gods of the profession.

Without a word of excuse, he left their table and went across the floor as though walking on air. Kassel and Hartenburg finished off the champagne, paid the bill and walked back to the *Beau Séjour*.

'Have a drink, Heinrich?' Kassel suggested.

Hartenburg shook his head. 'Bed for me!' He went up the stairs and turned left along the landing to Room 41. The door was open and the chambermaid was putting clean sheets and pillowcases on the cupboard shelf in readiness.

'Pardon, Kapitänleutnant, but you are leaving at five tomorrow morning. And the room must be ready for Kapitänleutnant Kretschmer who will be arriving only fifteen minutes later!'

'Slow astern!'

At five o'clock exactly, U888 slipped her moorings and edged backwards out of the phosphorescent brilliance of the U-boat shelter.

In the dark harbour basin, a minesweeper flashed at her impatiently, for the Tommies had been dropping mines. Still on electric motors, U888 swung round and followed her silently down the Scorff estuary.

Standing on the conning tower, Hartenburg felt that exuberant thrill of excitement. He did not mind that nobody had come to see him off, nor did he mind that his first patrol was a real horror – the sort they gave to the new boys, because no one else wanted them. His five torpedo tubes were filled with mines, and further mines were stacked up fore and aft – thirty-six in all. One slip, one touch of those dreaded snail's horns on the hull and up you'd go, exterminated by your own explosives. On top of that, you could claim no tonnage sunk, since you were never there to see whether any ships had hit your mines.

The crew had been very silent as they loaded the mines through the hatches. Even Kruger looked glum as they flashed goodbye to the minesweeper.

But via the Bay of Biscay, heading westwards, Hartenburg opened and read his sealed orders.

. . . PENETRATE INTO LOUGH FOYLE AND LAY YOUR MINES, CLOSE TO THE BUOYS THAT MARK THE PASSAGE TO THE FOYLE RIVER AND LONDONDERRY . . .

It was a real challenge – a real hair-raiser. True, Dönitz had recognised this and had added that should circumstances be unfavourable, he was not to risk his boat, but was to lay his mines instead in the twelve-mile gate of the North Channel to Liverpool and the Clyde.

'Exec!'

He called Kruger over to confer on their orders. Together they bent over the chart of the waters round north-western Ireland and made their plans.

The trip up the Irish Sea was easy. Hartenburg explained the absence of the patrolling destroyers with, 'They need all their escorts for the Atlantic convoys, Exec.'

Outside the entrance to Lough Foyle, they waited at periscope depth for the prevailing mist the meteorologist had promised and a ship, preferably an ancient merchantman inbound for Londonderry, to take them through the minefield.

Day followed day of glorious sunshine. Mirrored and enticingly enlarged by the periscope, Hartenburg had to let ship after ship pass through into the Lough without taking action. Worse, he also watched big convoys go though the twelve-mile North Channel between Scotland and Ireland, empty westbound for America, or filled with aircraft, tanks, lorries and crates of stores eastbound for Liverpool and the Clyde.

'See how the big ones keep to the middle course,' Hartenburg swung the periscope eyepiece over to Kruger. 'Deepest water there and the gap in their minefield! Look at that liner! Fifteen-thousand tonner! God, if only I had a torpedo!'

But there were other U-boats doing that work. On their fourth night, the sky was alight with red and yellow flames.

'Bet Prien's there!' Hartenburg growled. 'Schepke too. Lucky devils!'

For eight hours that night, U888 shook with depth-charge reverberations and the hydrophone operator took off the set to give his ears a rest from the continuous screaming of ships' screws.

There was another attack on their seventh day – in broad daylight this time, and Hartenburg watched six ships sink. Kruger counted 930 depth-charge explosions.

They were all far away. Nobody bothered. But then as Hartenburg pointed out sourly, U888 wasn't bothering anybody either.

And then on the ninth day – thick mist! They had spent the previous night on the surface, recharging their batteries and fresh air supply and allowing the crew up six at a time to stretch their legs and have a careful smoke.

Four hours after midnight, the black air went white. Droplets of moisture clung to Hartenburg's beard and bedewed his face. But at last he was smiling.

An hour after dawn, the hydrophone operator reported propeller noises. A foghorn started.

Twenty minutes later, a dark woolly mass loomed out of the mist and obligingly kept U888, now following astern, aware of her presence by continuous mournful hooting.

'Torpedo tubes open. Get ready to lay mines.'

The little duet threaded its way through minefields and sandbanks of Magilligan Point and down through the buoyed safe passage.

Every half-minute, there was a hiss of compressed air and a slight plop as a mine was launched from U888 just behind.

'Hard aport!' Hartenburg shouted down to the Coxswain.

They had reached the entrance of the Foyle river. Gravely, Hartenburg saluted their ghostly pathfinder now disappearing into the mist towards Londonderry. 'Thank you, my friend!'

The bows of U888 came right round and steadied on a north-easterly heading.

Slowly on the surface, still on electric motors, U888 crept back the way it had come.

Everyone in U888 held their breath. Eleven U-boats had already been lost minelaying. And now, at any moment, a lookout might spot them and sound the alarm. Even Hartenburg was sweating by the time Kruger called out, 'Last one gone!'

The sun was beginning to burn up the mist. Hartenburg could see the green Irish fields and the headless mass of high mountains. Over on the starboard side, near a tower that Kruger identified from his map as Kilkerry church, there appeared to be an aerodrome. The air shivered with the noise of aircraft engines. And then a big black Whitley lumbered up off the ground and began to climb, not half a mile away and on the same north-easterly course.

'Hasn't seen us, Exec.' Hartenburg kept his binoculars on the gradually retreating aircraft. 'All the same, we'll dive.'

The klaxon sounded the alarm.

'Flood tanks! Periscope depth, Chief!'

The nose dipped. The electric motors hummed.

'Four metres,' the man at the depth indicator called. 'Seven metres.'

'Steady!' Hartenburg was looking through the periscope. 'Hold her there. Full speed on both!'

At seven knots, U888 swished steadily through the water, her mission accomplished, back to the Lough mouth and home.

'Somebody emerging from the river behind us!' Hartenburg reported from the periscope. 'Faster, Chief!'

'Going flat out, sir.'

Hartenburg swivelled the periscope forward. 'Still another ten miles to go!' He looked back to the stern again. 'Couple more ships now. Convoy coming out! Catching us up fast!'

Another twenty minutes passed. Slowly Magilligan Point began to look larger.

'We're going to be all right, Exec. Starboard ten!'

The Coxswain was just turning his wheel and the bows were just beginning to respond when suddenly the boat began rocking.

A second later, a noise like thunder reverberated through the hull.

Hartenburg cursed. 'Leading ship's struck one of our mines! Now we're for it!'

From the hydrophone operator, 'Propeller noises! Destroyers at high speed!'

'Dive!' The periscope came whipping down. 'Take her to the bottom!'

Three men came crashing down on the oily plates of the catwalk as U888 tilted to a forty-degree angle.

The boat shuddered, continued diving.

Boom . . . *boom*.

'A hundred metres!' the man at the depth gauge was saying quite softly when a barrage of depth-charges flung the boat upwards. 'Ninety metres!'

'Faster Chief! Speed! More speed!'

The pings of the Asdic on the hull sounded like shrill death-watch beetles.

'Not far now! Depth?'

'Two hundred metres. Two fifty. Three hundred.'

Another burst of explosions made the steel hull clang like a church bell.

'Five minutes more,' Hartenburg said, 'and we'll be through.'

Kruger was watching the big-sweep second hand on the clock. One minute gone. Two –

'Seem to have stopped depth-charging, Sir,' he was saying, when there was a grinding noise of steel against steel.

U888 turned right over, shuddered, stopped.

All the lights went out. Men, tools, plates, pans everything not strapped down came rattling down like rain. Up from a fractured battery cell came the reek of chlorine.

'Anti-submarine net!' Hartenburg yelled. 'Full speed astern!'

The propellers raced in reverse. Pinioned on the ceiling, Hartenburg could feel a minute movement backwards. The emergency lighting came on. Everyone plugged in to the fresh air supply.

'Hydroplanes, can't you right her?'

'Trying to, sir!'

U888 stopped again.

'Chief, full speed ahead!'

'Batteries are low, sir.'

'You heard me! All the power you've got!'

They lay there, still turned turtle, see-sawing from full ahead to full astern like some vast salmon thrashing in a fisherman's net, trying to break through the steel mesh that now covered them. The scraping noise of the fractured wire, the high hum of the engines, the swish of the filthy water in the bilges, the tinkle of broken glass, oil dripping from leaking tanks, hammered through Hartenburg's head, as backwards and forwards, forwards and backwards, slithering one way, then the other, port, starboard, up, down, U888 fought for her life.

My first patrol as Captain, he was thinking, and my last.

Boom . . . boom . . . boom.

The destroyers had decided to administer the *coup de grâce*.

U888 throbbed, rocked, banged. The scraping noise to and fro, to and fro on the hull reached a crescendo.

And then suddenly as though from a catapult, the U-boat shot forward. She began righting herself, moved forward fast.

'We're through!' Hartenburg shouted.

'Thanks to those destroyers, Sir. They blew a nice hole for us!'

Back right side up again, slipping silently into safety, Hartenburg raised his eyes to the ceiling to where the sound of the propellers was coming. 'Kind of you chaps. Thank you.'

Behind them, the booming of the depth-charges was still going on. But gradually it grew fainter. Euphoria filled the boat. It was then, at the height of their triumph with everyone laughing and cheering, that for Hartenburg the real blow fell.

He had gone to lie down in his cabin, well satisfied, looking forward to some sleep, when the curtains parted.

'Pardon, Sir,' the wireless operator spoke softly so that only he could hear. 'Don't want to disturb you. But you should see this.'

Silently he handed over his Log.

16.10 Control calling U47.

The words looked innocuous enough. Dulled with fatigue, Hartenburg did not comprehend.

Then he looked at his earlier Log entries.

15.40 Control calling U47
14.15 Control calling U47
13.33 Control calling U47

He looked up into the wireless operator's eyes.

'No answer?'

'None, sir.'

Prien! Prien was lost! There were many differing views of Prien. That he was a Nazi. That he was arrogant. That he was cruel to his crew. But there were two views that everyone held: that he was brave and that he was the ace of aces. The U-boat arm was personified, would go down in history in that one fantastic feat at Scapa Flow. And to Heinrich Hartenburg, he was a god. And a god never dies.

It was at that exact moment, a strange juxtaposition which Hartenburg regarded ever afterwards as fated, that he heard further thunder.

Not depth-charges. Not propeller noises of the sort that he had ever heard before.

A new danger, a new assault, a new attack was approaching.

Immediately alert, he leapt from his bunk. He went out to the

Control Room, pushed Kruger away from the periscope, and peered through the eyepiece.

The first thing he saw was a Whitley rising up from that aerodrome he had seen. Such clamour could not come from that insignificant mosquito. Impatiently he swivelled the periscope right round.

Nothing! He could see nothing! Nothing but darkness! A vast chunk of black sky must have dropped into the sea, that was his first thought. But this chunk revealed itself as having two funnels, a sharp prow, lifeboats, and a hull like a vertical cliff.

'The *Queen Elizabeth*!' he whispered to Kruger. 'Christ, Exec, if only I had a torpedo!'

Awestruck, he watched 86,000 tons of liner cut a white swathe past him only yards away.

V JOHN
7 March 1941–23 November 1941

Blake shaded his eyes against the glitter of the sun as the Whitley climbed slowly over Magilligan Point.

He, too, had seen the *Queen Elizabeth*, from this height could still see the long white train of her wake curl north-east into the Clyde. Standing beside him, Bronski remarked, 'What a hell of a target!'

Blake turned the Whitley round Inistrahull and headed westwards towards the slow convoy SC456 at longitude 18 degrees west, unaware of the tiny pin of periscope just below him. 'No U-boat could sink her. Too fast.'

He was thinner than he had been five months ago, when the *Empire Excelsior* hauled him and the other four members of his crew up her rusty flanks. There had been no sign of Pomeroy, no sign of the Whitley. For two days the five of them had huddled in the dinghy, their faces stung by the icy wind, their limbs frozen, living on the Horlicks tablets and chocolate from their survival kits, not really expecting to be picked up.

Surprise rather than excitement had dominated Blake as the ancient ship hove over the horizon. She had heard Orton's SOS, had altered course away from the convoy, had put herself in danger, a defenceless wallowing old Canadian Lake steamer with a maximum speed of eight knots, braving the U-boat-ridden Atlantic.

Cosseted in blankets, filled with rum, Blake felt immense gratitude to the Scots captain and his rugged crew. With that same feeling, he remembered Pomeroy – that arm coming up out of the water holding the dinghy aloft before disappearing for ever. That last vision of him remained through the hours of mountainous seas and roaring winds, as they pitched and rolled their way to Lough Foyle and Londonderry, escorted by Whitleys from the squadron, one of them captained by Fanshawe.

They had given him a week's survivor's leave. A fraught leave, which in retrospect he knew must have been hell for Alexandra.

That was when it all came out. When all the muck that was inside you, spiritually more than physically, got sicked up. His fear, his sorrow for Pomeroy, his guilt about despising him, the sheer strain of what had seemed such a cold, long-drawn-out death, all came rushing out in Alexandra's arms. He had bawled like Maurice.

Christ, but she must have despised him! Yet if she did, she hadn't shown it. She had hugged him to her and wept with him. Ironically, for the first time, his love-making hadn't been clumsy. Perhaps because his need to lose himself in her had been so great.

At 7 Park Road, Maurice, of course, held centre stage. He cut a tooth while Blake was home, which Mrs Monteith celebrated with an extra tot of gin. He was growing into a hefty infant with his father's vivid blue eyes and strong features.

'He gets more like his grandfather every day,' Mrs Monteith said, holding his chubby chin in her fingers to emphasise it. 'He'll be a fighter,' she said, gazing at him fondly as if he was the real hope of Monteith's Reply.

Blake couldn't help feeling that Mrs Monteith regarded his ditching as a poor show. He had been brought down, his Captain killed – she could not accept that a Rolls-Royce engine, and not the enemy had been the killer.

He returned to Kilkerry more determined than ever on revenge.

At least he was now a Captain – taking over Pomeroy's old crew together with a boy of nineteen called Mallory, an ex-bank clerk, straight from General Reconnaissance School. Fortunately, Bronski more than compensated for Mallory's inexperience. The American was the lynchpin of the crew, the right-hand man on whom Blake depended for more than just his navigational skill.

Bronski, with his long nose, his hollow cheeks and mournful eyes, rarely smiled, never cracked jokes, but he exuded a strange lugubrious good cheer. He was quick, deft, and never flapped. He dressed execrably in a greasy flying jacket and a Dodgers sweatshirt, but he never got put on a charge for being improperly dressed, nor even had his attention drawn to King's Regulations. He was a law unto himself.

'Course 272 degrees, Skipper.' Bronski put the change of course slip on the throttle box. 'Estimate patrol area at 16.30.' He caught Blake's eye. 'And I gotta feeling we're gonna see a U-boat!'

They didn't. No one on the squadron saw a U-boat. Still no aircraft had actually sunk a U-boat.

The failure to sink U47, together with his experiences on board the *Empire Excelsior*, made his hate of U-boats even more obsessive. At the same time, he had developed a respect and affection for the British Merchant Marine. Whenever he went on the Liberty Bus to Londonderry, they would go down to the quay and see which ships were in.

His concern for the *Empire Excelsior*, still plugging at eight knots across the Atlantic, still miraculously unscathed, was almost fatherly. Twice he had found her tied up to a bollard, and gone on board and spent the day with Captain Rennock and his crew. At the end of February he had caught sight of the old lady laden with lorries, tucked up in the centre of a slow eastbound convoy being fussed over by an anxious corvette, and had had a chat in flashed morse with her.

That winter the weather worsened. Rain lashed down. Ice slung off the propellers clanged against the metal sides. A Whitley failed to return after reporting a glycol leak. Another hit the mountain above the aerodrome, trying to land in fog.

When Blake wasn't on Operations, he was continuing crew training – firing at drogues towed by Harvards, diving down on targets, dropping practice bombs on British submarines. Since no low-level bombsight existed, haunted by Pomeroy missing U47, Blake trained himself to become extremely accurate, dropping by eyes.

When he wasn't flying, he was down in Intelligence, studying the latest secret reports, U-boat positions from the Submarine Tracking Room. Although the German Enigma Code had not yet been broken, the Navy in Whitehall became adept at collecting information from radio bearings, experience of U-boats' idiosyncracies and reports from the French Resistance operating from Brest, Lorient and La Rochelle.

A windy March turned into a calm April. The Atlantic never looked so bad when the sun was shining. Blake's crew might not have seen any U-boat, but at least their leave was due. On 24 May Blake telephoned Alexandra to say he'd be home at the end of the week, and began packing.

Six hours later, in the middle of the night, he and his crew were called and told to report to the Intelligence Officer.

A flap was on, Flight Lieutenant Tarrant told them. The *Bismarck*, the most powerful battleship in the world, accompanied by the heavy cruiser *Prinz Eugen*, was out in the Atlantic and had already sunk the battleship HMS *Hood*. All available aircraft were being sent off to find her.

An hour later, Whitley A Able took off into pitch darkness.

'What do they expect us to do if we find her?' Mallory asked.

'Why, sink her, baby!' Bronski said. 'Sink her!'

Dawn came just as they started their square search at longitude 18 degrees west. The weather was cloudy with intermittent rain.

'She'll be easy to identify,' Bronski said. 'If we get a contact at fifty miles, that'll be *her*!'

But there was no contact. Nothing but rain and cloud for nine hours. Blake stayed out looking well beyond the limit of his range, landing back at Kilkerry with only five gallons of petrol in his tanks.

'*Bismarck*'s been found now, anyway,' the Intelligence Officer told them, as if he had lost all interest in the search. 'Swordfish have hit her and three battleships and an aircraft carrier are on their way to finish her off.'

He was in a remarkably cheerful mood. Blake soon saw the reason why.

Someone quite different gave Blake his hot cup of post-operation cocoa. This new Intelligence Officer had brown eyes and short dark hair.

'I don't think you've met my new assistant,' Flight Lieutenant Tarrant said. 'Jennifer Jones is going to be a real help to all of us.'

'Wonderful about the *Bismarck*, John!' Mrs Monteith's eyes glistened like sun on sea-water. 'Congratulations!'

Alexandra put her arms around him. Peter patted him on the back and baby Maurice blew bubbles generously all over his face.

Coming back to Oxford for his week's leave, Blake had not expected to receive a welcome that exploded all over him the moment he left the train and slipped out onto the platform.

A taxi took them to lunch at the Randolph Hotel.

'Tell me what you've been doing, John,' said Mrs Monteith. 'Apart from sinking the *Bismarck*.'

'The *Bismarck*,' he mumbled uncomfortably. 'Didn't have anything to do with the *Bismarck*. A Swordfish torpedo got her rudder and *King George V* and *Rodney* finished her off.'

'But you were out looking for her?'

'Oh yes,' he admitted.

'Did you see her?' Peter asked eagerly.

"Fraid not. Saw the ship that rescued us . . . the *Empire Excelsior*. She was in a bit of trouble, so we stayed with her.'

Mrs Monteith regarded that as 'very decent of you, John.'

'What's it really like in a Coastal Squadron?' Peter asked.

'Stop asking such questions, Peter!' Mrs Monteith said. 'John's work is very hush-hush.'

'Have you seen a U-boat?'

'Only on that trip we had to ditch.'

'Did you attack it?'

'Well . . . yes, we did.'

'Did you sink it?'

'Of course he sank it!' Mrs Monteith snapped at her son. 'Don't ask such silly questions!'

The RAF were high in her favour for winning the Battle of Britain, and now she fondly imagined the Navy were winning the Battle of the Atlantic. Peter was clearly earmarked for the Navy, and Mrs Monteith was sure that Alexandra's new baby would also become a Dartmouth recruit.

Blake was very much both the Head of the Family and the Man of the Moment. The sinking of the invincible German battleship had given Mrs Monteith the first paroxysm of pure joy that she had had in this war. The spirit of her revenge was at last beginning to bite.

Number 7 Park Road had welcomed him very much as the Commanding Officer come for inspection. If anything, it was more ship-shape and Bristol-fashion than ever. The chintz on the chairs was spotless. Paintwork gleamed. Not a speck of dust showed itself anywhere. Daffodils and tulips were arranged symmetrically in vases. All the books in height order, stood to attention in the bookcases. From the mantelpiece, even the stern photograph of Captain Monteith appeared to give him a respectful salute.

Up in their bedroom, it was the same, only softer. Alexandra's influence was apparent in the floral matching curtains and bedspread and the pictures on the walls. It was a dainty room, very much a girl's room. The silk and taffeta and cotton of Alexandra's dresses rustled invitingly as he hung his uniform on the same rail of the wardrobe after he had changed. The room smelled of expensive soap and perfume, so different from the dormitory at Kirkstone that the thought suddenly flashed through his mind, 'God, Sackville would go spare if he found us here!'

'Mummy thinks you're no end of a chap.' She said it teasingly – playfully rather than admiringly. None of the adoration that shone out of her mother's eyes shone out of hers. Then, seeing the hurt in his eyes, she added, 'Which of course you are!'

'You don't mean that.'

'But John . . . of course I do!'

Orders had gone out, Blake thought ruefully. He had been placed on a pinnacle. He could do no wrong. It was all epitomised in Mrs Monteith's words that night when they had sat down to dinner after sinking a considerable number of pink gins.

'You take the head of the table, John.'

It was like that throughout his leave. His mother-in-law continually made exaggerated claims of his war prowess to visiting friends. And yet he was grateful to her for boosting his ego. Constitutionally untidy, leaving papers, clothes, books all over the place in this too-neat house, he was aware that they were silently picked up and put away as though by an invisible servant. She asked his opinion, deferred to what he said, organised and made plans for the family, but gave him all the credit.

Alexandra was to take the week off from work, she had said. Neither of them was to do any housework. She would look after Maurice. They were to go out for walks, borrow the car (she had purposely saved up the petrol coupons), enjoy themselves and have a good time.

As a foretaste of what she intended, she produced like the fairy godmother two tickets for the Ball that was being held at the Oxford Assembly Hall that Saturday.

Coming back from that Ball at two in the morning, Blake said, 'I've never had so much fun in my life!'

'Yes, it was fun,' Alexandra agreed cautiously, as if afraid to admit to herself that she had enjoyed it. And in the same breath, 'Don't you have fun in Kilkerry?'

'Fun?'

'Yes, fun, John.' He felt her turn to look at him. 'You don't sit around in the Mess with all the other married bods, do you?'

That was pretty well exactly what he did do. But he was not sure where the conversation was suddenly leading, so he compromised. 'Sometimes.'

'I wouldn't want you to,' she said in a stilted voice. 'It wouldn't be fair. I want you to enjoy yourself, John. To have fun.'

'With other girls?' He tried not to sound like a typical Kirkstone boy, pious and shocked.

'Yes, with other girls.' Gently she mimicked his tone. 'With all that beautiful Irish talent.'

'Why?'

He must have sounded as profoundly miserable as he felt. She caught his hand. 'Because *I* want you to. You deserve some fun.' She tried to laugh lightly and teasingly, 'Don't you and the other bods go popsie-hunting?'

'Painting the town red? Oh, yes!' He did his best to enter into her half-teasing, half-serious banter. 'Every night!'

'With your Kirkstone friends?'

'Nobody's got a steady girl. Fanshawe's got six at the Derry Dance Hall!'

She laughed. Scornfully, it seemed to him, but perhaps he was mistaken. He knew he was inexperienced with girls, a 'real Kirkstone boy' she had once called him with a smile when he had apologised for the clumsiness of his love-making. 'You can't blame Kirkstone altogether,' he had told her. 'I'm clumsy at everything.' And she had kissed him and told him not to be so silly.

Now she was encouraging him to . . . what? Gain experience? Find someone else? Or enjoy himself before he got conveniently killed?

'Anyway, why do you ask?' he demanded truculently.

She seemed taken aback at his tone.

'I've told you, I want you to be happy. I've no right to expect . . . I mean . . . I wouldn't be jealous.'

He grabbed her arm. He wanted to shake her and tell her he wanted her to be jealous, *needed* her to be jealous, to want him. But instead, he gritted his teeth and said nastily, 'So I'm not supposed to be jealous of you?'

She answered in a low voice, 'You have no cause to be.'

But he had cause. He knew that. The incident passed off lightly enough, and they went to bed in each other's arms. Alexandra fell asleep almost immediately, but Blake lay awake for a long time, staring at the black ceiling.

Next day the incident appeared forgotten. They resumed the holiday programme that Mrs Monteith had in mind for them. They bicycled to Binsey. They sat on the same bridge as they had done when she told him about Swain in Germany. They watched the rooks wheeling over the elms, and picked primroses and violets. They went to the cinema, the theatre, dances and picnics together on the river. They visited his old room at Minton and walked in the college gardens. They went to the Radcliffe camera, and sat in seats E32 and E33 where they had studied together, and then went to the café in Carfax where the same silent waitress served them tea and toast.

'It's as though I've never been away at all,' Blake said.

'That's what you'd have really liked, isn't it? Never to have been away at all? To be still an undergraduate at Minton, working for your Finals. Instead of being made *paterfamilias* by me and having it rubbed in all the time by Mummy?'

'Marrying you was the best thing I ever did.'

'But –'

'But nothing! I've always wanted you more than anyone else in the world.'

She sighed. 'You've never had a chance.'

'To what?'

'To sow your wild oats! Have fun!'

He said wryly, 'I doubt I'd recognise a wild oat. But being with you is *my* fun.'

She persisted. 'To be shot straight from Kirkstone into an errant girl's bed with someone else's son tagged on –'

'That's nonsense.'

'– and a mother-in-law like Mummy.'

'But she's sweet! She's good for me!'

'Sweet? I wouldn't call her that. Steely, more like.' She suddenly covered her face with her hands. 'No, I didn't mean that. Not really. She's been marvellous! She *is* marvellous! She's brave and determined. She's done so much. And she looks after Maurice so well.'

'She loves him.'

'Oh, yes, I know! Too much.'

'Too much?'

'She expects too much of him. We have our rows. Inevitably, I suppose.' She paused. 'Of course the last person I should blame is Mummy. I couldn't take my degree without her. She's more a mother to Maurice than I am. The trouble is, she's working out something inside herself. She's got a complex.'

'We're all working out something. We've all got a complex.'

'Oh, John, not you!'

The name Swain had not come up during the whole leave. Nor had the name of Prien. That very omission, the studied avoidance of both names by everybody, had somehow underlined the real complex of them all.

'My dears, the most splendid news!'

The moment they had walked through the door, dripping wet, Mrs Monteith had fallen on them with delighted glee.

'It's been on the radio! Maurice and I heard it, didn't we, Maurice?'

Bewildered, the little boy looked up at her and stuck his thumb in his mouth, only to have it removed forcibly by his grandmother.

'But we're not going to tell them, are we, Maurice? They're going to have to wait until the six o'clock news!'

Up in their bedroom, as Blake changed his trousers and Alexandra her stockings, he asked her, 'What d'you suppose it is? That the war's over?'

'That the butter ration is going up by an ounce a week, more like. Mummy likes to celebrate the smallest thing.'

'I think it's rather more than that.'

When they came downstairs again, an air of expectant excitement hung over the lounge. Maurice had been given a quick bath and was perched on the tuffet, with his dressing gown over his pyjamas. Peter had come in from school and was sitting on the sofa, listening to Tommy Handley in *ITMA* on the radio. On a silver tray on the side table was a bottle of champagne in an ice bucket, a jug of orange juice and five glasses.

Tommy Handley made another quip. Mrs Mopp came in to ask, 'Can I do you now, sir?' The show faded out into studio laughter. Then Stewart Hibberd announced, 'This is the six o'clock news.'

'It'll be the first item,' said Mrs Monteith, reaching for the champagne bottle. 'Bound to be!'

The unhurried voice on the radio began calmly. It was something about the Battle of the Atlantic. They've probably got the *Scharnhorst*, Blake was thinking.

'. . . the news had been kept from the Germans for over two months, but has at last been released. Seven days before the ace Joachim Schepke in U100 was rammed and sunk by HMS *Walker* and the ace Otto Kretschmer captured from the sinking U99, another U-boat was sunk by the destroyers *Wolverine* and *Verity*. This was none other than –'

'Wait for it.' said Mrs Monteith, as the cork exploded from the champagne bottle and shot across the room.

'– Gunther Prien in u47. As the German press release put it, "The hero of Scapa Flow" has made his last patrol.'

Mrs Monteith was going round with the glasses, her grey eyes blazing. 'Prien's last patrol! That was worth waiting for, wasn't it? Here Alexandra, take this glass! That's yours, John. Peter . . . and that orange juice is for you, Maurice.'

Alexandra had gone deathly white. Peter was grinning. Maurice was switching his gaze from one adult to another as the radio voice announced that these three men had between them destroyed three-quarters of a million tons of shipping, and that Prien had sunk the battleship *Royal Oak*.

'And now we have been avenged!' Mrs Monteith raised her glass on high. '*Nemo me impune lacessit! To the death of those who harm us!*'

The glitter in her eyes, the high note of her voice shivered through the room. Then Maurice knocked over his glass and broke the stem. Orange juice poured over the carpet. Mrs Monteith was scolding him for being clumsy at the same time as Alexandra, her champagne untouched, searched his plump little hand for glass fragments.

Screaming and kicking, he was carried upstairs by Alexandra, with Mrs Monteith hurling warnings at him that 'Babies don't join the Navy!'

Things quietened then. Alexandra stayed up with Maurice, while the other three had dinner. Another bottle of champagne was produced. Blake said very little. Mrs Monteith and Peter kept up a continuous flow of exultant congratulations.

Alexandra called downstairs that she had a headache and was going to bed.

'She's tired, John,' said Mrs Monteith. 'Overwrought. The excitement has been too much for her.'

'I'll go up to her.'

'Good boy! Do that!' Mrs Monteith smiled at him as he left the table. 'Goodnight, John.'

'Goodnight, Mrs Monteith. Goodnight, Peter.'

Blake did not immediately go to their room. He went into the nursery and looked down at the sleeping infant. He leaned over and touched Maurice's flushed cheek. The baby stirred, opened his eyes, staring trustingly up at him. Blake felt a sudden protectiveness. Clumsily, he tucked the blanket round Maurice and tip-toed across the landing.

Alexandra was already in bed, her eyes closed. He undressed in the dark and climbed in beside her. She lay quite still, her breathing regular and quiet. She's asleep, he thought. He put out a hand and lightly touched her bare shoulder. She didn't stir. Fast asleep. Best thing for her. Her sleep seemed dreamless and unhaunted. But Prien's death must have opened up old wounds. She had loved her father, but she lacked her mother's vengeful spirit and would be unable to rejoice in Prien's last patrol.

As for Swain . . . she had got over him a long time ago, hadn't she? His death would make the end of that affair more final, wouldn't it? Just as his death had ended any hatred he himself had felt towards Swain.

Lying in bed, staring up at the darkened ceiling, he even felt pity towards Swain – the clever chap who'd lost everything in the end – Alexandra, his hope of fame, his life itself. Game, set and match, as Mrs Monteith would say.

It wasn't poor John any more. It was poor Henry.

He settled over on his left side and closed his eyes. But he couldn't sleep. He kept thinking about his leave, about going back to the squadron in the morning, about Alexandra, about Swain. Memories of the past, sharp and clear as the splinters of that broken glass, lodged painfully in his mind. He heard Mrs Monteith and Peter come up and go to bed. He heard the grandfather clock in the hall strike midnight, one o'clock, two.

Then he heard a softer, scarcely audible sound just behind him.

Quietly, with all the impenetrable containment of a disciplined but despairing child, Alexandra was crying.

John Blake returned to Kilkerry in a sombre mood.

He couldn't have analysed it, even if he'd tried, which he refused to do because he didn't want to think. Thinking about Alexandra and Swain was like touching something raw, a piece of burned skinned flesh. And thinking about Swain dead was worse than thinking about Swain alive. So you couldn't win anyway. As with the bods of the Squadron, when they were dead, you remembered what good types they were, and he certainly didn't want to remember anything good about Swain.

So instead of thinking, he stared out at the approaches to Liverpool and felt his sombre mood darken into downright gloom.

It was a dull overcast day, and Liverpool had been bombed the night before. Smoke still drifted over the city. The smell of rubble and leaking gas drifted in through the half-open window of the compartment.

As the train clanked past mean little streets razed to the ground, past piles of rubble over which ARP wardens and firemen were still crawling, Blake missed having Henry Swain to hate for it all.

He stared at a tram car lying on its side, the tracks simply wrenched up in front of it, at a shattered cinema, at half a house, its pink papered stairway leading nowhere. Nameless Huns weren't therapeutic enough to hate for it, though he did mutter, 'Bastards!' and an Army Major sitting opposite said, 'Amen to that!'

Like Blake, the Army Major was embarking at Liverpool, but for an unspecified destination. He'd left a family behind in London. He'd spent most of his leave down the shelter. Blake commiserated with him as one *paterfamilias* to another.

Leaving the train, their transport had a tedious time getting to the docks. A street was closed for an unexploded landmine, so they'd had to go round the houses, or what remained of them.

The last Blake saw of his railway companion was marching off towards a small ship close to the Belfast ferry. Blake hoped for the Major's sake that it was going to keep out of U-boat waters.

To add insult to injury, they had a scare on the crossing. Half an hour out of Liverpool, a bustling little tug came right across their bows and signalled *follow me*. Nothing was announced, but the rumour went around that a U-boat had been sighted. Apparently it had dived, and no one knew where the hell it was.

Wherever it was, if it did nothing else, it succeeded in making the entire saloon aboard the ferry as sick as dogs while she weaved and took evasive action all the rest of the way.

After an interminable train journey, Blake tottered into the Mess at Kilkerry and ordered himself a large brandy. The bar was half-empty. Most of the squadron had gone in to the bright lights on the Liberty bus. A few groups of ground staff loitered over their drinks. The Station Administrative Officer was propped up at the bar with the Station Adjutant. The Roman Catholic Padre and the Church of England Padre were sitting at a table, apparently seeing who could down the most Guinness.

Then at a table just beyond them Blake spotted the new WAAF Intelligence Officer drinking a modest coffee with the horse-faced Signals Officer, Flight Lieutenant Kenny. She didn't seem to be enjoying herself very much and immediately Blake thought, why not?

He made his way over, carrying his glass, and said boldly, 'Let me get you a brandy to help you swallow that muck!'

They both looked up at him. Kenny had a laugh to match his face. 'That's very friendly of you,' he exclaimed.

'Very,' the girl said drily.

Blake flushed. 'That's if I'm not interrupting?'

'Certainly not,' Kenny said. 'I was just boring Jennifer with shop.'

She shook her head. Her dark hair shimmered as if freshly washed, and when she shook her head, he smelled the soapy fragrance of shampoo.

'He wasn't boring me at all,' she said briskly. 'But do come and sit down. You look as if you could do with that brandy. And the coffee's hot. I'll go and fetch you one.'

'She's a grand lass. A real good type.' Kenny watched her as she moved over to the urn. 'She's married though.'

'So am I.'

'Husband's a prisoner of war.'

'Poor girl.'

'She takes it all very well though.'

'My ears were burning,' Jennifer said, returning and setting the cup in front of him.

'All very complimentary,' Kenny laughed, draining his brandy and looking at his watch. 'Well, I must love you and leave you. The wife likes a phone call at this hour of the day.'

He patted them both on the shoulder as he went.

They sat in silence for a moment.

'So how was leave?' Jennifer asked, resting her brown eyes on his face, as if she really minded what sort of leave he had had.

'So-so.'

'You didn't enjoy it?'

'I did and I didn't.'

'That sounds typically male,' she laughed. 'Don't tell me you're glad to be back? Or are you going to say I am and I'm not?'

'You took the very words out of my mouth.'

They both laughed. She had a nice mouth and even teeth, and in a quiet way she made him feel good. He found himself telling her about his leave, about Mrs Monteith, about Alexandra (although only the superficialities), about Maurice, about Oxford, about his anger at seeing Liverpool.

She was a good listener. Perhaps it was because of her job, but he thought it was also part of her personality. He ended up by asking her, 'Has anything much been happening while I've been away?'

She shook her head from side to side and said wryly, 'It has and it hasn't.'

He began to laugh and then saw the expression in her dark eyes. 'Tell me.'

She took a sip of her brandy. 'Well, I'll tell you the bad news first. Richardson and Hardaker have gone.'

'How?'

She shrugged. 'Just disappeared.'

'Any signal?'

'Some wreckage was washed up from Hardaker's kite. Nothing from Richardson's.'

'Has there been much action?'

'Several convoy patrols.'

'Uneventful?'

'Scarecrow mainly. Fanshawe attacked a U-boat.'

'Confirmed?'

'No. And he got shot up in the process.'

She stared gravely into her drink, her bobbed hair falling forward in dark curves over her cheeks.

'Have you come to the end of the bad news?'

She looked up. 'Oh, yes. Sorry. I was thinking.'

'Don't apologise. I'm just eager for the good news.'

'Well, it isn't very much really,' she shrugged, and went on lamely. 'But it seems that the tide's turning.'

His face fell. 'You could fool me,' he said irritably.

'It's all very hush-hush.'

'Yes, I've heard that before too.'

She glanced round the Mess thoughtfully. She looked at her watch. Then she leaned across the table.

'Look.' She spoke softly. 'It's time I got back to the Waafery anyway. Would you like to walk me as far as the door?'

'If you'd like me to.' He looked at her suspiciously. He was not at all sure that he wanted to walk the half-mile and back to the requisitioned Rectory that was the WAAF Officer's Mess, but anything to relieve the feeling of gloom that his leave had left him with.

He drained his glass and stood up. Together they walked out into the corridor. A young RAF Regiment officer wolf-whistled after them. Blake scowled at him over his shoulder.

In the corridor, they unhooked their peaked caps and slung their respirators, unlikely accompaniments to any seduction Blake thought, still scowling. Then they crossed the hall, negotiated the blackout trap and stepped out into a mild still overcast night.

The WAAF Officers' Mess was outside the camp proper, down a country road just beyond the church. They had to pass the guardroom. The Station Police on duty raised the gate and saluted. Mrs Jones, as a Section Officer and his senior, returned the salute.

The Station Police called, 'Goodnight, Ma'am. Goodnight, Sir.'

They walked a quarter of a mile down the road before she spoke. 'I shouldn't really be telling you this. But I don't see why you shouldn't know. It's your neck you're risking.'

'You can say that again.'

'We've only been told a tiny bit. A fraction of the story.' She fixed her eyes on the spire of All Saints now visible above the dark scalloping of the surrounding woods. 'But I have a friend who was on the course with me and she's at BP.'

The secret initials for the secret Bletchley Park decoding centre. Blake felt a tingle of excitement. For the first time he began to believe that she really had some good news to impart.

'The Navy have captured from U110 an Enigma machine. All intact. Code book and all. From now on, we can read their messages.' She drew in her breath. 'The tide *will* turn now. The U-boats' Happy Time really is over.'

'You say it with real feeling,' he said aloud. To himself he added, 'Almost as if you had a Heinrich Swain to hate.'

'Of course I do,' she said. 'I've got a husband. I want him back.'

She suddenly burst into tears. Though whether because she wanted her husband back or because of the enormity of repeating Top Secret information even to him, he didn't know.

Nor did he care. He put his arms around her and kissed her.

Their respirators banged and bumped between them like a couple of chastity belts.

Just as well, he thought, releasing her and walking her staidly to the door of the Rectory, kissing her once more on the tip of her nose, swearing that nothing would make him repeat that information to anyone.

But he made a date to take her out to dinner the following evening.

The following evening, Jennifer seemed ashamed of both her tears and the date. They left for Kilkerry on the Liberty bus, hardly speaking, as if conscious that they ought not to be doing what they were. Or as if they knew they might be starting something.

'I'm sorry about last night,' she said abruptly, as the bus rumbled over the Kerry bridge. 'I'm not usually the weepy type.'

'Of course you're not.' He patted her hand. He thought, again, as he had thought wryly last night, first Alexandra's tears, now Jennifer's. He seemed to have a helluva knack of inspiring girls' tears. For other men.

'It's only natural,' he said vaguely. And when she didn't answer, 'Not sorry you came tonight though, are you?'

She shook her head, 'No. I wanted to come.'

He felt immediately more cheerful. The evening was fine and the sun had not yet set. He suggested that before they went along to the Blathwaite Arms for dinner, they should have a drink at the Ferryboat Inn, and sit out on the terrace.

It was a mistake. Watching the slowly moving river reminded him of Oxford and Alexandra, and secondly, they were late at the Blathwaite Arms and had to wait ages for a table, which meant they would have to hurry to catch the last Liberty bus back.

But Jennifer was patient and sweet, and he warmed to her for it, and that was a mistake too.

'I'm not good at arrangements.' He shot an apologetic look across the candle-lit table at her when finally they were settled in.

'Well, you're good at other things.'

'Such as what?'

'Flying.'

'I'm afraid my instructors would not agree.'

'At least they've survived to disagree,' she laughed.

'True.'

'And you're good,' she said, studying the menu which the waiter handed her, 'at making other people feel good.'

It was the nicest compliment anyone had ever paid him. He didn't know how to reply to it. He studied the menu in his turn, hiding behind it for a moment or two, half embarrassed, half delighted. When he did get around to thinking about food, he found that most of the items had been crossed out. But at least in Ireland you could always rely on getting a good thick steak with all the trimmings. He attacked his, when it came, with enthusiasm. Certainly if he was good at making other people feel good, Jennifer was even better.

He ate in silence, comforted and contented. From time to time he looked up from his plate to find her eyes fixed on him in a curiously kindly and indulgent stare.

'I was hungry,' he said, pushing away his plate.

'So I saw.' She laughed. 'There's nothing nicer than seeing someone eat when they're hungry. One evening, you must come round to the Waafery. We've got our own kitchen. I'll cook you supper.'

'Will you? I can't wait. Are you a good cook?'

'Not bad.'

From that, she went on to tell him about cooking for her husband, Peter, so perhaps the invitation was partly a lead-in to remind him of the husband in the background. He was taken prisoner at Dunkirk, she said, in the Gloucester Yeomanry. That was where they both came from. Filton, near Bristol. He worked in a shipping office in Bristol – nothing very glamorous. But he was glamorous. Her tone became assertive as she said that, as if Blake had made some derogatory comment, which he certainly wouldn't have dreamed of. She herself worked at Filton. In the Bristol Aircraft design office. She and Peter had married when they were both twenty-three.

'I beat you. I married at twenty.'

'Twenty?' She looked doubtful and worried.

'Go on.' Blake smiled. 'Say it. I don't mind. Baby-snatching.'

She shook her head. 'I wasn't going to say that at all.'

'What were you going to say?'

She simply asked, 'How long ago?'

'Oh, nearly two years. We have a son.'

'That's wonderful.' Her eyes shone. 'Have you got a photo of him?'

'No.' He shook his head. He had never thought to take a photo of Maurice, let alone carry it around with him. He supposed that said a lot about him. And nothing very favourable either.

'You're just about the first father I know who doesn't.' She shook her head smiling. 'So that makes you twenty-two.'

'Yes.'

'I'm twenty-six.'

She said it so gravely that he laughed. 'And you're still able to get around, old lady?'

She laughed. 'With a stick.' She stopped laughing and eyed him seriously. 'But that makes me older.'

'Yes. I can do my arithmetic.'

'And wiser.'

He knew exactly what she was saying. She was saying, if ever I think we should call a halt to this, I must have my way.

'All right,' he said and lifted his glass.

But the days went by and she didn't call a halt. They were quiet summer days of delusory calm. Perhaps Enigma's capture was turning the tide. The squadron sorties were mostly scarecrow patrols. Blake criss-crossed the Black Pit. He flew up to Iceland. He went backwards and forwards over convoys. He collected several bullet holes from the Navy, but he only once saw a conning tower, and though he dropped depth-charges and reported its position, it vanished, and nothing disturbed or marked the waves around it.

Occasionally, he was debriefed by Jennifer. She was very efficient and clear-sighted. Occasionally, even when he was off-duty and she was on, he went over to Intelligence and sat drinking coffee with her till the returning patrols came in.

Whenever they could, they dined at the Blathwaite Arms. It had become their place. They had their favourite table and their favourite waiter, who was an elderly chap with flat feet, from Ballykelly. And when, at the end of September, the sun was hot, they took a picnic to the lake and swam in the deep icy water. They lay naked on the warm springy heather of the bank and made love. It seemed natural, unconstrained, inevitable at the time.

But it also seemed like a judgement from heaven when the next day a signal came through posting Blake to the Scientific Research Unit which experimented with secret anti-U-boat devices.

The RAF never allowed anyone to hang around. No sooner posted than you were off. Reporting date was in forty-eight hours.

So this time when they went to the Blathwaite Arms it was a farewell dinner, and a sad and guilty one.

'I shouldn't have . . .' Jennifer began, twisting her fingers round the stem of her wine glass.

'Yes! You should!' Blake said. 'We both knew what we were doing. And I'm glad. Very glad.' He paused. 'Will you write to me?'

She hesitated.

'Please. I shall miss you.'

'You'll be too busy,' she said. 'Much too busy. I remember you saying you'd like to go to a Research Unit. To gen up on sinking U-boats.' She smiled wryly. 'To get on with the war.'

'That was a long time ago. Before . . .' he stretched his hand across the table and touched her fingertips. 'Before I met you . . .' He didn't finish the sentence. Instead he added, 'And I'd rather get on with the war from here.'

'But I'm bound to be posted from here. Nothing ever stays the same for long, does it?'

He thought about that for a while. 'Well, I hope it's within striking distance of me if you do get posted.'

After a long pause she said she hoped that too. And when he kissed her goodnight, she promised she would write.

But packing his bags that night, he knew he should have let that be the end. He was ashamed of allowing the relationship to get as far as it had done. He lay awake for a long time pondering on that and many other things. He thought bitterly of a favourite saying of his mother's, 'The Lord provides you with all you want when you have ceased to want it.'

To his mother that meant, only when you have overcome your desires will God allow you to have them. But to Blake it meant the sheer perversity of the Almighty, the ashes to which He could turn the most desirable gift. Certainly Blake had wanted to go to the Scientific Research Unit, had wanted to make himself the king-pin, *the* U-boat hunter. But that had been when Henry Swain was still alive, when every U-boat he hunted was potentially Henry Swain's and before Jennifer.

He wondered ironically if the Lord might consider giving him Alexandra's love if he could ever cease to want it.

And on that sour note he drifted off to sleep. He dreamed he was already at SRU, testing their wonderful listening devices and their acoustic torpedoes and their Leigh Lights and strange magical gubbins, and flying their Very Long Range four-engined American Liberators.

But all of them were absolutely useless against a huge black impregnable submarine, on the conning tower of which was the triumphant face of Henry Swain.

VI HEINRICH
23 November 1941–July 1942

Chained to the conning tower rails, Heinrich Hartenburg rubbed the salt spray off his bearded face, screwed up his eyes and stared into the Atlantic mist.

An aircraft? A ghost? Or just a fragment of cloud?

Imagination more like, heightened by three days without sleep. Three days of being drenched to the skin, three days of icy wind tearing through his rubber suit and his layers of woollen sweaters.

Another great green wave came arching over the four men. About to close his eyes against the silent torrent, he suddenly saw the white blob was crystallising into a long thin wing on which were four big engines.

'Aircraft!' he screamed. 'Clear the tower! Diving alarms!'

U888 was vibrating with clanging bells as the Watch slithered into the Control Room. Last down, Hartenburg slammed the hatch shut.

Already the roar of the diesels had been replaced by the hum of the electrics. Bow and stern hydroplanes had been put to full dive. Men were wrenching open the valve levers of the diving tanks, calling out 'Five, four, three, two' as water poured in to the forward four tanks.

'Diving angle . . . thirty degrees!' called the man on the depth gauge.

Hartenburg stood with his arms folded, watching his crew carry out perfectly their much practised drill.

U888 took sixty seconds to dive. Nineteen had gone. For the next half-minute the boat would be at her most vulnerable.

Thirty seconds gone.

Now that all the vital actions had been done, the crew silently waited.

No one moved. No one seemed to breathe.

Consciously and slowly, Hartenburg controlled his own breathing. That way his heart held its steady rhythm. He studied the men cramped round him. Each had his own way of reacting to the approaching danger. Chief Petty Officer Brandt, the oldest man on board, held his head rigidly high, his shoulders squared, jaw out-thrust. The youngest midshipman's eyes had started blinking un-controllably. Kruger held his hands clasped in front of him as if he might be praying. The telegraphist's eyes were tightly closed.

The motors made so little noise, Hartenburg could almost hear the hammering of their hearts. Certainly he could smell the fear in their sweat, like the smell that hung over a fox's corpse. Round and round in his mind was going the knowledge that the Tommies were now using long-range four-engined aircraft. No U-boat had ever been attacked in the Black Pit before, so far out in the Atlantic.

Now he began to wonder what his crew were thinking. His own brain still continued to function with icy calm. He was known now as the iron man of U-boats. He was too hard, some people said. Suzanne complained that he was colder and more silent, though that was nonsense, as he had very soon shown her. It was natural and inevitable that his stays in Lorient were much shorter.

Forty-five seconds.

They were calling him the second Prien. He wore his hat at the same angle Prien wore his. He smiled that same rather superior smile. He had expressed a well-publicised ambition to sink the *Queen Elizabeth* – the subject of numerous newspaper articles and a favourite topic of Lord Haw-Haw.

He had sunk 60,000 tons already. Not quite as much as Varenfordt in his crown-emblazoned U181 – which was why he was always so eager to take the silver shark out hunting in the Atlantic again.

'Why?' Suzanne had asked him last Sunday. 'Why are you so anxious to go away from me?'

He had tried to explain something of the passion he had for his ship. However warm and snug on shore, he longed for the bass of the diesels, the softer sound of the electrics, the vibration through the soles of his feet, the smell of oil, the sudden excitement of smoke on the horizon, the hiss of compressed air as the torpedoes fired, the boom of a hit. He needed his feeling of power, that male cocoon of sweat and toil and fear, of discipline and brotherhood. He tried to explain to her that discomfort – the deck swilling with water, the overpowering heat and the stench of rotting vegetables, the conden-sation dripping down one's back – were as much a part of it as the thrill of stalking and hunting, the fear and excitement of being hunted, the pitting of wits of man against man.

'And when the Tommies have you cornered and the depth-charges come, do you also like them?' she had asked drily.

Fifty seconds . . .

Boom.

u888 rocked. All the lights went out. The hull shook and vibrated throughout its length, the stanchions and bulkheads creaked and whistled.

Boom . . . Boom.

The boat tipped right over, hissing with the sounds of escaping water. Men overbalanced, crashed onto the steel floor and slid along the oily catwalks.

Boom . . . Boom.

Emergency lighting revealed instruments smashed. Indicators were hanging half-suspended. Water was gushing out of a hundred pipeline leaks.

No more explosions. The aircraft had dropped its load.

The depth indicator was working – that was something. 150 feet.

'Level off,' Hartenburg ordered. 'Close all vents.'

The hydroplanes were adjusted on the big wheels till the spirit level showed steady on the trimming panel.

'Full speed.'

The hum became quieter.

'Full right rudder.'

Better to get the hell out of here. The aircraft could have sent a sighting report.

He turned to the Engineer. 'Damage Control, Chief. Check all compartments. Then bring me the report.'

As he made his way over the broken glass and debris to his tiny cabin, he could smell the reek of chlorine. Some battery cells are gone, he thought, I hope they're not going to gas us out completely. But aloud he simply said, 'Tell everyone to plug in to their oxygen.'

Thirty minutes later, the Chief came in to the cabin to hand in his Damage Report. 'We'll have to return to Lorient, Sir.'

The report certainly made grim reading. One of the bilge pumps gone. Compass cracked. Leaks in both oil and water pipes. Cracks in twenty battery cells and battery fluid sloshing round in the bilges. One of the diesel driving shafts twisted.

The damage was reported to Control. Back came Papa Dönitz's reply PROCEED. REMEMBER . . . I NEVER DESERT A U-BOAT.

'Nor does he,' Hartenburg said when Kruger showed him the signal. 'We'll be all right, Papa will see to that.'

The Chief looked aghast at being told to do makeshift repairs, but he was old enough and experienced enough and wise enough not to argue with a Captain like Hartenburg.

The air still reeked of chlorine. Water and condensation dripped down on sweating faces. The boat resounded with the clanging of hammers, drills, the tinkle of tools, feet slipping and sliding and men swearing.

When dusk fell, Hartenburg surfaced and let the cold air pour into the boat through the open conning tower hatch while the men went up on deck in turns. Then he gave orders to the cooks to dish out their favourite supper – beef soup and strawberries.

At midnight, the men were happily singing *Lili Marlene* to the accompaniment of the senior ERA on his accordion while u888, her interior still reeking of chlorine, many of her gauges still needleless, her starboard diesel crankshaft still groaning and wobbling, hobbled eagerly westwards through mountainous seas to join the Raubgraf Pack towards which – according to the message from Papa Dönitz which Hartenburg had deciphered on his Commander's Enigma machine – two large convoys were slowly but surely making their way.

'Tubes one to four ready, sir!'

Hartenburg gave a curt nod to the Torpedo Officer as he moved the periscope fractionally to port, trying to keep the dark shape ahead in the centre of the crosswires.

'*Verflucht!*'

Pitch black outside now. That wretched moon kept disappearing behind a bank of cloud! The temporary repairs were holding, but the boat was difficult to manoeuvre. The line of ships which had earlier been illuminated now disappeared.

u888 was running in the centre of the convoy at periscope depth. 'Real pickings here,' he had told his Executive Officer. 'Sixty ships at least!'

Varenfordt was also here in u181 – that was the trouble. Message after message had come over the radio from Kerneval as Dönitz positioned the Raubgraf Pack.

'Go in and sink!' had been his last order. The eleven captains had simply acknowledged – all except Varenfordt who had added, '*Heil Hitler*'.

'Damn!'

Darker than ever. Be hitting one of the ships next.

Not a sign of a light. Not a glimmer. Nothing!

Surely they must have realised there were U-boats around? What about their famous Asdic? Why didn't they oblige with star-shells and Snowflakes?

A light! A ship on fire in the centre of the column.

Searchlights, white tracer, yellow shell bursts. A Snowflake flare going up.

Immediately the dark shape reappeared in the periscope lens. A tanker. Beautifully close.

'Target central!' he yelled. 'Attack sight on!'

'Target Red 45, speed 8 knots, range 1,000 metres, torpedo speed 35 knots.' The Torpedo Officer linked the attack table to the gyro compass and attack sight. As the computer electrically transmitted the computed gyro angle to the torpedo, two red lamps went out, replaced by one green light.

'Fire at 500 metres.'

The tanker was still squarely in the sights. A ten-thousand-tonner at least!

The Torpedo Officer's order, 'Stand by to fire!' echoed throughout the boat.

As he waited for the range to close, Hartenburg felt the familiar, almost unbearable excitement. The excitement was far harder to control than fear. And he had to get everything exactly right. He mustn't miss. Missing meant losing face with his crew, losing out in the sinkings table to Varenfordt . . .

He pressed the button. 'Fire one!'

As the order boomed out over the loudspeaker system there was a hiss from the compressed air that fired the torpedo. U888 gave a little shiver.

The Torpedo Officer was watching the second hand on the clock. In the firelight thrown from the burning ship, Hartenburg could see the white slit moving forward over the moonlit sea.

Water cascaded up from the bow. *Boom!*

One to him. And with only one torpedo!

A ship blew up to starboard. Two more on fire. Destroyers

circling furiously, dropping depth-charges. He caught a sudden sight of a U-boat on the surface illuminated in a searchlight.

The familiar game had begun.

It went on for three hours before Dönitz ordered his Wolf Pack off, leaving only Kassel to shadow the remains of the convoy in UII.

With his sixteen torpedoes expended, Hartenburg had withdrawn to watch the battle on the surface from a safe distance and await further orders.

The weather had moderated. It was going to be a fine day, he reckoned. Down below, the crew were celebrating their successes. Another 18,000 tons chalked up.

Good, he agreed – but not good enough for Prien's successor. Six ships sunk, but tiddlers really. Nothing dramatic. After the exhilaration of battle, his mood sank down into dissatisfaction, as if a powerful drug had been withdrawn. Next time, he must do better.

He was pleased when the Executive Officer came up to the conning tower to tell him their new orders had come, and he went down to this cabin to decode them on the Enigma.

U888 . . . PROCEED TO PQ43 FOR REFUELLING AND REARMING.

He looked up the map reference. The Caribbean – sun and warm sea! Not too far away, either.

He called across to Kruger, 'Course 259 degrees. And full speed ahead!'

'. . . just before 8 a.m. today, 190 Japanese aircraft attacked Pearl Harbour, and in one hour and a half destroyed four and crippled two battleships, sunk six cruisers and destroyers, smashed 200 aircraft and killed and wounded over 3,500 civilians and servicemen . . .'

Listening to Miami Radio, lashed up to the big 1,800-ton milch-cow U-boat which was refuelling U888's tanks, not 400 miles away from American territory, Hartenburg could not believe his ears.

He had felt exactly the same when he heard of Germany's invasion of France, of Hitler's attack on Russia. France had been subjugated and Stalingrad, according to the Berlin Radio, was just about to fall. And now Japan had taken on America and had won an immediate and unprecedented victory!

Three days later, on Wednesday 10 December, while his crew swam and dived and sunbathed in the warm Caribbean, from the same source he learned that the Japanese had sunk the British battleships *Prince of Wales* and *Repulse*.

As Kruger said to him cheerfully, 'Looks like the war will be over by Christmas!'

It was not over by Christmas. Christmas was spent by U888, U181, U11 and three other U-boats in the Caribbean rendezvous alongside the depot ship *Nordmark* (where U888's engine shaft and other repairs were carried out) and two big milch-cows.

It was a strange sort of Christmas. The Captain of the *Nordmark* dressed up as Santa Claus distributing presents to all crew members. Carols and marching songs. Geese, fresh meat and vegetables, sweets, beer and wine. Hot baths, all clothes washed and ironed. Newly baked rolls, fresh milk, real coffee, oranges and bananas. Dinners and parties, drinking French champagne till the small hours. Then sunbathing and sea bathing all day.

While all around, every 20-millimetre, 37-millimetre, 40-millimetre and 88-millimetre – seventy-five guns in all – were manned by U-boat men wearing swimming trunks and steel helmets.

'Any idea what this Caribbean picnic is all about?' Kassel asked Varenfordt while the three ex-Trefeld boys were drinking brandy in the Officers' Wardroom two days after Christmas.

'Of course,' Varenfordt carefully knocked the ash off his cigar. 'The Commander told me.'

Varenfordt was now fourth in the sinkings table. As such, he was treated as a real celebrity by the crew of the *Nordmark*.

'And when is he going to tell everyone else?' Hartenburg asked.

'Only when it's absolutely necessary.' Varenfordt drew in a deep breath of Havana tobacco and exhaled it luxuriously. 'Security, you know. There have been so many leaks.'

In fact, the Commander told them the next morning. He had all six U-boat Captains into his cabin and announced dramatically, 'Gentlemen, we are about to begin Operation *Paukenschlag*.'

He was a plump, pompous little man who had been a U-boat Captain in the last war. It all sounded so much like Red Indians that at first Hartenburg had the idea – things had after all been so extraordinary these last few months – that they were going to stage an invasion of America.

'You know that America is now our enemy, that the Imperial Japanese Empire has joined our victorious forces. We are to make an immediate attack on all enemy shipping operating on the Eastern Seaboard. America is a newcomer to modern naval warfare. There is every reason to believe that we will find her as unprepared as the

Japanese found her at Pearl Harbour. You will be free to operate at will. And I promise you, there will be lush pickings for everyone!'

In that he was totally right. All six U-boats sailed that evening, every one thoroughly overhauled and checked, each with four tons of fuel and sixteen torpedoes.

U888, staying on the surface, proceeded at sixteen knots to a position just off Miami, reaching it at midnight the next day.

Hartenburg was amazed at what he saw. Lights blazed from houses and hotels. Red, green and white neon lights flashed. Across the water came the sounds of dance bands, the hooting of cars and the whistle of trains.

There were no naval patrols, no aircraft, no searchlights. Nobody appeared in the least interested in U888's presence, so Hartenburg stayed on the surface, enjoying the warm scented sultry air, the clear starlit night and the kaleidoscope of ever-changing colours along the beach.

Two hours later, making her way slowly between a line of buoys decorated with flashing white lamps, came a tanker.

'Not exactly the *Queen Elizabeth*, Sir.'

'But better than a French fishing boat, Exec. Give me tubes one to four!'

The Torpedo Officer opened the outer doors of the torpedo tubes.

'One to four ready, Sir!'

Unwittingly, her red and green navigation lights sending bouncing coloured balls on the choppy sea, the tanker came nearer.

'Seems a shame, Sir,' Kruger said.

'Remember she'll be carrying fuel to a destroyer.'

The Executive Officer smiled. 'That isn't going to get there.'

'And that'll be another 5,000 tons to us.'

The tanker was only 1,000 yards away.

'Just to be sporting, Exec, I'll fire by eye. Like darts!'

The only noise now was the swish of the tanker's bow and the whispering of the waves against U888's steel sides.

Hartenburg waited till the ship was less than 300 yards away.

'Fire one!'

A straight white line fizzed across the water.

A dull thud. Then a *whoof* as the oil ignited. Seconds later, a huge orange blaze.

'Our first American tanker, Exec!' The light from the flames flickered over Hartenburg's sun-bronzed face. 'Chalk her up!'

'Have done already, Sir.'

'And now let's get the hell out of here before they come to investigate! Course 090 degrees! Full speed ahead!'

But nobody came to investigate. Nobody appeared even to notice. It was the same week after week. The U-boats fired their torpedoes, went back to the *Nordmark* for replacements and returned. The tankers – still unescorted, still not in convoy – continued to come cruising slowly along just off the coast.

An occasional destroyer turned up and frantically dropped depth-charges. Now and again a flying boat flew over. Amateurs in fast speedboats turned out to try their luck at U-boat hunting. So did light aeroplanes from flying clubs, one of which Hartenburg shot down with a rifle as though it were a pheasant.

It was the weirdest way to go to war. Most of the American Navy, the U-boat men were told at their Intelligence briefings, had been sent to the Pacific. Admiral King who was in charge did not believe in the British convoy system.

'And long may he remain an unbeliever,' said the Captain of the *Nordmark*.

'Amen to that!' said Heinrich Hartenburg, actuated by some strange quirk of memory from his birthday party in Ceylon fourteen years ago.

Papa Swain's God certainly seemed to be on the side of his adopted son. During the first two weeks of *Paukenschlag*, 200,000 tons of shipping were sunk off the Florida coast by the six U-boats.

February, March and April saw the battle intensified as Dönitz trebled his fleet there. Those three months saw two and a half million tons of Allied shipping sunk for the loss of ten U-boats out of a fleet that now numbered 320.

The U-boat commanders operating from the Caribbean called it the 'Second Happy Time'. Hartenburg's own sinking score rose to 120,000 tons, well above Varenfordt's. Due to Hitler's belief that an Allied invasion of Norway was imminent, U181 and three other boats had been sent to kick their heels in Tromsö fjord, much to Varenfordt's fury.

But Hartenburg was happy.

Again and again, Hartenburg called. 'Attack sight on!'

Again and again, another tanker blew up in front of his eyes. The worst enemy was the heat – an inside temperature of 110 degrees.

Condensation dripped off the pipes. Stripped to the waist, men sweated and swore, sliding along the decks trying to grasp slippery stanchions, eating salt tablets and drinking gallons of iced water.

And all the time, Hartenburg's score mounted. It was only in July, when the Americans were at last using the convoy system, that sinkings fell.

In that month, u888 was heavily depth-charged five times. But by now, he was top of the sinking table, a household name throughout Germany, so his mother wrote in the only letter he had received from her.

'Heard this morning,' the Captain of the *Nordmark* told him as he finished reading his mother's letter, 'that u832 never reached Lorient. You remember Mercke . . .?'

Hartenburg nodded. One of the few married U-boat men. Always writing letters to his wife.

'God knows what happened to him. And you remember u599 and u119?' He shook his head angrily. 'Spies at work there!'

Both U-boats had been surprised on the surface by a British cruiser while they were in totally secret positions. The Security Chiefs of B-Dienst maintained that it was quite impossible that the British had broken their Enigma code. It must have been the French Resistance. Incidents of sabotage in Brest and Lorient were increasing. Five crewmen had been asphyxiated by a tampered exhaust.

When in July, u888's turn came up for return to Lorient for overhaul, the Commander of u1016, who had made the trip westward to replace him, warned Hartenburg of another increasing danger. Long-distance aircraft.

'I know.'

'Not only in the Bay. Now the Tommies have four-engined aircraft patrolling the centre of the Atlantic.'

'I've seen them.'

'And Dönitz said an aircraft can no more harm a U-boat than a crow a mole!' The Commander smiled wryly. 'But these aircraft are hawks and the mole can be killed if he pokes his nose up.'

In spite of the good weather, the trip home was a slow one, too much of it spent submerged. Hartenburg had managed to evade attack by the time he saw the tug waiting off the Ile de Croix to escort him up the Scorff Estuary, but aircraft had forced u888 to dive seventeen times.

Heinrich Hartenburg stood at attention on the deck of U888 as the U-boat sailed down the sunlight into Lorient harbour. Though the roofs shone and the windows glistened and the tiny wave tops glittered, that sunlight was misleading. The bands played with undiminished gusto – the Kretschmer march, the ace's march – and the ranks of *Kriegsmarine* blue were drawn up on the concrete and the flags flew in the breeze.

But there was something missing and there was something wrong.

Hartenburg narrowed his eyes. The frivolous pastel colours were missing. The girls in their summer dresses carrying flowers. Where were the girls?

His unspoken question was repeated aloud by Kruger, standing eager and alert on his left. 'What's happened to the girls from the *établissements*, sir?'

'I can see plenty of Administrative girls,' Heinrich said out of the side of his mouth. 'A big squad today!'

'Not so partial to German girls. It's French girls I like.'

'Shame on you!'

'Yes, Sir.'

When they nosed round the quay, the drums rolled and the crowd began cheering. But the cheering lacked the throaty depth he remembered from the days of Prien. And over the town hung an indefinable chill. Spending so much of your life deaf and blind to the outside world gave you a sixth sense.

Suddenly in the sunlit home port, he smelled danger.

As U888 manoeuvred alongside, he searched for any glimpse of Suzanne. The crew began shouting and laughing remarks to the girls. They replied with a certain heavy archness. The German naval girls were always much more uncompromisingly devoted to the regime than the sailors, much more rigid and Reich-minded. He could not blame Kruger. French girls were altogether more desirable.

When the gangway was rigged, Korvettenkapitän Thorman, the Flotilla Captain, came on board to greet him with a bouquet of flowers.

'Congratulations, Heinrich! Great news! You are to go to Berlin to receive from the Führer's own hands the Knight's Cross with Swords and Diamonds!'

Even that great honour didn't take away that strange sense of unease and suspicion.

It was only after the debriefing at Kerneval HQ that the explanation came. The *Esso Hamburg* and *Egerland*, the U-boats' vital supply ships, had been surprised and sunk. Surprised was the key word. The enemy had gained access to secret information. Spies and saboteurs must have penetrated the U-boat bases. As he listened, Hartenburg felt the hair on the back of his neck prickle. Fear of treachery fuelled his fury. So much for the occupied power behaving itself. Attacks on German personnel were feared. None of the crew must be allowed to go out in groups of less than four. And they must carry arms.

That was all they were told. But as he bathed and changed at the *Beau Séjour*, Hartenburg feared there would be much more to tell. Excusing himself on the grounds that he was the Captain and well able to take care of himself, Heinrich slipped out of the hotel after dusk and made his way to the *boulangerie*.

He knocked for so long that at first he feared Suzanne had gone. If she was there, she would know U888 was in and would have been, if not at the quay, at least rushing downstairs to greet him. He gave their special knock again, and then there were cautious steps and the door opened a crack, on a chain. The chain was something new, he thought, and said urgently into the crack, 'Suzanne?'

Still the door was not flung open. But the chain was unhitched and it was opened just wide enough to allow him to slip inside. It was shut again, and locked. Then and only then did she fling her arms round him and kiss him wildly.

'Come upstairs. Quietly though!'

She led the way, shut the door of the flat and slipped the two new bolts. She checked the blackout before switching on a small table lamp. In the upshadowed light, her face looked haunted and frightened. He took her in his arms.

'I've missed you so much, Suzanne. I've wanted you so much.'

He didn't want anything to eat, he said. He'd had something at the *Beau Séjour*, which wasn't true. He didn't want to hear any more about why Lorient was so tense or why she was afraid. He wanted just to feel her in his arms.

But lying back on the big white pillows afterwards, he knew he had to ask her and he knew he had to hear. He sipped the *pastis* she'd handed him and listened tight-lipped.

It was a long sad story. Yes, some of her countrymen, Communist agitators, had infiltrated the yard. She was most bitterly ashamed of them. They had put water and sand in the lubricating oil, or so it was said, thereby causing the death of U-boat personnel.

Heinrich got out of bed and pulled on his clothes as if to prepare himself better for the unseen enemy. '*Mein Gott*!' he exclaimed, holding his head in his hands, feeling a curious sensation, as if an icy hand had touched his shoulder.

'I have been sick with worry for you,' Suzanne went on in a low voice. 'One never knows which boat they will sabotage. Who they have a very particular grudge against. Two weeks ago someone threw stones through that window. And before that, I opened the door to a knock and a man . . .? I cannot see his face . . . throws acid. I duck down and it goes over my shoulder and my hair. I am not damaged, but I know they hate me because of you.'

Heinrich slipped his arm around her shoulders and kissed her forehead.

'Then,' she went on wiping her eyes, 'last week something very terrible happens. An armed German naval patrol disappears.'

'How?' he asked sharply.

She spread her hands. 'They were ambushed and murdered, their bodies hidden. Just outside Lorient. On the road to St Clair.'

'God!' He began pacing up and down in agitation. It was all much worse than he had suspected. 'I hope they found out who did it, and shot them.'

She said nothing. He saw a strange spasm of anguish twist her face. Then she covered her face with her hands. She remained like that for so long that he had to gently prise her fingers off her face.

'Tell me, Suzanne,' he said sternly. 'Tell me! Did they find out who'd done it?'

'No.'

'God!' He clenched his fists. 'So what did the authorities do?'

'They took hostages.'

The icy fingers on his shoulder tightened. He said nothing.

Then she went on, 'They ordered the municipal authorities to supply the names of all Lorient men over 19.'

Heinrich wanted to stuff his knuckles in his ears. He guessed what might be coming.

He heard her whisper, 'Then they shot ten Frenchmen for every rating killed. And twenty-five for every officer.'

He closed his eyes. 'I don't believe that,' he said, but he did believe it. 'That's enemy propaganda. The *Kriegsmarine* doesn't fight like that.'

'It wasn't the *Kriegsmarine*,' she said wearily. 'It was the military authority and the SS.'

'I don't believe it,' he said again.

She didn't argue. She put on her pink and white flowered peignoir, took his glass from him, refilled it to the brim and handed it back. He was not sure which he felt most shocked about, the French treachery or the German brutality. He told himself he was a fighting man straightforwardly fighting other men. But he knew he was deceiving himself. War was war. War was brutal. Unlikely as it might seem, all the terrors of fighting submarine war, the strange life of the boat, had encapsulated him from the real life on the surface.

'There must be some explanation,' he said. 'There *must* be.'

But he had begun to accept the necessity. Her next words completed his acceptance.

'The explanation,' she said fiercely, 'is that they dare not risk the safety of their U-boat crews. Examples had to be made.'

He put his hands on her shoulders and looked down into her face. 'And,' he asked her slowly, 'you can accept that? You, as a Frenchwoman, can accept that?'

'It was the Frenchmen who began the murdering,' she said with her endearing Gallic logic. 'Not the Germans.'

'And you don't feel differently towards me?'

'How can I? I love you.'

He pulled her into his arms and held her close. He felt sentimental tears spring to his eyes. She loved him. That he did believe. And, in the midst of all the treachery and reprisals, for that he was grateful.

He suddenly remembered over the years those English Literature lessons of Kirkstone – Shakespeare. The words echoed in his head. Suzanne's love was a good deed in a naughty world.

The Knight's Cross with Swords and Diamonds was the highest honour a U-boat man could receive, and the aerodrome was filled with reporters and photographers.

Heinrich stepped on the plane for Berlin with the cheers and the clapping still ringing in his ears.

He felt deeply moved by it all. A much-loved son of his country. The thought uppermost in his mind, as the aircraft taxied to the end of the runway, was if only his father could have seen him now.

He was the sole passenger in an aircraft used for ferrying the Führer's most honoured guests. His father had died fighting the enemy, but Heinrich had lived to repay that debt many times over.

His one regret was that he had been able to spend only such a brief time with Suzanne. 'Never mind,' she had said, 'it will be all the sweeter when you return.'

'But first I must visit my mother.'

'Of course. I shall be waiting. Tell the pilot to fly low over the town and I shall wave.'

As the Fieseler-Storch took off, Hartenburg looked back at the dockyard disappearing behind the port wing. Then the aircraft banked and headed into the sun, flying low over occupied France, then Luxembourg. Distance blurred the signs of war. A young *Luftwaffe* officer brought him coffee and some biscuits, and told him they were now crossing into the Fatherland.

Landing in Berlin, a large black Mercedes waited to take him to the *Kaiserhof*, the most celebrated, the most splendid hotel in Berlin.

A strange atmosphere pervaded in Berlin. It was like a high shrill note in one's ears. Fear and confidence went side by side. The hotel was filled with a cosmopolitan, expensively dressed crowd. There was an almost hysterical gaiety, strangely discordant to Hartenburg after so long in a submarine with its quiet disciplined order. He felt like a mole faced with noise and bright light.

After a luxurious soak in his marble bathroom, Heinrich was escorted into dinner by the Führer's naval adjutant, Captain von Puttkamer. The table was decorated with gold lilies and roses. There was champagne in an ice-bucket. The adjutant pointed out important people. Hermann Göring in the centre of a noisy group, General Gruber, the opera singer Lil Helendramm. Heinrich felt a not unpleasant sensation of mixing with the mighty on equal terms. Not a bad achievement for a boy who had swept up at the Blohm and Voss shipyard.

Over coffee, real coffe, not the ground acorn rubbish which was all his mother could buy, Captain von Puttkamer instructed him on the protocol for tomorrow's presentation.

'It's like meeting royalty,' Heinrich smiled.

'Indeed it is. And rightly so. The Führer is now the most powerful leader in the world.'

There was an air raid warning in the night, but Heinrich didn't hear it. No bombs were dropped. Von Puttkamer arrived punctually at ten in the morning in the official car to drive him in style the few hundred yards to the Chancellery. The morning was clear and fresh and the linden trees in full leaf. Heinrich felt excited and curious. The Führer, von Puttkamer had warned, could be unpredictable. Speak only when spoken to. Avoid contentious subjects.

The first thing Heinrich saw was the huge eagle that dominated the entrance at the top of the Chancellery steps. He raised his eyes to it. The shark greeting the eagle. As they mounted the steps, the eagle seemed to grow larger and more indomitable.

Inside was a vast marble lobby, then a high-ceilinged reception hall. Von Puttkamer whispered softly as if in some sacred cathedral, 'This is where our Führer gives audiences.'

Then he left him alone in its vastness. Punctually at ten-thirty the swing-doors at the far end opened and von Puttkamer reappeared, this time escorting the Führer himself.

Heinrich marched forward to meet the stocky figure dressed in army uniform. It was another of those profound moments of his life.

He found himself clicking his heels and giving the Nazi salute, as von Puttkamer had instructed. But not because von Puttkamer had instructed it, but because he wanted to.

'I congratulate you, Kapitänleutnant,' Hitler put the ribbon holding the diamond and silver cross round his neck. 'Germany is proud of you! Tell me, how goes the war in the Atlantic?'

'We are winning it, *mein Führer*.'

The Führer spread his hands and did a strange little jig. 'Excellent!' He waved Heinrich towards a velvet-covered sofa. 'Come! Tell me more!'

He sat beside Heinrich on the sofa, his curiously hypnotic eyes fixed on Heinrich's face. Heinrich could feel them travelling over his features as palpably as little brown mice. They gobbled up every crumb of information about the ships he'd sunk, the attacks, the sightings.

'So you saw their *Queen Elizabeth*?'

'Yes, *mein Führer*.'

'And you will sink her, of course?'

'Of course.'

Clapping his hands, the Führer stood up. The interview was over. But not quite over.

The Führer laid a hand on his arm. 'I know you will sink her, Kapitänleutnant. Great success is promised. To *you*. And to *me*. And very soon. Our stars are very favourable!'

Heinrich had heard that the Führer paid great attention to his horoscopes – his own and those of his leaders. He was simultaneously amused, disappointed and personally gratified.

'Thank you, *mein Führer*,' he said. 'I am proud that it should be so.'

It was only when he was on the train going back to Hamburg that he remembered those words of his with distaste and thought . . . yes, he'd come a long way since the boy who cleaned the Blohm and Voss shipyard.

But along what road?

His mother's welcome cast all doubts from Hartenburg's mind. 'This is the proudest moment of my life,' she said, cupping the gilt-edged box in her hands.

She had brought the photograph of his father down from her bedroom, and now it held a place of honour on the sideboard, flanked by her medals for being Heinrich's mother. She placed this greatest medal of all in front of it, and waved Heinrich to his chair at the dining table. She had baked a cake in the shape of a U-boat. Suddenly he was back to his birthday parties in Ceylon and the gingerbread men she used to make, and he felt gripped by a dreadful melancholy. For his vanished childhood, perhaps for his vanished self. Or perhaps it was Nature's see-saw after the euphoria of the last few days.

'And what was it like in Berlin, Heinrich?'

'I'm not sure. Very excited. Very shrill. I don't think I'd want to live there.'

'And the Führer, what is he really like?'

'That's even harder to say, mother.' He chewed a mouthful of food thoughtfully. 'One feels a charisma. One is drawn to him. Charmed by him. But underneath, there is something of which one could be very afraid.'

'Not you, Heinrich,' his mother said gaily. 'Everyone says you are afraid of nothing!'

And that was how he seemed to be known to everyone in Hamburg. The U-boat ace who was afraid of nothing. He was toasted in the cafés, girls came up and spoke to him in the street. And his mother's friends, of the few who still remained in Hamburg, like Mrs Goldman who kept the corner shop, shook his hand and said they were proud to know him.

The first night after he arrived home he took his mother to the *Caprice*, a small but expensive cafe on the waterfront. A four-piece band was playing under the pink lights. A moment after they entered, the band began to play the *Kretschmer* march. Every single occupant of the cafe got to their feet, and remained standing till the proprietor had conducted Heinrich and his mother to their best table. Throughout the meal, gifts of wine were sent over. The proprietor refused to present a bill.

Heinrich began to find the adulation irksome, an invasion of his privacy. He wanted to escape. But his mother basked in such reassuring glory. Her eyes shone. A flush warmed her cheeks. She looked less old and careworn than when he had arrived home. He could not begrudge her one minute of her triumph.

When the day for his departure came, she insisted on accompanying him to the railway station to make the most of their last moments together.

A stiff wind was blowing off the river. The skies were heavy with rainclouds. His train was not yet in at the platform. They stood side by side, watching a heavy-goods train shunting to the far end of the adjoining platform. Everywhere there were soldiers, and the black uniforms of SS men.

'You will take especial care, Heinrich?' His mother laid her hand on his arm.

'Of course. And you, mother, promise to go to the shelters when the bombers come?'

'I promise . . .' she began. Then her voice faded. After a moment she drew a deep steadying breath. 'I promise, Heinrich. I promise.'

He looked down at her sharply. Her face, which was normally pale anyway, had drained of every vestige of colour. She seemed to shrink inside her self. He followed the direction of her eyes. Along the next platform, a line of people were being herded by a squad of SS men. There were men and women of all ages and a few children. They each carried a suitcase. Several of them, perhaps all, for he couldn't see them clearly at that distance, wore the star of Jewry. What he could see was that they all looked cowed and afraid, like the remnants of a defeated army.

'Who are they, mother?' he heard himself ask, almost as if he were a child again.

'People being evacuated because of the bombing,' she whispered, her lips scarcely moving.

Then a profile, a manner of walking, of holding his head leapt out at Heinrich from the long anonymous line. He would have recognised that slightly limping gait anywhere, that shabby trilby hat on the back of the large drooping head.

'But there's Otto Lerner, surely,' he said, pointing to his grandfather's old friend.

She grabbed hold of Heinrich's hand, and held it against her. 'No, no,' she said. 'Otto has died. It was very sad. Months ago. It could not be Otto!'

Then his train came steaming in, cutting off the other platform from view. He settled himself into a corner seat, and folded his arms across his chest to stop himself trembling.

The man whom everyone said was afraid of nothing was suddenly afraid.

As the train steamed out of Hamburg station, Heinrich tried to rationalise away his fear. His fear was the result of a mistake. He was mistaken in thinking he saw Otto Lerner. Was he not also mistaken in thinking his mother was worried and distressed, that the little procession of people was anything more than she said it was? She had never lied to him. Why should she lie to him now?

Yet he could not but be afraid. Not for himself, but for her. His own position was inviolate. He was one of the most successful young officers in the most successful arm of the German Forces. He had been personally decorated by Hitler. He did not regard himself as being tainted by Jewish blood. Even had he so been, Admiral Raeder had resisted all attempts to dismiss Jews from the German Navy. The *Kriegsmarine* was an organisation apart. They were fighting men facing the enemy, not morbidly examining their distant heredity.

But he could not persuade himself that his mother hadn't been afraid. Afraid that he might acknowledge himself as a friend of the man who looked like Otto Lerner. Yet she was not Jewish. Not according to the Nuremberg laws. He remembered learning them in his days at Trefeld – the strict definition of what was a Jew and what wasn't.

Grandfather Mendelssohn had looked Jewish. But he was only half-Jewish, which made his mother a quarter and himself one eighth. Try as he might, he could not help doing this terrible arithmetic as the train clicked over the rails. A quarter and an eighth. Nothing to be afraid of. His mother was not even a mixed

Jew, she was German, because she had less than twenty-five per cent Jewish blood, had not married a Jew and had never practised the Jewish religion. Never been inside a synagogue. Never. She could not be assailed.

Yet as he did his comforting arithmetic, he kept seeing Grandfather Mendelssohn's face, kept feeling the grip of his hand and hearing his whispered words, 'Look after your mother.' Wouldn't Grandfather Mendelssohn despise him if he could see him now? Was this how he had to look after her? Or did he know there was much more of which to be afraid?

At Dortmund, the train was held up. He got down onto the platform to find out why. The RAF had carried out a raid on the Dortmund-Ems canal. Bombs had fallen on the city, close to the station. They would get the train moving, the station master said, as soon as the diversion line was clear. Outside the station there was the sullen smell of smoke.

He could see shattered buildings, hear the tinkle as shards of glass were punched out of broken windows. There was broken glass strewn over the forecourt of the station. It crunched under his feet like thin ice on winter pools. It was because of raids like this, Heinrich told himself, that those people in Hamburg were being evacuated. His mother hadn't lied.

As if to offset the damage, newspaper boys were yelling about good news on the Russian front. Heinrich bought a paper and retired back to the train to read it. The paper did indeed contain good news. The swastika had been hoisted on Mount Elbrus, the highest peak in the Caucasus mountains. Soon Russia would collapse. Before the year end, the Generals were saying. The German Army was now in command from Egypt to the North Cape of Norway, from Brest to the Volga river.

Heinrich folded away the paper. To add to that good news, the *Kriegsmarine* was winning the Battle of the Atlantic. So Russia this year. Britain next. Everything would be better when the war was over. And the Third Reich would not forget its heroes.

By the time the train steamed into Lorient station just before midnight, Heinrich was in a mood of considerable optimism. After leaving his bag at the *Beau Séjour*, he went straight round to Suzanne's. She opened the door quickly and drew him inside.

'I had almost given you up.'

But the flat was welcoming as if waiting for him. The furniture was polished, the curtains drawn, the lamp lit. A jug of wine and two glasses stood on the checked tablecloth. She led him in and kissed him tenderly.

'The train was held up. An air raid at Dortmund.'

She let out a spiel in angry French about the English, and then added, 'We had a raid the day before yesterday. They didn't do much damage though. The bombs bounced off the concrete. The boats were safe.' She laughed. 'They only damaged the canteen.' She kissed him. 'They are getting very frightened of the U-boats. The Tommies.'

'And well they might!'

'The Tommies are on the run,' she said, pouring the wine. They toasted the day when the war would be over, and then – 'Then,' she pretended, 'What then? What will you do with me then?'

'I shall marry you,' he said, 'if you will have me?'

'I will have you! I promise I will have you!'

He went to sleep in her arms. He must have been thinking again of his mother and the Nuremberg law, for he dreamed he was asking Suzanne if she had any Jewish blood, and telling her about the percentage added to a percentage and doing again the terrible arithmetic.

He woke to find Suzanne bending over him to say goodbye before she went to the shipyard. Coffee was ready and there were fresh croissants. In the clear sunlight of morning, his worries were plainly ridiculous. He had been worrying over a fragment of ancestry. He, and therefore his mother, were above such petty things.

After his breakfast, he walked briskly back to the *Beau Séjour*. The air smelled fresh and salty. Seagulls soared over the harbour. Life felt good. He ran up the steps to the entrance, crossed the lobby and pushed open the door of the bar. And there, sitting in the corner again, like a spider that had never left its web, was Kauffenstein.

'They told me you were usually back at this time, Herr Kapitänleutnant.' Kauffenstein waved towards the two glasses of *pastis* on the table in front of him. 'I hope you do not mind. I anticipated your order.'

'Thank you.' Heinrich forced a smile. 'You are most kind.'

He sat down at the table opposite Kauffenstein and tried to guess what now.

'We were all much gratified to hear of your decoration, Herr

Kapitänleutnant.' Kauffenstein lifted his glass and lightly touched Heinrich's. 'To many more!'

He swallowed the contents at a gulp.

Heinrich sipped his thoughtfully and studied Kauffenstein's impassive policeman's face.

'I was also very gratified, very personally gratified, to hear that you had taken my advice. About your name. Hartenburg is a fine name in a fine tradition. A successful name.'

'I hope so,' Heinrich said, and waited.

He watched Kauffenstein snap his fingers and point to the two glasses for the barman to bring over refills.

'You enjoyed your leave, Herr Kapitänleutnant?'

'Very much.'

'In Hamburg?'

'Yes.'

'And with your mother?' Kauffenstein managed a sentimental smile. 'We Germans are good to our mothers.'

'You seem to keep a close eye on me, Herr Kauffenstein.'

'We have to look after our U-boat heroes. Our survival may depend on them. *We* wish them well. Others do not.'

'More sabotage in the dockyard?'

'Yes. Three workers were caught by the French *Milice* and handed to us. They were shot. But still it goes on.' He paused and sighed. 'However, it is not the dockyard I am concerned with now.' He reached into the inner pocket of his coat. 'It is about *this*.'

He laid a letter on the table between them. With dismay, Heinrich saw it was addressed to Frau Swain. With even greater dismay, he recognised the handwriting.

He tried blustering. 'That letter is to my mother.'

'I know.'

'Then why has it been opened?'

'Herr Kapitänleutnant, this letter was found on a missionary gentleman coming into Danzig from Sweden. It was given to him by the Reverend Swain . . . your stepfather, no doubt?'

'The Reverend Swain adopted me. My real father was Kapitänleutnant Hartenburg, but that you will know.'

Kauffenstein inclined his head. 'You realize the seriousness of this, Kapitänleutnant? The letter came from Ceylon, a colony of a power with whom we are at war.'

'But it will simply be the letter of a husband to his wife!'

'But *is* it? How do you know? There are some strange sentences that could well be in code.'

'That is ridiculous! My adoptive father is a man of God. An unworldly man. He would know nothing to put in code.'

Kauffenstein smiled as if at Heinrich's naivety. 'He might wish to find out, rather to impart. He writes he is worried. He has heard ugly rumours.'

Heinrich put his hand across he table. 'Let me see.'

'No, Herr Kapitänleutnant. It is not allowed!'

'Herr Kauffenstein, what military secrets could my mother possibly know which she could pass on to her husband?'

'She has a very distinguished son who knows many secrets.'

'Which he does *not* repeat, Herr Kauffenstein,' Heinrich said sternly.

Kauffenstein inclined his head. 'But it is not just military matters. There are other things which must not be broadcast.'

'My mother, Herr Kauffenstein, broadcasts nothing.'

'This letter speaks of other letters.'

'I am sure she has not received any. She would have told me.'

Kauffenstein stared at him thoughtfully in silence, as if to allow Heinrich's thoughts and fears to gabble loud and clear in his mind.

He had thought his mother could be in danger from her slight taint of Jewishness. He had rationalised that fear away. Now this. Perhaps Papa Swain had heard exaggerated propaganda. Perhaps those were the ugly rumours. But how could he be so foolish and naive?

'I am sure it is all perfectly innocent,' Heinrich said to break the silence. 'Had you met my adoptive father, you would know it to be.'

Kauffenstein looked sceptical.

'I am sure also, Herr Kauffenstein, that this is an isolated instance. That it will *not* happen again.'

'And if it does?'

'No doubt,' Heinrich said grittily, 'you will get in touch with me.'

'We certainly will, Herr Kapitänleutnant! And if you find out she has received such a letter, *you* will get in touch with *us*?'

'I will.'

'Have I your word?'

'You have my word. I promise.'

Kauffenstein thrust his large hand across the table and shook Heinrich's. He rose, smiled and as if to sweeten the taste the interview had left, added in a friendly tone of voice, 'And you always keep your word, they tell me. Much was made of that on the radio, of your promise to the Führer. You will sink the *Queen Elizabeth*, they say. You always keep your word.' He took a few paces towards the door. Then he added over his shoulder, 'Success is a great shield, is it not, Herr Kapitänleutnant?'

Heinrich sat in silence. He suddenly thought of the photograph of his father in the little dining room in Hamburg, with his own decorations massed around. Now he had a vision of his mother with those self-same decorations surrounding her and keeping her as if within their palisade. Yet the palisade had to be constantly renewed, and there were still a few gaps through which the Englishness of her husband and the Jewishness of her great-grandfather could crawl through. But the *Queen Elizabeth* was a big ship, a prize that could plug up those and many other holes.

Heinrich drained his glass and went straight down to the quayside. He clambered on board U888 and ran his fingers over the silver-painted shark.

He couldn't wait to be gone.

It was pitch dark. Not a star overhead. Just a black blanket of cloud.

Standing with the four members of the Watch, leaning back against the conning tower rails, Hartenburg listened to the hiss of the bow wave breaking over the deck, felt the strong throb of the diesels through the soles of his feet.

This was better! His mind was quiet now, no longer assailed by the worries of the last few days. The challenge of the Atlantic always did this for him – reinvigorated him, reassured him.

Now he was doing all he could do. What he was happiest doing. At the same time, he was carrying out Dönitz's orders to stop on the surface all night to recharge the batteries, since it was now known, despite the scientists saying it was impossible, that the British aircraft had radar. They might get U888 on their scope, but they'd never be able to see her to make an attack.

Should they approach, however, his gunners would see the engine exhausts. And then –

He ran his hand affectionately over the barrels of the quadruple 40-millimetre. The men were talking in low voices to each other, joking the four hours of their Watch away. They seemed perfectly happy, too – proud of being the Number One U-boat, proud of his

Knight's Cross with Swords and Diamonds, only anxious to get back into battle and keep their position at the top of the table.

He had a good crew, better than Prien's, the best crew in the service. No Gestapo men here, as in some boats, so he had been told. All totally loyal to him, as he was to them.

Be successful, a veteran U-boat captain had told them on the Command Course, and your men will follow you anywhere.

There was a clatter on the ladder.

Kruger's voice called across to him. 'Your supper's ready! And it's best steak!'

He was smiling and had just started walking over the deck, when suddenly the sky caught alight.

A white-hot blaze was careering towards them, spitting sparks.

'Fire!' Hartenburg roared at his gunners. 'Fire at the light! *Das verdammte Licht*!'

He lifted his head.

Immediately a million candles burned into his eyeballs, as the vicious sun came screaming down towards him.

VII JOHN
22 July 1942–
4 November 1942

'Got her!'

Lying flat on the nose, Bronski directed the Leigh Light onto the sliver of steel ahead.

Tock-tock-tock-tock – Harvey started opening up with the .5s in the front turret.

'One mile, Skipper!' called the Radar. 'Dead ahead!'

Blake still kept his eyes on the instruments. The phosphorescent needle on the radio altimeter slid down to forty feet. One slip and they would catapult into the sea.

'Port, Skipper! *Port!*'

He skidded the Liberator left.

'Bomb doors open!'

Above the scream of the hydraulic pump, Blake could hear the 40-millimetre cannon tearing into the aircraft's skin.

'Half a mile,' the Radar shouted.

From the nose: 'Hold that, Skipper! Perfect!'

Blake looked up then.

Immediately the dazzle stung his eyes. A U-boat all right, ringed by a golden halo. And there on the conning tower glittered a jumping silver shark.

The same U-boat he had attacked ten months before. His gunners had sworn it was a kill, but the Navy had only allowed a 'possibly damaged'.

The Liberator lurched left as an 88-millimetre burst tipped up the starboard wing.

Blake kicked her straight.

'Quarter-mile!'

The aircraft gave a little bound upwards as Bronski pressed the tit on the new low-level bombsight.

'Depth-charges gone!'

Blake pulled back. Still pursued by red and silver tracers, the Liberator climbed back into the night.

'A straddle!' Rolf shouted from the rear turret. 'Right across her!'

'Let's hope the photograph comes out,' was all Blake said.

It did.

'If that isn't a kill, I'll eat my hat! Back at their Llanallan base, the CO of the Scientific Research Unit was jubilant. 'Best night photograph I've ever seen!'

It showed the depth-charges straddling the U-boat at an angle of thirty degrees across the boat. Five men could be seen on the conning tower. Smudged in spray but still clearly distinguishable was the jumping silver shark.

'Very interesting.' The Intelligence Officer pointed to it with satisfaction. 'We know about that silver shark from French Intelligence. That's U888, based at Lorient. And her commander is no ordinary U-boat captain. He's the ace who's stepped into Prien's shoes. Kapitänleutnant Heinrich Hartenburg.'

In spite of the photograph, the Navy's verdict was still only 'possibly damaged'.

'The body of the Captain,' Bronski grunted. 'Together with the periscope. That's what they want before they give you a kill!'

They were sitting with the rest of Blake's crew in the Crew Room at the edge of Llanallan airfield, waiting to do an evening exercise. The sun had just gone down in a blaze of scarlet, but from the windows they could still see all the Scientific Research Unit's aircraft – Beaufighter, amphibian Catalina, Wellington, Whitley, Hudson, Liberator – dispersed on the hardstandings, all of them arrayed with a bewildering collection of aerials, rocket-rails, searchlights and strange humps, none of them carrying Squadron markings.

Instead, beside the RAF roundel on the fuselage was a big yellow P surrounded by a circle, meaning *Experimental and Top Secret*. All of them had a guard.

Blake had been on the Scientific Research Unit for eleven months now. As far as family life was concerned, perched on the extreme south-west tip of Wales he was still a long way from Oxford. Far from getting leave because he was supposedly on Rest (though he did do occasional Operations with experimental equipment), he had only been home once and that only for five days.

Alexandra had been about to take her Final Examinations and had been nervous, though she seemed glad to see him. Their relationship, Blake thought, as they sat in her bedroom and he helped her to revise, had become a strange mixture of schoolboy and schoolgirl and staid married life.

They seemed to leap from one role to the other. But the part in the middle, the courtship, the wooing and the winning had got missed out.

Back at Scientific Research Unit, now that Swain was dead, life was better than on the squadron.

He enjoyed the total non-military attitude. No Air Marshals issuing orders, no laid-down work and hours for doing it. Everybody equal, everybody chipping in their twopennyworth. There was no imposed discipline because there was no need for it.

He had seen something of this attitude when he had collected the ASV Whitleys from Defford. But now he found that this same attitude prevailed in organisations which hitherto had been so secret that he had hardly known they existed.

In Bletchley Park, after the capture of U110's Enigma, they were decoding Dönitz's signals to his U-boats. Blake had been sent on an eighteen-hour trip to check if a decoded signal was correct and a German milch-cow U-boat was in a position 300 miles south-east of the Azores.

It was. Two British cruisers were sent out of Freetown to intercept. And that was the end of it.

The BBC, he knew, openly broadcast to Germany and Occupied Europe. But he had no idea that dozens of British Lord Haw-Haws were broadcasting scurrilous half-truths in fourteen languages, some of them spiced with invented pornographic detail to make them more palatable. Then he captained another Liberator filled with radio men checking on their reception and range.

One of the stations was the *Atlantiksender* which sent depressing news of losses to U-boat men interspersed with Flotilla football scores, American Jazz, and information on promotions, sailings and new tactics obtained from the French Resistance.

But it was on the new devices side that Blake was particularly concerned with on the Unit. He had come in on the tail-end of the Leigh Light development. His new job was the testing of a totally new torpedo dropped by parachute from an aircraft that homed on propeller noise from a U-boat. This was to be used in harness with sonar buoys, also dropped by parachute, which could pick up sounds and transmit them to aircrew listening on four special receivers.

It was to make a further test of this combination that Blake and his crew were waiting that evening in the Crew Room. The Scientific Officer who would be accompanying them was replacing four radios and then retesting the receivers.

Blake looked at his watch. 'Wonder when Doc Picton will finish?'

Joe Orton shrugged his shoulders. 'He said an hour.'

'Two already.'

'Should we have supper first?' Rolf suggested. 'I'm hungry. And you know what those spam sandwiches are like.'

In the end, they took off supperless just before nine o'clock and rendezvoused with a British submarine fifty miles south-west of Strumble Head.

They dropped their sonar buoy. On receiving unmistakable sounds of propeller noises, from the bomb-bay they dropped Fido, which fell on its white parachute into the sea. If the practice torpedo connected, a shrill bell-like signal was supposed to be transmitted. But they heard nothing and Blake brought the Liberator back to Llanallan.

He carried out further tests throughout August, with no better results. Then, since his crew were well overdue for ten day's leave, the CO took over, and they went off.

After an overcrowded night journey of thirteen hours, during which he had spent most of the time standing in the corridor, Blake arrived at Oxford station in summer morning sunshine.

He'd just jumped down onto the platform and was searching among all the khaki and blue for the first sight of Alexandra, when he felt his arm grabbed. A voice, instantly recognisable as Wagstaff's, said as he turned, 'It is John, isn't it? John Blake?'

Poor old Wacky looked wackier than ever. Thinner, if that were possible, and even more out of step with the world.

'You look well. The RAF must suit you,' Wacky said generously.

Blake wished to God he could have said the same with conviction. He tried saying it without, and Wacky just grimaced. He was dressed in what looked like brown battledress without any flashes. A plain forage cap was perched on his dome of a head.

'And what're you doing, Wacky?'

'Well, I was in the Orkneys. Building roads. That was grim. The wind never stops blowing. But I'm on the move. Just had a spot of embarkation leave.'

'Not more road building, I hope?'

'No. Seems they're going to let me drive an ambulance.'

Blake began to say, well that'll be better. Then the sheer inanity of such a remark shut him up. Thankfully Alexandra shoved her way through the crowd at that. She came up breathless and smiling.

'I remember you,' she said, shaking Wacky's hand warmly when Blake tried to effect introductions. 'Androcles and the Lion.'

'Happy days,' Wacky said. 'Were you one of those girls that laughed?'

'Only when John fell over his dress.'

'Well, he doesn't look much like Lavinia now,' Wacky said.

'That's because I feed him so well,' Alexandra laughed. 'I've got a stew waiting for him now. Have you time to come and join us?'

Wacky seemed quite overcome. The poor sod actually blushed. But no, he had a train to catch. They parted with mutual admonitions to take care.

Alexandra had the car waiting. Mrs Monteith was a dab hand at getting extra petrol coupons. She was very well. So was Maurice. He wanted to ask her if she'd heard anything about her Finals. She had written that the papers hadn't been too bad, which was confidence indeed for Alexandra. But he didn't want to bring the subject up in case it was a sore one.

As she put the car in the garage however, she whispered, 'No news yet, John.'

The following morning, Alexandra's tutor phoned to ask her to be good enough to call in at his office that afternoon.

'You've either done very well or very badly,' Mrs Monteith said crisply, voicing what Blake himself suspected.

He was not sure, when he came to think of it, that he wanted her to have done either. Certainly he didn't want her to have done badly, but if she'd done brilliantly, she would move a little further out of his reach and her fairy crown would acquire more diamonds.

'We'd better have the bottle out either way,' Mrs Monteith said, as they awaited Alexandra's return.

It was a warm afternoon. Mrs Monteith told Blake to carry the drinks tray out into the garden, where Maurice was playing in his playpen.

'I'd rather have tea,' Alexandra said rather dispiritedly when she found them there. 'If you don't mind. I'll go and put the kettle on.'

'I will,' Blake said. 'You sit down.'

'Before anyone moves,' Mrs Monteith snapped, 'What did he say? Are your results bad or good?'

'Good.' Alexandra permitted herself a little smile. She looked from Blake to her mother like a small girl basking in parental approval. 'Yes, they're good.' She ran her hand through her hair nervously. 'And he's offered me a job.'

'Well, that's good too,' Mrs Monteith said. 'I can cope with Maurice. Get her the tea, John dear, let's hear all about it.'

When he returned, Mrs Monteith had extracted the details from her and was jubilant.

'It's a wonderful job, John,' she told him gaily. 'Wonderful! You mustn't let her hesitate over it. It's to broadcast in German on one of our enemy broadcast units. Aimed at the German Navy. '

Blake was glad he had already handed the tea to Alexandra, for he felt his hands shake. He subsided into his chair, gripped the arms and tried to look judicial.

'On something called the *Atlantiksender*, John,' Alexandra said. 'Have you heard of it?'

'Yes.'

'The Radio Unit's at Woburn. Only nineteen miles away. Transport provided. My tutor broadcasts from there. Now they want a woman's voice, too.' She paused. 'What d'you think, John?'

What did he think? My God, what did he think! He looked around the garden, at Mrs Monteith's curious mixture of roses and potatoes and marigolds and beans, incapable of thought of any kind. Just a terrible feeling of some capricious but immutable pattern that had them all in its web.

'I think,' he said at last, 'that you must do whatever you think you should.'

Mrs Monteith obviously thought that was a very unsatisfactory answer.

'I see it,' she said, 'as a tremendous contribution to the war effort. This war is a woman's war too.' She poured herself another gin. 'I think you owe it to your father.'

She raised her glass and smiled warmly at Alexandra, as if she was another recruit for Monteith's Reply.

Alexandra drew in a long breath. 'I shall take it then, if you both approve. But,' she licked her lips, 'I can only do it till Christmas. You see, I think I'm pregnant again.'

Pregnant again. The metal wheels of the Llanallan train rattled the four syllables rhythmically in Blake's ears as the engines gathered speed down the straight run through the Severn valley.

Outside the carriage window, the telegraph wires danced. Clouds of white steam fled past. He had made Alexandra pregnant. Not intentionally. Just rather carelessly, as one might expect. Nevertheless, however he had done it, he had done it, and he couldn't help feeling naively pleased with himself. A man, not a boy. In some absurd way, he had equalised with Henry Swain, indeed excelled him, because Henry was dead and he was alive.

Since Alexandra had announced the news, this was the first opportunity he had had to examine it on his own. At home, he had to maintain the role of father for the second time round. It wasn't like that at all.

Fatherhood was quite different from what he had expected. Awesome in fact. A feeling that you'd started something you couldn't stop. Not unlike going in on a bombing run and not being able to pull out.

So that below the childish pleasure and self-congratulation lurked a gnawing anxiety. He had worried about Alexandra when she was expecting Maurice, but not like this. And he had worried about what would happen to Alexandra if he got the chop. But not with the urgency he did now. He had never thought he must stay alive to look after her. But he did now. He began to feel thankful that SRU was slightly less dangerous than being on Ops, which a little while ago he would have thought a shameful thing to feel.

Months ago, he could remember thinking that the ethos of SRU gave him real hope the Allies would win the war. Now, as the train halted at Llanallan station, Alexandra's pregnancy gave him real hope that one day they would make their marriage work. They would grow to love each other as he had told Alexandra three years ago. Now with Henry Swain dead and the new baby coming, they were a real family. He could almost see them going off, hand in hand into the sunset, while the cinema curtains swished shut.

In the Liberty bus from the station to the airfield, he kept a lookout for chicken farms within cycling distance. He'd bike around like some of the older ground crew did, buying off-the-ration eggs for the family. Alexandra would get an extra egg a week for being pregnant and cod liver oil, Mrs Monteith had said, but that wasn't enough. He hoped she wouldn't overdo things with the

Atlantiksender. But Mrs Monteith would never let her escape doing that, even if she'd wanted to, which he was sure she didn't.

He arrived at the airfield in good heart full of uxorious plans and looking forward to renewing the Fido tests. The first person he saw in the Mess was Bronski, propping up the bar, his long nose sunk in a pint tankard.

'When did you get back?' Blake asked, cheerfully punching him on the shoulder, and ordering himself a half.

'Coupla hours ago.'

'Good leave?'

'OK, I guess.'

Blake waited, smiling, for him to ask about *his* leave. He had decided he would tell Bronski that his wife was pregnant again. He knew his navigator thought him quite a guy.

But Bronski didn't ask. Instead he said soberly, 'Skipper?'

'Yes, Bronx?'

'Something that isn't OK.' He paused. 'The Wingco and his crew got the chop.'

He went on to tell Blake that three days before, the Wingco's crew were on trials with the same submarine. They had dropped Fido. But the strings had become entangled when the parachute opened and had wrapped themselves round the tailplane, jamming the elevators.

The Liberator had dived straight down into the Irish Sea. There had been no survivors.

There being no Liberator and no Fido experts, SRU's research into the acoustic homing torpedo was shelved. Blake and his crew were sent on a Joint Anti-Submarine Course at Western Approaches Command in Liverpool.

It was only a three-week course, but representatives of all units involved in the Battle of the Atlantic were there – coastal aircrew, radar and radio experts, technical boffins, gunners, submarine, destroyer, corvette and Merchant Navy crews.

The course was run by the Navy and involved taking alternately the parts of the Germans and the British in a typical Atlantic convoy attack. Blake was a U-boat Commander, a British Merchant Skipper, the Captain of a *Focke-Wulf* Condor, the Captain of a British destroyer, Grössadmiral Dönitz in his Berlin U-boat Headquarters and Admiral Noble here in Liverpool.

The final lecture, on the careers of the U-boat aces, was given by the Captain who had organised the course.

'The men I shall be telling you about were trained and dedicated killers, though not all of them were Nazis. When Schepke, Prien, Endrass and Kretschmer were operating, Dönitz had only just over fifty U-boats. Now he has nearer four hundred. But numbers are not important. In the final analysis, it's all in the skill and character of the *men*. It was the few aces who did most of the damage.'

He went on to sketch the careers of each of the early aces, all of them either dead or captured. Then he turned to the aces who were still operating.

'The most successful and dangerous of these is Kapitänleutnant Hartenburg. His boat is U888, with a jumping shark painted on her conning tower. I understand that Flight Lieutenant Blake's crew on this course have twice attacked him.' He looked towards Blake sitting at the back. 'Isn't that so?'

Blake nodded. 'We've attacked a boat with that insignia.'

'Hartenburg was on Prien's crew,' the Captain went on. 'And he has assumed Prien's mantle. He changed his name from Swain to Hartenburg on obtaining his own command.' He looked at his watch. 'And at this particular moment, we know from our French friends that Kapitänleutnant Heinrich Swain Hartenburg is about to leave Lorient on his ninth patrol.'

VIII HEINRICH
4 November 1942– 28 February 1943

Heinrich Hartenburg woke shouting. 'Dive, dive, *dive!*'

Then he recognised his familiar *Beau Séjour* bedroom, and sank back again on the pillows.

Just a dream.

The Tommies were back again, that was all. Still trying to penetrate the twenty feet of concrete over the U-boat shelters.

He looked at his watch. Only eleven o'clock. For another hour, he could lap up the soft feel of clean sheets. All his things were packed. The car to take him to the quay wouldn't be arriving till after lunch.

The last couple of trips had been bad ones. *Das verdamnte Licht* attack had been a nasty shock. The Chief had wanted him to return Lorient, but makeshift repairs had got them through the patrol. Worth the effort – 22,000 more tons sunk.

But aircraft were making life hell. Thank God they had the Metox receiver – the *Biscayakreutz*, the crew called the cross-shaped aerial. Now they could hear the Tommies' radar twenty miles away – and dive.

Sinkings were still high – 800,000 tons last month. But so were U-boat losses. Three a week, mostly by aircraft.

U532, U39 and U776 had not returned last week. Just before he went to bed the previous night, he had heard that U232 was overdue.

Sabotage, the authorities were saying. No other possible reason. The Enigma Code couldn't be broken, the cryptologists were certain about that. If a machine were captured, there was a special code which the survivors were to use in their Red Cross letters home. No such notification had been received.

Result – spy mania. The SS and the *Abwehr* were beginning to suspect their own ugly shadows. So, at times, did he. Two nights before, slipping out from the *Beau Séjour* to see Suzanne, he had found himself stopping every few yards, flattening himself against the wall and listening. He had heard nothing but the distant sound of the sea, seen nothing but an alley cat searching for fish-heads.

Suzanne would have laughed if she had seen him. She had amused him that evening with a description of the *Abwehr* and the French *Milice* doing their regular security check of the Todt organisation. She herself had above average clearance and as a chemist she was treated with respect. They had arrested a Polish cleaner and two Arab cooks for stealing soap and beans. Suzanne was a good mimic. He had laughed uproariously. What clowns the police were! He had thought of the ridiculous fuss, happily now done with, that the *Abwehr* had made of poor Papa Swain's letter. But he hadn't told her of it. She hated the English so much, he thought wryly. She would not approve of an English stepfather.

Hours later, the RAF had dropped their nightly incendiaries. He had made love to Suzanne in the crimson glow through the crack in the shutters. Clasping her to him, he momentarily forgot his need to succeed and whispered emotionally, 'I would be happy to die now. Like this.'

'So would I,' she had whispered. 'So would I.'

But the incendiaries had burned themselves out and the bedroom had become pitch black. No high explosive bombs had followed.

Now, there was a blessed silence, followed by the All Clear. For thirty minutes more, he lay comfortable in the luxury hotel that would have to last him over a fortnight's patrol.

The maid brought him some coffee just after twelve. He dressed leisurely, went downstairs, picked up his mail and took it into the dining room.

A request from Berlin Radio to give a talk. Two publishers were suggesting he wrote his memoirs. The big fat letter from his mother he opened last.

There was an enclosure. He recognised the writing. He felt his heart stop.

. . . *from a Swedish missionary friend*, she wrote. *You see that Papa Swain is very anxious. He has heard things and is worried about us. He talks of another letter. That I did not receive. What should I do, Heinrich?*

She did not seem really worried. She had such unbounded faith and confidence in him.

Papa Swain's letter was full of love and caring – and foolishness. Feeling irritated and frustrated, he finished his meal, went up to his room and burned both letters in the empty grate.

Then he sat down and wrote his mother a short note, saying simply that he had her letter and would deal with the matter she had raised on his return from patrol. Then he posted it in the hotel box before getting into the waiting car and driving to the docks.

Inside the U-boat shelter, Kruger was waiting beside U888 carrying their sealed orders. Next in line was Varenfordt's boat U181, back from patrol with the dents of cannon shells all over the golden crown painted on her conning tower.

'Any idea where they're sending us, Sir?'

'North Atlantic, I hope!'

There was no farewell ceremonial.

They left the tug off Ile de Croix. Hartenburg decoded the orders on the Enigma.

He swore softly. '*Verflucht!*' Over his shoulder, he called out, 'It's the Med, Exec!'

Kruger grimaced. 'Lots of destroyers and aircraft!'

Five days later, after hugging the Spanish and Portuguese coasts without interference, they saw through their binoculars the lion-shaped shadow of the Rock of Gibraltar, speckled with grey silhouettes and buzzing flies.

One of the flies started coming towards them. Immediately Hartenburg sounded the Alarm and dived.

For the next two days, he reconnoitred the approaches to the Straits, searching for a way to get through. No way appeared. Destroyers and aircraft were constantly patrolling.

Others were having the same problem. His radioman handed him an intercepted message: BEING ATTACKED IN STRAITS OF GIBRALTAR. HYDROPLANES DAMAGED UNABLE TO DIVE U732.

'Poor old Schultze,' Hartenburg said. 'Hope he's all right.'

It was a faint hope. Two hours later, there was another message: U732 SINKING.

In the evening of the third day, Hartenburg went over to the Moroccan bank, hoping to use the tide current to help him through.

The coastline was shallow. U888 crept along at five knots. There was nothing on the Metox, nothing on the hydrophones. Hartenburg was beginning to think they were through when the hydrophone operator passed across a message. 'Propeller noises.'

Five minutes later came the Asdic pings on the hull. Then a pattern of twelve depth-charges.

u888 shook all over. Rivets burst. All the lighting had gone, even the emergency. The darkness was filled with the sound of water pouring into the boat. Then the smell of chlorine came flooding up from the batteries.

His torch piercing the darkness, the Chief Engineer came up to report. One of the diesels had been shifted off its mountings. The electrical panel was smashed. There was water a foot deep in the engine room. The air was getting poisoned with fumes. The men were panting and choking.

'We'll have to go up soon, Sir.'

Hartenburg waited till dark. Then, very carefully, he brought u888 to periscope depth and took a good look round.

'Nothing but stars, Exec! Surface!'

Compressed air hissed into the ballast tanks. Kruger opened the lid. Fresh air came pouring in.

'Give me all the speed you can, Chief!'

u888 limped back to the lee of the Spanish coast. There they stayed stopped while the Chief Engineer and his ERAs assessed the damage.

Hartenburg gave orders that the men were to have their favourite meal – beef soup, strawberries and chocolate – his usual reward after they'd had a tough time.

Immediately they started eating, they became as cheerful as schoolboys. He stayed in his cabin and wrote his report on the patrol so far. He was sitting, pen poised, frowning down at his own words, irritated that they would make such melancholy reading, when he heard the faint furtive sound of a carefully turned-down radio.

It was not their wireless. It was not morse. By the softness of the transmission, by the clapping and cheers that punctuated it, he realised the seamen were listening again to the *Atlantiksender*, the British propaganda service to U-boats.

Hartenburg's frown deepened, but he didn't move. He'd had his command long enough to know when and when not to exercise it. The seamen were only interested in the American jazz and their local teams' football scores. Let them listen! It was a treat, like the strawberries and chocolate.

Then someone must have turned up the volume. Above the static came the voice of the announcer as clearly as if she sat in the cabin with him. He would have recognised its timbre, its cadences, its beguiling faintly accented German anywhere.

Alexandra's voice. He sat transfixed.

'. . . Third Flotilla, one . . . Sixth Flotilla, two . . .'

Then, as if she knew she had their attention, she changed her tone, speaking gently as if she really cared about them all.

'All you crew of German U-boats, why do you fight for Hitler? For an evil regime? Don't you know you will be sacrificed? Like your comrades on U732 and U39? They are already dead. They will never return to Lorient again!'

It could have been Alexandra speaking earnestly to him alone, speaking as if she minded what happened to him. Alexandra on the hilltop of Kirkstone, Alexandra at Hamburg, Alexandra in his mother's house. He tried to feel anger, outrage, betrayal. To visualise Alexandra now as the enemy. The propagandist. The spreader of lies.

At that point, he must have yelled for the radio to be turned off. He couldn't remember so doing. But he felt the sharpness of the sudden silence. Even felt Alexandra's sudden absence like an exorcised ghost.

But she had not been exorcised. It was as if she had transported him out of the foetid cabin, back to Ceylon and his childhood again. He sat with his arms folded across his chest, remembering their little group, mourning their innocence.

He thought of his mother and Papa Swain and Papa's elderly and abiding innocence. He no longer felt irritation towards his adoptive father, only pride in his love and faith. Poor Papa Swain going about his calling as if the world were not a wicked place, and man was still human, still redeemable.

Five minutes later, the Engineer Officer came up to report that they would need heavy lifting gear and a dockyard to move the port diesel back on its mountings. He pointed out it would be suicide to attempt the Med in their crippled state. He suggested that they take advantage of the two days' grace allowed to combatants and put in to Cadiz.

Hartenburg agreed. It seemed quite clear then what he must do.

Alone again, he took out paper and envelope and wrote a letter to his dear Papa Swain. He told him that both he and his mother were well and sent their love, but regrettably he *mustn't* contact them any more. Such contact would be very dangerous. In happier times, they would see him. Till then.

He sealed the envelope, grateful now that Papa Swain's God had given this opportunity to him, and climbed the ladder up onto the deck.

The cold fresh air poured into his lungs like nectar. He felt simultaneously disturbed and exalted by hearing Alexandra's voice.

Looking over the phosphorescent crests of the black waves, he wondered what she looked like now and whether he would ever see her again, and if she would recognise him if he did, and whether they would ever cease to be enemies.

u888 took three hours to limp into Cadiz. He thought of Alexandra for most of that time, and of the strange and mixed-up world they lived in. For the first time, he thought that dear foolish Papa Swain was the only sane one in it.

The Spanish were very friendly. They gave Hartenburg and his Chief Engineer every cooperation, providing tools, winches, lifting gear, main electric power, even six of their own submarine technicians.

The Spanish Navy entertained u888's crew to a lavish dinner ashore in their own Mess. The wine flowed. Señoritas were invited. Warm and fulsome speeches were made. The historic friendship of Fascist Spain and Nazi Germany was toasted. So was Spain's gratitude for Germany's staunch support in the Civil War.

Just after midnight, Hartenburg made the excuse that he must get back to u888 to check on the repairs to the engine mountings. He walked down to the barracks' main gate. He returned the sentry's salute and turned left down the wide avenue towards the town centre. In his pocket was his letter to Papa Swain, now with the right Spanish stamps affixed.

He stopped outside the Post Office. He waited till a group of people on the other side of the avenue had disappeared down a side street. He looked left and right.

No one was coming. There was no sound of cars. The place was totally deserted.

He took the letter out of his pocket, dropped it into the postbox and immediately walked briskly up the avenue again and down to the harbour.

The whole diversion had only taken him five minutes. He was back on board, joking with the Spanish technicians and the members of his own crew on Watch long before the revellers returned from the party.

Before he turned in, he left a note for the Duty Officer to remind all hands that listening to enemy propaganda was *verboten*, and would be punished.

Then he climbed into his bunk and fell dreamlessly asleep.

u888 stayed in Cadiz the permitted two days. Then she went out to sea again and entered Sanlucar fifteen miles further up the coast. After two days there, on she went to Huelva. Hartenburg was determined not to go back to Lorient empty-handed. News was coming in from the Atlantic Wolf Packs of massive sinkings. Varenfordt had added 15,000 tons to his score.

After two weeks of this cat-and-mouse game, with the Spanish winking a blind eye at International Law and u888 becoming healthier every day, Hartenburg finally left his hosts with many expressions of gratitude and reported to U-boat Central that sufficient makeshift repairs had been made to fit the boat for further duty.

To everyone's relief he was not sent to the Mediterranean, but up into the central Atlantic to join the south end of the Dolphin Wolf Pack.

Five days later, the Watch reported masts on the horizon. A convoy of sixty ships hove into sight.

But so did two Very Long Range Liberators. Only at the north end of the Wolf Pack could an attack be made.

The Wolf Pack followed the convoy. But that night while travelling on the surface, with no Metox warning, down came a Liberator, illuminated u888 with its searchlight and dropped six depth-charges that flung the boat on her side.

After they had righted her, the Chief reported the clutch between the diesels and the engines was jammed, the hydrophones damaged and the main oil tank ruptured.

'Have to go back this time, sir,' the Chief Engineer said.

Hartenburg ruefully agreed.

It was a nightmare journey. Attacks by single-engined Avengers indicated that the American aircraft-carrier USS *Bogue* was around. Nine times u888 had to crash-dive from aircraft for which there had been no Metox warning. There was every indiation, Hartenburg wrote in his Log, that the Tommies had new and sophisticated radar on frequencies outside those received by the Metox.

They arrived at Lorient in a damaged boat with all their torpedoes, after being away for five weeks. It was a particular humiliation to Heinrich Hartenburg to come in to harbour with only his Commander's pennant flying and no other flag for naval or merchant ships sunk.

The usual welcome committee was there in the U-boat shelter – the Flotilla Commander, the band blaring, the administrative girls cheering and throwing flowers. There was the usual champagne dinner.

Hartenburg left early. There had been three letters from his mother at the *Beau Séjour*, the first one acknowledging his note. All of them circumspect and guarded, as if she had sensed without him telling her of the need for discretion.

Now that he had been able to send the letter to Papa Swain from Cadiz, with luck there would be no more repercussions.

It was Suzanne he longed to see now. As he changed into flannels and sweater, for the first time he thought of her in connection with Alexandra, acknowledging their similarity and disparity with one another – Alexandra now the enemy, and Suzanne the loyal friend. He wondered wryly and romantically if his mature love for Suzanne was grafted onto the old adolescent love for Alexandra. An interesting idea, he thought, and a not unpleasant one. He brushed his thick hair, smiling at his own reflection in the dressing-table mirror, anticipating Suzanne's warm and loving welcome.

He was still smiling as a knock sounded on the bedroom door. The chambermaid, no doubt, to rinse out his bath and replace the towels.

'Come in!'

He saw the reflection of the door behind him opening with momentous slowness. Not the neat fingers of the chambermaid, but Kauffenstein came in.

Heinrich put down his hairbrush with a sharp rap. He felt the back of his neck tingle with a premonition of danger. He turned round, shoulders squared, feet apart. He opened his mouth, about to object, but the *Abwehr* officer forestalled him.

'Please forgive the intrusion, Herr Kapitänleutnant.' Kauffenstein smiled affably and apologetically. Running his eyes over Hartenburg's clothes, he added, 'I hope you were not about to go out?'

'No.' Hartenburg replied shortly.

'Good. May I sit down?'

'If you wish.'

Ponderously, Kauffenstein unfastened the buttons of his overcoat and settled himself into one of the two armchairs that flanked a small oval table by the window.

'I would feel easier if you also would sit down, Herr Kapitänleutnant.' He waved invitingly towards the other chair. 'Then . . .'

'Then,' Hartenburg said crisply, 'you will tell me the reason for, as you rightly called it, this intrusion.'

Kauffenstein nodded. 'I will, Herr Kapitänleutnant, I will!'

He watched Hartenburg walk slowly towards him, 'It is better you are comfortable. We have a long night in front of us.'

Hartenburg said nothing for a moment. No words were needed. As sharply as if Kauffenstein had tapped Grandfather Mendelssohn's tuning fork, the conversation took a sombre note.

A fearful note. A threatening note.

'Well?' Hartenburg lifted his chin and narrowed his eyes, 'Well? *What* is your reason?'

Kauffenstein met his gaze steadily for several seconds. Then he dipped his hand into his coat pocket, brought out a white envelope, *the* white envelope, with the Spanish stamps affixed, and laid it on the table between them.

He made no comment. The silence seemed to go on and on. Outside, in the street below, a lorry trundled past, then another. A tug hooted across the harbour water.

Then Kauffenstein said mildly, 'You said that your mother would not receive any more letters.'

'I did not expect she would. On the other hand, I could not promise she wouldn't.'

Kauffenstein inclined his head. 'But what you could promise, what you *did* promise, was that if she did receive such a letter you would inform me.'

Hartenburg said nothing.

'But you didn't,' Kauffenstein prompted.

'I hadn't the time.'

'One can always make the time.'

'I had to go on patrol.' Hartenburg clenched his fists. 'The war doesn't wait!'

'But you have been so foolish!' Kauffenstein managed to look genuinely regretful. 'So foolish! To post this in Spain. Surely you must know our *Abwehr* Chief, Admiral Canaris, is himself a Spaniard! He has the closest links with Spain.'

Hartenburg said stiffly, 'I did what seemed best at the time to bring the correspondence to an end.'

'But you have flouted your country's laws! You have been discovered! We must act. If not, the Gestapo assuredly will!'

'So how do you propose to act?'

Kauffenstein sighed. 'We must investigate.'

'Investigate me?'

Kauffenstein nodded. 'Bearing in mind your eminence and my
admiration, I am truly sorry to –'

Hartenburg cut short his apology. 'How investigate?'

'Cryptologists.' Kauffenstein studied his own fingernails and did
not look directly at Hartenburg. 'You will know well what such
people are. They will examine the letters for codes.'

'What nonsense!' Hartenburg jumped to his feet. 'What absolute
rubbish!'

'And while that is being done,' Kauffenstein began to button up
his overcoat, 'you must be kept under surveillance.'

Hartenburg was so angry that at first the words didn't penetrate.

'*Mein Gott!*' he exclaimed. 'There's a war to be won! We're right
at the turning point! And *you* investigate my mother's letters for
codes!'

Suddenly the words *under surveillance* penetrated his tiredness and
anger.

Under surveillance? Him? Kapitänleutnant Hartenburg? It was
impossible! Unthinkable!

'There is also an underground war.' Kauffenstein stood up. 'Just
as deadly as the war you fight.' He drew himself to his full height. 'I
suggest you pack a change of clothes and your toilet things.'

His tone had become cold, curt now and menacing. 'I must ask
you to accompany me to Brest gaol. We have a car waiting.

Kauffenstein drove the ninety kilometres from Lorient to Brest at
top speed without saying a word. Fitful moonlight chequered the
U-boat shelters as they rounded the bay, sped past the massive stone
French Naval College, now the Headquarters of the First U-boat
Flotilla, and clanked over the canal drawbridge to the prison in the
centre of the town.

'I am truly sorry,' he said again to Hartenburg when he handed
him over to two uniformed warders.

'Am I in for a long stay?'

'That will depend.'

'On what?'

'Our enquiries.'

'Well,' Hartenburg said angrily, 'tell me what you find out, because *I* don't damned well know.'

'We will, Herr Kapitänleutnant. We will.' Then he gave the Nazi salute. *'Heil Hitler!'*

Hartenburg said bitterly, *'Auf Wiedersehen.'*

The prison reeked of urine and disinfectant, but the guards were courteous. He was put in a hospital cell. The bed had clean sheets, but he could not sleep. He kept wondering what had happened to his mother, if he could or should have acted otherwise.

Next morning, the Prison Governor, an SA colonel, came to see him at nine o'clock and asked solicitously about his comfort.

'I want to know why I'm here at all.'

The Colonel shrugged his shoulder. 'Well, of course, I do not know the answer.'

'But you must!'

'I do not.' The Colonel drew himself up stiffly. 'You have my word.'

He's lying, Hartenburg thought. But as the day went by, he wasn't so sure. He was treated gingerly with care and respect, like an animal they didn't quite know how to handle. Excellent food was brought him from a local restaurant. No ordinary warder, but the Governor himself accompanied him on his exercise round the prison yard. He was given newspapers. He could listen to the radio. He was allowed books and writing materials. He could send one letter a week to his mother. This would be censored. But it would be posted through the ordinary mail and he must give the *Beau Séjour* at Lorient as his address. In his first letter, he had to tell her that he was assigned to a special mission and would not be able to visit her for some little time.

'You don't want it known that I'm in prison?' he asked the Governor.

'Nor, I imagine, do you,' the Colonel countered.

No, nor did he, Hartenburg thought, as he began his fifth week in this cold white cell.

His mother would be frantic. He had received two letters from her. Guarded letters. No code or cryptologist was needed for him to know that she was afraid.

If only he could get out! Escape was out of the question. He was an officer of the Reich. He must be released with honour. To add to his fame. For he must indeed, as he had memorised from those Shakespeare lessons of Kirkstone days, be 'seeking the bubble reputation even in the cannon's mouth'. That reputation was his and his mother's only shield. It was an embarrassment to the prison staff and the authorities that he was here. As a household name, a top U-boat hero, any stain on him would be a blow to German morale. The last thing the Führer would want publicised was that his leading U-boat ace was a traitor. For the successes of the U-boats were the only good news in the German papers. Varenfordt was top of the league and now, ominously, his own name was not mentioned.

'It would appear,' the Governor said on the brisk morning march early in the New Year, as the frozen puddles cracked like glass under their feet, 'that our advance into Russia must be halted for the winter.'

Hartenburg said nothing. Edgar, the warder who brought him his meals, a stout little Bavarian, had told him the Governor chafed to be back on active service, disliked prison duties and confining such as the Kapitänleutnant.

'Are there many such as me?' Hartenburg asked him, but he wouldn't say. Edgar was respectful, but frightened himself. He did not share the Governor's desire to be sent to the front.

'May I at least be given access to my superior officer?' Hartenburg demanded of the Governor, when the seventh week of his confinement began.

The cell was growing smaller, the white ceiling pressing down like a box lid. He was beginning to hear cries and strange sounds at night. He felt a claustrophobia which he had never felt in a U-boat.

He clenched his fists with frustration, paced up and down the tiny room, and only by a supreme effort of will stopped himself gripping the iron bars over the windows and screaming his pent-up rage to the grim façade of the prison block opposite him.

On the Friday of that tenth week, there was a bomber's moon. The air-raid sirens sounded in Brest. Hartenburg put his eye to a crack in the blackout behind the window bars, peering up at the bright flashes of gunfire, the blue-white searchlights. He glimpsed a Lancaster bomber caught like a black moth in their cone, saw it explode in incandescent orange, flaming red. The stone prison shook to the crump of bombs. Shrapnel and glass splinters rained down.

The following day, he read that the RAF had attacked not only the Brest peninsula but also the Ruhr. Whole cities were set ablaze in brutal saturation bombing, which was nevertheless leaving the German people undismayed. In an inside page of the paper, he saw that Rommel had retreated to Tunisia and that General Paulus and his entire Army had surrendered to the Russians at Stalingrad.

All this would be reversed in a short time of course, but meanwhile the German people must spare no effort.

'*Mein Gott!*' Hartenburg crumpled up the paper. The German army was caught like Napoleon's by the Russian winter. The Ruhr was ablaze, Rommel in retreat, his supplies cut by the British navy, while the *Abwehr* or the SS tried to make out that Papa Swain was a cryptologist and their leading U-boat ace a traitor! If it hadn't been so tragic and dangerous, he would have laughed out loud.

He was reminded of Fische four years ago at Kirkstone, and his secret weapons mania, culled from his father who was a friend of Goebbels. And suddenly he was back at Kirkstone School, to the hilltop with Alexandra again. Alexandra in black stockings and gym slip and neat white virginal blouse, laughing provocatively up at him. Alexandra lying beside him behind the hedge.

Alexandra the enemy, he reminded himself sternly, closing his mind to anything except the present. But when he finally got to sleep that night, it was of Alexandra that he dreamed, and the Midshipman's Cup and the cracking of Varenfordt's mast. He actually heard the crack and woke laughing.

But that crack was repeated, a merging series of cracks. A volley.

Disorientated, still half in his dreams, he blinked his eyes. It was still dark. Now his ears caught the sound of voices, orders, stamping feet. Now another volley.

He felt for his watch and looked at its phosphorescent numerals. Six o'clock. The time for executions. He clenched his fists and lay back on the pillows, sweating.

That morning, the Governor did not appear to accompany him on exercise. Edgar marched round with him. He refused to answer any questions. His solid face was set. He had heard nothing. The Kapitänleutnant must have had nightmares. Many prisoners did.

And when the Governor appeared three days later, he was relaxed and affable.

'I am happy to say, your informal request has been granted, Herr Kapitänleutnant.'

Hartenburg's spirits soared. Hoarsely, he asked, 'I'm to be released?'

'Not now. Not precisely now. But very soon. It was your other request. To see your superior officer.'

He beckoned behind him, and in came Korvetten-Kapitän Thormann.

The Commanding Officer of the First Flotilla was a bluff red-faced Navy man who found the situation quite beyond him. He perched on the edge of his chair saying over and over again, 'It's all a big balls-up, Heinrich. We'll get you out of here double-quick.'

'How quick is double-quick?'

'Well, very quick.'

'This week?'

'I wouldn't like to say. But now we know . . .'

'Does Grossadmiral Dönitz know?'

Thormann seemed appalled at the very idea. 'No, no! Certainly not! The Grossadmiral is so very busy. He has succeeded Admiral Raeder and is now in charge of the whole *Kriegsmarine*. As you know, he moved from Kerneval to Paris. Now he is moving again.'

'Where to?'

Just for a moment, the Korvetten-Kapitän hesitated. That hesitation pierced Hartenburg more than anything that had so far happened to him. He's not one hundred per cent sure of me – he of all people!

He didn't press the Korvetten-Kapitän. He simply folded his arms across his chest, stared at his superior officer and waited.

After a long pause, Thormann said, 'To Berlin.'

'I would like Dönitz to be informed. I formally request that he be informed.'

'He can do nothing, Heinrich.'

'On the contrary, he can do *anything*! Second-in-command to Hitler. Of course he can!'

'There have been several attempts on our Führer's life,' the Korvetten-Kapitän said, in a low anxious voice.

'That doesn't concern me.'

'It concerns us all, Heinrich,' Thormann said tersely. And then more kindly. 'But let us talk more cheerfully! Varenfordt has been awarded the Knight's Cross with Swords and Diamonds. Our sinkings last year totalled eight million tons. And soon we shall have the new Mark xxi U-boats. Perhaps you' – his voice was uncon-vincing – 'will command one.'

'And how is my Exec Kruger and the rest of my crew?'

'They are well. Very well. '

Hartenburg smiled wryly. 'Straining at the leash, I imagine?'

'Straining?'

'Anxious to get going. Impatient at kicking their heels while I'm in here.'

The Korvetten-Kapitän's red face went redder. His blue eyes looked unhappy. 'Impatient? Ah, no! We have been careful of that. We have not let your crew stay idle. That would indeed be bad. They went out on patrol last week.'

'In U888?'

'That's right.'

'Under whose command?'

'Kruger's. He's been promoted to Oberleutnant.'

Hartenburg said nothing. He felt very cold. For the first time he wondered seriously if he would ever leave this little white cell alive.

IX JOHN
28 February 1943–26 March 1943

Oh God, Blake thought, are any of us going to get out of this alive?

Below him, the CO's Liberator, on fire from nose to tail, was literally flinging itself at the leader of the three formating U-boats.

From his side window in K King, peering through the Bay of Biscay mist, he followed its flaming progress into the hail of red and white tracer from the multiple pom-poms on the *Wintergartens* of the three conning towers.

Three hundred yards away now. Two hundred. Suicide he thought! Bloody suicide! Another Charge of the Light Brigade. But he's going to take that U-boat with him!

A hundred yards. Fifty . . .

Suddenly a burst of white water. A flash of orange.

Then nothing . . . *nothing*! Just the three U-boats continuing at full speed westwards into the Atlantic.

On the VHF, Blake called up the other Liberator circling the formation just out of range of the guns. His mouth still felt dry, his heart hammering.

'The CO nearly got her!' he said. It sounded inept and inadequate. But what else could he say?

'So I saw.' Fanshawe's voice came over loud and clear from S Sugar.

'Our turn next.' That was one octave more cheerful than 'Us next'. End product the same, though. Yet one of those might be Swain/ Hartenburg, and that spurred him on.

He could still remember the shock that had gone through him at Western Approaches when he had learned the true identity of Hartenburg, the name of the man behind the silver shark painted on the iron mask. At one time, he had been conscious of a certain pity, even a certain superiority. All that was over now that he knew Henry Swain was not only alive but was dealing death and destruction wholesale. All the old hate had revived. All the old secrecy that he had to maintain with Alexandra.

'The sooner we go in, Foxy, the better,' he called on the VHF. 'Delay, and they'll dive!'

Certainly he'd acted soon on the Swain/Hartenburg news. The moment he'd got back to SRU, he'd put in for a posting back to Operations. That hadn't been easy. As a trained scientific test pilot, Command had wanted to keep him where he was.

Not till a month ago had he managed to get posted as a Squadron Leader to 656 Squadron at St Edzell in Cornwall, operating VLR Liberators in the Bay of Biscay and the Black Pit in the centre of the Atlantic.

He was glad to see Fanshawe again, glad to be back at last on Operations. Becoming proficient in the latest scientific anti-U-boat devices had been both fascinating and necessary, but now he particularly wanted to put them into practice.

Intelligence was reporting Hartenburg very much alive, still amongst the three or four aces at the top of the sinkings table. Over Berlin radio, Lord Haw-Haw was calling him 'the second Gunther Prien, who will sink the *Queen Elizabeth*'.

'Now the sun's going down' – again Fanshawe's voice over the VHF – 'the mist's getting worse!'

'Certainly difficult to see 'em.'

'Shall we go in *now*?'

Through the gloom, Blake saw S Sugar's starboard wingtip lift ahead of the three white arrowheads. Fanshawe's voice, 'Going in!'

Blake tipped up his port wing, 'Going in too.'

Still hugging the water, he skidded K King right round, linking up two miles behind the three U-boats.

All hell had broken out in front. Puffs of heavy flak weaved themselves into a black blanket threaded with long streams of red, white and green tracer.

Bronski peered through the windscreen. 'No sign of Fanshawe.'

'There he is now!'

As Blake pushed the throttles against the stops, the Liberator's white wings emerged like a ghostly bird flying out of a thunderstorm, forward and upper turret guns spitting silver beads into the leading conning tower.

'Giving as good as he's getting.' Bronski moved to go forrad. 'Going to man the low-level bomb sight, Skipper.'

Suddenly everything went dark. K King was flying over on her port side. An 88-millimetre had exploded.

'In line with the U-boat now, Skipper.' Bronski's quiet voice over the intercom. 'One mile.'

'Watch out for Sugar, Skipper! Dead ahead of us now!'

Fanshawe was still airborne, rocketing up to the U-boat's bow.

'Got my eye on him.'

Suddenly it all happened.

A huge orange flash appeared ahead of them. Liberator and U-boat disappeared in flames and smoke.

'Sugar!' the front gunner screamed. 'Crashed into the conning tower!'

Blake had already seen. Pulling the starboard wing vertical, he kicked the Liberator right round away from the holocaust.

'Attacking the portside U-boat, Bronski!' he yelled. 'See him?'

'I see him.' The American's voice was as matter-of-fact as ever.

'We'll attack from the beam.'

A crash like thunder as the starboard outer was hit. Blake pushed the red feathering button to stop the windmilling propeller screaming. Sweat poured down his face as he jammed his left leg on the rudder to keep her straight.

'Two hundred yards.' Bronski seemed to be talking from another world. 'One hundred . . . getting ready to drop . . . depth-charges gone!'

'Terrific, Bronx!' the rear gunner was shouting. 'A straddle . . . a beautiful straddle! God, those explosions!'

Blake waited till they were well out of range before putting on full port bank to have a look behind.

The orange fire was still burning – that was what riveted his eyes. The bows of the U-boat that Fanshawe had attacked were right up in the air like an obelisk, garlanded with pieces of burning Liberator.

Even as Blake watched, it began sliding backwards, down, down, down – till everything had disappeared.

Where his U-boat had been was a massive oil-slick.

'At least Foxy got the bastard,' Blake thought. 'He didn't go empty-handed.'

A bubble of near-hysterical laughter rose in his throat. Sharply, he called over the intercom.

'What's the damage?'

The outer starboard engine feathered, oil streaming over the wing, the rudder responding like two frozen feet. But what else?

Bronski came up with the list. Shell holes right down the fuselage, the top half of the tailplane shot off. But nothing through the hydraulic system and none of the crew hurt.

'We'll make it, Skipper, I guess?' It was fifty-fifty statement and question.

'I guess.' Blake gently parodied him.

A curious detachment now seemed to possess him. A mechanical doing of what had to be done. All part of the training. All part of making the fighting man out of the schoolboy. For another fifteen minutes, they circled the scene, sending wireless homing reports to other aircraft.

Come in and kill! The tigers are half dead! Their U-boat, the one with the crown on the conning tower, was lying on the surface, stopped, surrounded by a sea of its own oil. The survivor was alongside trying to help.

It had altogether been a major victory, Blake thought, as he set course for home. But he felt tired and morose. He experienced none of the exhilaration he'd occasionally felt after a successful battle, none of the euphoria of just being alive. He felt almost guilty at being the lone survivor while Foxy and the CO had gone in.

Foxy of all people, the typical survivor, getting the chop just when they were winning the U-boat war. Poor old Foxy!

Blake stared down at the grey empty sea, trying to summon up again the warmth of revenge. But there had been something about that line of U-boats, grimly remaining surfaced, fighting to the death, that had excited his admiration as well as his hatred, and that made a bloody bitter mixture.

He was almost glad of the numbness of the rudder. He could fume and curse and labour with the bloody thing. It gave him the same satisfaction as biting on a bad tooth and was just about as stupid.

When Bronski put the box of sandwiches on the throttle pedestal and asked cheerfully, 'D'you reckon they'll give us a spot of leave, Skipper?' Blake looked at him as if he were from another world.

So he was. Or at least, leave was. He hadn't had leave since the forty-eight hours at the end of December when William was born.

This time it had been Alexandra who had signed the telegram. YOU HAVE A SON. WE'RE ALL FINE. LOVE, ALEXANDRA.

Not, he had noted, *you* have *another* son, or *we* have another son, but *you* have a son. *Yours*. Even before he had gone home on that forty-eight-hour pass, he had begun to wonder if she would love his son less than she loved Heinrich's. What a petty-minded bastard he was becoming!

He took a mouthful of chicken sandwich, and mumbled, 'Probably' to Bronski.

This time, he thought, the leave would go better. Alexandra had been tearful after the baby. Perfectly natural, Mrs Monteith had assured him.

A physical symptom. *Not* depressed, *depression*. For what had Alexandra to be depressed about? Two fine sons and a splendid husband. Blake had the feeling she was repeating a brisk pep talk she had given Alexandra herself before he arrived.

Funnily enough, till William was actually born, things had been better between Alexandra and him. He had even begun to think that she loved him a little. Her German broadcasts seemed to have given her a new identity, a new importance of herself to herself.

He couldn't explain it. But it was as if now she was someone in her own right. Not Mrs Monteith's daughter, or Heinrich's mistress, or Maurice's mother, or Blake's wife, but herself. Herself – conscientious, painstaking, discreet, fulfilled. Even the fact that she was pregnant had not unduly depressed her. She would go on working at Woburn for as long as she could. And after she had the baby, she would go back, if they would have her.

For himself, Blake had experienced a strange secret pleasure in Alexandra's pregnancy. He felt more grown-up, more of a man. He had enjoyed trying to look after her. He had cycled round the local farms and bought eggs and if he were lucky, butter and the occasional chicken. He had become expert in rolling eggs in newspaper and putting them in boxes he bagged from stores and posting them back home. Alexandra wrote to thank him very sweetly, and he telephoned her as often as he could.

But with William's birth, all the old barriers came back up. He wasn't a very prepossessing baby. He was much smaller than Maurice had been, a fact ascribed firmly by Mrs Monteith to wartime rationing and to arriving a bit ahead of schedule – 29 December.

'He'll be a press-on type,' she said.

But Maurice was her darling. A sturdy, noisy three-year-old. More than a bit of a handful. Needing a man's heavier hand. Like his father, always demanding to be the centre of attention.

To see in the New Year, Mrs Monteith and Blake had gathered round Alexandra's bed with the two bottles of gin he had managed to buy in the Mess. Maurice was safely tucked in bed.

Then, just after midnight, Maurice had wakened.

'I'll go,' Blake had said.

It was logical that he should. Alexandra couldn't and Mrs Monteith was well away and shouldn't. When Maurice argued, Blake had done what he'd wanted to do for the past forty hours. He put him over his knee and let him feel a man's hand.

Alexandra had been angry at first and then tearful.

'She never could take her gin,' Mrs Monteith had said apologetically, when she resumed her New Year celebrations downstairs.

He had returned quite thankfully to SRU the next morning. Alexandra had written only once a week since then.

Now the thought of leave stirred up the same apprehension of failure as the bloody landing he would soon be called upon to make.

Outside, sea and sky had merged to one opalescent horizonless grey. Birds'-feather grey, muffling and suffocating. Not the bloody weather to be coming down in without a rudder. Talk about up Shit Creek without a paddle, and you had there a pretty accurate description.

Just behind him, Bronski was whistling through his teeth, but he wasn't missing anything. His eyes were checking the instruments, the density of the cloud racing past the windows, Blake's hands on the stick.

He got them down all of a piece. Just. With the fire and the meat wagons racing after them. When he brought the Liberator to a halt, Bronski punched his shoulder in mute congratulation and stretching his arms, sighed, 'Now for that leave! London, here I come!'

Going home on the train to Oxford, Blake sat opposite a plump handsome woman in ENSA khaki, who was going to organise a camp concert at Heddingford. He found himself telling her about his wife and his sons and his crew. He was desperate to unwind.

He didn't tell her about the DFC. That bit of news, the immediate award, had been broken to him as he picked up his travel warrant from the Adjutant. He had been overwhelmed. He didn't feel he deserved it, and the whole business embarrassed and yet very secretly delighted him. He couldn't help asking himself, who would have thought it? Me, of all people? And indeed, who would?

As he was leaving the train, the ENSA lady dived into her respirator case, brought out a handful of lipsticks and gave them to him for Alexandra.

'I hope she knows she's a lucky girl to have a fellow like you,' the lady called after him.

He shook his head and blew her a kiss. He had not told Alexandra which train he was coming on, so there was no one to meet him. He felt he still needed more time to adjust before going home.

He took a bus part-way from the station and walked the rest. There were daffodil shoots poking up in the park, some crocuses already out and fat leaf buds on the winter twigs, an indefinable aura of coming spring.

At 7, Park Road, Mrs Monteith had anticipated his arrival. The garden was tidy, the paths swept, the hedge clipped. The house was immaculate, fragrant with the scent of bowls of hyacinths.

Alexandra came running downstairs to greet him. William was pressed up against her shoulder. His wife and his son. What a vision of perfect bliss! Yet like a vision, he felt he couldn't touch them, or reach them.

'Let me take William,' Mrs Monteith said briskly, 'Then you can greet your husband properly.'

Alexandra put her arms round him. William howled. Mrs Monteith paced up and down with him patting his back. Maurice toddled in from the garden and scowled. He clutched his mother round the thigh, glaring as if he saw a monster.

Blake had taken the precaution of buying a hand-made red engine from one of the armourers, who'd been doing a roaring trade now that toys were so scarce in Britain. Now he produced it from his suitcase.

Maurice was delighted. Gave him a kiss. Round one to Blake.

Then he produced the gin for Mrs Monteith and told them diffidently and with genuine self-deprecation about his DFC.

Rounds two, three and four all went to Blake. Mrs Monteith could not have been more pleased. She spurned the usual gin. This was a very special occasion. More special even than the birth of her grandsons. Not just an immediate DFC, but one for sinking a U-boat. Monteith's Reply had been given. Her cup did indeed run over. Only one of the hoarded victory bottles of champagne would do.

'You have a hero for a father,' she told Maurice, allowing him to have a sip from her glass. 'And so do you,' she said smearing William's soft blueberry lips with a finger dipped in champagne.

'To your husband, Alexandra! And to *my* hero son!'

She raised her glass. For a moment, she looked suddenly old, as if attaining her revenge had taken some of the stiffening out of her.

She went to bed early that night to give them an evening by the fire together. They sat on the sofa, holding hands.

Or rather, he held Alexandra's. She still looked wan. William didn't let her get much sleep, and Maurice was at a difficult stage.

'You do love them, don't you, John?'

'Yes, yes.' He had never had time to think about it. He supposed he did. 'Of course.'

'Both the same?'

'Why, yes! Don't you?'

She nodded and then added, 'But I'm their mother.'

'And I'm not their . . .' he began to say, when she put her free hand over his mouth.

'I didn't mean that. I really didn't. Don't say it. I just meant that it comes more naturally to a mother.'

He didn't believe a word of it, but he wasn't going to start an argument.

So he asked her if she missed going to work, and that started her off. She'd like to begin again, as soon as she finished breast-feeding. They wanted her back to Woburn and Mrs Monteith was willing to look after both boys. She was on a number of committees for the war effort, Wings for Victory, the Spitfire Fund, the WVS, but she could hold a lot of the meetings here.

Blake didn't listen. He felt resentment stir inside him. 'I think it's a bit hard on William,' he said tersely.

'But *why*? Mummy's marvellous with children.'

'She's not his mother.'

'She looked after Maurice.'

'William needs you. Someone young. Besides,' he added unforgiveably, 'she drinks.'

'That's a horrible thing to say.'

'Horrible but true.'

Alexandra was furious. But she kept a tight rein on her temper. They went to bed that night in a state of armed neutrality. But half-way through the night, he flung his arm round her, and woke with his head pillowed on her shoulder.

The next day he remembered to give her the silk stockings and the perfume he'd bought in the NAAFI, and the lipsticks the ENSA woman had given him. She was delighted. Lipstick was in such short supply that some of the girls she knew were making their own from lard and cochineal. On their walk through the park that afternoon, Blake insisted on tasting the lipstick.

They sat on a bench under a beech tree, while Maurice crunched noisily around amongst last autumn's beechmast, and Alexandra gently rocked William's pram with her toe. She held up her face obediently like a good child and Blake kissed her lingeringly.

'Good. Very good,' he said. 'Delicious!'

'And was she very good too? Delicious?' Alexandra asked teasingly. 'The ENSA woman?'

For one happy moment, he thought she might be jealous. He toyed with the idea of making her even more so. A good-looking lass, he might say. All these ENSA girls are always very glam, like Rank starlets.

Instead he told the boring truth. 'She was fair, fat and fifty, if a day.'

'I don't believe you,' Alexandra smiled.

But she did.

He wondered what she'd say if he told her about Jennifer. Nothing at all, most likely. But he hated himself for not saying a word all these months. She had written to him regularly. She was still at Kilkerry, still hoping for a posting to the mainland. She was on his conscience and tentatively, the next day, he did broach the subject.

Alexandra was pushing Maurice on one of the swings in the recreation ground, and Blake was lolling against an upright. A squad of the Home Guard were drilling at the far end of the park, the sound of their boots ringing across the frozen ground.

'You remember you told me to take out other girls?'

Imperceptibly, Alexandra seemed to stiffen. In a quiet neutral voice she corrected, 'I didn't *tell* you to. I said if you *wanted* to, I had no right to be jealous.'

'Same thing.'

'*Not* the same thing.' There was a pause while she thumped Maurice higher on the swing. 'Why? *Have* you been?'

But he was so put off by the tone of her voice that he said, 'No. Of course not.'

'Then why bring it up?'

'I wondered if you felt the same?'

'Yes.'

The walk back home was broken by Maurice asking what taking out a girl was.

'Oh,' Alexandra answered patiently, 'going to the pictures. Or a party. Or out to dinner. Something nice like that. Isn't that so?'

She turned to John and smiled quite sweetly. But he felt vaguely got at by the pair of them, and his own inability to do, or to think, or say, or feel the right thing. He began to count the days before he could go back to St Edzell. He invented a stint as Duty Officer to return a day before his leave was up.

The train back to St Edzell kept stopping and starting, and it was after ten when he walked into the Mess to have a few noggins before bedtime. About to hang up his cap and respirator in the corridor, he suddenly saw a neat clean WAAF officer's cap perched against the battered squadron headgear.

Absurdly, his heart leapt. He unhooked the cap and examined the name tape sewn inside.

45867 Jennifer Jones.

He couldn't believe it. He went in search of her as in a dream.

She was not in the bar or the ante-room. He finally ran her to ground in the deserted dining room. She was seated at a long empty table, looking dog-tired and listlessly eating a sandwich.

'John!' Her face lit up when she saw him.

'I thought you were a mirage.' He slipped into an empty chair beside her and helped himself to one of her sandwiches. 'How come? But first tell me if you're real?' He kissed her to make sure. Then, 'Are you here to stay?'

She nodded.

'Posted?'

'Yes, Air Ministry posting. With effect from today.' She beamed. 'I've been due for a move for ages. But I didn't think I'd be sent here.'

Privately, Blake thought he felt the touch of that old web again. The web of Fate. But aloud he said, 'It figures, though. Action hotting up hereabouts and all that.'

'I suppose so.'

'All the same, what luck! God bless the faceless ones at Air Ministry. Never thought I'd live to say that.'

He trotted off to the bar to fetch a couple of scotches so that they could toast the faceless ones in style. He felt very mellow by the time he escorted her to her quarters. She had found it a long tiring journey from Northern Ireland, and he kept a supportive arm round her all the way. They kissed each other tenderly at her door. 'I can't tell you how glad I am to see you,' he whispered.

'You have done,' she smiled back. 'You have a very revealing face.'

'See you tomorrow,' he said, relinquishing her, and thinking how much better that prospect made all his tomorrows.

He supposed he should have stopped and asked himself the question . . . why?

X HEINRICH
26 March 1943–30 November 1943

'There are one or two questions, Herr Kapitänleutnant . . .'

Hartenburg struggled to his feet and stared into the face of the SS officer whom the Governor had shamefacedly ushered into his cell. Dapper in the black and silver of the hated *Sicherheitsdienst*, the officer was a head shorter than himself, but a compact, confident, intrinsically menacing man. His pale unremarkable face was dominated by the same sort of eyeglasses as his master Himmler, his voice smooth and clipped, his movements precise.

'There are one or two questions I would like to ask *you*,' Hartenburg growled.

'Please,' the SS officer inclined his head, and waved Hartenburg back to his chair. 'I am sure you would prefer we asked questions of you than of . . .' he drew out the silence to its uttermost. 'Your mother.'

The questions were the same. Why had he posted the letter to his stepfather in Spain? How would he explain this correspondence between his mother in Germany and his stepfather in an enemy country?

He answered perfectly truthfully that the correspondence had started as a result of his stepfather's natural anxiety over the welfare of his mother. And he had posted the letter in Spain simply to put an end to that correspondence.

The *Sicherheitsdienst* officer pondered his replies in silence. Then he asked, 'You are aware that there have been plots against the life of our beloved Führer?'

'If there are, it is regrettable. But I fail to see the connection. I am a loyal servant of the Führer. On active service, Herr Oberleutnant. Not in some chairborne brigade.' In his anger, he got to his feet. His hands trembled like an old man's.

The SS officer's glasses flashed as he turned his head to watch Hartenburg's angry perambulations. In an altered, more conciliatory tone of voice, he said, 'We have intercepted a number of coded letters.'

Hartenburg stopped in his perambulations, and turned to glower at the SS officer. 'Not in my letter or my stepfather's letters! *Mein Gott*! That is too stupid.'

He was about to add, 'even for the SS', but he stopped himself.

'Secret information of U-boat milch-cow tankers has been transmitted to the enemy.'

'How?'

The SS officer didn't answer.

'By my mother?'

'I am not saying so.'

'No. I doubt if you would be that stupid. By me then?'

'I am not saying that either.'

'Good! So why then am I in prison?'

The question was too much for the *Sicherheitsdienst* officer. He jumped to his feet, clicked his heels, raised his right hand in the Hitler salute and departed.

But his menace remained. And Hartenburg's question remained unanswered. Now nobody visited him. No contact with the outside world was allowed. Hartenburg felt the walls of the prison closing in on him.

'How long am I to be kept here?' He went on asking Edgar, because there was no one else to ask.

Of course in his heart of hearts, he knew how long. He was to be kept until all his achievements were forgotten, till all the safeguards of his mother and himself were expunged and he sank into oblivion. Then he would be got rid of. The six o'clock rattle of machine guns that now sounded out every few weeks would be for him. Then the lime-pit. Why, he didn't know. Some gigantic bureaucratic mix-up, most likely. Some neurotic *Dummkopf* like Fische decreeing that a head must roll because the enemy had stolen a march. What a way for a man to go!

He began to develop a nervous tick. He took to biting his nails. He lost his appetite. He slept badly.

Twice in the first two weeks of March, the Tommies had raided Brest. The second time he found himself praying to Papa Swain's God to make them drop their bombs on Brest prison with him in it. To let him die with some dignity, at least at the hands of the enemy. But Papa Swain's God got his navigation wrong.

At dawn there came the sound of voices and of bureaucratic confusion and argument. Slopping out was painfully delayed. Finally, the cell door was unlocked.

But not by Edgar. The doorway was filled by a middle-aged man of his own height but built like a blacksmith. He had a hefty jaw, small blue peasant's eyes and hands like bricks. Edgar, he announced, had been killed, cycling to his billet during the raid, and he, Kurt Klemke, would be taking over.

At first sight, it seemed another relentless change for the worse. Then, when Kurt rolled up his sleeves, he saw a tattoo of an anchor on his forearm.

Yes, Kurt said, he had been to sea in his youth, and his only son was in the *Kriegsmarine*. It grieved him, he said, stiffly, that he stood in this capacity to the Kapitänleutnant. The *Kriegsmarine* needed such officers.

Hartenburg discovered as the days went by that something else also grieved Kurt. Sometimes he talked about it freely, sometimes reluctantly, shying away from the heart of the subject as if denying its reality.

It had happened exactly fifteen months ago. Due to a clerical error, he had been posted to a camp called Auschwitz. 'The Kapitänleutnant might have heard of it?'

'No.' Hartenburg shook his head.

It was not usual for German prison officers to be sent there. But the error had been made and he went. When he arrived, he thought indeed he was lucky. The camp was well laid out and recently built. It looked very clean and pleasant in the snow. Then he had found . . . then he had had to . . .

For days, Hartenburg didn't discover what he had found, or what he had had to do. The account stopped there.

Kurt was the proud possessor of a small chess set. They played in the evenings. If I survive this war, Heinrich thought, I shall never be able to play again. For as he made a move, Kurt was able to allow a little information to dribble out.

Bloody, horrifying, nauseating, inhuman information. Surely, surely, the product of a disordered mind!

Torture. Terror. Beatings. Starvation.

'They have gas chambers there, Herr Kapitänleutnant, with which to exterminate people. Thousands of people. Six thousand in one day. Children too, Herr Kapitänleutnant. I had to cart away all their bodies and their shoes.'

'Nonsense! Evil nonsense!' Heinrich was so angry when Kurt tried to tell him such rubbish that he jumped to his feet and scattered the chessmen to the floor.

Another night, it was naked men and women Kurt spoke of, left in icy cold water to see how long they took to die. A medical experiment, the Auschwitz doctors called it. The doctors checking every hour how near death they were.

'You are sick, Kurt. Sick! These things are happening in your *sick* imagination!'

'No, Herr Kapitänleutnant. We are *all* sick!'

Now, to add to all his other miseries, Heinrich couldn't decide just how mentally sick Kurt was. He couldn't decide if his stories were entirely the product of his sadistic fantasy, or containing the germs of an unacceptable truth.

'Each camp keeps *Totenbücher*, Herr Kapitänleutnant. The death books. Like score books. There is a spirit of competition between camps.' And then he added, 'People don't think of the victims as human beings because so many are Jews.'

Heinrich lay awake all that night, pasting together in his mind the grim fragments Kurt had told him, making a deadly and gruesome picture. Little by little he was beginning to believe.

Not all of it, but some of it. Enough. All the vague suspicions he had pushed to the back of his mind over the years now solidified and came forward to join the picture. He could no longer pretend to himself that the camps and the persecution of the Jews didn't exist.

Something had gone wrong with the bright image of Germany resurgent, of clean young Aryan manhood taught at Trefeld and fostered in the *Kriegsmarine*. He had been too long in his own encapsulated ship with a crew one trusted and specific tasks to do.

It was as if now his submarine was surfacing in a changed and hostile world. Deep down, he knew he believed Kurt. Not believing him was trying to continue his own make-believe. Worst of all, he believed and was not just angry, but terribly afraid.

His mother's letter was late coming that week. He read and re-read it for signs of distress. But she wrote cheerfully, if stiltedly. A good German mother to her good German son.

But she couldn't write and say that she had been so proud to hear his name on the radio. Or read it in the newspapers. For Hartenburg had vanished. Varenfordt reigned supreme.

And without him to protect her, would the SS in their black and

silver discover that she had not only received a letter from Papa
Swain, but was also a quarter Jewish? Night after night, he was
haunted by that fragment of Jewishness and woke sweating and
shouting, dreaming of seeing his mother's shoes outside the concrete
gas chamber, or being checked hourly in the icy water to see how
long she would take to die.

'If I don't get out of here I shall go mad!' he told Kurt as they
tramped round the exercise yard. 'I must get out! Or go mad!'

'We are all mad,' Kurt said stolidly again.

Three mornings later, just before dawn, he heard the march of
boots down the corridor, a door unlocked, a muffled cry, boots
marching away again. Twenty minutes later, the volley of shots.
They have executed someone from this hospital wing. Heinrich's
blood froze. The tide was creeping closer. One morning the steps
would carry on just a little further.

And that would be that.

He had to get out! Had to!

Mere physical escape was useless. He must be given release and
reinstatement. With the chance to be a public hero again. And there
was only one man who could help him to do that.

Papa Dönitz.

Before Kurt came on duty that morning, Heinrich wrote an
impassioned letter to the Grossadmiral. He reminded him of his
career, he pledged his undying loyalty to the Grossadmiral and to
the Third Reich and begged him to use his good offices for his
release so that he might continue to serve his beloved country.

Even as he wrote the letter he knew that part of him had died the
death, that part of him had decided to keep its eyes closed to what
Kurt revealed. But he had to survive.

Afterwards, he thought Kurt agreed too readily to take the letter
and post it at the busy Central Post Office in Brest. Kurt was
probably an SS Unteroffizier. God knew, they even had them in the
Kriegsmarine disguised as ship's crew. Heinrich had probably played
right into their hands. First, posting the letter illegally in Cadiz.
Now Brest. Always supposing Kurt wasn't just a *Dummkopf*, taking
the bribe of his watch and throwing the letter in the rubbish.

'I posted it, Herr Kapitänleutnant. I promise you. Without
attracting notice. Though whether it will get there is another matter.
Your watch keeps excellent time, Herr Kapitänleutnant.'

March went out that year in Atlantic storms that lashed the coast of Brittany and seemed to shake even the stout walls of the prison. Heinrich's restlessness reached fever pitch. By his reckoning, in a few more days there would be another firing squad. He was reluctant to let himself fall asleep because he was afraid of waking to the sound of approaching feet.

One thing he'd learned in his twenty-five years of life was that nightmares, not dreams, come true.

The real secret nightmares that lie at the bottom of one's soul. The ultimate dread we know is coming.

He woke on 12 April to hear the march of two pairs of heavy feet. They stopped outside his door.

Keys were produced. The lock turned. The door was flung open. Light flooded in and blinded him.

This was it. 'I shall die with dignity,' he told himself, jumped out of bed, and stood to attention.

'Ah, you expected us!' said a familiar voice. His Flotilla Commander's voice. 'Dress quickly, Heinrich! We have a car waiting! You are summoned to the Grossadmiral's office in Berlin!'

'When did HX91 alter course south?'

Grossadmiral Dönitz stood very erect, his gold-braided arms folded, looking down at the plotting chart on the table. Flanking him on each side, Rear-Admiral Godt and Kapitänleutnant Schnee both had their heads bent so that the little group reminded Hartenburg of the head and paws of the Egyptian Sphinx.

After a month at the Berlin U-boat HQ in the Tirptz Ufer, the trauma of Brest goal was beginning to heal. Increasingly, Hartenburg was able to push Kurt's hoarsely whispered revelations to the back of his mind, and to come to terms with the horrors and dangers of life as he and his mother must live it. He did not totally reject what Kurt had told him, but neither did he totally accept it. The truth, he told himself, must lie in the middle. And as the tide of war boiled this way and that, the scum came to the top.

How could Papa Dönitz possibly know of such places? A family man, fond of children, fond of his dog Wolf that accompanied him everywhere. It was a joke amongst his HQ staff how much he idolised that dog!

'There is nothing in the world more faithful than a dog,' he told them. 'He believes in his master unconditionally. What *he* does is right!'

U-boat HQ was a tight little professional cell, embodying all that was best in the officer tradition, dedicated simply to the winning of the Battle of the Atlantic.

'Four hours ago,' Godt said.

'Do we know why?'

'B-Dienst have decoded a signal from Western Approaches to the Commodore, warning him of the *Pfeil* Packs, east of Greenland.'

'How many U-boats?'

'Twenty.'

'Where's the *Raubgraf* Pack?'

'Here, sir.' Godt pointed to nineteen blue pins on the huge map of the Atlantic on the green baize-covered wall. 'Waiting at 35 west. Shall we send them north?'

Except when the British Lancasters came over Berlin during the night, it was quiet in Operations. During the daily nine o'clock conference when the up-to-date Atlantic situation was studied, the British signals decoded by B-Dienst taken into account, the bad weather, gales, snow and ice were weighed, it was quieter than a church. Rarely was there need for words. Sinkings of Allied ships were greeted with a slight smile, U-boat losses with a tightening of the lips.

At a moment like this, when the Grossadmiral was in the process of taking an important decision, the silence could go on for many minutes.

It was not, as Hartenburg had thought when he was operating in command of U888, a kind of poker game. Rather, it was a chess game between two Masters. Opposing the Prussian ex-U-boat Captain now was a Great War submarine commander, a devout Catholic with Jewish forbears. Instead of Godt and Schnee, Admiral Horton had as his right hand an American WRNS officer from Ohio called Kate Halloran.

Now, as everyone in the green baize room stood stock-still and silent, they were putting themselves in the British shoes, trying to deduce what they would do, before deciding the U-boats' next move. Allied shipping losses in the year that had just ended totalled nearly eight million tons. British new construction was less than a quarter of losses, and consumption so far exceeded losses that in less than two months Britain would grind to a halt. With 400 U-boats now in service, victory was in sight.

'Leave the *Raubgraf* where they are!'

Dönitz had broken the silence. Now he looked at his watch, murmured something to Godt, and left for further problems in the big *Kriegsmarine* HQ in the centre of the city.

If Dönitz was right, the prize was huge. And Papa Dönitz was usually right. In Hartenburg's eyes, these days, *always* right. As an officer, he had from the beginning revered and admired the Grossadmiral. Had his own father survived, he would have been such a man.

But added to that now, he also felt a deep personal attachment. No one else but the Grossadmiral could have got him out of Brest gaol alive. Yet Dönitz had waved away Hartenburg's attempt at thanks, had eyed him coldly as if he didn't know what he was talking about, had said stiffly, 'I sent for you, Kapitänleutnant, because I expect even greater service from you.'

'It goes without saying . . .' Hartenburg had begun emotionally.

'Yes,' the Grossadmiral had cut him short. 'It goes without saying.'

But a week later, momentarily relaxed and reminiscent, Dönitz had told him, 'Years ago, I myself paid an official visit to Ceylon. Aboard *Emden*.' He smiled. 'I formed the opinion that the English were a very foolish lot.'

So he had known about poor foolish Papa Swain and the letter and put it all in perspective. What a leader! A great man who could still concern himself with his individual men!

That morning passed slowly. Signals came in from U-boats off the Brazilian and African coasts. But everyone was thinking of HX91.

Most of the HQ staff worked round the clock, snatching sleep and meals when they could at the *Hotel am Steinplatz* close by.

Coming back from a quick lunch at three that afternoon, Hartenburg enquired, 'Any news?'

Schnee shook his head. 'Weather's bad. Slowing them up.'

Neither mentioned the other possibility – that HX91 could slip through the *Raubgraf* Pack under the camouflage of Atlantic mist and rain.

At seven o'clock Schnee went off for a bite. It was Hartenburg's turn to say 'Nothing yet' when he returned.

'Not long now, and –'

Schnee had no need to finish his sentence. Night would come down and save HX91. At eight o'clock, with no sighting from any of the *Raubgraf* Pack, Hartenburg had all but given up hope when suddenly the Duty Orderly brought in a signal.

SS MORNINGSTAR SINKING SOS.

And, ten minutes later, SS KEMPENFELD BEING ATTACKED.

Schnee smiled across the plotting table at Hartenburg. HX91 had gone back onto the Great Circle course, just as Papa Dönitz had said it would.

Nine ships totalling 62,000 tons were sunk. Then night and the weather closed the battle down.

'We are winning, Heinrich!' the Grossadmiral told him.

But British aircraft were now increasingly being fitted with the new radar which the Metox could not pick up and warn against – the sort that had attacked and crippled Hartenburg's U888.

Agonised conferences were held. U-boats were equipped with multiple anti-aircraft guns. *Stay on the surface and fight it out* was the order.

Down went many Wellingtons and Liberators. But down also went U268, U615 and U376.

That Spring 100 U-boats were sunk in four months – mostly by Very Long Range Liberators and *Das verdammte Licht*.

Papa Dönitz's face became more drawn, his eyes more tired. Yet reverses simply inspired him. The talk now in U-boat HQ was all about the new wonder weapons.

'There are the new devices and the new boats that will win us the war,' Dönitz told his staff. 'I have ordered three hundred. And they will be built from pre-fabricated sections in less than three months each.'

There was the new schnorkel, a periscope-type device that was in effect an air intake above the surface, enabling the diesels instead of the electrics to be used when submerged.

There was the new Walter boat, powered by hydrogen peroxide, capable of staying underwater indefinitely with a surface speed of thirty knots.

But it was the new Type XXI U-boat of 1,600 tons that captured Heinrich Hartenburg's imagination.

When the bombs rained down on Berlin, when the U-boat losses mounted, Heinrich Hartenburg clung to the vision of commanding a XXI – and fighting back!

But monthly sinkings of Allied shipping came down to less than 300,000 tons, while over forty U-boats had been sunk. Almost every day from the Atlantic came agonised cries.

U732 – ATTACKED BY AIRCRAFT.

U664 – SINKING.

U901 – UNABLE TO DIVE.

On 21 May, the radio room in U-boat Headquarters echoed with one signal over and over again: U954 REPORT YOUR POSITION.

Hartenburg heard the remorseless tapping of Morse when he came back from a hurried lunch. Seven hours later, the same message was still going out.

U954 – REPORT POSITION.

Papa Dönitz came in late that night, which was unusual. His face was white with fatigue.

'Any news?'

Godt said quietly, 'None, sir.'

Dönitz left. Hartenburg asked, 'Who's the Skipper of U954?'

'Loewe.'

'Don't know him.'

'Know who his Executive Officer is?'

'No.'

'Dönitz's son, Peter.'

There was no further news. U954's last message read: BEING ATTACKED BY LIBERATOR IN POSITION 35.09 NORTH, 35.18 WEST.

In the Black Pit, 1,000 miles from land, previously the happy hunting ground of U-boats.

Two weeks later, another callsign was being repeated. U888: REPORT YOUR POSITION.

U888 was considered lost with all hands – with man and mouse, as the German sailors say.

Kruger had gone, and all his crew!

It seemed a long time since he had commanded U888 at Lorient. A long time since Suzanne. The memory of her still had the power to excite his desire and to move him profoundly. But neither for her sake nor his own dare he get in touch with her.

Not that he had lived a monastic existence since those Lorient days. Far from it. There were beautiful and glamorous girls in Berlin, and he could take his pick. They were just as blonde, just as pretty and much more attractively dressed than Suzanne. They danced well, they flattered assiduously and considered he was doing them a favour by sleeping with them, which he did with dutiful frequency.

But they lacked something – Suzanne's piquancy, her intelligence, her Gallic unpredictability, or perhaps what he missed was the intriguing spice of their situation – he the conqueror, she the conquered.

He tried very hard to fall in love with Mitzi, whose father was a General serving in the Ukraine, and whose uncle was on Goering's staff. She was beautiful and suitable.

But she wasn't Suzanne. Suzanne herself had probably forgotten all about him. Given him up for dead. Or worse still, she might have been murdered by the Resistance or killed by the fearful bombing.

He worried too about his mother in the terrifying Hamburg raids. Though he telephoned her regularly, it wasn't till the autumn that he would get leave to see her. She had been overjoyed to hear that his 'special mission' was now completed. She had asked cautiously about it. And he had told her even more cautiously that it was now complete.

'You will find Hamburg very changed,' she warned him on the telephone, when he told her that he was at last coming home. 'The bombing, you understand. But the spirit is unchanged.'

Humping his bag from the station, Hartenburg thought that the spirit seemed very changed. There was a furtiveness, he thought, even a prickling of terror that hung in the air like dust from the toppled buildings and the reek of a burst sewer main.

'It is you who are unchanged, Mother,' he said, kissing her in the hall.

But that wasn't true either. Her fine dark eyes were shadowed and netted with wrinkles. A nerve twitched spasmodically under her left eye. Her movements were agitated. She seemed unable to sit for more than a couple of seconds, getting up to straighten the antimacassar on the armchair or smooth the table runner or rush into the kitchen to stir the soup.

That first night, he heard her crying out in her sleep, screaming and whimpering. At meal times, she was unable to concentrate for long on what he was saying. A glazed, inward-turning look came into her eyes. She screwed them up as if trying to summon her concentration back to him.

Towards the end of a long patrol, Hartenburg had seen men with stress symptoms like that, and he asked her gently if the bombing was too much for her.

She seemed relieved that he had brought up the subject.

'No, Heinrich, no. I always go to the shelter. And I am a fatalist. But . . .'

'But what, Mother?'

'There is a hostel where I might go if the bombing gets worse.'

Hartenburg drew in his breath sharply. He felt as if he'd been plunged back into Brest prison again.

'Who told you about this hostel, Mother?'

She shrugged. 'A gentleman, I think he was from the city hall.'

'In uniform?'

'They are all in uniform of some sort, Heinrich.'

'Black uniform?'

'It might have been.'

'Was it the same man who came to see you about Papa Swain's letter?'

'No. He was from the *Abwehr*. He never came again. You must have satisfied them, Heinrich. The hostel is for elderly people living on their own. Frau Goldman who used to keep the corner shop, she was bombed out and she has gone to this hostel.'

'Frau Goldman was a Jew.'

'But I am not, Heinrich.'

'Of course not.' He felt very sick and cold inside. He was afraid to alarm his mother. And at the same time, afraid not to. 'It was not likely you would go to the same hostel.'

His dilemma was resolved for him. Just before supper on his second evening, while he was sitting reading the evening paper and his mother was stirring the soup in the kitchen, a knock sounded on the front door.

'I'll get it, Mother,' he said, and adjusting the blackout, drew back the door.

In the filtered light, he saw the gleam of silver. The SS uniform. His heart dropped to his boots.

'Is this the Mendelssohn house?' a nasal voice demanded.

'It is my mother's house. What do you want?'

'We require to interview Frau Swain.'

'What about?'

'That is not for you to ask, nor for me to say.'

'And the time is too late for any interview.'

Hartenburg made to slam the door, but the SS officer's foot was in the way.

'I am Kapitänleutnant Hartenburg,' Heinrich said imperiously.

The name obviously meant nothing to the SS man, but the rank did. It disconcerted him. He hesitated.

'Tell your Obersturmbannführer, my mother is not to be disturbed tonight. I forbid it. Tomorrow, I myself shall call on the Obersturmbannführer. At ten precisely. Be sure and tell him that.'

The foot was hastily removed. He slammed the door shut. He stood for several seconds, leaning against it, his eyes closed, his whole body wet with sweat, shaking like a man with malaria.

His mother came out of the kitchen wiping her hands. She took one look at his face.

'Heinrich,' she said softly, 'I'm sorry, I should have told you.'

She let him pull her into his arms, and out it all came.

Yes, the man had been before.

Yes, she was afraid. Very afraid. Not of the bombings. She was not afraid to die. She was afraid of what people said sometimes happened to you before you died. Of terrible people, petty bureaucrats, who now seemed to be in charge. Of course it was probably all rumour. Propaganda put out by the British. Germans were not by nature cruel. They would not starve and beat and maim. But nearly all the people she knew had now left the city. She never heard from them.

'Did this man say you might *have* to go to the hostel?'

'Only for my own good.'

'Don't go, Mother! I forbid you! Tell him your son has ordered you to stay here. Tomorrow I shall see this man's Obersturmbannführer. I will use my authority to make sure you are not disturbed again.'

Heinrich tried to rehearse what he would say to the Obersturmbannführer as he walked quickly to the Gestapo HQ in the centre of Hamburg. He tried to escape the shadow of Brest gaol, to concentrate on better things. He reminded himself of Trefeld, of cadet training, of the tenets of the new awakening Germany. A Germany whose honour was held in trust by the officer class and by the courage of its Armed Forces. There were scoundrels, God knew, among Himmler's men. But there were scoundrels everywhere. Every rising nation harboured them, used them, had cause for shame. The British for all their piety and good sportsmanship had massacred and corrupted to gain and hold their Empire. So had the French and the Dutch. The American settlers had slaughtered the Indians. Perhaps blood had to be shed for the birth of greatness. Yet his own reasoning failed to convince.

It was a breezy day with golden sunlight sparkling on the familiar harbour waves. It seemed a hundred years since his cadet days. All was changed. He knew more clearly even than in the miseries of Brest gaol that the new Germany was a myth.

His uniform with the Knight's Cross with Swords and Diamonds at his throat, guaranteed him a respectable reception even there. He returned the salutes of the guards, climbed the steps under the heavy portico, lifted his hand to his cap peak as the inner sentries presented arms and he was ushered into the outer office of the Obersturmbannführer.

The whole place smelled of fear and suspicion. Or was it his own fear and suspicion bouncing back at him from the drab painted walls?

A blonde secretary was typing as he was shown in. She carried on with her work for a moment or two in typical secretary manner.

Then she looked up. She gave him a long speculative stare, as if recording, not without interest, that he was a handsome virile young man, but she was clearly suspicious of his errand.

'I have an interview with the Obersturmbannführer at ten,' Hartenburg said brusquely. Too brusquely.

'Obersturmbannführer Mueller does not usually grant interviews before eleven.'

'Then today he is lucky. Kindly tell him I am here!'

But it was a mistake to try to argue with the Obersturmbannführer's secretary. She kept him waiting till eleven before leading him in.

A fat red-faced man in the black and silver uniform of the SS came from behind a large desk.

'Heil Hitler!'

His skin was shiny and moist like boiled ham. He had little pig's ears and wore steel rimmed spectacles. 'Herr Kapitänleutnant.' He held out his hand. 'My name is Mueller. To what do I owe this honour?'

The little stars of eyes behind the spectacles seemed genuinely puzzled. Perhaps the underling had not in fact conveyed the message. Whether he had or not was momentarily irrelevant. Hartenburg ignored the fat red hand.

'I will come straight to the point of my visit, Herr Obersturmbannführer!'

'Of course. Of course! Please be seated.'

'I would prefer to stand. What I have to say I can say briefly.'

Sensing danger, the Obersturmbannführer's smile congealed. But his voice continued bland and unruffled.

'As you wish, of course, Herr Kapitänleutnant.'

He re-established himself behind his desk, leaned his elbows on it, and put the tips of his fingers together.

'I can see you have something on your mind. What, Herr Kapitänleutnant, is troubling you?'

'One of your men has been bothering my mother.'

'Bothering your mother?' The red face looked genuinely astonished. 'What do you mean by bothering? It is impossible that one of my men would bother your mother.'

'This man has been to her house.'

'No, no. There is some mistake. None of my men would bother your mother.' He shook his head. 'Only with the greatest respect would she be treated.'

'There is no mistake. I was there when he came last night. He had been before. I refused him entry. I sent a message by him that I would see you today. At ten.'

'I know nothing of this. It is an error.'

Mueller picked up the phone on his desk and began speaking rapidly. Hearing the name Hartenburg, Heinrich interrupted. 'Her name is Swain. Frau Swain.'

Mueller's brows wrinkled. 'Is that not an English name?'

'Her *second* husband,' Heinrich said, 'was an English missionary. My father was Korvettenkapitän Hartenburg. He was killed in the Great War.' He had to use everything he could. 'You will have heard of him.'

'Of course, of course,' Mueller said, glueing the telephone receiver to his ear, listening intently.

Hartenburg saw the red face darken.

'There are certain difficulties, Herr Kapitänleutnant.'

'There are no difficulties at all, Herr Obersturmbannführer.'

'You must let me be the judge of that. We have our enquiries to make.'

'Then make them of me.'

'My men did not know at the time that you were her son. So many departments, you understand. So much work.'

'I would have thought,' Hartenburg said sharply, 'that you would have had some more valuable work to do in the war than bother lonely old women.'

'For their own good, Herr Kapitänleutnant.'

'I doubt that, Herr Obersturmbannführer. And as her son I claim the right to be judge. She will not go to any hostel. Our Führer commands respect to our mothers. She will live where she chooses. And if I hear of any more visits from your men, I shall complain to Grossadmiral Dönitz that my war effort is being undermined.'

'Harsh words, Herr Kapitänleutnant!'

'You would receive harsher from the Grossadmiral. And as you know, he is now only second to the Führer.'

'Heil Hitler.' Mueller got to his feet and raised his right hand. 'You have my word that your mother will not be troubled again.'

The Obersturmbannführer accompanied him to the door of his office. 'And when are you back on duty, Herr Kapitänleutnant?'

'Tomorrow.'

'Then I wish you well.' This time Hartenburg took the proffered hand as the sealing of a bargain. 'Good hunting!'

'Good day, Herr Kapitänleutnant.' The secretary smiled coquettishly, deciding he was after all an acceptable person.

He touched the peak of his cap to her and ran down the steps. The interview had gone reasonably well. He had managed to achieve a little grace for his mother perhaps. But it was no more than pasting sticking plaster over a gigantic hole. The real menace would not be kept out. The tide was coming in over them. Hartenburg wondered if the Obersturmbannführer had realised, indeed had intended, that the sting of the interview was in the tail.

'Good hunting, Herr Kapitänleutnant,' he had said.

Good hunting indeed! While he could hunt and kill, he had the power. Without it, he had nothing. And certainly he would not sink enemy shipping while sitting at a table at U-boat HQ.

Three days after he returned to Berlin, Hartenburg managed to speak to Dönitz.

'Request permission, sir, for posting to one of the new XXIs.'

The Grossadmiral eyed him keenly. But he seemed unsurprised, even approving.

'I will do my best, Heinrich.' He patted his shoulder. 'Now, more than ever, is the time for our real heroes. The Allies may invade. But with such as you we shall win!' His smile relaxed into one of playfulness. 'And we have not forgotten your promise to sink that fat *Queen Elizabeth* prize!'

XI · JOHN
30 November 1943–5 June 1944

The anti U-boat patrol continued from St Edzell, but now far fewer U-boats were sighted. Dönitz had withdrawn many of his men away from the murderous attacks of aircraft. Blake and his crew saw nothing but sea.

But now the Invasion was coming.

Everyone in Britain knew it and was impatient for it, though few people knew precisely where, nor who would be involved, nor when. Weather maps were scrutinised, moon charts and intelligence reports read and re-read, the radio monitored. While over the Atlantic there was a brief lull. The breathless uncanny hush before the man-made earthquake.

'The worst part of the whole thing,' Blake told Jennifer over their usual noggin in the Mess, 'is the waiting.'

'I know,' she said fervently, and he could have kicked himself, for what else did the poor lass do but wait. Wait for news of POW husband Peter, wait for the crews to come back for debriefing, or not come back as the case might be. Wait to see who got the chop and who didn't.

He patted her hand in apology and she smiled acros the table at him. They understood one another very well, Jennifer and he.

'There are far too many men on too small an island,' he complained the following Saturday when he took her to the local pub for a drink and a hot cheese and onion pie. The whole of southern England was becoming altogether too crowded for his liking. An armed camp. Troops, tanks, guns, armoured cars, ships and aircraft were all waiting for the spring good weather.

The Cornish roads were full of Yankee transports and wolf-whistling Yankees. The pub, like all the rest, was full of Charles Boyers in Free French blue and Polish princes in Army drab, not to mention Canadians, Aussies, New Zealanders, Dutchmen, Belgians and Danes.

'A woman's paradise,' Jennifer laughed, eluding a very free French hand, and snuggling closer to him at the bar.

Blake resisted a temptation to punch the Frenchman's smirking face. Perhaps he was getting jealous now of Jennifer. Or was it simply that his temper was bloody short these days. All part of the tension. They were nearly half-way through May and it couldn't be long now.

And into this electric atmosphere Alexandra had thrown her little unintentional firecracker. Her letter crackled in his tunic pocket as he searched for the money to pay for the pies.

'I've got something to tell you, Jennifer,' he began brightly when the pies were despatched, watching her dust the crumbs off her uniform skirt.

She smiled up at him. 'Something nice?'

'*I* think so.'

'You don't sound very sure.'

'Don't I? Oh, I am. At least *I* think it's nice.'

'But I won't?'

'I flatter myself,' he said attempting lightness and failing dismally, 'that you might not.'

'Oh,' she drew in a long breath. 'Something about your wife?'

'How did you guess?'

She gave a short laugh, swirled her drink round and stared into it. 'Not very difficult, John. Your face gives you away. You have a very revealing face.' She touched his cheek with her free hand.

'They want to come down and take a holiday bungalow. She and the boys.'

Jennifer nodded sagely several times as if she'd guessed that.

'You'd better start looking,' she said briskly, sliding off her stool as if there wasn't a moment to lose. 'I'd offer to help you,' she laughed uncertainly, 'but that might not be a good idea.'

In the event, he didn't need help in finding a bungalow. Many of the holiday homes were standing empty. He chose one with a big garden, next door to an already occupied house which, by the look of the swings and slides in their garden, held the promise of playmates.

He managed to borrow the Squadron van to go to the station to meet Alexandra, and Maurice was thrilled at the prospect of travelling in a vehicle with an RAF roundel on its side.

Alexandra's skin was pale, she was very thin. In contrast, the boys were sturdy and boisterous. 'You did want us to come, didn't you?' she asked, when he kissed her.

She looked so uncertain, standing there, holding onto a boy with each hand.

'Of course I did. It made my day when I got your letter.'

He bundled the boys in the front seat beside him, and made Alexandra sit in the back.

'You see,' Alexandra leaned forward to explain as he started up the van again, 'we were all getting a bit too much for Mother.'

'I'm not surprised,' Blake said with humorous hollowness, as young William tried to push Maurice off the seat.

Alexandra laughed and patted his shoulder and said, 'Dear John!'

But he was absurdly disappointed. He had hoped that she had come to Cornwall because she wanted to see him. Not because Mrs Monteith needed a well-earned – and God knew it *was* well-earned – rest.

All the same, he, Blake, had got used to picking up the crumbs that fell from a rich German's table. And in any case, his own behaviour was not beyond reproach. If Alexandra had come to see him, then he was going to enjoy it. For a while, he was going to forget about Heinrich and the war, and Jennifer and what if anything Jennifer and he felt about each other. That last was a question he pushed to the back of his mind because it was too complex to answer.

Everything started splendidly. Though the beaches were mined and surrounded with coils of barbed wire and the cliffs thick with gun posts, the garden had a sand-pit and there were indeed children next door. Blake enjoyed getting away from the Mess and the talk of invasion and living out, waking up to the sound of the seagulls with Alexandra clasped in his arms. No matter why she had come down, it was something very close to bliss.

He was free for the first week, and did little, except for one duty crew when he took a Liberator up on air test of a new starboard engine. Now promoted to Squadron Leader and a maker rather than breaker of rules, just for a couple of minutes he tossed his Establishment hat over the windmill and dived down on the bungalow, sweeping inches over the roof, while the two boys and the next-door children jumped up and down with excitement waving from the garden.

Maurice was particularly excited at the size of the aircraft and the noise it had made. He clamoured to be taken up to the airfield and shown round a Liberator.

'Some day,' Blake smiled down at the eager upturned face. Maurice had grown into a sensible, attractive boy more like Alexandra at the moment than his father, thank God.

'And me,' William clamoured. 'And me.'

Those were his favourite words, Blake had discovered. *And me.* He was too young to know what an airfield was, but what Maurice had, he had to have. Thereby no doubt hung a tale, but one he didn't want to think about.

In any case, Alexandra was not keen on either boy going up to the airfield, so the matter was dropped and alternative treats planned. After a Biscay patrol, he took the family on a picnic on Dartmoor. The boys bathed in the stream, and Alexandra lay on her back in the warm sun. Bees hummed. The war seemed a million miles away.

He had seen Jennifer at the Biscay de-briefing. She had been smiling, friendly, detached. Like the first time he ever saw her. As if their relationship had been run like a cine-film into reverse. She had even asked politely, in front of the crew, if his wife and family had settled in well. You couldn't get much more distant than that. And that was no doubt as it should be.

On his day off, he lounged in the garden. Maurice and William and the trio from next door appeared to be playing perfectly happily, when suddenly a fight started.

Blake had dozed off to sleep. He woke abruptly at the noise but kept his eyes shut, hoping the fracas would die down.

'Go on, John,' Alexandra called to him through the kitchen window. 'Do something.'

He opened his eyes, got to his feet and walked over to the sand-pit, where bigger and smaller boys were shoving and pushing and squirming in the sand.

'Hey,' he said, laughing, trying to make it all a joke, 'is this a private fight or can anyone join in?'

Their faces flushed and panting, the boys took no notice. He picked them off one another, brushed them down none too gently and said severely, 'What's this all about?'

William kicked sand over Maurice and shouted accusingly, 'It's him!'

'Maurice is spoiling our game,' said one of the boys next door. 'He won't be a German.'

Clearly they were playing the popular war-time version of cops and robbers.

'Oh, come off it, Maurice! Don't be a spoilsport!'

But Maurice was adamant. Aware that he was being watched by the neighbours next door and by Alexandra, and anxious to shine as a peacemaker, Blake whispered something in the boy's ear.

It worked like a charm. Maurice accepted the hated role. The interrupted game went on peacefully.

'Whatever did you tell him?' Alexandra asked when he came back again into the house.

'Oh,' he said evasively, 'nothing much.'

Thinking it was just a money bribe, Alexandra merely smiled.

Next day, when she was out shopping in Newquay with the family next door, taking William with her, Blake seized the opportunity to fulfil his promise to Maurice and take him to the airfield.

'Don't tell your mother, mind. Or William.'

Maurice promised.

In all fairness to him, the boy kept his promise. But luck was not on John Blake's side.

Unfortunately, the night before there had been a raid on the U-boat pens at Lorient. One of the Lancasters had been so shot up it had made a belly landing on St Edzell, and was now the centre of attention.

Maurice couldn't help seeing the shattered rear gun-turret, covered with blood and spattered with flesh. He kept manfully quiet, gripping Blake's hand and stumping silently round the Lancaster, not asking any questions.

In the middle of that night, he woke from a nightmare, screaming and vomiting.

Alexandra went to him. The whole story came tumbling out.

Blake had never believed it possible that she could be so angry.

'I realise,' she said, by way of reconciliation the next day, 'that you couldn't have known that was going to happen. But it was a clottish thing to take him there in the first place!'

'I know,' he cupped her face and kissed her, 'and I'm sorry.'

She caught his hand, looked up earnestly into his eyes and whispered, 'It must be awful sometimes for *you*. Awful!' She brought his hand to her lips, and said softly, 'I love you, John. In my own way. You know what I mean, don't you?'

Whatever way that was, he supposed, it was considerably better than nothing.

Then the following week, the Officers' Mess put on an informal dance. The last one, in all probability, before the invasion so the liquor would flow. The next-door neighbour agreed to baby-sit and Alexandra, well-trained Navy daughter that she was, had brought a long dress suitable for the occasion. It was blue, very simple and well-cut, and she looked stunning in it.

For some reason, it reminded him of the dress he had worn for Lavinia in 'Androcles and the Lion', and he and Alexandra laughed about that all the way in the taxi to the Mess. The amusement stopped Blake from thinking about whether or no he should introduce Alexandra to Jennifer.

The matter was decided for him. By ill-luck the taxi dropped them outside the Mess just as Jennifer was getting out of the Chief Intelligence Officer's old jalopy. Flight Lieutenant Henderson and Jennifer and Blake and Alexandra walked up the steps of the Mess together, and in the bright lights of the hall, introductions had to be made.

Henderson said heartily, 'We were wondering when we were going to have the pleasure.' He thrust out his hand and grabbed Alexandra's. 'Very pleased to meet you, Mrs Blake. Jennifer and I are good friends of your husband.'

Once teamed up like that, it was difficult to come apart again. Jennifer took Alexandra off to the Ladies' cloakroom. Henderson and he waited in the corridor for them, the Intelligence Officer beating time appreciatively with his hand to the strains of the five-piece band in the dining room, and occasionally, to Blake's horror, winking.

When the girls emerged, Henderson found them a table for four at the edge of the ballroom. Bronski came up and asked Alexandra for a dance. Then Rolf. One could always rely on the crew to do their stuff.

'Don't take any notice of me,' Henderson said each time, 'I'm just here for the beer. I don't know how to dance. You give Jennifer a whirl, John, old boy.'

'You're embarrassed,' Jennifer said when he put his arm round her.

Like all the WAAF officers, she had to be in uniform. The barathea of her tunic felt unyielding and prim after Alexandra's soft bare skin. Yet the male-style uniform enhanced rather than detracted from her femininity. He felt a wave of tenderness for her.

He shook his head. 'I feel a heel.'

'Well, you're not.' She sighed. 'Or at least no more than the rest of us.' She looked across the floor at Alexandra, laughing merrily as she danced with Rolf. 'Except your wife. I'm sure she's not a heel. She's very pretty. Prettier even than I thought she'd be.'

He laughed. 'A cut above *me*?'

'Oh, no! Nothing like that. But I can understand why you're so in love with her.'

'I am, am I?' He whirled her round. 'How d'you know that?'

'I told you before. You have a revealing face. I can tell by the way you look at her.'

Half an hour later, when he danced again with Alexandra, she said exactly the same words. 'You've had an affair with that little Section Officer, haven't you? I can tell by the way you look at her.'

'As a matter of fact,' he said stiffly and with dignity, 'she is a colleague. A first class Intelligence Officer.'

'Bully for her!'

'And bully for me. For all of us. We depend a lot on our Intelligence Officers.' He sounded pompous even to himself.

Alexandra raised her brows but said nothing.

'She is also,' Blake said ponderously, 'a friend.'

'How close a friend?'

'I have taken her out to dinner.' He spoke slowly as if searching his memory for absolute accuracy. 'I have talked to her about you and the family. I have bought her the odd drink in the Mess. And she has bought me one.'

'Have you been to bed with her?' Alexandra asked crisply.

'No,' Blake answered promptly. That time by the lake they had not actually been to bed. And since then, nothing. A few good night kisses. Companionship. Affection. A deep affection, even.

At that point the dance was brought to an end by a loud roll of drums. The jaunty playing of Sir Roger de Coverly indicated the next number was a Paul Jones, men and women joining a circle and skipping round to take as partner whoever was opposite them when the music stopped. Alexandra was whisked away by Mrs Medical Officer and the WAAF Catering Officer, while Blake resisted the men's hands and slunk off to the bar and bought a whisky-chaser. Then another. He needed them.

By the time he got back to the table for four, Bronski and Rolf were sitting there dutifully. Alexandra was dancing with the Station Administration Officer, who had his great hand right in the centre of her bare back.

'Jennifer had a headache, Skipper,' Bronski told him, 'so Henderson took her back to the Waafery. We said we'd keep the table for you.'

'What happened to you, John?' Alexandra came up, fanning her cheeks with her handkerchief.

'The demon drink got me. I prefer it to dancing with strange women.'

'*I'd* have preferred it to dancing with strange men,' Alexandra said.

For the next two dances everything went well. But as in most RAF parties, the men congregated round the bar with their tankards while the invited civilian girls sat around waiting for someone to condescend to dance with them.

As the evening wore on, the men began to sing. Nothing really offensive to begin with. Just a few bawdy songs sung to hymn tunes, not loud enough at that stage for the Mess President to decide to get the ladies off home.

But eventually the boozers got around to their choicer numbers.

The band was playing a quickstep. Blake was whirling Alexandra round the floor.

When this blinking war is over, sang the boozers to the tune of '*What A Friend We Have In Jesus.*' Then more loudly, they began one about Hitler and Goebbels, set to '*Praise The Lord For He Is Glorious*'.

Momentarily Blake was carried back to Kirkstone, to the time when the Trefeld boys sang *Deutschland Uber Alles* to that self-same hymn tune.

The tune must also have touched some sombre chord of memory in Alexandra. He felt her stiffen in his arms.

'What's the matter, Alexandra?'

'Nothing.'

'Don't give me that! I can always tell when something's up.'

She shrugged.

'You don't like the singing,' he persisted.

'Is one supposed to?'

Blake made a little irritated exclamation.

'You wouldn't get the Navy behaving like that,' Alexandra let out furiously.

They went home soon after that, and somehow he couldn't let the matter drop.

'What's so wrong with letting off steam and singing bawdy songs?' he asked her in the taxi.

She didn't answer.

'You're not a prude.'

She still said nothing.

Stupidly he went on, 'Or wasn't it the words?' he asked nastily. 'Was it the tune?'

She side-stepped, which was unusual for Alexandra. 'You would think they'd look after the girls they'd invited. Dance with them instead of –'

'Well, we can't all be little gentlemen like the Navy.'

'You can try,' she said icily.

Out of such a trivial moment, a row loomed. He felt so aggrieved and guilty and disappointed that instead of saying something pacific he made matters worse.

'And I suppose the *Hun* Navy does it even better?'

'Yes,' she snapped. 'They do.'

Then she drew a deep breath and covered her face with her hands. Through her fingers, she gulped, 'I'm sorry! I shouldn't have ever said that! It was unforgiveable. Not true, either. I was reminded of . . . something . . . that's all.'

But her apology, heartfelt as it was, made it worse.

Though she had never mentioned Heinrich and didn't mention him this time, his name hung in the air. The man himself seemed to actually sit in the seat between them.

The taxi ride finished in silence. Perfectly polite silence. He had been again considering telling her that contrary to her belief, Swain was still alive. He had even thought of telling her about his pre-eminence as a U-boat ace, about his potential for devastation if he got hold of a Type xxi U-boat. But he didn't. And that taxi ride finally put a clamp on any such resolutions.

Two days later, the holiday was over. Alexandra and the children returned to Oxford.

Blake moved back to the Officers' Mess. It was better, he told himself, while he was on Operations, to live with the Squadron boys – and pick up the old friendship with Jennifer again.

To while away the waiting time, the officers ran a sweepstake as to when the invasion would be. Dates were drawn out of the Mess President's hat.

Blake drew 5 June.

XII HEINRICH
6 June 1944–9 June 1944

'Sorry to wake you, Sir.'

Hartenburg snapped the side lights on, sat up and took the three signal flimsies from his Executive Officer's hand.

His cabin on U2452 was spacious. Everything was modern in his new wonderboat – including his very young crew. His Executive Officer, Busch, was the eldest at twenty-one. During the last six months of training, testing and modifying, he had worked them hard. But he was as pleased with them as he was with his XXI.

He was not so pleased with other things. Yesterday, they had brought U2452 from Danzig to the Blohm and Voss shipyard at Hamburg for minor modifications. He had been glad of the opportunity to visit his mother, glad to be in Hamburg again.

But Hamburg was even more changed than before. Despite the confidence of the shipyard technicians in the new U-boats and the new secret weapons, the city seethed with rumours of an imminent Allied invasion, with suspicion and gloom. As for his mother . . . he had lain awake for most of the few hours before Busch came in, trying to interpret to himself his own impressions of his mother.

'What's the time, Exec?'

'Three a.m., Sir.'

He waved the flimsies. 'What's in them?'

'Commander's code.'

In other words, Top Secret. He felt a little thrill of excited anticipation.

'So I'll have to put them through the Enigma myself.'

''Fraid so, Sir.'

He swung his feet off the bed. His mother had said she had been resting in bed yesterday afternoon. That was the reason for the drawn curtains, the letter-box stuffed with hessian, the barricaded doors. That and the bombing. He had had to clear the letter box, put his mouth to it and call, 'Mother! It's me, Heinrich!' before she would come hesitantly to answer the door.

She was so thin too, and nervous-looking. She had alternately wept in his arms and laughed for joy. He wondered if she was a little deranged.

Over supper, she told him she had heard bad news of Mrs Goldman and her family. They had all died. Of some epidemic or accident, perhaps. No one knew exactly. There were rumours. Rumours about so many things.

When they drank the wine Heinrich had brought from the wardroom, she lifted her glass and thanked him for his wonderful achievements. 'Without them . . .'

'Without them what, Mother?'

'Oh, nothing.' She had shrugged. She seemed to have got into a habit of not finishing her sentences, of losing track of what she was saying. She had changed the subject. She chided him for not telephoning her first. One day, he might come and find her gone; no, not to Mueller's hostel. She had heard no more of him. But she had received the most splendid invitation.

Had Heinrich not known her truthfulness, he would have sworn she was making it all up. Her eyes shone like a child's as she told her story. It was a fairy story come true. The Hartenburgs, his father's people, had come forward to claim her. It was all because of Heinrich's exploits. Yes, there were some of them alive. She had been mistaken in thinking them dead. They were still very rich and powerful. Still in their huge castle. And there she would be if ever he came to find her and she was gone. He was not to worry. She would be safe in the Hartenburg castle.

'Let's waste no time, then,' he said sternly, more to himself than to Busch. He put the flimsies beside the machine and began battling with the decoding.

The first was short.

The invasion has started.

The second was longer. It was a message from the Grossadmiral.

Every enemy vessel is a target demanding full commitment of your boat, even if it is put at risk. No thought must be given to the danger of shallow water or possible mine barriers.

The third signal simply said, *Proceed immediately at full speed into the English Channel and intercept troop transports in the Solent.*

He shouted to Busch, 'Otto!'

'Sir?'

'Prepare to leave port. Crew to action stations!'

He dressed hurriedly, put on his lambskin coat, and climbed out of the boat onto the quay. All around was the clanging of machinery and the lights were blazing as the men worked round the clock on the new Type XXIS. Blohm and Voss had never failed to deliver a new boat once a fortnight throughout the war.

In the main office, he told the night manager that U2452 would be leaving in ten minutes.

'I want a letter sent to my mother. She lives quite close to the main gate, if you wouldn't mind delivering it personally.'

'Of course, Herr Kapitänleutnant!'

He wrote: *We've been sent off at short notice. I will telephone you as soon as I can. Always go to the air raid shelter when the sirens go. If there is any trouble at all and you cannot contact me, get in touch with Grossadmiral Dönitz in Berlin. He will see you are all right.*

He didn't mention the Hartenburgs. In the cold darkness of morning, they seemed even less likely than yesterday.

The manager took the letter. 'Good trip, Herr Kapitänleutnant.'

'Thanks.'

Hartenburg walked back to his boat. The men were already in their yellow life-jackets.

'Let go bow and stern ropes! Both motors slow astern – rudder amidships!'

The arc lights looked smudged in the oily waters as U2452 glided stern first into the main channel of the Elbe.

It was beginning to get light.

Building by ruined building, the city of Hamburg slipped by – cranes, warehouses, factories, houses, trees. This was where he had been born. This was where he had been educated, brought up to love the sea. Over there by the lakes in the parks, his grandfather had taken him to sail his paper boats. Behind him, getting further and further away every minute, was his home where his mother would be sleeping.

Once out of the Elbe and into the North Sea, they were totally on their own, in complete and deadly unity with their twenty-four torpedoes. Along the coast of Holland, they went down to schnorkel depth, the head of the air-intake just above the water.

Inside, it became hot and oil-scented. Vibration from the pounding of the diesels shivered through his body. On they roared at fourteen knots.

'Where are we now, Exec?'

'Off Dieppe. Any sign, Sir?'

Hartenburg swept the horizon ahead with the periscope.

'None. All very peaceful!' He moved away. 'You take over.'

It was the hydrophone operator who first gave the alarm. He cried out with pain, the noise was so intense.

'Screws! Hundreds of destroyer screws at high speed!'

He knew then. He didn't need Busch's shout from the periscope. 'Look, Sir! Look! The whole world's against us!'

He looked. Prepared as he was, he could hardly believe his eyes.

A forest of masts, a bridge of boats. Lines of transports and landing craft as far as he could see. An outer screen of destroyers and corvettes practically bow to stern. A high cover of Spitfires and Mustangs. Every few minutes a Liberator passed over, low down on the water.

'What are we going to do, Sir?'

One glimmer of the conning tower above the water, and it would be shot to pieces. One attack and they'd be pinned down by escorts for days.

A cruiser was coming towards them.

Furiously he slammed the periscope down, lest it was spotted. 'Shadow till night!'

Throughout that day, nothing but bad news.

U618: SINKING.

U871: ATTACKED BY AIRCRAFT.

U464: DAMAGED RETURNING TO BASE.

At dusk, he surfaced and got a better look.

The landing craft and escorts still seemed unending. Just before darkness fell, a white column of smoke shot up from a line of transports.

'Someone's got one, Otto!'

Minutes later, U181 reported sinking a 5,000 tonner.

'Varenfordt.' So he was back from instructing and on Operations again. The old rivalry stirred inside him. 'Now it's our turn! Diving stations! Tubes one to four ready!'

But he did not fire. He could not. Wherever he went, there were aircraft overhead and naval escorts round him.

His only hope was to get a straggler, and there was none.

Dawn broke and he had still not attacked.

Next day was the same. In the morning, over the hydrophone, came the continuous sound of depth-charges.

Watching through the periscope, still schnorckelling on the diesels, he saw a U-boat bow coming up at a sharp angle. Seconds later, a U-boat surfaced into a hail of fire, and men in yellow life-jackets began jumping into the sea.

At midnight, another signal. U181 SINKING.

Varenfordt! Varenfordt had gone! In action, as it should be, he thought. Of the old dependables on whom Papa Dönitz relied, now there was just Kassel and himself.

Next day, attack was still out of the question. They went down to 200 metres in the middle of the convoy lanes. Myriad screws grinded above them. He felt frustrated, balked of his prey.

A bitter fury possessed Hartenburg. He would not be defeated. He would not be overwhelmed by sheer weight of numbers. Not while he had his wonder U-boat and was still able to strike.

'We could get a destroyer, Sir,' Busch suggested.

Hartenburg turned on him angrily. 'It's troop transports Papa Dönitz wants!'

His mind was in a turmoil. How could anyone think straight, pinioned here under 1,000 ships and 2,000 aircraft?

'Exec!'

'Sir?'

'Pitch-dark outside now. When does the moon rise?'

'Half an hour, sir.'

'Better get cracking then! Surface!'

'*Surface*, Sir?'

'You heard me!'

He had to stop the Asdic finding him. He had to surface right inside the lines of merchant ships like they used to do with the Atlantic convoys. Only then could he identify the big troop transports and accurately send his torpedoes into them.

'Blow tanks!'

The nose came up steeply. On the surface, Hartenburg flung open the hatch, and scrambled out onto the conning tower, followed by Busch and the gun crews.

It was like being in a gorge. Black cliffs of transports rose up on either side of him. No sign of any escorts. They were on the *outside*, their duty never to let through any such as him.

And here he was, on the same southerly course as the merchantmen. No one expecting him.

He felt his heart beat faster. A sense of exhilaration and power drained away his frustration, cooled his fury. The Allied Invasion looked mighty, but it would fail! Back in such ships as survived would go these troops in another inglorious Dunkirk! The very size of his opponent inspired him – a David against a steel Goliath that was nevertheless just as vulnerable to a well-aimed stone.

He had at his fingertips the power – and the U-boat service would have the glory.

He felt calm now. Cool, detached, determined, as he surveyed the plethora of targets.

Landing craft were too small. The biggest, he must go for the biggest!

Carefully he surveyed the dark silhouettes and selected a transport to port with a tanker just behind her.

'Fire a fan of four!'

With luck, he would get both of them.

Standing beside Busch in the darkness, he heard the hiss of the compressed air, the *whoosh* as the torpedoes left the tubes, followed their white wakes across the black water.

'Fire stern tubes!'

There were two fat merchantmen behind.

'Reload!'

Even as he said the words, it was as though a volcano had erupted. An orange tongue licked the sky. Ammunition went off – blues, reds, verdigris greens illuminating tanks and lorries plunging into the sea, burning men jumping off the decks, masts falling, bows tilting vertical.

A searchlight flashed on. Then another. Snowflakes burst above U2452, making day of night.

'Dive!'

A silver stream of tracer was coming towards them. From the stern of a sinking merchantman, a four-inch gun was firing at them.

In half the time of the old boats, U2452 was underwater and streaking to the bottom.

Not a moment too soon. The hull reverberated to the sound of screws at high speed, the pings of Asdic. The escorts had arrived. Down came the depth-charges. Pattern after pattern vibrated the U-boat sides till the whole hull shook with a palsy.

There they lay for the next four hours while an exhilarated Hartenburg made plans for his next foray against the invasion.

'They'll soon tire, Exec. When they've gone away we'll surface again and . . . yes, what is it?'

The telegraphist was holding a signal flimsy.

He snatched it, glared down at four words? RETURN TO LORIENT IMMEDIATELY.

'This'll be Thormann's doing!' he shouted at Busch. 'Bringing us back just when we've begun!'

A barrage of depth-charges and Asdic pings accompanied them on a westerly course as Hartenburg weaved in and out of the islands along the coast.

Gradually the noise of the explosions faded, and the frigates and the aircraft disappeared.

Using schnorkel, Hartenburg continued southwards till in the moonlight he saw the low silhouette of the Ile de Croix, and heard on the hydrophones the soft swishing of the tug he had radioed for.

'Blow all tanks!'

Back on the surface, Busch flashed their recognition. U2452 followed the tug up the Scorff estuary into the familiar Lorient harbour.

This time there was no welcoming committee, no guard of honour, no military band, no girls with flowers to welcome him. U2452 slid silently into the dimly lighted shelter.

It was a ghost cathedral. Empty except for U11.

Kassel's boat was secured to bollards by metal ropes, lest she sink. Bows a mangle of twisted steel, conning tower riddled with shell holes, guns smashed to pieces, the white sea-bird insignia on the side stained with blood.

An Oberleutnant hurried up to Hartenburg. 'Korvetten-Kapitän Thormann sends his apologies for not meeting you, Sir. But – '

'I understand.'

'You are to report to him at Kerneval Flotilla HQ tomorrow at noon. A car will be sent to the hotel.'

Hartenburg simply nodded and turned away to speak to the dockyard engineers who would be refuelling and servicing U2452.

It was past ten o'clock when he left the bunker. Outside the docks, a whole street of houses was knocked flat as a pack of cards.

Lorient had changed since he was last here. The whole world was changing. Shifting under his feet like a ship that had slipped anchor. But, he reminded himself sternly, the anchor was Germany. Germany and victory. Were he to see the British ports now, Southampton, Portsmouth, Bristol, he would no doubt find them a mass of rubble.

He suddenly remembered his first sight of Bristol – that ridiculous expedition to the chocolate factory with those ridiculous boys from Kirkstone school.

The Invasion was bound to fail, he told himself, hurrying through the blast-damaged entrance to the *Beau Séjour*. As at Dieppe, the Allies would be slaughtered.

Heavy air-raids, the desk clerk told him, handing him the key to Room 72. Many casualties. The Place Vicennes? That too had suffered. Only last week, a land-mine. The Todt Organisation office? That was no more than superficially damaged.

'Can you get me a telephone line to Hamburg?'

The clerk looked doubtful. 'I can try, Herr Kapitänleutnant.'

But there were no connections.

'It is the same every night. The bombing, the Resistance . . . who knows?'

Hartenburg walked upstairs to his room, had a bath, went into the empty dining room, and picked at a steak a listless waiter brought him before going into the bar.

It too appeared deserted. Then from the corner by the window a voice called out, 'Hello, Heinrich!'

It was Kassel.

Hartenburg walked across to him.

'Saw U11, Victor. Had a bad time, eh?'

Kassel simply nodded.

'I came through the Channel.'

'I heard. In a XXI,' Kassel said grimly. 'We were in the Channel too. In a VIIC without a schnorkel.'

'Must've been hell.'

'Hell? It was murder! The whole thing was one big muddle. Dönitz ordered all the boats off, cancelled the order, then three hours later reissued it. All eight non-schnorkel boats were to stay together on the surface and fight it out.' Kassel raised his voice. '*Fight it out*! The sky was black with rocket-firing Mosquitos and Liberators! Half the boats sunk before we reached the Channel! Dönitz's orders were that we should fight until we died!'

'Only thing Papa Dönitz could do.'

'Papa Dönitz! That's a laugh. Hitler's toady now! That's why he gets U-boat priority. He's promised that the XXIs will save Germany.'

'And they will, Victor.'

Kassel turned blazing eyes to him. 'Nothing will save Germany! Nothing! In the Invasion, the U-boats were totally defeated.'

'All that will be different, now we have the xxis. I promise you!'

'Nothing will be different! Because Germany has been led into rottenness! I was listening to the *Atlantiksender* – '

'That *Giftkuche*? I'm ashamed of you.'

'Come off it, Heinrich! I've seen things. You've seen things.'

'*What* things?'

'The Jews. The way the SS – '

'The *Kriegsmarine*'s outside all that. No prejudice against the Jews ever, Victor. Papa Dönitz is dedicated simply to winning the war. He knows nothing of that.'

'But he does! How else could he be second now to Hitler? That speech of his. Ranting about the 'poison of Jewry'. Didn't you hear it?'

'No, I didn't.' Heinrich was furious. 'You misheard! You're distorting the truth.'

'And now he has issued an order. Instead of the *Kriegsmarine* salute, we are to give the Nazi arm raise.'

'Don't believe it. You're overwrought. You don't know what you're saying. About Papa Dönitz, of all people!'

This was treason! This was the same as happened in the last war! He remembered his grandfather telling him about the shameful mutinies of the *Kriegsmarine*. And now it was about to happen again.

Horrified and disgusted, Hartenburg left the man and went to his room, to wait till it was late enough and safe enough to venture out to the Place Vicennes.

He had planned to go to the *boulangerie*. More than ever now, he needed to see Suzanne again, hoping against hope that she would still be there.

But when he opened the hotel door, he found the street full of military police.

'It is midnight, Herr Kapitänleutnant,' their *Feldwebel* told him. 'So?'

'After curfew.'

'*Curfew*?'

'There have been disturbances, Herr Kapitänleutnant.'

He had no choice but to return to the hotel and go back to his room.

But not to sleep. He lay restless on his bed, his mind full of the sounds of exploding depth-charges, the sights of sinking ships, the smells of cordite and burning oil. It was the same the next morning, pacing up and down the deserted hotel corridors, waiting for the Kerneval car to arrive.

It was a relief when it did, when again he had a role. Korvetten-Kapitän Thormann greeted him warmly. The news wasn't all bad. True, the Allies had a beachhead at Arromanches. True, the girls in the *établissements* were stitching up Union Jacks and Stars and Stripes and changing their names from Helga and Gertrud to Mary and Flo. But the Panzers were holding the line.

'And I got a couple of transports.'

'We know, Heinrich. Papa Dönitz has been on the phone. He is delighted. Now what is needed is a grand defiant gesture. In U2452 he feels he has the boat and in you, Heinrich, the man.'

'My crew and I are eager to go.'

'He knows that, Heinrich. Your next operation is being planned. Already B-Dienst has sent us the latest decoded British orders. The Allies are in for their biggest naval catastrophe.'

He had half guessed. 'Is it . . .?'

'You must not ask me, Heinrich. You must wait till tomorrow. Tomorrow you will have your Top Secret Orders. One thing only I can tell you.' Korvetten-Kapitän Thormann smiled. 'You will be pleased.'

Now Hartenburg had three-quarters guessed. 'That is good.' He paused. 'There is just one thing I ask you.'

'*Anything*, Heinrich.'

'I have only one relative.' He hesitated. 'My mother . . . she is in Hamburg. The *Kriegsmarine* . . . Papa Dönitz would look after her?'

Thormann put his arm over Hartenburg's shoulder. 'Papa Dönitz would be proud to do so. Remember his words, Heinrich?' "I never desert a U-boat"!'

Those words were certainly true. In a dense maze of falsehood, they shone like a beacon. Hadn't Papa Dönitz got him out of prison, shared sorrow with him over the loss of his son and U888? Hadn't he given *him* exactly what he wanted . . . command of the first XXI?

Now it was up to him to bring honour back to the U-boat service, give Germany inspiration to win, above all give his mother the iron protection of a real hero household-name son.

There was one thing that disturbed him. Very small really. Could be explained in all sorts of ways. But right there at the back of his mind it worried him.

When Hartenburg gave him the usual *Kriegsmarine* salute at the end of their meeting, Korvetten-Kapitän Thormann had raised his right arm and shouted, 'Heil Hitler!'

Hartenburg waited till dusk before leaving the *Beau Séjour* for the *boulangerie*. All the way along, he saw signs of destruction. There were great gaps where buildings had been. As he approached the Place Vicennes, he began to be terribly afraid of what he would find.

His first feeling was one of relief, for here the houses were still standing. And though the roof of the shop next door had been stoved in, the *boulangerie* itself had suffered no more damage than to its windows, which were boarded up, and the front which was pitted with shrapnel.

The brown door still survived. But he could smell no hot bread. He waited till the square was quite empty before giving his usual knock.

It seemed to echo emptily. No one came.

He knocked again. Still no one.

For the third time, he gave that knock.

And then unbelievably, as if he were back in a childish Aladdin pantomine again, the door swung open. A hand, surely a familiar one, was laid on his arm, drawing him inside. The door shut behind him, and he was in Suzanne's arms again.

'I can't believe it.' She hugged him to her. 'I couldn't believe it! I heard only today that the famous Kapitänleutnant Hartenburg was back in Lorient again.'

Upstairs, she cupped his face in her hands and studied it in the lamplight.

'It's been bad, hasn't it,' she said. 'I knew something had happened to you. I knew. Otherwise you wouldn't stay away.'

It was only little by little, when they lay in bed together, and then like poor Kurt in the prison at Brest, that he could bring himself to tell her what had happened.

The air-raid sirens sounded, and still he went on talking. The sky reverberated to the sound of the Lancasters. Holding her tight when the crump of bombs rocked the building, he forgot about his own war long enough to say, 'It must have been very bad for you too.'

'Not as bad as it has been for you. And the bombs are not as bad as the Resistance. They are getting very bold now. Because of the Invasion. They think the Germans will lose. Now they do dreadful things to . . .' she buried her face in his chest, 'to such as me.'

'But the war won't be lost, *Liebchen*. It is the invasion that will be lost. The Allies will be thrust back into the sea. Our new U-boats will send their ships to the bottom. Dear, dear Suzanne,' he felt suddenly very strong and confident, 'you have no cause now to be afraid.'

The bombs sounded further away now. Like a child being told a comforting story, she snuggled down in his arms, listening wide-eyed to the mechanical wonders of his new boat. She obviously understood very little of it, but she was naively impressed.

'And then too,' he smiled down at her, 'we have other weapons, which the British will soon feel on their backsides. Flying bombs that don't need aircraft to deliver them. Rockets. Jet engines.'

As if conspiring with his comforting words, the bombers' engine noise had died away. There were no more bombs.

'It is the Resistance who should be afraid, *Liebchen*,' he finished up. 'Not you.'

'I am never afraid when you're here,' she said, getting out of bed to refill his glass. 'But soon you will sail away again. In your new wonderboat. Won't you?' She drank out of the wine glass and then held it to his lips. 'To . . .' She paused, half-smiling, half-pouting, her eyes provocative and teasing. 'To . . .' she repeated, 'to try to sink the *Queen Elizabeth*. Isn't that what you always wanted to do? Isn't that what you promised to do? And you always try to keep your promises.'

'Not *try*, *Liebchen*. Not try.' A note of deliberate disbelief in her voice angered and aroused him. 'I shall! I shall keep my promise! I *shall* sink the *Queen Elizabeth*.'

He snatched the glass from her, pulled her roughly to him and took her with a fierceness that made her scream out.

Clenching her fists, scowling at his ruthlessness, she pulled away from him and said, 'But they say it is impossible! Utterly impossible! That she is too fast even for you to catch. Even you, Heinrich. *Even you*!'

His momentary anger melted away. He smiled and kissed her pouting lips. 'I shall catch the *Queen Elizabeth*. No, don't shake your head! I shall!' His mind turned to the master plan for his next operation which Papa Dönitz was already preparing and which already he reckoned he had almost guessed. 'I *promise* you.'

Suzanne looked unconvinced, but admiring. Then with her usual quick change of mood, she smiled, 'I'm sure, Heinrich, if anyone can catch her, *you* will. But let's not talk about the *Queen Elizabeth*. Let's talk about *us*.' She stroked his face. 'How much time have we before you go away?'

He said nothing. But she knew.

'I'll come tomorrow,' he said comfortingly, 'if I'm still in Lorient. If not,' he stroked her left breast close to her heart, 'keep me *here*.'

He left before midnight to escape being caught in the curfew. That night, he slept well, but in the morning he was back impatiently tramping the hotel corridors, waiting for his orders to come in from Kerneval HQ.

When at last they arrived that evening, he snatched them from the despatch rider and read the covering letter from Korvetten-Kapitän Thormann: *You are to sail at midnight. Open the sealed packet of orders when you are well clear of Lorient. Good luck!*

They were still keeping him in suspense, but now he was so sure, he did not mind. His bag had already been sent to U2452, and he wasted no more time.

Without saying goodbye to anyone in the hotel, without a backward glance he hurried down the street to the docks just as the air-raid siren went.

BOOK THREE
10 June 1944 – 20 April 1948

Sweeping in from the Atlantic, a deep depression had roughened the surface of the Irish Sea. Though all that day the area was patrolled by Allied aircraft and destroyers, those on watch could see nothing but waves and whitecaps, and no echo showed up on any radar screen.

Camouflaged by sea water, the periscope of U2452 moved further and further north, unseen and unmolested.

'That's the twenty-eighth Liberator I've seen, Exec!'

White hat at a jaunty angle on his head, Hartenburg was in high spirits. After the traumatic experience of the Invasion, the bombing of Lorient and the threat of their destruction from *Atlantiksender*, they had slipped safely out of harbour, and were already half-way to the target rendezvous.

'Peace, perfect peace, eh Busch?'

'Safe as houses, just as you promised, Sir.'

'And the Tommies have no idea where we are!'

Hartenburg was allowing all the crew to come up one by one and look through the periscope at the futile efforts of the aircraft trying to find them. All on board could hear the sound of screws as the destroyers raced round in circles. And five times had come the *boom-boom-boom* of depth-charges being wasted on mistaken targets miles away.

Now darkness was falling, they would be safer still.

'What's our new estimate of the *Queen Elizabeth* target area, Otto?'

Busch measured the distance with dividers on the big navigator's map. 'Twenty-three hundred hours tomorrow, Sir.'

Hartenburg had assembled his crew together and explained exactly what they were going to do and where they were going to do it. Just as he had guessed, Papa Dönitz had given him what he wanted. That his ambition was the sinking of the *Queen Elizabeth*, all of the crew knew. That they were going to have the privilege of carrying it out had immediately been greeted with enthusiasm and cheers.

'We shall attack in the narrowest part of the North Channel,' he had told them. 'In the twelve-mile strip of water between Scotland

and Ireland. She is bound to slow down for the minefields. With our fast underwater speed, she will be unable to outmanoeuvre us. And in the confusion of her sinking, we will turn tail full speed ahead back home to Lorient!'

Hartenburg was always careful to explain to his crew how he intended to escape from a successful attack.

'They'll never catch a glimpse of us! They won't even know we've been there!'

'Aircraft approaching, Sir!' The last of the crew in the line-up pushed the periscope in his direction. 'Another Liberator.' Looking into the eyepiece, Hartenburg read out the letters on the side of the fuselage. 'JK–Z Zebra. Where's that from, Exec?'

Busch looked it up on the Intelligence sheet. '656 Squadron at St Edzell, Cornwall, Sir.'

'She's a long way from home.'

Listening on the latest Naxos-U search receiver, the Radio Officer reported loud signals from the aircraft's new ten-centimetre band radar. 'Coming right at us, Sir!'

'I can see him.'

'Won't he see us, Sir?'

Hartenburg could actually make out the heads of the two pilots through the cockpit perspex as the Liberator passed overhead. 'All he'll see are waves.'

'Signal getting weaker, sir!'

'He's going away now. Giving up! Going home!'

In all these predictions but one, Hartenburg was correct. Neither Blake nor any of his crew had seen any sign of U2452, either on the sea or on the radar. They were giving up their search for the day, but they were not returning to St Edzell. The course on the compass was 290 degrees and they were going to Blake's first operational station, Kilkerry beside Lough Foyle, to rest and refuel while the search was carried on throughout the night – none too hopefully – by other Coastal Command aircraft.

Altogether twelve aircraft from three squadrons, all on the same assignment and all with the secret 'Mark XXIV mine' nicknamed Fido in their bomb-bays, landed at Kilkerry and were immediately put under heavy RAF Regiment guard. All the crew had simply been briefed that they were doing a special Stopper Patrol as the northern defence against possible U-boat infiltration southwards against the Invasion shipping traffic.

'See anything?' Blake enquired.

'Damn all,' replied another Squadron Leader.

'Nothing there!' said a red-haired Flight Lieutenant. 'It's one big hoax! Jerry intelligence is keeping us all up here so the U-boats can bash the landing-craft in the Channel!'

For the last three days along with the other crews, Blake had been doing Cork Patrols, so-called because they bottled up both entrances to the English Channel, between which sailed the Invasion ships. This was where the action was – U-boats sinking transports and destroyers being torpedoed. Short sharp *Luftwaffe* bombing attacks against a background of bursting shells along the Falaise peninsula. All of them were anxious to get back to where 'the fun was', and resented simply wasting their time on what they reckoned was 'another Command balls-up'. There was nothing more lowering to the spirits than staring at an empty windswept sea for fifteen hours, then being diverted from your home base, being given a scratch meal in an overcrowded Mess, told you'll be sleeping in billets on dispersed mountain sites, and finally informed you'd be doing exactly the same in the morning.

The crew were assembled that night in the Operations Room for their combined briefing. This time, they were given considerably more information.

'You'll be looking for U2452, a type XXI U-boat,' the Chief Intelligence officer told them. 'And the Captain is the ace Heinrich Hartenburg.'

Hearing the name again, Blake felt once more that same anger, the same desire for revenge. But this time it was mixed with a strange awareness of inevitability, of an intertwined destiny. As he sat listening, pictures came into his mind, walking the plank that day in Colombo, the fight on the hillside at Kirkstone, the White Bull of Scapa Flow painted on the side of Prien's U47 in which Swain was serving, the glitter of the jumping shark under the Leigh light – trademark, so the Captain of the Liverpool anti-submarine course had told him, of Swain/Hartenburg.

'Several of you have had a crack at the Jumping Shark,' the Intelligence Officer was saying. 'But this time, it's absolutely vital that it's found and killed.'

'How are we supposed to find it,' asked the other Squadron Leader, 'if the XXI boats don't surface?'

'How do we know it's there at all?' asked the red-haired Flight Lieutenant.

'Oh, it's there all right! And Hartenburg will leave his mark . . .'

'I'll say he will!' the Flight Lieutenant interrupted.

'. . . which will be a greeny-yellow stain on the surface of the sea.'

'That's what I call real obliging,' Bronski murmured amongst the groans of disbelief.

The Intelligence Officer remained unshaken. 'What I am telling you now is the highest possible Secret Priority – which is why you haven't been told before. The French commandant of the Lorient dockyard is not the collaborator the Germans think he is, but one of our two most trusted agents. The other is a woman chemist in the Todt Organisation whose eldest brother was shot by the Germans. Most of our information on Hartenburg over several years has come from her, including his obsession to sink the *Queen Elizabeth*.'

The Intelligence Officer paused. 'That obsession Dönitz is now going to exploit. The *Queen Elizabeth* will be passing through the North Channel at twenty-three hundred hours tomorrow. And Hartenburg will be under orders to sink her.' Again the Intelligence Officer paused. 'This time you've *got* to get him.'

'How?' Blake asked.

'Our ingenious French friends have injected a phosphorescent chemical dye into one of the U2452's huge batteries. Underneath, a plastic time-bomb is fused to go off before the *Queen Elizabeth's* arrival.'

'He could still schnorkel on diesels,' objected the Flight Lieutenant.

'Immobilising his electric power isn't the idea. Liquid will pour out of the fractured battery, producing clouds of lethal chlorine gas. He'll *have* to get rid of it. Normally he would use his bilge pumps, but not in enemy waters. But it'll be that. . . or surfacing . . . or being gassed to death.'

A silence fell over the Operations Room.

'So now you know what's to be done.' The Group Captain of the Station finished off the briefing. 'You will be taking off at different times during tonight and tomorrow so that the whole of the North Channel and its approaches are patrolled continuously. Any questions?'

The stunned silence still persisted.

'Right then! Trucks are waiting outside to take you to your Sites. Goodnight . . . and good luck!'

Blake and his crew were to take off at ten o'clock next morning, 'a civilised time' Bronski called it. The truck lumbered up the mountain and dropped them at the same Nissen on Three Site that had been Blake's home on his first posting to Whitleys nearly four years before.

Standing at the door of the hut, looking at that same view over Lough Foyle and the Atlantic, Blake felt a weight of inexorable doom, of shared fate with Henry Swain. Blood brothers Swain had made them. Bloody it was certainly going to be.

Blake slept badly that night. Lying on his bunk, he listened to the small movements of his crew, the creak of their beds, and watched the dying moon creep across the uncurtained window of the Nissen and disappear into gathering cloud.

He was glad enough when it was morning and they were taken first to the Mess for a bacon and egg breakfast and then via Operations out to their aircraft on Dispersal.

At ten o'clock exactly, Blake lifted the Liberator off the runway into the morning mist that was still hanging over the mountain.

'Kyle of Lochalsh . . . 012 degrees, Skipper.'

'Turning onto 012, Navigator.'

The appearance of Z Zebra materialising out of the morning mist was immediately registered by Hartenburg through the sky periscope.

'That same 656 Liberator from St Edzell's turned up again, Exec!'

'He's a trier, sir.'

'But he won't succeed, Otto. Not with this sea.'

Neither man was worried. They were well ahead of schedule. U2452 would be on station, and then they would tuck themselves down on the bottom and simply wait till they heard the unmistakable sound of the huge ship's screws.

Meanwhile they took turns watching Z Zebra and three other Liberators going to and fro between Scotland and Ireland, at the same time keeping an eye on four destroyers dropping enthusiastic depth-charges close to the coastline.

'Seem to be expecting us, Sir.'

'It'll be just the usual protection screen for the *Queen Elizabeth*, Otto.'

Lunch was steak and fresh strawberries. Afterwards one of the engineers brought out his harmonium, and the crew off watch sang old U-boat songs before carrying out a final inspection that everything was working and on the top line.

'I want all the batteries checked, Chief,' Hartenburg told his Engineer Officer. 'We may have to use the electrics for hours after the attack.'

Twenty minutes later, just before he took U2452 down to the bottom of the sea, through the sky periscope Hartenburg had one last glimpse of a Liberator diving down at the choppy sea.

'It's that Z Zebra, Exec. Thinks he's seen a periscope. Wonder what the devil it really was?'

In fact it was a battered old biscuit tin, sole survivor of a torpedoed freighter that had been swept by the current from half-way across the Atlantic to the North Channel.

Blake had seen it glittering in the late afternoon sun, and taking it for a periscope, had immediately dived.

'Better luck next time, Skipper,' said the front gunner as Blake pulled the Liberator up from the surface of the sea.

They had been doing a perpetual merry-go-round of the gap between Scotland and Ireland for seven hours now and the monotony was beginning to tell.

'Do you really think he's down there, Skipper?' his second pilot asked doubtfully.

'I'm sure of it, Mallory. Dead sure.'

Blake could sense him, almost smell him down there. His own breathing quickened. He felt the hairs on the back of his neck bristle, the saliva dry up in his mouth. His eyes were never still, scanning each wave crest, sweeping the surface of the sea for the glint of a periscope or the slightest sign of a wash.

Five times before, something had caught his eye and he had dived. Two seagulls, a large dead fish, an oil stain, broken boxwood. As hour by hour went by, he did not relax his vigilance, his mind sharp and alert, possessed with an exciting certainty that the final confrontation was imminent.

The sun sank. The mountain range that led to Ben Nevis and the Caledonian Canal disappeared in the twilight. Now he would have to pin his hopes on a sonar pattern.

'At least it's calmer,' Bronski said as he prepared to drop a centre buoy with two flame floats at the western end of the shipping lane through the minefield.

Two minutes later, he dropped another buoy and one flame float, finishing ten minutes later with a square marked by a sonar buoy and a flame float at each corner, with a fifth buoy and two flame floats in the middle.

Mallory, his second pilot, flew to each of the five flame floats while Blake adjusted to each of the five frequencies and clamped his hands over the earphones to catch the least sound of a swishing propeller.

An hour of intense concentration followed. Then Blake saw Bronski raise his eyebrows questioningly.

He shook his head. 'Only sea noise. If he's down there, he's not moving.'

A further two hours went by. More sonar buoys and more flame floats were ejected. Still there was nothing over the earphones.

The coffee thermos was brought out. Bronski poured a carton for Blake, but it stayed on the throttle pedestal, gradually getting stone-cold.

On the flight deck, nobody said anything. As round and round the sonar pattern they went, there was only the hum of the engines as a background to Blake's thoughts.

'He's lying doggo,' said Bronski.

At twenty-three hundred hours, Rolf reported from the W/T position, '*Queen Elizabeth* estimating at 00.25, Skipper.'

'Drop another sonar pattern!'

Listening over the southern-most buoy an hour later, Blake thought he heard the very slightest scratching sounds.

He passed the earphones over to Mallory. 'Hear anything?'

Mallory jammed the earphones hard over his head. He closed his eyes.

After a full three minutes, he took them off again and passed them back.

'Sorry, Skipper. Not a thing!'

Blake glanced across at the clock on the instrument panel. 'That bomb should be going off soon.'

'That'll give us a clue,' Mallory said.

'You never know,' Bronski put in as they began trying out another sonar buoy pattern, 'might hear his propellers yet!'

'Wind's dropped.' Mallory peered down into the darkness. 'No white caps.'

But half an hour went by, and still there was no sound from the sonar buoys, no sight of the phosphorescent glow in the blackness below.

'Either he's not there,' Mallory said, 'or the bomb hasn't gone off.'

They went on circling the flame floats, watching and listening.

'*Queen Elizabeth*'ll be here in half an hour,' Bronski said. 'What're we going to do, Skipper?'

'We'll try the Leigh Light.'

Bronski went forward into the nose as Blake descended to fifty feet.

'Turning the light on now!'

The dazzling white beam pierced the night, fingering each yellow flame float in turn.

'Can't see anything, Skipper.'

Blake swung the Liberator's nose to starboard.

'Still nothing, Skipper.'

Blake took the aircraft right down to the water.

'Port, Skipper,' Bronski suddenly shouted.

Blake skidded the Liberator round.

'There!' Bronski yelled excitedly. 'At ten o'clock. Can you see it?'

Looking out of his side window, Blake saw a greeny yellow smudge glowing on the dark water.

He was there! Not a thousand feet away from him now, moving around in his own U-boat, making final preparations for launching his torpedoes, was the quarry he had been stalking for years, the target for Monteith's Reply.

'Drop another sonar pattern!' he called over the intercom. 'Should be able to hear him this time!'

But still they heard nothing.

'He'll have stopped his engines, Skipper,' Mallory said. 'He won't move again till he has the Q.E.'s screws on his hydrophones. Then he'll have to get into attack position!'

Blake looked at his watch.

'Radar, any sign of the Q.E.?'

'Got a blip at thirty miles, Skipper.'

'Probably her. Keep an eye on it.'

He went round the sonar buoys again, but there was still no sound. Again the sonar buoy batteries would be exhausted.

'Drop another pattern!'

This time there was the very faintest scraping noise. He said nothing, just passed the earphones to Mallory.

'Hear anything?'

'Nothing, Skipper.' He passed them to the navigator, 'Bronski?' Bronski shook his head too.

One begins to doubt one's hearing, Blake thought. I may have been hearing what I both want and fear to hear. Or it might simply be my imagination.

'He's bound to make a move soon,' Bronski frowned, 'if he's down there.'

Blake clenched his fists over the controls. 'He's down there!'

'I'm not sure, Skipper.'

'I am!'

He was certain Swain/Hartenburg was there all right. And this time he wasn't going to get away.

Breathlessly, Blake continued to listen, his ears registering and magnifying every crackle of static, every creak of sea sound, his mind coldly aware that every minute the *Queen Elizabeth* was steaming closer and closer to Hartenburg's torpedoes.

'*Queen Elizabeth* fifteen miles away,' Radar called, 'closing fast.'

'We'll have to drop Fido blind on the flame floats,' Blake said, 'otherwise it'll home on her screws.'

'Shall we—'

Blake put his finger to his lips. Excitedly he clapped his hands over his earphones. 'I can hear him now!'

He passed the headset over to Mallory. 'Listen!'

The second pilot nodded. 'Like a heartbeat,' he said. 'He's moving!'

Blake pushed the stick right forward. Over the intercom, he called 'Bomb doors open! Prepare to drop Fido!'

At fifty feet, he flattened the aircraft out two miles away from the last flame float to be dropped. Still hearing the propeller noise on the sonar buoy, he steered the aircraft at a steady 150 knots towards it.

'Drop!'

That was all. One word.

'Parachute's opened,' reported the Rear Gunner. And seconds later, 'Fido's entered the water fine!'

'What next, Skipper?'

'Drop another pattern of sonar buoys!'

The sound of the U-boat's screws was still there. Now the sensitive head would be searching, altering the torpedo rudder accordingly.

He waited, still listening.

Suddenly, the noise of the screws stopped.

'Can't hear *anything* now!' he said to Mallory. 'If he's switched off his engines, it's us who are sunk!'

The second hand on the instrument board clock circled five times. Still there was nothing.

'Eight minutes since we dropped!' said Bronski.

Suddenly the noise of the propellers came back.

Blake breathed again. Now Fido's automaton metal ears would be turning on their pivots. The amplifiers would be magnifiying the least vibration. The computer would be taking over – calculating, deciding, acting. Cogs would turn, steel rods would move. Minute adjustments would be made on the rudder, to the speed, to the angle of dive, all the time moving forward that thousand pounds of explosive warhead, closer, closer . . .

The seconds ticked by. The bloody thing's missed, Blake was thinking, when suddenly over the phones came a noise like thunder.

He saw Bronski and Mallory watching him expectantly.

John Blake said nothing, because now it was all over and he had no words to say.

All he did was to put up his thumb.

That water earthquake went on echoing in his ears. The incongruity of that upturned thumb went on appearing to him suddenly in dreams. At the victory celebration in the Mess bar, that noise drowned the songs. Everything upright turned into an upturned thumb.

Through the tag end of the war, while he was on patrol, searching for the U-boats that still went on fighting, over the intercom would come thundering the frightful symphony of that explosion.

Now there was no Black Pit for the U-boats to bask in. Almost every time they surfaced, day or night, an aircraft would attack, or a string of escort vessels would depth-charge for hours. Now the air was filled, not with the SOS's of merchant vessels, but the last messages of U-boats.

More U-boats were being sunk than ships. Now when the *Atlantiksender* radio told them that a U-boat crew's life expectancy was fifteen days, the German submariners believed them. But still they went on fighting.

The war in Europe was moving to its close by the time their daughter Charlotte was born at the end of March. The United States

Ninth Army were about to envelop the Ruhr from the Wesel bridgehead, while the United States First Army was poised from the south. The Canadians were blasting the Germans out of Holland. On 30 April, ten days after celebrating his fifty-sixth birthday, Adolf Hitler shot himself. He had nominated Admiral Dönitz as his successor. But the new wonder XXI prefabricated boats, which might have won the war if they had come earlier, were bombed out of existence.

And as the Allied armies advanced, the prison camps were broken open. Blake and his crew had just arrived back from a patrol and were drinking the cups of coffee Jennifer handed them prior to debriefing, when her telephone rang. She answered it formally, then incredulously. She put out a hand weakly to find a chair and subsided into it.

All she could say into the phone was, 'Thank you, thank you, thank you, thank you.'

She put down the receiver slowly, and then carefully controlling her voice said, 'That was Dover Clearance. Stalag 11B has been taken by Canadians. Peter's alive and well.' Then she walked stiff-backed and white-faced to the Section lavatory, and the silent men heard the sound of her being violently sick.

She emerged apologetically. 'Sorry about that,' she said, and began the debriefing.

In the Mess that night, they really celebrated. They all reckoned Jennifer was a good type, and the rationed spirits were brought out, and the beer flowed.

Blake stuck close to her side. He'd got used to her company since she had been posted to St Edzell, though they'd never been lovers again. After she'd met Alexandra, their relationship had changed. They had distanced themselves from one another, and yet paradoxically had become closer. As Jennifer had once said, they'd hung onto one another for mutual support, each grateful to find one other person who could do that.

'You're pleased too, aren't you, John?' she asked him suddenly in the midst of the party.

'Pleased, yes, of course,' he answered truthfully, for who could not be pleased? 'And envious.'

'Of me or Peter?'

'Of both.' He stared down into her eyes, which were glowing with a still-disbelieving happiness. He was going to say, 'I'd give anything to see Alexandra's face lit up like that', but it sounded disloyal and begrudging, so he said no more.

Yet he felt his pleasure for her tinged with real sadness. It was the end of something, he supposed. He walked her back to the Waafery for the last time, and kissed her chastely on the forehead.

Almost exasperatedly she said, 'Don't *you* ever realise how lucky *you* are?'

Three days later, she went on compassionate leave to join her husband. He saw her off at the station. Buying a newspaper on the way back to camp, he read for the first time the names of Dachau and Ravensbrück.

The British public began to hear of Nazi atrocities. Victory in Europe, when it came, was celebrated with righteous euphoria.

The church bells rang. People danced in the street. To be in uniform was to be hugged, kissed, bought drinks, made a hero.

Then came the atomic bomb-blasts of Hiroshima and Nagasaki that heralded Victory in Japan Day, the Nuremberg trials at which twelve German leaders were condemned to death, and Grossadmiral Dönitz received a ten-year prison sentence.

And still the noise of the U2452 exploding was like tinnitus in his head, the upturned thumb still a gesture that haunted him.

'What are you going to do now?' Alexandra asked him.

'What am I going to do now?' he replied, as though he were answering her question.

What *could* he do now? A married man with three young children, a wife anxious to use her talents in life, a mother-in-law who wasn't exactly well and wasn't exactly ill, a disgruntled brother-in-law who was beginning a belated University education after being released from an undistinguished two years in the Navy, *what* could he do?

The answer to the question would have to be sorted out by him, and him alone. After all, he was the *paterfamilias*, he would have to dictate the future, not only for himself but for the others. That was his responsibility. He couldn't get out of it.

All his previous actions added together made up the sum of this. And in those previous actions, could he have done any different to what he had done?

He had been caught, just as Henry Swain had been caught. Their education had conditioned them to do what they did. So he had killed Swain. But in a war. If he hadn't killed Swain, he would have killed *him*. Then why did he feel guilty? In a war, each side took their young and turned them into killers. He remembered learning for Matriculation Henry V's speech before Agincourt: 'In peace there's nothing so becomes a man as honest stillness and humility. But when the blast of war blows in our ears, then imitate the action of the tiger.' And the transformation into tigers began in that humble peacetime. At school, do as you're told. Kirkstone had taught that, all right. Just as Trefeld had done. Do not question authority. When we want you to be humble, be humble. When we want you to be a tiger, be a tiger. Kill.

But with Henry Swain, his one-time friend, his childish blood brother, it had been more than that, more than obedience to orders, more than deference to authority, more than defending his country. For if it was only war, why did he not tell Alexandra?

'What are you going to do?' Alexandra went on asking.

Of course he could never tell her. The ace Hartenburg must remain a ghost throughout their lives. He had sunk a U-boat – that much Blake released – adding that it hadn't *really* been him, it had been a marvellous mechanical 'thing' that had sniffed the U-boat, nosed it out, and destroyed it. All he'd done was to drop the 'thing'.

But what about Mrs Swain, he had thought. Alexandra knew her, had told him she'd visited their home opposite the Blohm and Voss yard in Hamburg. Wouldn't they meet some day? Wouldn't Mrs Swain tell her about her ace son Hartenburg?

After the war, along with other pilots of bombers, John Blake dropped food to Belgium and Holland, took supplies in to Hamburg, landed at the *Luftwaffe* aerodrome, stayed the night, heard of the thousands of civilian casualties, saw the terrifying desolation – flattened, nothing left. No, Mrs Swain would not be telling anyone about her son.

But the Reverend Swain, wouldn't he find out about his ace stepson? Blake's parents had stayed in Ceylon, when the clamour for independence from Colonial rule intensified after the war, trying in vain to protect the Church's schools and property from being taken over in an atmosphere of rioting and violence. Returning home three months later, after the island's independence had been officially celebrated, his father had told him that Papa Swain was still living in his old school, now entirely Buddhist-run. More unworldly than ever, no longer the headmaster, he spent his life in prayer and contemplation, cut off from the world. He was looked after by the Buddhist community and was now revered as a saint.

So then it was his secret. That earthquake sound in his ears, the shadow of the upturned thumb, would be his and his alone, to be told to no one, to be shared by no one.

'What are you going to *do*?'

'What am I going to do?' At last he answered her question. 'Why, get a job, of course!'

He had thought of going back to Oxford to finish his degree, but decided he couldn't face reading History, and anyway he had a family to support. He had thought of staying in the RAF, but he'd had enough of being under the orders of others. So he joined British Overseas Airways on the North Atlantic run – a military pilot turned civil pilot, flying the same old faithful Liberators over the same old Atlantic battleground.

Butting through rain and cloud, clattering through storms on his way to New York and London, he could look down on the grey Atlantic – and think.

Hundreds of U-boats lay under that icy pall, together with fifteen million tons of ships. 29,000 merchant and naval seamen. 10,000 Coastal Command airmen. 32,000 U-boat men – 71 of them along with Henry Swain close to Inistrahull in the North Channel, which he often flew over those first years after the war.

They had been strenuous years, years of trying to lay the civil foundations of their family life. In some ways successful, in some ways not. They had bought a house in the village of Avonfield, under the shadow of the Berkshire downs. Only half an hour from London Airport, with a stream that ran through their large garden on its way to join the Thames nine miles further down.

The house was old and Alexandra liked it, near enough to the village school which the two boys attended and where Charlotte would be going in two years' time. Peter was back at Oxford, taking Politics, Philosophy and Economics at Balliol College, and living at 7 Park Road, an arrangement which delighted Mrs Monteith. It was Blake's mother-in-law who had been the real success – a Vice-President of the Navy League, a Justice of the Peace, a pillar of the Oxford Conservative Party and extremely busy for every hour of every day.

And Alexandra? Was she happy? John Blake often wondered. Occasionally, he brought himself to ask her. Since he had killed Swain, he had never dared to ask if she loved him.

Yes, she was happy, she always said. She had the children and was the best of mothers. When Charlottte went to school, she planned to get a mother's help and go back to the University to take her Ph.D as a living-out student.

'You don't mind?' she asked John.

'Mind? Why should I mind?'

She had tried to explain. 'You seem so . . . so . . .' she had searched for the impossible right word.

Her face had crumpled. She had shrugged and given up. For how could she possibly describe that shadow that lay over everything he did, that severed their conversations, their plans, their love-making. His *Doppelgänger*. Sometimes, he was afraid that he would talk about Swain in his sleep, or in a moment of weakness confess how he hated him and what he had done.

He had forced himself to laugh as she had searched for the impossible word. 'Jealous? Don't tell me I seem so jealous?'

'No, of course not.'

'So why should I mind? I'm lucky to have such a brilliant wife.'

She often went up to London University to a lecture and to buy books – as she had done that day nearly three years after the war had ended, that day that he would always remember.

That day he wondered, as she prepared to leave for London, whether *she* had remembered. Every year, like a wedding anniversary. This year, would she forget? This year, would the healing begin?

He never really knew, of course. She never let on. Perhaps he was too isolated in his guilt for her to confide in him. She never mentioned Swain. She never told him whether she remembered that day all those years ago in Ceylon.

The twentieth of April – the day Henry Swain never let anyone else forget. Certainly John Blake would remember Henry Swain's birthday till the day he died.

'John.' Alexandra had put her hand on his arm. 'You look tired. Would you like me to stay?'

Her voice had been gentle, tender, almost loving. Sometimes he had the strange, hopeful idea that she did love him, that it was his own feelings and memories, not hers, that lay between them.

The previous evening he had flown in from New York. He had arrived, laden with food, for Britain was still rationed, with nylons and perfume for Alexandra and toys for the children.

He had longed to say, 'I've hardly got home. Yes, I am tired. Stay with me. I want you.' But he couldn't let himself. He saw the cold fixed shadow behind her clear eyes, the reflection of the *Doppelgänger* that would always haunt him.

'Of course I'm not tired.' He had smiled down reassuringly into her earnest upraised face, and patted the hand that still rested on his arm. She was, he noticed, searching his face as hungrily as he searched hers.

'Of you go!' he said briskly. 'You need a break!' He turned to the children. 'We're going to have a good time, aren't we?'

They were too busy playing with the toys he'd brought to answer. Maurice was already fighting with William, trying to take away the Chattanooga-choo-choo train John had bought for him. Blake said nothing. He always treated the boys equally. But that didn't mean you loved them equally, Alexandra had once unfairly exclaimed.

'Mine boys,' Charlotte was shrieking, stamping her foot, hugging the doll he'd given her. 'Stop it, mine boys! Stop it!'

Not that they did. They just went on. Maurice was banging William's head.

'Lunch is in the fridge.' Alexandra brushed his cheek with her lips. 'See Maurice eats his spinach.'

And then she was off. He heard the car depart. It accelerated as if she was glad to be gone.

It was raining that morning, as it had rained all week. They played elephants and game shooting. Then he tried draughts. Then he had to go into the kitchen to boil the vegetables and set the table.

He could hear Maurice and William still fighting in the lounge, until there were actual tears, but he would not interfere.

Lunch passed with William kicking Maurice under the table.

'Mine boys!' Charlotte put up her finger in admonishment, intercepting as she did so a sharp kick on the shins from William intended for Maurice which provoked howls of rage and pain, and which had to be soothed by her sitting on John's knee, being fed her bread-and-butter pudding.

It cleared after lunch and the sun started to shine. The children trooped out into the garden while John Blake started the washing up. In through the open window came the sound of whispering, chasing and fighting.

Why, he thought, *why* do boys do it? Why did we do it – Henry Swain and I?

Why indeed? What was to stop them? Would they go on for ever?

One day, would circumstances direct their fight? Would governments conspire to enslave and slaughter them? Would they, in their turn, be haunted by their own private ghosts?

Would yet more names be carved on the Kirkstone War Memorial? Weren't another twenty dead including Fanshawe, Nash, Jenkins, and ironically, Wagstaff, enough?

Poor Wacky, killed when his ambulance was blown up in Burma. He would have been so angry to see his name on that Memorial in that waiting empty space. There had, in fact, been some argument amongst the Governors as to whether he should be included at all.

He had been a Conscientious Objector, one governor had pointed out. He hadn't actually *fought*. But the majority had been in favour and Wagstaff's name had gone up, a co-recipient of the mountains of poppies on that first Armistice Service after the war ended. All ex-service old boys were earnestly asked to attend.

As he washed up the children's lunch dishes, he remembered that day. 'I wonder,' he had thought as they filed out of Chapel, 'if sometime they will put up the names of the visiting pupils, the Trefeld boys?'

Maybe one day, he answered himself, cynically perhaps, when we have found another mutual enemy.

The washing up finished, he dried his hands. He walked into the garden, down the path, and over the lawn. The sun had come out and the rain on the blades of grass was sparkling. Feet crunching on the gravel of the path, he walked past the flower beds, yellow with daffodils and fragrant with wallflowers. He noticed they needed weeding and was going to the tool shed when he heard a shout from beyond the barrier of the laurels.

He didn't move at first. It was the silence, the sudden suspicious silence that made him go on. Rounding the corner of the bushes, he saw the boys had found a plank – and like that time, twenty years ago in the Swains' garden in Colombo – had put it across the stream, swollen with the rain, thin side uppermost, putting in stakes to hold it firm in that upright position.

The silence was simply explained. Maurice was half-way across like an acrobat on a tightrope, watched breathlessly by Charlotte on the other side, while William waited his turn.

He was taken back over the years. The bright frail sun seemed to deepen into a hotter, sultrier light. The laurels shimmered into oleanders. Maurice had inherited his father's grace and surefootedness. He knew he could do it – step by step, like Henry Swain had done before him, till he jumped off lightly at the other side and Charlotte was calling, 'Now it's your turn, William!'

William. Young, clumsy William. If he fell down that gully he would hurt himself. Alexandra would be furious. These days, Blake tried his damnedest to avoid angering Alexandra. He meant to step forward to stop William. But somehow he couldn't.

Then, William was on the plank. Wobbling as John Blake had done – tremulously foot by foot, not gracefully at all, but like a small elephant, every second promising the probability he'd fall off.

Half-way across, there was a deathly silence, as backwards and forwards like a clown doing it on purpose, he swayed. His face was white. He was scared.

John Blake caught a glimpse of Maurice's face on the other side, frowning.

Was William going to give up half-way? Was he going to shuffle back to the beginning? Was he going to fall off?

Time stood still. It had become strangely imperative to John Blake that William should continue. Not because he was his son or Maurice was Henry Swain's son, but because it was important for all of them, an omen for the future. This was their tenuous hold on something. This was the way . . . but to what?

William was struggling on. Less than six feet. Three feet and then he was over—

No, he wasn't. He looked down, tilted, saved himself by shooting his arms backwards, and put one foot in front of the other, painfully slowly but surer now. One final wobble, and then . . .

For his last step, Maurice stretched out a helpful hand. William grasped it as he jumped onto the bank.

He was there!

Maurice punched his shoulder in congratulation. Charlotte clapped her hands. 'Mine boys!' She laughed admiringly. 'Mine brothers.'

Blake saw the boys' two profiles turned to one another, grinning, so different and yet so alike, so exasperating, but so beloved.

'My sons,' he said softly, knowing that this was the tenuous hold, this the way back to other love, to Alexandra, to life together. 'My sons.'

For the first time, he felt gratitude towards Swain for Maurice, for Alexandra and for many things. His guilt and hatred vanished. He recognised that the shadow between Alexandra and himself had not been *her* memory of Swain but his own. He experienced the beginnings of peace with himself.

Beyond the laurels, he heard the clock chime five. Alexandra would be back soon. Now that the shadow was receding, they would begin again. He would take those first tentative steps. He went back inside their house, eager to welcome her home.